Murder in Piccadilly

Murder in Piccadilly

Charles Kingston

With an Introduction
by Martin Edwards

Poisoned Pen Press

Poisoned Pen Press
6962 E. First Ave., Ste. 103
Scottsdale, AZ 85251
www.poisonedpenpress.com
info@poisonedpenpress.com

Printed in the United States of America

Introduction

Murder in Piccadilly, originally published in 1936, is a lively mystery with an appealing final twist. In many respects, it forms a companion piece to a book which first appeared four years later. *A Scream in Soho*, by John G. Brandon, has also been included in the British Library series of Crime Classics, and the novels share elements in common, notably locale. But the pseudonymous Kingston was not quite as prolific as Brandon, and is even less well remembered today.

Kingston's book should not be confused with *The Piccadilly Murder*, an excellent whodunit written seven years earlier by Anthony Berkeley, one of the leading lights of the Golden Age of Murder between the two world wars. Whereas Berkeley was an innovator in the detective fiction genre, Kingston had a more traditional approach to his craft. He set out to write unpretentious entertainment, and won a modest but loyal readership. His work is competently plotted, and infused with a quiet sense of humour.

The central situation in *Murder in Piccadilly* is typical of many crime stories of its time, in that a wealthy older person stands in the way of an impecunious younger relative. Massy Cheldon, a waspish sceptic, is rather more neatly characterised than many of the innumerable elderly misers in Golden Age detective fiction. When his widowed sister-in-law Ruby asks why he remains a bachelor, he parries the question by retorting, 'With a Socialist government composed of alleged Conservatives in power the landowner is a prisoner within his paltry income'. Ruby's son Bobbie, amiable but weak, lazy and none too bright, is by no means a conventionally attractive protagonist. Bobbie is infatuated with Nancy Curzon, a pretty young dancer (at the splendidly named 'Frozen Fang' night club), but it is a truth universally acknowledged in books of this era that a girl like Nancy will only contemplate marriage to a single man in possession of a good fortune. His naive adoration of Nancy, rather than mere greed, propels Bobbie into the clutches of the engaging but ruthless Nosey Ruslin, who quickly realises that he too can benefit if Bobbie inherits Massy Cheldon's fortune sooner rather than later. Ruslin is shrewd, but not quite as shrewd as he thinks.

The murder promised by the book's title does not occur until halfway through the story, but Kingston describes the victim's last hours alive with a touch of irony that lifts his writing above the merely functional. The crime is committed at the crowded Piccadilly Underground station—this just two years after the Tube station homicide recorded in Mavis Doriel Hay's *Murder Underground*, another obscure book revived as a British Library Crime Classic. The stage is set for the appearance of Kingston's series detective, Chief Inspector Wake of Scotland Yard. Wake is a nicely drawn character, genial but remorseless, and soon he is causing alarm amongst suspects with guilty consciences.

Musing on the notion of a crime committed with great daring in broad daylight, Wake recalls the case of Vera Page—one of those real-life murder mysteries that fascinated Golden Age writers, and influenced their work. Vera was a ten-year-old girl from Notting Hill who was raped and strangled five years before this novel was written; sadly, there is nothing new about child sex murders. The Vera Page case made headlines in its day, but nobody was ever charged with the killing, whereas with Wake in charge, there is never any real doubt that the killer in the fictional investigation will be brought to justice. Wake takes false confessions, misconceived accusations, diatribes against capital punishment, complaints about police incompetence, rubber-neckers who have trebled the population of Piccadilly, and '"shrewd guesses"—that was the invariable phrase—as to the identity of the criminal' all in his stride. Calmly and methodically, he works towards the moment when he will be able to make an arrest.

Murder in Piccadilly echoes some aspects of a novel Kingston wrote two years earlier. *Poison in Kensington* was reviewed by Dorothy L. Sayers in *The Sunday Times*, and also had a romance at the heart of the narrative, while a rich old uncle was once again the murder victim. Sayers was mildly impressed: 'we know that everything must end happily and virtuously in spite of all appearances. None the less, the tale…is worked out quite entertainingly for those who do not mind taking a good dose of sentiment and melodrama as a substitute for probability.' The plot twists in *Murder in Piccadilly* are contrived quite artfully, and the result is pleasing, even though Kingston was by no means working at the cutting edge of Thirties crime fiction.

So who exactly was Charles Kingston? Little information is available; he was one of that army of journeymen writers whose reputations fade once they have stopped producing new books. Allen J. Hubin's monumental bibliography of crime fiction indicates that, from 1921, Kingston published at the rate of about one book a year for a quarter of a century. His full name was Charles Kingston O'Mahoney, and it seems that, before turning to crime in the fictional sense, he wrote a book called *The Viceroys of Ireland*. His surname suggests Irish origins, but his favoured setting for fictional crime was London. His portrayal of the 'Frozen Fang' and Soho nightlife indicates that he found the capital rather more attractive—gangsters and all—than the green and pleasant acres of the Broadbridge Manor estate. This is not a cerebral country house whodunit of the kind so often written during the Golden Age, but a good-natured, old-fashioned thriller that retains a warm period charm.

Martin Edwards
www.martinedwardsbooks.com

Chapter One

"My dear Ruby," said Massy Cheldon with a vinous good humour derived from a delectable lunch for which he had not paid, "falling in love is like falling downstairs—you don't mean to do either."

"But Bobbie's got it badly this time, Massy," she said nervously, her eyes on the door which divided her son from the only person he detested as if fearful that it might open.

"Who is the girl?" The tone was a trifle hard now, and Ruby Cheldon observed apprehensively the sudden stiffening of the short, lean figure and the hardening of the habitually suspicious expression of her brother-in-law's microscopic eyes. "Did I understand you to say that she is a dancer in a night club?"

"That's where Bobbie met her," she murmured, trying to bring her nerves under the control of her tongue. All the signs of a dangerous explosion were apparent to her, and she knew that she must placate, whatever the cost to her pride and veracity might be, the only man who had the power to lift her son out of the slough of despair into which his latest love affair had plunged him.

"What is her name?" As he barked the question at her she started out of the reverie into which she had been lured by irresistible memories of Bobbie's numerous affairs with women, ancient and modern.

"Nancy Curzon," she stammered.

"Street or family?"

She laughed so as to flatter him.

"I don't know, Massy. Bobbie hasn't brought her to see me yet."

"So you don't know her? But I might have expected it. However, it's really no business of mine." He glanced from side to side of the attenuated room with its incurable furniture and faded oil paintings, the relics of an imaginary grandeur which Ruby Cheldon chose to regard as proofs of her gentility. But she was not following her brother-in-law's gaze. An analysis of his thoughts demanded all her attention now. She knew what "it's really no business of mine" meant. It was his way of declining to accept any responsibility in a cash sense for his nephew's vagaries. His presence there this afternoon had been the result of a conspiracy between herself and Bobbie, and they had rejoiced when he had accepted the invitation to call on his way from his club in Piccadilly to his mansion in Sussex. Between them they had drawn up a programme of tactics which they believed augured success, although both realised it was a forlorn hope to expect his uncle to disgorge anything of the large income he derived from the Cheldon Estate. Still, there was ever an outside chance of Uncle Massy creating a precedent and Bobbie was so passionately in love that he was only too willing to take a minor part in the conference and even eager to be conciliatory and submissive. For if at twenty-three he had some of his mother's pride he had none of her tact and discretion, while instead of her courage he had only the imitation of that virtue which is called recklessness.

"Cosy place you've got here," said Massy Cheldon, who disliked silence even when he had nothing to say.

"It's the best we can afford," she answered, a restless expression passing across her pale, faded face. She dare not retort with Bobbie preparing what he called a subtle appeal to his uncle's generosity. Yet if there was one word she detested it was "cosy" applied to her portion of the human rabbit warren which filled a corner of two of Fulham's least pleasing thoroughfares.

"If Bobbie could earn his own living you'd be able to afford something much better," he snapped back at her. She knew he was thinking of the small allowance he made her and winced. "What with my contribution and your pension even a little assistance from your son would make all the difference in the world, Ruby, and you know it."

He shifted his position to the right of the fireplace and stared at the remnant of his cigar.

"He has been so unlucky, Massy." She flushed as she suppressed her anger.

"Nonsense. I can't understand why you should be clever enough in everything except the one thing that matters, Ruby, and that is your son. You've spoilt him from the day he was born, and look at him now. And in spoiling him you've spoilt your own life too. Don't tell me you couldn't have married. Why, you're still handsome and attractive with a son in the twenties. How do you keep your figure without giving your face that drawn bloodless look which so many women have? Fulham must be healthier than Broadbridge." He sighed with self-pity. "Life's nothing but worry on top of worry. A landowner nowadays, Ruby, is a compulsory philanthropist." He sighed again and added the unsmokable portion of his cigar to the lingering fire.

Ruby Cheldon winced as she detected the hint not to broach the subject of further assistance.

"How can I help spoiling him?" she asked abruptly. "He's all I have. You've never done him justice, Massy, you've never appreciated the fact that he never knew his father." There was pride and pity in her large dark grey eyes as she looked him straight in the face.

"I've never forgotten that his father was a gallant soldier and that his mother is only foolish when her son is being criticised. She wants all the world to believe that he is perfect."

"Everybody likes Bobbie," she said, almost sullenly. "And he's a gentleman."

"Are gentlemen scarce in the Cheldon family?" he asked curtly.

"He ought to have gone into the army," she said, ignoring the question.

"But the army means examinations and hard work and obeying orders. And if I may say so, my dear Ruby, you've brought up Bobbie on the principle that the only orders worth obeying are his own. Come, Ruby, it's time you wakened up. Here's your son without a penny of his own proposing to marry a dancer from a night club. Do you seriously tell me that you approve?"

"Of course I don't." A new note in her voice impressed him.

"Then you don't wish me to make it possible for him to marry this lady from the lower regions of some insanitary building in the environs of Piccadilly? Of course, I shouldn't do anything of the kind," he added hastily, fearful lest her sense of humour should fail her.

She moved from her chair and stood beside him.

"Bobbie is bringing Nancy Curzon to see me next week, and I wish you could see her too."

"I'm perfectly willing to meet the lady, but supposing she captivates us all and we become anxious to rope her into the family, the question will then arise, what can Bobbie do?"

She looked pensively into the air.

"It goes without saying that he can drive a car?" he said drily.

"He drives beautifully," she answered, the irony in his tone escaping her. "And he knows how to dress," she added irrelevantly.

"And I bet he also knows half a dozen night clubs and how to mix at least ten different cocktails. These alleged social accomplishments, my dear Ruby, have the merit of impressing the lower middle classes, but in a sordid age are not regarded as qualifications for the salary Bobbie naturally expects in his capacity of gentleman."

She was not listening, a life-long familiarity with his vocabulary and humours as well as humour rendering such attention unnecessary. She had caught a sound from the next room and guessed that Bobbie had decided that her allowance of time for the purpose of bringing his uncle into the frame of mind essential to the experiment in generosity had elapsed and that he must now make his appearance on the scene.

"Bobbie's got to realise the unpleasant fact that he must take off his coat and forget his gentility. It's useless his thinking that I'm going to die to suit his convenience. The Cheldon estate has been his curse. Waiting for dead men's shoes always is. I'm good for another twenty years at least, although there are moments—" He turned mechanically to survey his features in the mirror over the mantelpiece. "If only the tenants would be reasonable, but they don't leave me a shilling. What with repairs and reductions and all the other encumbrances life's a burden. And now my nephew wants to marry a dancer at my expense."

"Not at your expense, Massy," she said quickly. "Naturally he looks to you for help and advice."

"He can have the advice," he said sharply, picking out the word that involved him in no liability. "Yes, he can have the advice," he added, as if speaking to himself. "But it'll take the form of plain speaking and straight from the shoulder home-truths. He must be taught that sponging on his mother—"

"Hush!" she whispered, "here he is."

As Bobbie Cheldon closed the door behind him and was in their midst the atmosphere became electric. Yet in that moment the older man could see, had it forced on him, in fact, that it was not altogether the awkwardly lazy, pleasure-tackling, colourlessly cynical youth of old who now extended towards him with composure and confidence a delicate hand which pressed his own firmly.

"Good afternoon, uncle," he said, and his mother's heart ached with a delicious remembrance of his childhood, for in his voice there was something to remind her of the days when he had been so lovable because of all those dear faults of which a child is so delightfully unconscious. He had been a lovely boy whose every action savoured of a grow-ing masculinity, sensitive to praise and blame, defiant and repentant, enchantingly original in his remarks, explorer, engine driver, pirate, cowboy, soldier and sailor, and all in a little back garden in a Surrey suburb.

"You're looking as healthy as a young giant ought to look," said Massy Cheldon enviously. "But sit down. I haven't more than a few minutes to spare and I've heard your news."

Bobbie glanced inquiringly at his mother, but did not speak. It was common knowledge that Uncle Massy disliked being overlooked and that Nature having fashioned him as a monologist, dilettante, poseur and valetudinarian, he chose to regard his lack of inches as a handicap and a grievance. He could not, therefore play the role of heavy uncle with a nephew whose seventy-two inches dwarfed his own sixty-eight unless that nephew sprawled on the hairy sofa while he stood before the fireplace and frowned and fumed as his humours enjoined.

"Yes, Fulham must be healthier than Broadbridge," he said again, envying the attractive, open countenance of Bobbie, his strong shoulders, balanced limbs, and the eager vitality in his eyes.

He resented the insurgent jealousy which compelled him to catalogue all the advantages his nephew held as against his own age, wealth and worries. Underneath it all, too, there was a dread that sooner than either of them knew the Cheldon estate might pass to Bobbie, and youth and health with unusual powers of enjoyment would be reinforced by great possessions. It was enough to make a mean man meanly irritable.

"Why is it, Bobbie," he asked testily, "that the moment a man discovers he has the best mother in the world he wants to leave her?"

"Because, uncle, it's time I married and settled down," was the mild reply. Ruby Cheldon interpreting the motive, marvelled at the transformation that even an ignoble love could effect in her son.

"I'm glad to hear you intend to do something." He moved a couple of paces forward and returned to his original position. "It's about time."

"I agree with you uncle." Bobbie rose, and then remembering that his uncle had the "chair" sank back on to the lifeless conglomeration of horsehair, defunct springs and faded tapestry. "I can see now what an ass I have been, but I mean to make up for lost time."

"Let me think," said Massy Cheldon, wondering what had happened to Bobbie, ignorant of the fact that youth can work miracles when animated by a pure idealism, and unable to share his sister-in-law's belief that it was all the doing of the unknown Nancy Curzon.

Ruby Cheldon was too conscious of the presence of the men to have to scrutinise their faces as she reviewed the situation and its immediate past. Bobbie's hatred and contempt for his uncle were ingrained and nothing had ever happened to weaken them. The boy had grown up to idealise a father who had died in action on the very day that Massy Cheldon had received the O.B.E. for his eminent services as the Food Controller of a small provincial town. There had been nothing for the soldier except a shell which had torn him to pieces, but for the civilian there had been a reward for successful evasion of military service. That had been a bad beginning to their relations during the years when Bobbie had been at his "prep" school and worse when Massy Cheldon visited him at lengthy intervals at Marlborough and managed to collect some of the credit that accrues to the brother of a hero. It had been cheaply acquired, too, for Bobbie's school fees had been paid out of the meagre savings of his father, savings religiously preserved by his mother for his education, and Massy had gone on his way rejoicing and economising.

But Bobbie's hatred lost something if not all of its virility when he was old enough to appreciate the financial importance of his uncle and his exact place in a scheme of things which included all the male descendants of Jonathan Cheldon, merchant adventurer in India and founder of the family fortunes. For Jonathan, returning home with profits and plunder and a record comparatively venial in an age of wholesale corruption, determined to force the yeoman Cheldons into the ranks of county gentility by purchasing and amply endowing the mansion and estate known as Broadbridge Manor. Ever since then his descendants had buttressed and strengthened the family pedigree. Two of Jonathan's sons had entered the army and the younger had risen to the rank of general. A son of the general had become an ambassador and another had achieved a little fame at the Bar. Meanwhile, the Cheldon estate, losing something every decade by the advance of taxation and the failing strength of the pound, had descended with the solemn inevitability of a dukedom from heir to heir until Colonel Henry Cheldon held sway for nineteen years and departed, leaving his elder son, Massy, in possession of Broadbridge Manor, and a younger son in the army.

That younger son was Bobbie's father, and unless Massy Cheldon married and had a son the Cheldon estate must pass to Ruby's only child. She recalled now the wonder and the pride with which Bobbie had received the news that only one life stood between himself and the family estate. In almost the same breath she winced as she remembered his bitter railings against the Fate that permitted "that pompous bore" to keep him out of the money that he was certain guaranteed happiness.

The net result had been the tightening of the tension between uncle and nephew that had never really slackened. In vain had Ruby pointed out that Bobbie owed something to the uncle who avoided matrimony as carefully as he avoided generosity. "No woman would have him," was Bobbie's contemptuous retort, and so the guerilla warfare had continued.

Now, however, Bobbie was in the position of suppliant and a very humble suppliant at that. He was in love and an uneasy, tremulous, agitating love it was, too. Whoever this Nancy Curzon might be it was evident that she had many admirers and that competition for her hand in matrimony was keen. Only the fear of losing her prevented Bobbie meeting his uncle's fussiness and contempt with insolence and ill-temper. Well, that was to the credit of the night club dancer. Ruby sighed. She wished she could do something, but then since Bobbie had begun to talk vaguely of "doing something" on his own account she had been helpless.

Perhaps, Massy was right and where Bobbie was concerned she was foolish. But could she help it?

She half-wished there was no Cheldon estate and no entail. The zeal of Jonathan Cheldon had become a curse after a century, a curse to herself and a danger to her son. How often had Bobbie grumblingly adverted to the fact that every day his uncle lived he, the misunderstood heir, lost a day's income. There lay the explanation of his unwillingness to study, his failure to pass the preliminary examinaton for the Bar, his diurnal dissatisfaction with all the world and its inhabitants except a small coterie of imitation intellectuals which infested the purlieus of Fulham and Chelsea.

"What's the use, mother, when I'll have ten thousand a year when Uncle Massy dies of overeating?" had been his invariable rejoinder to her mild suggestions that a more active life would make him happier.

"Your uncle may live another thirty years," was a checkmate which he always refused to admit.

She was rescued from further depression by the voice of her brother-in-law.

"There are other risks in marriage besides financial ones," he was saying in that pedestrian, self-opinionated manner of his which had earned for him the petrified dislike of all the other bores ensconced in armchairs in St. James's Street, Piccadilly and Pall Mall. "How can you be sure that you are marrying the right woman? You can't tell until you've married her and then it's too late if you've made a bloomer."

"I suppose that's the reason you've remained a bachelor, Massy?" said his sister-in-law with a laugh that did not lighten the atmosphere.

"I cannot afford to marry," he answered gravely. "With a Socialist government composed of alleged Conservatives in power the landowner is a prisoner within his paltry income. It's all very well to quote Harry, but he was lucky, Ruby."

"Thank you," she said, merrily. Massy Cheldon's compliments were rare, omitting, of course, those he paid daily to good wines and good food.

"But how would the world get along without women?" Bobbie asked with an earnestness that indicated that he believed he was the first to coin that question.

"We are not talking of the world—we are talking of you," was the unexpected retort. "You want to marry and you haven't a shilling. At twenty-three you've still got to earn your first week's salary." He very nearly said wages but recollected in time he was speaking to a Cheldon. The tone and manner were bitter, even savage, and Ruby trembled, but the spirit of Nancy Curzon was there although none of them knew it. "I quite agree, uncle," said Bobbie, humbly, "and that's why I want you to put me in the way of earning my own living."

At this unexpected surrender Massy Cheldon, suspecting that the victory was not actually his, moved uneasily. He was too accustomed to lecturing and hectoring his nephew to be able to fit in with a state of affairs in which friendliness and politeness predominated.

"Didn't Schopenhauer say that love was a species of insanity because it made a young man unable to keep himself voluntarily undertake to keep another man's daughter for the rest of her life?" he asked, falling back on sarcasm.

"Well, anyhow, uncle, you're sane enough, according to the Schopenhauer standard," said Bobbie with a laugh.

Massy Cheldon scrutinised him again, and again resented the frank youthfulness of his open, sunny manner, and the flushed, animated cheeks and shining happiness of expression. Resentment deepened into something lower than mere jealousy when he reminded himself that all this youth and vivid enjoyment might one day—perhaps, soon—be allied with wealth. A street accident, poisoned food, any of the ordinary ills of life—the middle-aged man who was obsessed by meanness shuddered at the thought of being parted from his museum of coins, banknotes, share certificates and rents. Hitherto he had disliked Bobbie, and Bobbie had gone out of his way to justify his dislike, but now with his nephew apparently reforming and shedding all his weaknesses Massy Cheldon realised that there was nothing left for him to do except to hate his heir, nakedly and primitively.

"Marriage is expensive," he said aloud, "unless, of course, you can manage it at someone else's expense." He laughed alone.

"Now that I have Nancy to live for I am a different man, uncle," Bobbie exclaimed, in his excitement rising and standing over him. "She's a girl in a million, beautiful, clever, original, a living poem. When you see her you'll not be surprised I fell for her at first sight. I wish I could describe her adequately, uncle." The glowing face and the boyish enthusiasm made Ruby Cheldon tremble again, though not with fear.

"She's a dancer, isn't she?" Massy Cheldon shifted to the stance which intimated to the knowledgeable that he was about to talk about himself. A heavy gripping of the floor, slight drooping of the shoulders, far away look in his fish-like eyes, and the outline of a grin about his too thin lips—Ruby saw all these signs and sought consolation in the hope that however boring the reminiscence might be their simulated interest would wheedle him back into a good humour.

"A dancer, eh?" He seemed to fall into a reverie. "That reminds me of a girl I met when I was a fresher at Oxford. A wondrous specimen of female divinity minus any sort of intelligence. I used to rave about her, and so did others. I remember I nearly fought a duel with young Allen on her account the day before she chucked me in favour of Tubby Kelshaw, who succeeded to the family peerage the following year. Dolly is a grandmother now and a pillar of the High

Church party, but I think she'd have married me if I hadn't been a pauper compared with Tubby. That was fifteen years before I succeeded to Broadbridge. A dancer? They haven't changed, Ruby, and neither has human nature."

"You ought to have married, Massy," said his sister-in-law, compelling herself to be complimentary. "I'm sure you'd have been a successful husband. But I suppose you've preferred to leave a trail of broken hearts behind you, and yet you're angry with Bobbie because he's in love."

"I'm angry with Bobbie because he's talking of marriage when he ought to be doing some remunerative work."

Bobbie moved away to hide his resentment and to stifle the retort which had sprung unaided to the tip of his tongue.

"But I'm not cut out for matrimony, Ruby, and that's a fact," Massy Cheldon continued as soon as it was obvious that his nephew had no intention of turning the discussion into an argument. "Most of my pals have had a shot at it and missed badly. Look at Tom Hedley who's been married four times and—"

"Four times!" Ruby exclaimed. "Why, it's polygamy on the instalment plan."

His smile of appreciation was confined to his mouth while he made a note of the remark for use later on.

"Tom wouldn't listen to me, and all four marriages were failures. No, Ruby, you must leave me to my lonely bachelorhood, and twenty or thirty years hence when Bobbie is older and wiser he can step into my shoes at Broadbridge and try and make something out of the Cheldon estate."

"I'd rather have Nancy and poverty than all the wealth in the world," said Bobbie with an earnestness pathetic rather than convincing.

"That's very romantic, Bobbie," remarked his uncle almost tolerantly, "but would the young lady agree with you? My experience of dancers is that they prefer to love all the wealth of the world."

"Nancy is different, uncle, quite different from the sordid, mercenary type you knew." The enraptured speaker smiled pityingly at fifty-three years of ignorance. "She's a sprite, uncle, ethereal, all spirit, a child of nature. Every time I see her dance I think of a love poem, a sonnet. She's put life into me, uncle, and with her as my daily inspiration I feel I can achieve almost anything."

"Can you achieve a job at five pounds a week?"

The rhapsodist crashed back to earth.

"That—that's what I—er—I hoped, uncle—I—er—" he stammered.

"In coherent language that means you want me to place you in a well paid position so that you can begin life in a style superior to that of Galahad Mansions."

The hostility and contempt were having their effect on Bobbie's temper, but he strove hard to keep to his pact with his mother.

"I can only do my best," he muttered.

"That's something anyhow," said Massy Cheldon sarcastically. "Though it's a pity you didn't think of trying to do your best a little sooner. You might have been at the Bar now or in a well paid post in the Civil Service, and—"

"Need we have all this again, Massy?" his sister-in-law asked in the gentlest tone she could assume. "We want to discuss Bobbie's future—not his past."

"Do you really wish him to marry?" he asked in astonishment.

"I want him to be happy," she replied, giving Bobbie an affectionate glance. "I know my son better than anyone else knows him, and he'll do the family credit yet."

Massy Cheldon made a dramatic gesture by flinging his hands in the air.

"Oh, you mothers!" he cried, as if helpless and hopeless. "You'd march to hell with your sons rather than go to heaven without them."

Bobbie took his mother's arm in his, and the sight infuriated the friendless, warped, self-centred miser.

" 'Pon my word, Ruby, you almost persuade me that you're more to blame than the young cub himself."

Bobbie released his arm and took a step forward.

"Bobbie!" His mother's exclamation was a piteous cry of terror which restrained him in time.

"Oh, all right," he said and threw himself on the sofa.

Massy Cheldon, believing that his personality had triumphed, reverted to his usual role of crabbed, critical and sarcastic relative.

"I won't waste any more of my time," he said fussily. "That reminds me, Ruby, to ask you a question which I can't find the answer to. Why is it always orange peel time in Fulham?" She laughed. "I'm serious. It goes on all the year round. The entrance to Galahad Mansions was strewn with orange peel and children when I arrived, and it'll be orange peel and children the next time and the time after that. It can't be pleasant for you."

"Galahad Mansions is not Broadbridge," Bobbie retorted and strode out of the room in a rage.

When they were alone Massy Cheldon laughed harshly.

"I'll tell you what we'll do, Ruby," he said. "Invite this Nancy Curzon to enable me to see her. Not a dinner party, for I won't put you to the expense and the trouble. Make it an evening party, as informal as you can. Don't give it the appearance of a court martial on the girl. Get some young people and make it a jolly affair with nothing suggestive of an ulterior object."

"I think I'll try it," she murmured, and sighed. "But what will happen, Massy, if she passes the test?"

He smiled to himself.

"When the unexpected happens it is wise to do the unexpected," he replied, oracularly.

"You mean you would make Bobbie an allowance—a generous allowance?" She stared at him with a sort of dazed wonder.

"Exactly." He smiled again, but this time it was a smile expressing his contempt for her ignorance of the world and its worldlings. He could have laughed at her unsophistication. Fancy, not being intelligent enough to envisage the type represented by "Nancy Curzon!" He always clothed the name in inverted commas. The girl would of a certainty prove as false and as artificial as her acquired cognomen. She would giggle, talk and think at the top pitch of her voice, betray herself in a dozen different ways in as many minutes, and in the very act of struggling to conceal her vulgar origin ostentatiously expose it.

"The party shall take place," she said, suddenly ending the unnecessary silence. "I'll ask Sylvia, Freddie Neville, Mrs. Carmichael and one or two others."

"And no reference to me, please." Massy Cheldon gathered himself together preparatory to departure and in a moment changed from the intimate friend and relation to the patronising, rather pompous visitor from another region.

"Not at all a bad little place this," he said, without taking his eyes off his gloves. "Used to know Fulham in my youth but had forgotten it. Nice neighbours, I hope?"

"The flat overhead is occupied by a conjurer who beats his wife and the one opposite by a retired doctor. We have a dipsomaniac on the floor beneath, and there's a man and wife with nine children next to that." Ruby Cheldon laughed. "We're all living beyond our means in Galahad Mansions." She tried to laugh and failed. "But that can only bore you,

Massy, and, after all, nothing matters except Bobbie's future. I haven't slept through a night since he told me about her."

"I'm glad you called me in," he said after the manner of a doctor. "But now we'll forget the worst side of it and try to think of the best. I must be off. I have a new chauffeur and he isn't conversant with the shortest route to Broadbridge. Good-bye, Ruby." He took the extended hand and raised it in a finicky, affected manner to his lips. "You can rely on me once I hear from you the date of the party."

He went to the door and threw it open. A moment later Bobbie could be heard emerging from the dining-room.

"I'll think it over," he said to his nephew as they walked down the three flights of cemented staircase. "I expect to be in town again early next week, and if it is necessary I'll drop you a line asking you to call at my club."

They had reached the pavement before Bobbie could bring himself to mutter in an ungracious tone, "Thank you, uncle," but the sight of an obviously costly motorcar, with a tall, soldier-like chauffeur in attendance, banished his surliness and replaced it by a bitterness which was inspired by self-pity. In silence, and motionless, he watched the car drive out of the sombre street, oblivious of the awe-inspired stillness of the children in the gutter and the tired women in doorways.

A tennis ball, black with age and ill-usage, awakened him out of his reverie as it slid from his arm and dropped like a sodden potato at his feet.

"Sorry, mister," said a voice, and a small, grimy face was upturned in the direction of his unseeing eyes.

Bobbie, without acknowledging the apology, turned into Galahad Mansions, absorbed in a scurrilous analysis of the one life which stood between himself and wealth and luxury—and Nancy.

He found his mother staring into the weakening fire that had been lighted only because it was necessary to make a burnt offering to Uncle Massy on an afternoon in early May that had threatened to be chilly.

"What did he say?" he asked, thinking only of himself as only an expert can.

"Nothing practical, Bobbie," she answered, restlessly. "But if he won't do anything you must do something for yourself."

"I wish I could." He dug his hands into his trousers' pockets and held himself with a vicious intensity that reflected his state of mind.

"I blame myself, Bobbie," his mother continued, "for letting things come to this pass. I should have insisted on your getting work of some sort. You have brains and personality. But, of course, it's this cursed Cheldon inheritance—waiting for dead men's shoes, and your uncle won't die for a long while yet."

He started rather guiltily, for at that very moment he had been thinking of his uncle's chances of prolonged mortality. Fifty-three was a tremendous age to twenty-three, and yet there was Billy Annan's uncle, Sir Percy Annan, who was ninety and going strong. It was very disheartening.

"I shouldn't have let you refuse that appointment in South Africa three years ago."

"When Uncle Massy was seriously ill—dying," he reminded her. "Had he died I'd have had to come straight home on the next boat."

"It was a mistake—our mistake," she murmured, her thoughtful expression adding dignity to her natural beauty. "I haven't been ambitious enough, Bobbie. I ought not to have been content just to have you. In spoiling you I have spoilt myself. To think that we've been living in Galahad Mansions for five years! To think that I was once happy to be here!"

He laid a hand on her shoulder.

"It's not your fault, mother, it's just luck. If father had been a food controller instead of a soldier you'd be rich and happy, and—"

"You'd never have met Nancy Curzon, Bobbie," she said flippantly. "Don't forget that. It's places like Galahad Mansions that bring you into contact with girls like Nancy Curzon. That reminds me, Bobbie. What about a little party for me and our friends to meet Nancy?"

The ecstatic look in his eyes hurt her.

"The very thing, mother," he cried, all his envy, hatred and uncharitableness forgotten. "I'd love you and everybody to meet her and tell me how lucky I am. What about next Tuesday? Nancy is dancing at nine and at one in the morning so she could come either at seven or at half-past ten. At least, I think she could. I'll have to ask her."

"Splendid." She was recovering under the spell of his boyish enthusiasm. "I'll ask Freddie Neville and Sylvia Brand. I think Freddie's keen on her. And Mrs. Carmichael."

"Who's keen on Uncle Massy?" He laughed ironically. "I can't imagine the pompous old ass marrying that modern Lady Sneerwell. But still, you can ask her. But, of course, you won't invite uncle?"

"I'll not send him an invitation," she said truthfully. "Have you any special friends you'd care to ask?"

"I'll wait until the day. Depends on whom I meet. And Nancy might want to bring along a pal, perhaps, her dancing partner, Billy Bright."

"Don't forget, Bobbie, we can't invite more than eight as we've only got ten tumblers, to say nothing of chairs. Galahad Mansions isn't Broadbridge Manor with its salons."

When she observed the quick change in his expression she regretted her humorous comparison, and to save the situation she added hastily, "We'll have a jolly little party with no frills and no pretence, and we'll make Nancy feel at home the moment she arrives."

"That's just like you, mother," he cried, and kissed her. He never knew why she averted her eyes and why she trembled. Fortunately, at that moment the hall door opened to the accompaniment of a creaking key.

"That's Florence," his mother said quickly. "You tell her we'll have tea in here. I'll see her later."

Florence was the daily help who "obliged" by working whenever it suited her own convenience. She was a sturdy girl with an inclination to stoutness, but undeniably pretty and with plenty of assurance. She was greatly in demand in the neighbourhood of Galahad Mansions and could be relied on for a not too inaccurate résumé of the news that the newspapers dare not print. She knew the inside history of all the families which could afford to employ her in instalments, but she specialised in the royal family, particularly their matrimonial alliances. This week she was doing duty for Mrs. Cheldon from four to eight.

Bobbie had hitherto regarded Florence with aversion though not because she herself deserved or provoked it. But she was evidence of their ghastly poverty, and he resented the evidence as much as the fact itself. Uncle Massy did not pay a woman eightpence an hour for four hours twice a week to keep his mansion clean. Uncle Massy did not....

He strode into the kitchen with the determination of a man whose time is precious and who must be economical with it.

"I say," he began, and stopped. "Why, what's the matter?"

For Florence, seated on a chair and with her head on arms resting on the kitchen table, was sobbing convulsively.

An ever-present consciousness of superiority over the rest of the human creation and especially that meagre portion of it which laboured to lessen his discomforts was responsible for the detached curiosity with which he regarded the noisy, truculent figure. There was accompanying that curiosity, however, a growing feeling of resentment that anyone else should indulge in sorrow to an extent comparable with his own.

"What's the matter, Florence?" he asked, shoving his hands into his pockets and watching her with an amused interest that never came within approachable distance of embarrassment. "Dry your eyes, and let's hear all about it. Mother ill?"

"No—no, sir," she whimpered, unable to maintain the sobbing to a pitch satisfactory to her fury. "It's Tom—my young man."

"Oh, of course." Why it should have been "of course" he did not know, but young men had always formed the staple population of Florence's life. How often had he heard his mother express a wish that her fragment of a domestic would take a vow of celibacy!

"He's been and gone and chucked me," she gulped.

"I am sorry." It was the regulation remark. "Bit of a cad, eh? Never mind, Florence, there are plenty more, and a popular girl like yourself, you know, eh?"

She smiled faintly.

"I expect by next Monday you'll be booked up for the remainder of the year." She smiled appreciatively. "The young men like you." She nearly laughed over the tear drops. Bobbie, enjoying the patriarchal and patronising role, sought for further words of encouragement. "After all, it's Tom's loss and not yours, you know."

Her expression became cloudy again.

"I'm not quite so sure about that, sir," she said, threatening to lapse into watery sentimentality again. "It's because he's come into lots of money that he's jilted me."

"Lots of money?" Bobbie echoed, excited as well as interested.

Florence completed the drying of her eyes before replying.

"It's that uncle of his, the rich one." Bobbie thought of his own and scowled. "Mr. Welt owned a newsagent's business in Chawdon Street, one of the best in Fulham. Well, on Sunday Tom's cousin took the old man out in his motor car and they had an accident and Mr. Welt died. Tom heard about his will yesterday. He gets the shop and nearly five hundred pounds." She dabbed at her eyes. "The shop's worth six quid a week clear, and Tom won't have no more to do with me. I'm not good enough for him." She repeated the phrase with a vicious emphasis. "I've a good mind to sue him for breach of promise even if he's never written me any love letters and there's never been a ring. But Ethel and Gladys and Harry Smith all have seen him with me and he told them…"

Bobbie listened with his thoughts at Broadbridge Manor….

"And if you ask me." He awoke as the lengthy narrative took another turn. "If you ask me." She paused impressively.

"Yes? What is it I've got to ask you?" He spoke mechanically.

"I tell you what, sir," she said, apparently dropping the interrogative style which was a favourite of hers, "it's my opinion that it was all a put-up job between Tom and his good-for-nothing cousin, Bert Cronen."

"Indeed!" He threw the word in to satisfy her.

"An absolute put-up job." Florence approached nearer and lowered her voice to the requisite conspiratorial level. "Nearly a week ago Tom got the sack from his job. Cheeky to the foreman, he was. Well, he's finished there and he owes his landlady for five weeks. The dogs got the money, sir. I know that 'cause he told me. Well, Tom's in a rare fix, no weekly wages and nothin' to come. Then it occurs to him that he's still his uncle's favourite. Isn't it likely that he got Bert Cronen to take the old man out in his rotten car and purposely had an accident? You're not going to believe that it was just chance that made Tom a rich man inside a couple of days? He knew his uncle would never have died in the ordinary way so soon. Good for twenty years and—"

"How old was he, do you know?" There was a curious hush in his voice.

"Fifty-five, but young for his age," she answered promptly. "I saw him only a fortnight ago when me and Tom went to tea with him. Mr. Welt was always saying he was going to touch eighty. That's how he would put it—touch eighty. Why, in many respects, sir, he was younger than Tom. You know these printers, sir."

Bobbie did not, but he was not listening, and she took his abstracted air for profound absorption in her shattered but still dramatic romance.

"They're never fit." To his surprise she burst into tears again. "I always hoped that when me and Tom married we'd be able to help his uncle with the shop. I didn't want a husband who might be at work all night. But there, I'm silly. Tom's rich now and I'm not good enough for him. It was all right when he was broke and I could help him a bit. It's different now. He's killed his uncle and got the shop and nearly five hundred quid. And I wish I was dead, I do indeed."

With a sympathy animating him that astonished him he laid a hand on her arm.

"I'm sorry, Florence," he said feelingly, "really sorry. But there are better men left than Tom, and one of them will find you soon. There, I can see you're a sensible girl."

She looked gratefully at him.

"Thank you, sir," she whispered. "I never thought you'd bother about my trouble. But I'll sue him, that is if he ain't—I mean, if he isn't had up for murder. He wasn't in the car—that's his slyness—but it was a regular do, that was. They ought to hang him and his precious cousin for murdering the old man for the money and the shop. I'm not good enough for him!" She concluded with a scream of derision that frightened herself as well as Bobbie. "Sorry, sir," she said nervously. "I—"

"That's all right. Better think of something. And that reminds me. Mother says we'll have tea now." He turned to leave the kitchen. "Oh, by the way, Florence, what's the name of the gentleman with the car?"

"Bert Cronen, sir. Why?" Her surprise temporarily banished her sorrow.

"Oh, er—I—well—I want to tell mother the whole story. But get tea at once, Florence."

"You've been a long time," said Ruby when he re-entered the room. "Anything happened?"

He flung himself into the sofa and set in motion its dead springs.

"Just a little human drama, mother," he answered with an affectation of laziness. "Another of Florence's love affairs has terminated in tears and tatters."

"I suppose he drank—the last one was a gambler—so it was the turn of a drunkard." She smiled reminiscently.

"Oh, no, nothing of the kind. Real human drama, mother. Nemesis has overtaken the chucker of young men. A young man has chucked her."

"That's interesting." She sat up in her chair. "Usually they are afraid of Florence."

"This one isn't or wasn't. Mother, money has come between them. It appears that the young man has or had a rich uncle who was taken for a ride—strictly innocently, of course—in the car belonging to Tom's cousin, Bert Cronen."

"And the uncle was so infatuated with the car or its driver that he cut Tom's name out of his will and made Bert his heir?"

"Wrong again." Bobbie was enjoying himself in a dour, self-pitying way, but his mother was unconscious of that. "Bert, the cousin, took the opportunity to kill the rich uncle, and lo! and behold, Tom is now the owner of a six quid a week newsagency in Fulham and nearly five hundred more quids in the bank. The immediate consequence of this sudden accession of fortune is that Tom considers he ought to look higher in the social scale than our tri-weekly obliger, and Florence is heartbroken."

"That means she'll be emotional for a week at least, and I want our party to take place next Tuesday."

"We can do without her. I'll help, and so will Nancy for that. She's wonderfully domesticated considering she's an artiste. Besides, we can rope Freddie Neville in, and Mrs. Carmichael will be unhappy unless she's nosing around all the time. Oh, here's Florence approaching, so exit young master in search of silence."

Ruby watched the girl arrange the tea things and did not speak until the seventh sniff.

"Sorry to hear of your disappointment, Florence," she said, trying to infuse something else into her tone than politeness.

"Thank you, ma'am. But Mr. Robert has been so sympathetic-like and kind. I thought he'd have laughed at me but he didn't. You should have seen his face when I was telling him how Tom and Bert had killed their uncle for his money. At least, it's my opinion that they did."

A horrible sense of discomfort pervaded Ruby. She shrank from the association of "murder" with "uncle," and she escaped from panic only because it was so obvious that the girl was utterly incapable of discovering a parallel in Galahad Mansions to the temptation which must have assailed the alleged murderous Tom during the weeks preceding the profitable tragedy.

"You mustn't bring charges you can't prove, Florence," she said, severely. "The cousin wouldn't have risked his own life to help Tom."

"He didn't ma'am," was the unexpected retort. "Mr. Robert guessed that as well as me. Wanted to know particularly what Bert's name was."

Ruby seized an empty cup and rattled it unwittingly against a saucer.

"We'll have toast for tea," she said weakly.

Chapter Two

The preparations for the party by providing a diversion for Ruby Cheldon's oppressive and apprehensive thoughts quickly restored her to her usual serenity of outlook and manner. She loved entertaining, and was, therefore, always at her best no matter how poor her surroundings or how inferior the ingredients of the feast might be. A gracious friendliness towards all, attentiveness to everybody, combined with a tactful avoidance of iterated invitations to eat and drink, an unobtrusive supervision, and yet a total absence of dominance gave her the control and leadership of every party of which she was the hostess without anyone suspecting that she was something more than one of those present.

But then she left nothing to chance, not even the apparently smallest details. The commandeered rooms were with their contents subjected to a disembowelling cleansing which rendered parts of them almost as shiny as the "payway" products of the new era. Even the sofa, thrust into the least conspicuous of corners, was nearly redeemed from passive hideousness by gaily-coloured cushions distributed at strategic points. A couple of rugs from the bedrooms broke the drab monotony of the drawing-room floor, and the shaded electric light mercifully reduced the three engravings to symmetrical frames and nothing else. Flowers in glass vases were assigned positions where Ruby thought they would show most effectively, and whenever possible inartistic evidences of their poverty were banished to the kitchen.

Her chief glory and pride, however, were her photographs, those relics of gentility which the poor wear like medals. The photograph of General Sir Hildebrand Cheldon complete with Crimean whiskers and cast-iron regimentals. ("Oh, yes, he was my husband's uncle.") Hubert Cheldon in his uniform as a deputy-lieutenant. ("I've got a book about him somewhere.") Jonathan Cheldon in the dress of the late eighteenth century which the twentieth regards as a uniform. ("That's a photograph of his portrait. Painted by Sir Thomas Lawrence. Yes, he does look like Lord Clive. Lots of people have remarked it.") Broadbridge Manor with its extended frontage and vast lawns. ("Belonged to the Dukes of Weybridge before Bobbie's ancestor bought it. Lady Emily Cheldon. Daughter of the Earl of Ditton. Married Bobbie's grandfather. His aunt, who jilted a marquis, used to tell me that Disraeli was crazy about Lady Emily.") Thomas Delaforce Cheldon in his legal robes. ("Yes, but all the Cheldons are handsome. That book in his right hand? I don't know, but probably it's one he wrote himself. He was always writing.") And in the place of honour a large photograph of Colonel Henry Bertram Cheldon. Ruby had no need to voice her pride in her husband, neither was it necessary for her to parade his virtues or add to them by invention. His silver frame was always the centre of the array of Cheldon memorials and reminders that it was a distinct come-down in the world for a member of that illustrious family to dwell in Galahad Mansions, Fulham. They formed a goodly company for the edification and sneers of guests according to their degree of humility or jealousy.

"I don't think we've forgotten anything," Ruby said pensively to her aide-de-camp, Florence, at half-past eight on the night that was to witness the appraisement of the girl who was a candidate for entry into the exclusive ranks of the Cheldons. "I don't suppose anyone will arrive for another hour." She had been ready herself since a quarter to eight when Bobbie had gone off to offer himself as escort to Nancy Curzon.

"Don't forget, ma'am," said Florence, who could enjoy a party no matter how complicated her amatory troubles might be, "that Mr. Davidson mustn't use the sofa. It won't bear his eighteen stone."

"I'll head him off," Ruby promised with a smile. "What's that?" The front door bell rang twice with an impatience to which only a genuine Cheldon was entitled.

Ruby moved to the front of the fire where for a few moments she watched the reflection of the infrequent flames in her soft dark blue silk dress. She was feeling excessively nervous, certain in her mind that it was Bobbie who had rung the bell and that soon she would be facing the ordeal of an interview with a common, aggressive young woman with Bobbie looking on and, perhaps, discovering the real reason for the party and hating his mother for it ever afterwards.

The door opened and Florence, who had been carefully coached in the respectful formality due to the Galahad Mansions branch of the Cheldon family, announced the caller with the stateliness of a veteran butler.

"Miss Hyacinth Curzon."

Ruby advanced with a dignity of which she was unnecessarily conscious, and the instant she saw her son's fascinator her heart sank. For there was nothing common or flamboyant in her visitor's appearance. Here was a convincing imitation of the real thing, and, above all, here was an unusual and magnetic beauty.

Forty-eight involuntarily stared at nineteen and in one full scrutiny took in her five feet six inches of perfect and healthy womanhood, her head of brown hair, pale cheeks slightly touched with colour, broad, clever-looking forehead, bright, challenging dark eyes, firm and yet dainty chin, expressive lips vibrant with an earnest appreciation of life. She was certainly very pretty, this dancer of the night, and Ruby, vaguely summoning the ghosts of Lady Emily Cheldon and other aristocratic wives of dead and gone Cheldons, felt hopeless as she contemplated the possibility of convincing Bobbie that mere beauty did not guarantee the standard of bluish blood which she had a right to expect in the girl he intended to elevate to the position of her daughter-in-law.

"Miss Curzon?" she began nervously, when she found her visitor's eyes wandering round the room.

"Yes, that's me," came the response set to the discordant music of a superfluous giggle. "Isn't Bobbie here?"

"I thought that he'd gone to meet you. Won't you sit down?"

Nancy smiled her thanks and lapsed into a momentary reserve which made her feel ill at ease.

"I expect he'll be back at any moment now, Miss Curzon," said Ruby, as she became aware of several wave-lengths of a scent of penetrating virility. There was another pause.

"Nice room you've got here," said Nancy in a toneless voice.

"It might be better." The words were used merely to pass the time. The battle had already begun but only in skirmishes, neither being yet prepared to launch heavy artillery.

"I like the quiet colour scheme." She giggled again, forgetting in her nervousness that she had resolved to show Bobbie's mother what a perfect lady could be or ought to be. "You'll excuse my curiosity, won't you?" The lower part of her face grinned.

"Curiosity is often a form of politeness." Ruby Cheldon was feeling on top now and completely unafraid. The girl was common and her beauty and obvious cleverness merely underlined that fact.

Suspecting that she was losing ground Nancy regained her self-possession by initiating a discussion about herself.

"Of course, Bobbie's told you all about me, Mrs. Cheldon? He's such a dear boy. Quite unspoilt and a perfect lamb."

"Bobbie did mention that you were a dancer." Ruby's voice and manner would have earned the approval of Lady Emily Cheldon and her sister, who had married a colonial bishop. It was concentrated dislike touched with a veneer of contemptuous interest.

"I'm professionally known as Hyacinth—Nancy to my pals—Curzon of Curzon and Bright, speciality dancers. We do all the tip-top night clubs and our act is a regular riot."

"That means it is a big success?" It was the grand lady of the manor evincing an interest in the under-gardener's daughter.

"I should think so." She leaned forward in order to assume a more confidential attitude. "The managers will be fighting to get us soon, and don't you make no—I mean, don't you forget it."

"I'm afraid I hadn't intended to remember it," said Ruby, impulsively, and instantly regretted her rudeness. Fortunately, Nancy, accustomed to the curious humour of her underworld, chose to treat the remark as exquisitely funny.

"That's a good come-back, Mrs. Cheldon," she said wiping her eyes.

"She can act," thought Ruby, and for some unknown reason shivered.

"I'm very fond of Bobbie." Bobbie's mother thought the tone oddly impersonal, even detached. "He's a gentleman—

you can tell that at first sight. A perfect gentleman, I don't hesitate to say. None of your common crowd like the Belbills and Marjorie Grimes' pal who runs a cigar shop in the Edgware Road. No, Bobbie's a perfect gentleman, just as you're a perfect lady."

"Only a lady—I don't claim perfection," said Ruby ironically.

Nancy ignored the emendation.

"When Bobbie and I met in Bohemia—"

"Bohemia—is that a night club?"

The dancer wriggled in her mirth.

"Excuse me, but you are a one." She laughed for several seconds. "Bohemia is where bohemians meet."

"Oh, I see. And what are bohemians exactly?"

"Now you've got me, Mrs. Cheldon." She laughed. "I suppose bohemians are people who live the sort of lives other people don't live—do unconventional things and—er—have their own views about everything. Oh, dear, I never thought before or tried to think what it does mean exactly. Perhaps Bobbie could tell you better than me."

"If bohemians are persons who do unconventional things then I'm afraid you're mistaken about my son. He's the most conventional young man in London."

Nancy laughed the laugh of superior knowledge.

"Do you really know Bobbie, Mrs. Cheldon? Oh, yes, of course, you've known him all his life and I met him for the first time three months ago, but I'll bet I know something more about him than you do. Why, he's said things to me he wouldn't say to you."

"I expect he has."

The dryness of her tone was a challenge, and Nancy Curzon decided that it was time she brought into action the superiority with which her conquest of Bobbie Cheldon endowed her.

"I can do anything I like with Bobbie—he's crazy about me." She rose and opened her handbag. Ruby leaned forward and took a silver cigarette box from the table near her.

"Try one of Bobbie's," she said quietly.

"Thank you." The girl gracefully posed for her own satisfaction as she went through the preliminaries necessary to smoking.

"Look here, Miss Curzon," Ruby resumed, "I'm expecting a few friends soon and so time is precious. I want to talk to you about Bobbie and his future. As his mother I'm naturally anxious. Please don't think I'm your enemy or your friend. There, I'm very candid. But Bobbie is all I have, and we've got so little." There was a chance for a compliment here, but Nancy, too busy thinking of herself, missed it. "Bobbie has proposed to you, I suppose?"

That faintly cockney giggle pervaded the room again.

"You won't believe me, Mrs. Cheldon, but he actually went down on his knees. Delightfully old-fashioned, but so perfectly sweet. That was two days after we met in the 'Squealing Pig', and I've taught him a lot since. He wanted teaching."

"What he wants most of all is an opportunity to earn his living so that if he marries he'll be able to keep his wife in decent comfort."

"Do you mean a job? Bobbie working! Oh, my hat!" She uttered a piercing scream.

"You know the world, Miss Curzon, and it must be obvious to you that we are poor. At present Bobbie can't afford to marry."

"That's what they all say." She wheeled round to face her. "Isn't Bobbie heir to a title and estate bringing in ten thousand a year?"

"There's no title—only a property."

"Oh, I thought all estates had titles stuck on to them. Still it doesn't matter. Ten thousand a year will do to be going on with. After all, it's nearly as much as Happy Blibbs makes, but he's a top-liner."

"No doubt Bobbie has told you exactly how he stands." Her tone was one of suppressed irritation. "The Cheldon property is at present in the possession of his uncle, who is only fifty-three—"

"Fifty-three! Ye gods! Isn't the old man saving up to buy a wreath for his own funeral?" She stopped in her laughter, conscious that the atmosphere had become icy. "Sorry. Just a joke. But fifty-three! It's terribly old, isn't it?"

"Mr. Massy Cheldon may live for another twenty or thirty years. The Cheldons live long. But there is another possibility to be considered. He may marry and have a son, and in that event Bobbie would never get a penny or an acre."

"I'll lay the odds against the old man marrying and having a kid, but the twenty years frightens me. I'd be thirty-nine then, and living in a bath-chair. That's not the game for me, Mrs. Cheldon, and you can tell Bobbie so. He only talked of coming into ten thousand a year, and I believed him. It wasn't fair—" She walked over to the fireplace and stood staring into the grate, and in spite of her feelings Ruby Cheldon envied the lovely young life which had so much that was unlovely and common about it.

"A young man in love is always optimistic, Miss Curzon," she said, almost apologetically.

"Bobbie's talked as if he was a millionaire." The voice was sulky. "I was very nearly chucking Billy Bright my partner, and retiring from the profession altogether. I thought Bobbie had pots of the ready. Why, it was on account of Bobbie that I refused last night an offer for a continental tour with Billy Bright."

"From your point of view there must be better fish in the sea than my son," Ruby began.

The girl turned on her angrily.

"You don't mean that—no mother could mean it." The termagant peeped through the glistening eyes. "It ain't—it's not fair, Mrs. Cheldon. After all, I didn't propose to Bobbie, did I?"

The older woman went to her side and laid a hand on her arm.

"Why should we quarrel, Miss Curzon? We're both fond of Bobbie and want to do the best for him. We're two women of the world—you're nineteen and I'm forty-eight."

"Forty-eight!" she exclaimed. "Aren't you afraid of death?" Nancy was back in the Whitechapel of her childhood with its coffins, fish and chips, beer and policemen.

"It's only life we're afraid of as we grow older. When I married, nearly thirty years ago now…" She paused to sigh reflectively, and the girl seized the opportunity to take the stage.

"Thirty years ago! I've seen pictures of what people looked like then. Wearing long skirts and going about in hansom cabs."

"We weren't always wearing long skirts or going about in hansom cabs, Miss Curzon." Ruby's smile was genuine for the first time. "Life was pretty much the same then as it is now. We had much the same affairs and adventures as the young people of today have. Foolish and rich young men got entangled with common women. There were elopements, quarrels about money, divorces, even night clubs."

"Night clubs thirty years ago?"

"Yes, night clubs. I'm told they were even worse than they are today. I wonder is that possible? My cousin says they were. So you see, Miss Curzon, we're going round in a circle. In my young days there were fast women and fast hansoms. Today there are fast women and fast motorcars."

"I suppose that means me?" The glare was so intense that Ruby could detect physical danger to herself in it.

"I'm trying not to be personal, Miss Curzon. I'm not saying anything against you—only against the notion of my son marrying. He's penniless, and you don't want a penniless husband."

"Not on your life." The snarl was unmistakable.

"I want Bobbie to work and work hard before he even thinks of marriage. I want him to regard the Cheldon estate as out of his reach. The Cheldons have always been work-ers. Bobbie's father did his bit and a bit over, and I want Bobbie to follow in his footsteps. He's in love with you, and I'm not surprised. You live in a world of which he knows nothing. You're all light and brightness and adventure—he's compelled to live in a dull flat with a dull mother."

"Bobbie's no snob," she muttered.

"We're all snobs, Miss Curzon. By the way, would it be an impertinence to ask which branch of the Curzon family you belong to?"

The unexpectedness of the question discomfited Nancy and made her forget her grievances and her anger.

"Well, you see, in a manner of speaking, I belong to them all—if you go back far enough. Curzon's a sort of family name."

"But perhaps it isn't your family name?"

"I'm as good as anybody else." The sulky hostility beto-kened retreat.

"For your own sake, Miss Curzon, I hope you're better than a great many people I know. But I think this is Bobbie."

Two doors made a rushing noise and Bobbie, flushed and excited, stood over Nancy with an arm around her shoulders.

"Sorry to have missed you, darling, but I'm glad you and mother have had the room to yourselves. You've told her everything? Mother, isn't she wonderful?"

"She is very clever."

Nancy, interpreting the last word as only another woman could, stiffened.

"Why didn't you tell me, Bobbie, that you hadn't a bean?" she said, releasing herself from his embrace.

"But I never said I had money, darling!" he protested. "I told you all about the Cheldon estate and that I was hoping my uncle would help me to get a job and—"

"A job? I don't want to marry a man with a job. I want to marry one who can afford to do without one. I work like a damned nigger and where am I? When the agent's paid and the landlady and the bill at the clubs where I've got to spend or they won't have me, there's nothing left."

"Marriage founded on love—" he attempted, but he had two women against him now and speech was almost illegal.

"Miss Curzon is talking sense, Bobbie, and marriage founded on commonsense is the sort that succeeds."

"Love is the first and only essential, mother," he retorted, "and—"

"Let's leave love out of it," Nancy exclaimed petulantly. "I've been listening to insults and putting up with them because I thought you'd got the cash, Bobbie. If I'd known the truth I'd have let your mother know exactly where she got off."

"But, darling—"

"Need we prolong the discussion, Bobbie?" his mother asked.

"But, mother. As Bernard Shaw once said—"

"Only once?"

"Oh, never mind about Bernard Shaw. He gives me a pain in the neck. You two talk like a couple of gramophones. I won't—" Nancy spluttered.

The voice of Florence announcing Miss Sylvia Brand relegated to well below the surface all contentious subjects.

"Hello, Mrs. Cheldon, and there's Bobbie." The introduction was affected in the usual slipshod and hurried manner.

"Good evening, Miss Curzon."

Sylvia gave her a smiling glance while the dancer looked her up and down with something between a sniff and suspicion. But she need not have done more than ask herself if here was a possible rival. That Sylvia Brand liked Bobbie was obvious, but nothing more. She was pretty enough, but her efforts to aid nature with a touch of paint here and there had the effect of detracting from her good looks. Nancy, who used none outside her working hours, seemed fresh and natural now, while her possible rival was a shade too artificial in appearance to have a chance in the silent beauty contest now in progress. Actually there was no comparison between them, for Sylvia imitated badly and inexpertly a type not worth imitating and in her efforts to appear smart and be smart deprived herself of all the advantages derived from superior education and social position. But then Sylvia Brand, having been over-educated, really knew very little. She had gone through the conventional educational mill and had emerged a slangy, filmised, genteel paraphrase of an unconventional modern girl. Could she have afforded to be natural she would have confessed that she wanted to marry Bobbie and have a family somewhere in a western suburb. As it was, South Kensington veneered by Wardour Street had her in its grip and she was compelled to move with a small crowd which considered life a failure unless "doing something" every day and every night.

Physically she was half an inch taller than Nancy and had a figure nearly as good. She dressed with credit at the expense of a doting father and studied the art of self-possession under every conceivable circumstance. At this moment she was thrilled and alarmed by the presence of Bobbie's "latest" in the fastness of Galahad Mansions, but she affected a nonchalance which she never abandoned.

Ruby Cheldon murmured something about seeing Florence and left the room; Bobbie rushed out when the telephone bell rang with a "That may be uncle or someone."

Sylvia smiled when she found herself alone with Nancy.

"Volatile youth," she said, with a languid air. "Suppose you and he have fixed it up?"

"Haven't got past his mother yet—that is, if I want to." The reply was a trifle enigmatic, but Sylvia believed she understood it.

"Didn't know it was necessary to ask permission of mamma nowadays?" she drawled, but her heart was beating faster.

"One must be unconventional sometimes." Nancy was astonished at the ease with which she could imitate her and her set. "It strikes me she'd prefer him to marry you or someone like you."

The unexpected addition staved off Sylvia's embarrassment.

"Oh, that's only your joke. Bobbie and I are great pals, but nothing more. I expect he thinks I'm immature. He's a bit of a poet, you know, and looks down on us poor girls."

"Well, he looks up to me—crazy about me."

"Not surprised. You're a bit out of the ordinary and we're all ordinary here. I had a birthday party the other day—nineteen of us because I was nineteen."

"I was nineteen in March."

"Then there's a month between us. How interesting."

"Where were you born?" They had never taught Nancy Curzon, née Soggs, reticence in Paradise Alley, Whitechapel.

"Mount Street."

"That's near Grosvenor Square?"

"Mother used to say it was about a thousand miles away." She laughed. "When I was ten we emigrated to Knights-bridge."

"I was born in Paradise Row, Whitechapel," Nancy retorted with aggressive and false pride, "and Mrs. Cheldon knows it or guesses it and tells me politely I'm common and ignorant."

"I should say you were most uncommon, Miss Curzon," said Sylvia, in her youthfulness overrating her power to sup-press an offensive patronage.

"All that matters to me is that Bobbie loves me." She said this to remind Sylvia that if she entertained any hopes in that direction or if she imagined she could ride roughshod over her she was mistaken. "He's told me a thousand times that I'm the only girl he has ever looked at, but I'll bet many have looked at him." Again the giggle betrayed her.

"Bobbie's very popular," said Sylvia calmly. "We all think he's a dear. It's a pity he can't get a job."

"Get a job?" The reference coupling Bobbie with work always had an exasperating effect on Nancy, and she exploded. "I wish to God you wouldn't talk that rot about Bobbie as if he were a twopence ha'penny clerk living in a back street. Bobbie's a perfect gentleman. Why, the other night at the 'Frozen Fang' when a drunken ass threw a plate at him Bobbie instead of throwing the pieces back picked them up and handed them to a waiter. Bobbie's a gentleman who oughtn't to have to work." In her anger and speed she over-employed words. A rattle of glasses on the other side of the door warned her and she subsided into a windless growl.

It was Sylvia who opened the door and disclosed Bobbie bearing a tray containing the familiar furniture of a cocktail diversion. Behind him as if acting as acolyte was a tallish, fair-haired youth reverently walking, both eyes and hands ready for emergencies.

"Be careful, Bobbie," he was saying when the procession arrived. "There isn't too much sherry in any of the glasses, you know. Hello!" He stared at Nancy and grinned appreciatively.

"Hello!" Nancy returned carelessly. Whoever he was individually she knew his kind in bulk, hundreds of them.

"Freddie Neville—Nancy," was Bobbie's mode of introducing them.

Freddie grinned again. Grinning was a hobby if not a speciality of his, although it mattered nothing to him that it served to distract detection of the narrowness of the space between the extreme boundary of his chin and his too prominent teeth.

"Tootle-oo!" he chirruped and handed her a glass of sherry. "Spotted you at once, though I couldn't quite fix the name. Don't remember to have seen the Nancy."

"It's Hyacinth on the bills," she explained.

"Of course. Well, here we are, Nancy, and the best of pals. Gather round before the Old Brigade arrives."

They moved in a body towards the corner of the room furthest from the door, and once she found herself in the company of youth Nancy's self-possession and confidence returned to her. She was supreme in that little coterie, and she knew it. Freddie Neville, whose mission in life was to combine pleasantness and good humour with an utter lack of anything approaching brainwork, installed her as their leader, and Sylvia, barely conscious that in the presence of the real thing of which she was only an imitation, it would be discreet to merge into the audience. When Kitty Manson, Sylvia's usual partner in their nightly pursuit of what they called "life", arrived and proved to be an animated beauty photograph with a fondness for "chipping" Freddie, the party's temperature rose a trifle higher. Laughing and shouting, pausing to appreciate Nancy's own particular scream with which she heralded or emphasised her funny stories, and sometimes talking in chorus they paid no heed to the more elderly of the guests whom Ruby was receiving while her thoughts were as far away as her brother-in-law.

Florence interrupted with a collection of plates containing sandwiches and cakes. Freddie captured two and held them before Nancy. To prove that he had a sense of humour Bobbie immediately wrested them from him and presented those cakes and sandwiches which had not reached the floor to his divinity. The chorus laughed; Kitty said something which was considered witty, and Sylvia hit Freddie on the head with her empty glass. Somewhere in the background there was a murmur of voices, and Bobbie glancing over his shoulders saw his mother's crony and toady, Mrs. Elmers, the widow of a clergyman, and Galahad Mansions' acknowledged authority on Debrett. Beyond her was Mr. Davidson complete with his eighteen stone of a lifetime's over-indulgence in food, and listening to Mr. Davidson's recital of his unflattering opinion of Mr. Stanley Baldwin was the tall and gaunt Miss Shamley, a female of almost unblemished reputation.

"We're filling up," said Bobbie sarcastically.

"I'm not," said Nancy instantly. "Can't afford to. I have to dance in an hour or two."

The humour appealed to them, and in the midst of the storm of laughter Mrs. Cheldon came across to speak to Nancy. At once a chill fell upon the revellers, a chill caught from the resentful discomposure of the dancer.

"Mr. Davidson and Mrs. Elmers would like to make your acquaintance," said Ruby with a smile.

Nancy, suspecting that Mr. Davidson and Mrs. Elmers were only two members of the jury trying her that night, suppressed an instant desire to snub Bobbie's mother, but something in the calm, set pallor of her face and the serene determination of her expression checked her.

"Right-ho—I mean, of course." She nearly stamped her foot in her vexation at this lapse, but it was difficult to maintain perfect ladyism in the presence of so much sugared hostility and covert criticism.

Mr. Davidson shook hands enthusiastically, and Mrs. Elmers fishily.

"Fine weather we're having?" said Mr. Davidson.

"What a charming dress!" said Mrs. Elmers, who in spite of a vocabulary of exaggerated adjectives produced to please, seemed to take winter with her wherever she went. Nancy looked at the pointed nose, white and wrinkled skin and carnivorous mouth, and retreated a step or two.

"Yes—er—I mean—" she murmured, and to her relief the struggle towards politeness was mercifully ended by the sensational entry of Massy Cheldon.

"Why, Ruby!" he exclaimed as he took her hand between his own, "I'd no idea you were giving a party. I hope I'm not in the way?"

"Of course not, Massy. We're delighted to have you. Bobbie, a whisky and soda for your uncle. Not a cocktail. You know he hates them. Mrs. Elmers, I needn't introduce my brother-in-law to you. Mr. Davidson. Oh, Massy, I want to present you to Bobbie's friend, Miss Nancy Curzon."

It was only accidental, but to Ruby at any rate it was disturbing that the others should form a ring while Nancy extended her hand.

"Pleased to meet you," she said fatally.

"It's an honour," Massy responded gallantly, and looked over her head. "There's Sylvia and Kitty, and, of course, Freddie. Hello, Freddie!"

Really the great man was in a most friendly mood. "Charming!" whispered Mrs. Elmers. "Wish I had his money," was Kitty's comment, "I'd start the screamingest night club in London and bar everybody over twenty-five."

"Must come and see you dance, Miss Curzon," Massy resumed when the party had recovered a little from his importance.

"But haven't you?" she asked seriously. "I seem to remember your face. Must have seen you before."

"Now you're trying to make me vain," he retorted, and Nancy was so puzzled that when Freddie came up to claim her she suffered him to lead her back to the exclusive coterie in the corner.

As Massy Cheldon moved away with Ruby, conversation became general, and Mr. Davidson, invading the Freddie Neville group, broke it up. Sylvia wandered towards Mrs. Elmers, and Freddie, taking a hint consisting of a muttered threat in his right ear, left Nancy to Bobbie.

"I know your uncle well by sight," she said, and said it so seriously that Bobbie stared at her in astonishment.

"Why the tragedy, Nancy, and the gloom?" he asked, seeking refuge in facetiousness. "Of course, you've seen my uncle. He's one of London's most famous bores and is often on view in Piccadilly and Pall Mall, to say nothing of St. James's Street."

"Now you're talking like Freddie," she protested. "It's something more than having seen him, Bobbie. When I started dancing I used to be one of a troupe called the 'Seven Fairies.' I was the youngest—only fourteen—and the eldest was a girl named Hortense Delisle. Her real name was Annie Smithers, but that wouldn't have looked well on a bill. Of course." She uttered an exclamation of relief and her face cleared. "It was your uncle who got keen on Annie, dead nuts, in fact. We girls used to tease her about him."

"Well?" His lack of surprise astonished her.

"Why do you say 'well' like that?" she whispered, wishing she could shout. "Is your uncle that sort of fellow?"

"Always has been, according to his own account." Bobbie laughed. "He's been a lady-killer from the day he left Eton, perhaps before. But he's always seen to it that the killing has cost him nothing."

"I think he spent money on Annie."

"Oh, so that's why you're melodramatic. My dear Nancy, you must learn to be surprised at nothing. Uncle Massy is a bore and a miser who fancies himself as an Adonis. But he's always been too mean to marry, which I suppose I ought to be thankful for."

"I wonder," she murmured pensively.

"Wonder what?"

"What your uncle would say if I asked him what had become of Annie. She was going about with him a lot when she suddenly disappeared."

"To be continued?" said Bobbie, ironically.

"Let me think, you idiot," she said with a smile. "Annie was a beauty." She sighed. "Oh, here's Freddie." She made a face at him.

"Nancy," said the irrepressible intruder, "Sylvia and Kitty and I want you and Bobbie to join us in a midnight visit to Whitechapel. Rather a lark! Whitechapel's an awfully interesting place, you know."

"It's awful, but not interesting, Freddie. But do take your face away. Oh, who's that?"

"Mrs. Carmichael," heralded Florence from the doorway.

The newcomer entered on the run, uttered a laughing apology to Ruby and instantly rescued Massy from Mr. Davidson and Mrs. Elmers.

"That's the queerest widow in Fulham," Bobbie whispered. "Wants to marry my uncle, and yet she's well off."

Mrs. Carmichael, who at forty-three had to some extent got the better of her age, was now chatting to both Ruby and Massy. She was of good figure and height, with handsome features and a warmth of expression which gave a semblance of youth to her appearance. Her feeble egotism induced her to arrive late at every party, believing that a solitary entry with all the other guests forming a chorus would give her an outstanding position in any company. She had at her finger-tips the gossip of fifty drawing-rooms and about as many families, which she retailed with an artistic hesitancy and pretence of ignorance which convinced her—but no one else—that she was a listener to instead of a retailer of scandal.

"I'm so sorry I'm late, dear," she purred to Ruby.

"Oh, we all know, Mrs. Carmichael," said Massy chaffingly, "that you take good care to avoid whatever dangers may lurk in punctuality."

"Nasty, clever man," she cried, affectionately.

"What about a livener-up, Mrs. Car?" asked Freddie, intruding where even a devil would have feared to tread.

"Thank you," she said with the sourest of her ready-to-wear smiles. "A weak, very weak whisky and soda."

To her annoyance Mr. Davidson, observing that Freddie Neville was apparently basking in the smiles of the eclectic Mrs. Carmichael, joined the group and was speedily followed by Sylvia, Kitty and Mrs. Elmers. The widow of multiple butcher shops smiled her hardest to keep her thoughts at bay.

"A wonderfully pretty girl, Massy," said Mr. Davidson, anxious to please.

They started at his loudness of voice until they discovered that Nancy and Bobbie had disappeared from the room.

"Of course, she's pretty, Davidson," said Massy curtly. "What else is there to infatuate Bobbie?"

"When a man thinks only of a girl's beauty he's apt to forget himself," said Mrs. Carmichael, but the remark missing fire because Massy Cheldon continued to look severe, she added hastily, "Not that I approve of this constant running down of our sex. An incurable bachelor like yourself, Mr. Cheldon,—"

"Incurable? There's no such thing or state, Mrs. Car!" retorted Mr. Davidson who was sufficiently well-to-do to be able to afford to discount Massy Cheldon's standing in his own family. "Cheldon is merely taking the longest way round to St. George's, Hanover Square. I used to think I was one of the incurables. Didn't marry until I was forty-three, and I did it again at fifty-six."

"And yet you're always sneering at our poor sex, Mr. Davidson. You deserve to be punished for it," said Mrs. Carmichael severely.

"I was," he answered curtly.

The widow sought a chair and Massy Cheldon dropped into the one next to hers. Mr. Davidson sprawled himself on the decayed sofa, to Ruby Cheldon's horror, and Mrs. Elmers occupied part of a chair. Freddie, ready to serve, stood between them and the door.

Ruby longing for the time to pass so that she might take counsel with her brother-in-law, inspected the array of bottles and decanters on the sideboard.

"Perhaps Mrs. Elmers would like some tea," she whispered to Florence who had appeared in response to the pressing of the bell. "Oh, there's the front door. Who can it be?"

She had forgotten the vanishing of Bobbie and Nancy, and their return was very welcome, for somehow even the inventive and resourceful Mrs. Carmichael was finding it none too easy to keep the conversation alive.

"Sorry, mother," said Bobbie, "but the cigarettes gave out. Have one, uncle?" He presented a large box. "Oh, of course, Mrs. Carmichael. You too, Nancy."

"I must rush," said the dancer. "Just come back to say good night. Goodbye, Mr. Cheldon. Have my work to do before I try and forget Freddie and his grin."

"Oh, come now, Nancy!" that youth protested good humouredly.

But the murmuring "good nights" and "good byes" and the temporary disappearance of Bobbie blotted him out of the picture until Bobbie had come back and in a feverish attempt to compensate himself for the loss of his fascinator led Freddie to a determined assault on the solids and liquids.

"Thank you, Bobbie," said Massy Cheldon, accepting the scientifically adjusted whisky and soda. "I wanted it."

"A toast, ladies and gents," said Freddie, believing his assumed cockney accent was exquisitely correct and therefore exquisitely funny. "To the health and happiness of Nancy Curzon, and I am sure you will all agree with me that Bobbie has found a distinct number one."

Massy Cheldon nodded, and Mrs. Carmichael therefore nodded to. But they did not fail to notice that Bobbie's face reflected a sort of angry pride that threatened a scene.

"So she's dancing in a night club," Massy Cheldon remarked in an undertone with a sentimental flavour about it. "Dear me, why I could have been only a boy when I was last in one."

"But I thought night clubs were only invented during the war," exclaimed Sylvia.

"My paternal grandmother eloped with a man she met in a night club in the Haymarket in the early years of Queen Victoria's reign. It's curious to think that if that hadn't happened I mightn't have been here."

"Oh, night clubs are not the curse some people make them out to be," said Freddie Neville, helpfully.

"Thank you, Freddie," said Massy Cheldon ponderously, and Mrs. Carmichael duly provided the necessary laughter. "By the way, how is your mother getting on at Hollywood?"

"First rate, thanks. She's just got a fresh contract at two hundred a week—pounds not dollars—and is going great guns. You should see her press notices. But I can tell you that I was a trifle worried until I got the cablegram, for if she hadn't secured the contract I'd have had to take that job in the city my cousin offered me."

"That was a narrow escape, indeed," said Mr. Davidson sarcastically.

"It was. Quite knocked me off my grub with anxiety and nervous strain." Freddie Neville was incapable of identifying sarcasm even when it was being aired at the expense of others. "But won't it be jolly when Bobbie's married to Nancy? We'll all be able to see her dance for nothing. A jolly crowd these night club birds, and quaint. One's an ex-pug, you know."

They did not know, and Mrs. Carmichael, in particular, did not wish to know. Freddie's oratory only bored her, but then so would have the most polished of speakers if Massy Cheldon happened to be in her company.

"You'll marry one day, Freddie," she said sweetly. "All you men want looking after, particularly Mr. Cheldon."

"I have twenty servants to look after me," he said, and growled as he reminded himself of their cost to him.

"They only look after themselves," said Ruby, with a laugh.

"It's not good for a man to be alone," Mrs. Carmichael ventured. "That's in the Bible, but it's not one of the Ten Commandments although it ought to be."

"Why will you women always bring up the subject of marriage?" said Massy Cheldon testily. "One would think it was the best substitute for paradise. You should see some of the married couples at Broadbridge. They live like pigs."

"Is that their fault?" asked Bobbie, moodily.

"Of course it is," snapped his uncle. The tone angered Bobbie who had to find revenge in a pose of philanthropist and idealist.

"If I owned Broadbridge I'd be ashamed to admit that some of my tenants lived like pigs," he growled. "I'd give them decent houses."

"And have them turned into pigstyes within a year! But then, Bobbie, it's so easy to be generous with another man's money. Of course, I'm not popular at Broadbridge, and don't I know it! They would prefer for their landlord some romantically-minded young ass who would pauperise them and at whom they'd be the first to laugh. They don't want a shrewd, level-headed, clear-thinking man who keeps them up to the scratch."

"People who live in pigstyes must have to do an awful amount of scratching," said Mrs. Carmichael in an effort to ease the situation.

"And, of course, they grunt," said Ruby.

"They grunt right enough—at me," said Massy Cheldon gloomily. "But unfortunately or fortunately all the pigs are not at Broadbridge." He glared at his nephew.

"I say, populace," protested Freddie Neville in a plaintive voice, "aren't we getting a bit personal talking about pigs?"

"Speak for yourself, Freddie," interjected Sylvia Brand.

"Perhaps, you're right, Freddie," said Massy Cheldon rising.

It was the signal for the breaking up of the party, and Mr. Davidson began the farewell proceedings.

"Just see Sylvia and Kitty home," whispered Ruby to Bobbie. Her brother-in-law still lingered, the last of the guests after Mrs. Carmichael had been conducted to the custody of her chauffeur.

"Well what do you think of her?" Ruby asked with a wan smile.

"My dear Ruby," he answered, seizing the whisky decanter, "there's not the slightest need for me to tell you that. You've been too long one of the Cheldons not to know the Cheldon standard. Can you fancy her at Broadbridge Manor? Does she fit in with our rules and traditions?"

"She's dreadfully common." Ruby sighed. "Oh, dear, I do wish she was even passable. Massy, you remember her 'perfect lady' and 'perfect gentleman' and her manners!"

"She's clever though, Ruby, devilishly clever, and we've got to bear that in mind. Bobbie is infatuated with her. We both know what a young snob he is, and yet he gloated in her gaucheries. Was actually proud of them."

"She certainly helped to make things hum so far as the young people were concerned," she remarked. "And she's very pretty."

"If she were merely pretty she wouldn't be dangerous, Ruby, but with her cleverness she'll play the deuce with Bobbie and—you."

He laughed and drank a libation to his sense of the ironic.

"But what am I to do? Thank Heaven, she won't marry Bobbie unless he can afford to keep her."

"She's dangerous," he repeated, leaning against the sideboard and staring at her. "Ruby, you'll think I'm an old fool, but I'm afraid of Nancy Cheldon."

"You are certainly foolish," she retorted with a laugh. "What is there to be afraid of?"

"I hope you're right, but you can't look at things from my standpoint. You're the fond, doting mother who can think no evil of her son, and I am the not too affectionate uncle who can think anything good or bad of his nephew. Ruby, this girl has done more than make Bobbie fall in love with her—she's transformed him, and I believe she's got sufficient influence over him to drive him to any extreme."

A haunting dread passed over her like a spasm of impulsive terror, and she tried to banish recollections of it by endeavouring to be facetious.

"You're an incorrigible leg-puller," she said, speaking rapidly because her state of nerves would not allow her to think first. "Why, you'll be hinting next that to get the Cheldon property Bobby would—" She stopped dead, frightened by what she had already blurted out, and her fright was not lessened when her brother-in-law caught her by the left arm and drew her towards himself.

"So it's occurred to you, too, has it?" he asked, in a voice consistent with the sudden return of greyness to his cheeks. "Ruby, the position is too serious for us to play hide and seek with mere words. Let me put it this way. Bobbie has not only to be saved from this adventuress but from himself. He's weak and easily influenced, and his weakness is all the more apparent because he poses as strong. There's no knowing what he may try to do to gratify this harpy. He may even—"

"I won't listen," she cried, putting her hands to her ears.

He smiled to reassure her.

"I'm not angry with you, Ruby, and certainly not with Bobbie. I don't believe I've anything to fear from him, but if you allow him to get into bad company there's no knowing what he may do. The weak can often become strong in the hands of the unscrupulous. Bobbie will never injure me—he won't have the pluck. Now you're making a face." He laughed again. "Do you wish me to say that he will attempt to abbreviate my existence on this earth? Oh, you women, there's no pleasing you." He turned and removed from the decanter the inch of whisky it contained.

Ruby Cheldon went over to the window, not because she wished to inspect the curtains or by parting them feast her eyes on Juniper Street by moonlight. The act was due entirely to a wish to get as far away as possible from her brother-in-law and to escape from her disturbing thoughts. The latter, however, only doubled in strength and numbers.

Until the last few days she had never quite realised the exact importance of Massy Cheldon to her son. For one thing she had never thought of the possibility of her brother-in-law dying. He was only a few, a very few years older than herself, and to have contemplated his decease would have meant coupling with it musings on her own. To her the Cheldon inheritance had been something which in the ordinary and usual course of events might devolve on her son when he was middle-aged. The last three holders of the property had been round about sixty when they had succeeded. Bobbie was twenty-three. It would be time to indulge in golden daydreams when he was in the late forties. But now!

She shrank from repeating the word "Murder" to herself, but it had forced itself on her that afternoon Bobbie had casually related an epitome of Florence's latest amatory problem, for as he had spoken of the sudden accession to wealth of Florence's faithless follower she had seen in his eyes the envy and longing created by the irresistible comparison with his own problem. The hated word had then swum into her brain and there it had lurked ever since. And now it repeated itself so distinctly as to be almost vociferous.

Murder. Murder. Murder.

The murder of Uncle Massy. Florence had lost her lover because he had come into money by means of an accident which she continued to characterise as a deliberately planned crime.

Murder. Murder. Murder.

"Oh. I wish you wouldn't talk about it!" she exclaimed, forgetting that she was not alone.

"About what?" She quivered. "Bobbie's affair with this soiled fairy from the underworld?" She looked her relief.

"Please, don't be so hard on her," she pleaded, momentarily generous because she was under the sway of a feeling of relief bordering on ecstasy.

"I apologise, my dear. After all, I mustn't forget that one day she may be your daughter-in-law and a Cheldon. Shades of Lady Emily!"

"Don't be ridiculous!" Ruby protested. "Really, Massy, you might be more helpful. You're the only male member of the family I can appeal to, and I thought with all your cleverness and knowledge of the world—" She paused to wipe her eyes.

"I'll do what I can," he said, without emotion and quite unaffected by her tears. "But I'm certain you'll not approve of anything I'll do for you. First of all, you wish me to break the engagement between your son and the night club dancer; then I'm to find Bobbie a job that'll enable him to be independent and rush into the girl's arms. For heaven's sake, don't worry about anything I've said about Bobbie and the Cheldon property. It was only a mere surmise of mine without any foundation. Bobbie hasn't the pluck to earn a living and he hasn't the pluck to imitate the gentlemen who specialise in the higher walks of crime. I'm not afraid of him and you needn't be either. But, as I have said, he needs to be protected against himself."

With a sudden stiffening of her body and a look of determination he had not seen in her face for years she confronted him.

"Massy, I won't have this creature kidnapping Bobbie. Something's got to be done to part them, and I look to you to do it."

"But what can I do?"

"Your brother appointed you his guardian," she reminded him.

"Until Bobbie was twenty-one. He's now twenty-three."

She threw up her arms in despair, but she had not the opportunity to speak, for a familiar banging of a door heralded Bobbie.

"Sylvia and I've been chatting at the corner," he explained as he explored the whisky decanter without success. "But at last I got her a taxi. Mrs. Carmichael took Kitty. I say, uncle, you and mother have walked into the whisky."

He flopped on to a chair.

"Bit of a frost, mother, eh? What a collection! If Nancy hadn't turned up what a ghastly binge it would have been! But that reminds me. Uncle, what do you think of her?"

"Assuming that by 'her' you mean the young lady whose acquaintance I made tonight," Massy Cheldon began with an effort at one a.m. pomposity. But Ruby interrupted to save him from blundering.

"Your uncle has been admiring her, Bobbie," she said hurriedly. "He thinks she's very pretty and very clever."

The boyish features glistened with the pleasure and pride that animated him from crown to sole.

"Everybody says the same," he murmured, too happy to be more than articulate. "Nancy's one in a million." He bent his head over his knees, his hands clasped before him. "Can you wonder I'm crazy to marry her? Don't you see now that I must marry her—that without Nancy hell would be preferable to life?"

His uncle patted him on the shoulder.

"Bobbie, the first move is to get you a job." He would have continued in the same avuncular strain and pose had not Bobbie jumped to his feet and seized the limp hand in a double grasp.

"That's awfully good of you, uncle!" he cried, in a paroxysm of affectionate gratitude. "Of course, I must have a job. Without one I couldn't marry Nancy."

Massy Cheldon recaptured his physical freedom.

"It's too late to talk now, and my chauffeur must be swearing at me. Look here, Bobbie, come down to Broadbridge for next Friday to Monday and we'll talk things over then."

"Thanks awfully, uncle. I'll be delighted. Yes, we'll have a good pow-wow. I can see it's all Nancy's doing, but I knew she'd win you over at first sight. She does that with everybody."

"Bobbie," said his mother with a cold detachment of manner, "will you see if your uncle's car is waiting outside?"

He raced out of the room and Ruby's thoughts went back to her son's schooldays and her eyes became moist.

"Massy," she whispered, almost angry with him now for some reason she did not wish to discover, "is this invitation a trap or a—?" She stopped, unable to complete or further interpret her suspicions.

"Or a test? Is that what you mean, Ruby?" He smiled slightly, and the best of his smiles was never pleasant to look upon. "That is for Bobbie to decide. But perhaps you don't wish him to come?"

"Of course I do." She stiffened again. "I must face realities, as you've been fond of telling me. Here's Bobbie." She held out her hand. "Good-bye, Massy, and thanks for dropping in."

She was alone in the room for nearly five minutes, but was quite unable to do anything with her solitude. Her thinking faculties failed her and she could only listen for the sound announcing that her brother-in-law's car was moving away from the front of Galahad Mansions. The moment, however, Bobbie re-entered she became alive with doubts, anxieties, disturbing thoughts and perplexing questions.

"Now, mother, will you ever say again that there's no such a thing as a miracle?" He positively danced around her. "Just think of it! Uncle Massy falling for Nancy! Isn't it wonderful? But then, Nancy's one hundred per cent wonderful and I'm going to tell her so!"

"What, now?" she exclaimed, as he made for the door.

"Absolutely." He came back and kissed her. "Nancy's got to be told the amazing news that Uncle Massy is going to help me to a position which will enable me to marry her."

Words of warning clamoured for enunciation, but she had not the courage to disillusion him.

"Oh, all right, Bobbie," she murmured, weakly and wearily. "Don't be too late." She yawned in spite of her efforts.

From the doorway he smiled back on her, and when the outer door closed she was still reproaching herself with cowardice.

Chapter Three

As he strode through the too infrequent streets Bobbie lost himself in the happiness of realised dreams. Even the first ecstasies of his capitulation to Nancy Curzon seemed tame in comparison with the sense of triumph and achievement which animated him now. Life was something more than mere living; earth, including the Fulham particle of it, was more to be desired than heaven; he was a conqueror with wealth and success at his mercy because Nancy was his forever.

She had captivated his uncle, and that meant that the path to the altar would be strewn with roses; he would taste many of the pleasures of Broadbridge long before the Cheldon property was his own; he would be able to crown the girl he loved with luxury, and, above all, she would be his alone forever and forever.

Inspiration failing him he was more than satisfied to fill in the spaces of his mind with a mechanical repetition of his plans and prospects. To Massy Cheldon he gave a large size in wings and a larger portion of virtue than that incorrigible egotist had ever claimed for himself. To everyone else he would have given something of his happiness could he have done so, for it was of the kind that increases as it is shared.

In a turning off the King's Road he found a taxicab, and although it was bearing him to Nancy he half regretted the curtailing of his delightful fantasia. But behind all his delirium of joy was a dread which he contrived temporarily to suppress, a dread lest he was deceiving himself and was too much of a coward to give his intelligence full rein.

The cab stopped outside a tobacconist's shop in one of the offshoots of Shaftesbury Avenue and Bobbie stepped out and sought a lamp-post and under its guidance selected the essential coins. Then he glanced around him, glad of the unusual loneliness, grateful for the shutters of the adjoining shops, and happy in the solitude that seemed to make Nancy exclusively his. Somewhere underground and below a ham and beef shop was the "Frozen Fang", London's newest night club or at any rate the latest addition to Bobbie's list of nocturnal refuges. Suddenly he became uneasy. Would Nancy be waiting for him? He had had no idea it was so late. London appeared to be empty or unconscious, and the policeman in the light of a distant street lamp a swollen toy. It must be nearly three, and the "Frozen Fang" was not sufficiently well known to last much beyond two in the morning. He listened anxiously and heard nothing except the patter of the policeman's boots. By now the cab had disappeared and save for fitful lights on top floors London had ceased to exist.

He took a step forward and paused as a well remembered voice floated towards him from the basement. It was Nancy's and she was cursing someone, but the infatuated lover heard only the voice.

"What, you?" was her ungracious greeting as Bobbie presented himself at the top of the stairs leading from the subterranean imitation of Bohemia. "I wonder the lady-mother let you out of her arms."

The sneer was as coarse as the voice was tired and angry, but Bobbie was not in the mood to quarrel with anyone, and certainly unable to discover blemishes in the most perfect of creatures.

"I've got wonderful news for you, Nancy," he whispered, as yet unaware that two men were emerging after her.

"You don't mean to say that someone's shot that skinny uncle of yours?" She half turned her head. "Nosey, listen to the bearer of good news!"

Before Bobbie could attempt to interject a pleasantry of a kind likely to restore her good humour a stoutish, heavily-built man with a flavour of the forties about him panted to her side. As the street lamp was directly in front of the exit from the "Frozen Fang" Bobbie had no difficulty in guessing that the reason for his sobriquet was the pronounced flattening of his nasal organ. But as if to compensate he had large and bulging eyes, a sensual mouth, and ears that resembled a couple of cauliflowers waiting their turn to be washed. Bobbie took an instant and fearsome dislike to him, but the dislike lasted little more than a moment, for Nosey as soon as he reached the pavement extended a brawny hand and shook his sympathetically.

"Don't you mind her, Mr. Cheldon," he said in a voice pregnant with good nature. "She's in one of her tantrums. Best little girl in creation but apt to go off the deep end if everything doesn't come her way."

Nancy gave him a playful tap on the cheek.

"I can't be angry with you, Nosey," she said, and when Bobbie heard her careless laughter he could have hugged the ex-pugilist.

But the "Frozen Fang" now disgorged Billy Bright, Nancy's dancing partner, a young man of sallow complexion and dressed in evening clothes and grease. He was only Nancy's height and looked a couple of inches shorter, but Billy Bright bore himself with conscious pride, and his attitude towards Bobbie was one of patronising toleration.

"Hello, Cheldon!" he said lazily, giving his dark moustache a twist and a pat at either end. "Quite a little party. I suppose you'll come along to my rooms? We're going to discuss a new contract over a bottle of whisky." Bobbie shuddered in the safety of the gloom.

"Thanks," he said, feeling that nearly all the romance had been rubbed out of his fairy story. "I could do with a livener."

With an insolence too blatant to be resisted Billy took possession of Nancy, and Bobbie was compelled to follow with Nosey, who had the easiest of tasks in widening the distance between them and the couple in front. The ex-pugilist walked slowly, but of a purpose, and it was only when he could speak without being overheard that he opened a conversation on the only subject that interested his companion.

"She's a fine girl, Mr. Cheldon, a top-notcher. Got a great future before her in the profession—unless, of course, she marries."

Bobbie's heart had sunk, but now it rose.

"Perhaps, she's told you I want to—to—"

"Marry her? Of course. We've been talking about you all the evening, Mr. Cheldon." Bobbie warmed to him. There was no familiarity, no coarseness and no insolence. Nosey might not be of the Cheldon type of gentleman, but he spoke and behaved like one. Bobbie could award him no praise greater than that.

"And why shouldn't you marry her if you can give her a better time than she can give herself?" Nosey continued. "You're a gentleman and you have education and position. Nancy talks as if you hadn't any money, but as soon as she told me all about the Cheldon estate I said to her, 'Don't you be a fool and chuck away the chance of a lifetime. The lad's the right sort and the money will be there or thereabouts.'"

"Thank you, Mr.—er—" Bobbie laughed from sheer embarrassment. How could he address him as "Mr. Nosey?"

"Ruslin—Peter Ruslin," said Nosey introducing himself. "Partner in the firm of Ruslin & Oakes, theatrical agents. Used to be a pug."

A great light dawned on Bobbie, but it was not a comforting light.

"Have you got her the contract she mentioned?" he asked nervously.

Nosey Ruslin nodded expressively.

"A chance to make her name in two continents," he answered, oracularly. "Name in electric letters. You know the sort of thing. If she produced the goods her salary would jump sky-wards. But, of course, you'll marry her, and you're to be envied." He lowered his voice. "Between you and me, Mr. Cheldon, I want to get her away from Billy Bright. I can't stomach foreigners. It ain't English. Not a good influence. No, not at all. D'you know, tonight she was actually talking of marrying Billy if there was nothing better for her." He knew Bobbie was shivering but pretended not to notice it. "Of course, my contract is for the pair of them. After all, Billy does know how to dance, and he's got ideas. It's Bright & Curzon, you know. They'd have to travel Europe together, and that would mean marriage first. Then there's America and—"

Billy Bright's flat had now been reached and it soon engulfed them.

"Whisky? Nosey, I've a bottle of champagne to celebrate." Billy was doing the honours as if posturing in front of an audience.

"Better not open it until we've decided one way or the other," said Nosey genially. "But I'll join you in a whisky."

Nancy had disappeared, and the three men were looking at their empty glasses when she returned.

"Got anything to eat, Billy?" she asked in a voice that sounded hoarse and disagreeable. "Well, Bobbie, what's the news? Uncle in the pink and feeling fit to live for another fifty years?"

Bobbie tried to smile, but he failed to do more than produce a slight distortion of his features.

"Uncle's the goods, Nancy," he said impulsively. "After you went he promised to do his best for me. Couldn't say too much about you. You should have heard him. Pretty and clever and fascinating." He was not the first editor to improve on his text.

The girl eyed him suspiciously. At nineteen she knew something about men and their world; at twenty-three Bobbie knew nothing about women and their intuitions.

"He said that to you, did he?" she muttered. Then aloud, "I wonder what exactly he meant by it?"

A grating laugh from Billy Bright emphasised the sympathetic silence of Nosey Ruslin.

"What you ought to ask, Nancy," said her dancing partner, "is, what did he mean in hard cash by that?"

"You mind your own business!" snarled Bobbie, losing his temper.

Billy Bright, yellow-streaked through and through, was not afraid with a girl on the premises.

"Whatever concerns Nancy is my business," he retorted truculently. "And it's because it's my business we're here now. Nosey, tell him about that contract."

"No, you won't." Nancy stepped forward into the centre of the room. "I'll have no quarrelling about poor little me."

"I'm sorry, Nancy," said Bobbie, penitently. "I shouldn't have forgotten you were present. I wanted to see you alone and—"

"We're all friends here," she declared meaningly, but her wink was reserved for Billy and Nosey, and Bobbie was unaware of it as he was ignorant of the meaning she put into her tone.

"That's right, Nancy, that's right," wheezed Nosey, selecting the only armchair and filling it completely. "Let's sit down and have a quiet chat. Nice rooms you have here, Billy."

The diversion was diplomatic, and by the time the tenant had expatiated on the advantages of living above a grocer's shop Nancy was back again in her usual humour.

"Now listen to me," Nosey said when he had emptied his glass for the third time, "I want to talk business and I want Mr. Cheldon to butt in whenever he likes. I'm a business man first and last, and I want to link up with Bright & Curzon."

"Curzon & Bright," murmured Nancy, who had her pride.

"I can give you two the chance of a lifetime—a long continental tour beginning in Paris and ending in Monte Carlo with a possibility of America to follow." He stopped to glance covertly at Bobbie's uneasy expression. "Now, Nancy, I know you too well to talk big when there's nothing really big on the premises, and so I'll not be coy in mentioning the actual salary. It'll be a hundred a week, and when you've deducted my commission there'll be ninety left. Out of that you'll have to pay your own expenses, and these will average twenty quid a week."

"That'll be thirty-five a week clear for each of us," Billy Bright translated to his partner.

A cry of delight burst from her lips.

"Oh, Nosey, I could hug you!" she cried, springing up and suiting the action to the word. "You're a perfect dear! Thirty-five quid a week and living in the best hotels! It'll seem like fairyland."

"But if you score a win, Nancy," the agent explained, "it'll be double thirty-five for the American tour, and I'm certain you and Billy will be a wow. Your act is distinctive—a sure winner."

Bobbie's heart was making his boots feel overcrowded, and his depression was not lightened by an impression that his companions had forgotten he was in the room.

Thirty-five pounds a week plus luxury in first-class hotels, continental travel with all its novelties and allurements! It would be ridiculous to offer in competition the salary he would earn in the situation which Uncle Massy had almost guaranteed to obtain for him.

"Nosey," said Billy, rising, "I want you to see some photographs I've had taken and framed. They're hanging up in the dining-room."

For the first and only time in his life Bobbie's heart warmed towards Nancy's dancing partner, but the moment he was alone with her he had no thought of anything except the crisis which confronted him.

"Nancy," he said in a tone of supplication, "you won't sign that contract? You won't go abroad with Billy Bright?"

"If you mean I'm likely to do the tour without first marrying him then all I can say is that you're a—"

He stopped the verbal garbage with a kiss.

"I meant nothing of the kind, darling," he said, "I only want to hear you promise to marry me and let me take care of you."

She melted into his arms according to plan.

"I don't want to leave England and I don't want to dance, Bobbie," she whispered with an attempt at the intonation of a child. "But what else is there for me? I hate poverty." She shivered and the shiver was genuine. "It's all very well for you to talk, but you don't know what poverty is. Ten living in a room and meat once a week if you're lucky. Dirt and starvation and misery. I'd rather die than be poor. I want the best things life has to give a girl."

"I will give you the world if only you will wait," he said earnestly. "Nancy, can't you realise how much I love you?

I've been in love before, but my love for you is different, higher, purer. I'll slave for you."

"Slaves don't get paid," she said impatiently.

"Uncle Massy is our friend." He was pathetically serious and proud. "With him behind us everything will be all right."

"He's going to make you a fat allowance?" She sat up involuntarily. His face told the truth before he could frame a half-lie. "I thought so. What's the use of wasting time, Bobbie? You think your uncle cottoned to me? Well, I know he didn't. He and your mother are the same—they think I'm common."

"Common?" he echoed, aghast. "If they think that they must be mad, but I'm sure they don't."

She rose and shook herself.

"What a life! And fancy having to marry Billy? Ugh!" She gesticulated dramatically. "Life is hell without money, and don't I know it!"

"But listen, Nancy, I'm going to spend next weekend with uncle to talk over arrangements for our wedding."

She stared into his face as if seeking a clue to what she suspected was a new and subtle form of humour.

"Say that again—I forgot to laugh," she said aggressively.

"I mean it," he answered, unable to lose his temper with her. "We had a chat about you before he left. Uncle is director of a bank and has lots of influence. I might get an opening—"

"The only worth while opening in a bank is the one that leads to the strong room," she said with tired humour.

"I'm sorry, darling," he whispered humbly.

She stroked his hair and smiled down at him as he sat transfixed with gloom on the arm of Nosey's vacated armchair.

"Bobbie," she said, and her voice had tears in it, "I want to tell you something. I hate Billy."

The surprise brought him to a standing posture.

"You mean it? Then why not leave him?"

"Because without him I'd be penniless. He's made me. It's him the agents want. Nosey is very kind, but it's Bright & Curzon he wants too—not Curzon & Bright. I'm no fool and I know it."

"Well, let me take you away from him?"

"To what? From thirty-five quid a week to—your uncle's promises? Oh, Bobbie, you're a darling and a pet, but if only you had the Cheldon property! If only!" She covered her face with her hands.

"Darling!" She seemed pathetically light, almost gossamer-light in his grasp. "Can't you trust me? Won't you give me a chance?" She began to sob. "You make me wish I could send uncle into the next world," he muttered to himself, but she overheard and a smile came into dry eyes hidden by the upper portion of his waistcoat.

"I don't think there'd be many mourners," she ventured to say when she had concluded the ceremony of pretending to wipe her eyes. "But, of course, I'm only joking, Bobbie. You know that, don't you?"

"You couldn't have an evil thought, darling," he protested.

"Just think of what it would mean to your mother, Bobbie," she murmured in a voice which was dreamy with sympathy, "to have plenty of money. She was meant for something better than that rotten flat."

"I'm so glad you like her, Nancy," he said gratefully.

She returned to the subject which was uppermost in her mind.

"I know if the worst came to the worst you could always earn a decent living, Bobbie," she resumed in an enticing tone, "but with your mother it's different. You're young and clever, and she's growing old. Oh, dear, what a curious world it is when an old bachelor is allowed to keep decent people out of their rights."

He did not trouble to remind her that his and his mother's rights did not begin until his uncle died. Romance seldom demands precision.

"More than a hundred persons are killed each week by motor cars," said Nancy reflectively. "Funny that should occur to me," she added and laughed.

Bobbie for once was not thinking of her, for a vision of Florence and her blighted hopes was encircling him.

"Oh, well, it's nearly daylight and we're both fools to be thinking we'll ever be rich." She stretched herself and yawned. "Billy." Her shrill cry was immediately answered by Billy and Nosey in person. "I want Bobbie and Nosey to see me home," she explained. "I'm dead beat."

Nosey was first with the fur coat, but Bobbie was allowed the honour of escorting her down the rickety staircase, Nosey following close behind with elephantine fussiness.

To Bobbie's disappointment the walk had to be short as Nancy's rooms were less than a quarter of a mile away, and it was with reluctance that he turned from the doorstep of the unsavoury building.

"Isn't she amazing?" said Nosey Ruslin enthusiastically. "Isn't she worth taking any risk for?" He produced a nearly gold cigarette case and when they had lighted up they strolled leisurely towards Shaftesbury Avenue.

"I tell you what, Mr. Cheldon," said Nosey, pausing as if he had just made a momentous discovery and must record it vocally, "if I were twenty years younger and built a little more on Ronald Colman lines I'd commit murder if there was no other way to get her."

Bobbie meant to greet the remark with a laugh and tried his best to carry out his intention, but all he could do was to blink at the speaker.

"But I suppose I'm talking rot," Nosey added in a different tone. "I'm middle-aged and if it came to the point it would be Safety First with me from start to finish. But she's a marvel, Mr. Cheldon, and a regular knock-out."

Bobbie's opinion of Mr. Ruslin was rising every minute. He was the cleverest man he had yet met.

"I can't tell you how I feel about her," he answered under his breath.

Nosey Ruslin stopped again. They had not only the pavement to themselves but apparently the whole of London. Somewhere in the background there was a policeman and a pedestrian or two, but their immediate boundary was formed by the periphery of the light from the street lamp.

"I'm not in love with Nancy and never have been. But I'm fond of her. She's got that touch of genius that appeals to the artist in me." He repeated the tapping of Bobbie's chest. "Between you and me, Mr. Cheldon, I think Billy Bright a cad, and if Nancy's fool enough to marry him she's finished. You know what it is with these dancers—the men, I mean. They select a pretty girl, train her and tour with her for a year or two. After that she is too well known to be any longer a draw. The public require youth and beauty and freshness—particularly the freshness—in a girl. So the male gets rid of her and finds a substitute."

"But supposing she's his wife?"

"Then so much the worse for the wife." Mr. Ruslin laughed as harshly as he could.

They resumed their walk and in another ten minutes they were standing outside another of London's imitation mansions.

"I'm home, Mr. Cheldon," said Nosey genially. "Hope you haven't far to go. But remember what I've said. I like the look of you and if you're in love with Nancy you'll save her from the clutches of that dago Billy Bright. I've spoken freely to you because you've got sense, and if you want to hear me talk more Nancy will tell you where to find me if I'm not at home."

To his astonishment Bobbie clutched him by the arm.

"What about that contract? They didn't say what their decision was."

"Oh, the contract." Mr. Ruslin threw away half a cigarette. "Nancy insisted on my giving her a week to think it over." He laughed. "Think it over, indeed! What she really meant was that she wanted time to consider if you could prove you were in a position to marry her. She's dead crazy on becoming Mrs. Cheldon but not in a tenth-rate flat. She can keep herself in luxury—"

"For a time," Bobbie interjected.

"Exactly—for a time. But do you think she knows that? Nancy is like all of them—she's under the delusion that she's got about twenty years of dancing ahead of her." He held out a massive hand. "Good night, Mr. Cheldon, and take my advice."

"What advice?"

"Don't count the cost if Nancy's the prize, and don't waste your time imagining that she'll give up thirty-five quid a week for a husband and a fifth of that sum. But I do want an invitation to your wedding." He chuckled with all the force of his ever-present good humour. "I know—we all know, Mr. Cheldon—that you're a bit above us. You belong to the upper ten and we're just—well just ordinary people. You would raise Nancy to your level, and she's ambitious, believe me, yes, sir." He held out his hand again, and Bobbie animated by the flattery he had had poured into him, pressed it gratefully.

"Good night, Mr. Ruslin," he said in a shaky voice, "and if I may I will have another chat with you before I go down to my uncle's place at the weekend."

Nosey vanished into the darkness of the entrance to Ambassador Mansions and Bobbie strode homewards keenly alive to the soothing properties of the wind that blew gently on his face. His thoughts took him in turn from the extremes of triumph to the depths of despair and in between he found innumerable reasons for doubts and fears which clamoured for remedies. By the time he reached Galahad Mansions they had grown in number and strengthened in persistence.

"Anyhow I've got a real pal in Mr. Ruslin," he muttered to himself by way of escape from his worries.

By a coincidence Mr. Ruslin was at that moment discussing Bobbie, who might have been troubled had he known that when Nosey climbed the stairs to his third-floor flat a shadow congealed and became Billy Bright.

"I saw you on the other side of the street," said Nosey cheerfully, opening the door with his latchkey. "Once I thought that young fool would have spotted you."

"He'd never have recognised me," said Billy, entering the living-room which with a bedroom comprised ninety per cent of the flat. Without troubling to ask permission he began to operate with the whisky decanter and the soda siphon. "What happened, Nosey?"

His host rubbed his hands.

"Planted the seed, my dear Billy, planted the seed," he exclaimed with enthusiasm. "Dropped a hint that he ought to scrag his uncle and the next moment laughed at the notion. Then I flattered him. Compared him to you to your disadvantage."

The dancer grinned.

"I've never met a bigger ass in my life," he said, but without heat or jealousy. "But what can you expect from a chap who's been brought up in a hothouse by his darling mamma? You heard Nancy's description of the old lady?"

"A scream. Billy," he lowered his voice not because there could be any danger of an eavesdropper but in order to impress on his companion the seriousness of his words. "Billy, it's a cinch. I thought when we first mentioned the affair that there was going to be some risk for us, but now I know there won't. He believes everything, even that hundred quid a week tour on the continent."

Billy laughed spontaneously.

"If he believes that he'll believe anything," he remarked, unconsciously paraphrasing Macaulay.

"He's so much in love with Nancy that he'd believe the crowned heads of Europe were fighting one another to secure her for their state theatres. He can't see that at her best she's only second-rate. Billy, don't yell when I tell you that he believes it's her dancing that makes the partnership—that if you lost her you'd never get another engagement."

Billy, lounging in an armchair, did no more than wink.

"Poor Nancy!" he said pityingly. "I haven't told her yet that when our engagement with the 'Frozen Fang' ends next Saturday week there's nothing more. I don't want to chuck her unless—"

"You can get someone better," Nosey added. "My dear Billy, she's a rotten dancer. Her youth and good looks have helped her, but there are so many girls with looks and youth who can dance better that there's no future for her."

"Unless I married her," said the dancer lazily.

"Billy." Nosey's voice was almost stern. "It's no use going on with our little scheme unless you stick to business. I can't have you working in Nancy's camp as well as in mine. You understand? Marry her by all means, but let's finish here and now."

Billy stared at him in surprise.

"Now you're the fool!" he growled. "How can I marry Nancy or anyone else? I'm up to my neck in debts; next week I may be kicked out of my flat; there's not a restaurant in London that'll give me credit, and the agents are getting so tired of me that they send the office boy out to say that there's nothing doing at the moment. Nosey, when agents do that it's as good as a signed statement that I'm not worth a cent in the dancing market, that no one wants me."

"What about me?" asked Nosey dolefully. "I've been fighting to stave off bankruptcy for months and—" he paused and forced a smile.

Billy nodded understandingly.

"That little affair with Jack Fraddon? Still worrying about the money he invested in that theatrical agency?"

Nosey became positively grim.

"The last letter I had from his solicitor hinted at criminal proceedings." He raised the growl to something akin to a shout. "What if I did use the partnership money to pay off a private debt; does it amount to theft? Of course not. Fraddon's solicitor may say that I forged his client's signature to three partnership cheques, but—"

"Don't worry about that," said Billy. "Keep all your energy and brains for the scheme that's to make us rich."

Nosey's equanimity returned. Optimism suited him better than pessimism.

"He's weak and he thinks he's strong. I worked on his passion for Nancy, hinted that she was in danger from you, and appealed to his sense of chivalry without letting him guess my object. 'You're above us in class' I said, and, Billy, he swallowed it all. He'll go down to see his uncle or he'll get at him in some way and all the time he'll be thinking that it's his uncle's life against Nancy's. That's how I dropped a seed here and there, my boy." He leaned back to chuckle appreciation of his finesse and subtlety.

"But supposing he doesn't do the uncle in?" asked Billy doubtfully.

"I'll lay any odds he won't," was the surprising answer.

"But I thought everything depended on that."

Nosey Ruslin solemnly secured further liquid refreshment.

"Billy, you don't know the world like I do," he said, poising the glass in front of his face. "Didn't I tell you this fellow Cheldon is weak but that he considers himself strong—the strong, silent man type?" He laughed before drinking. "He's just the sort to make for the family mansion breathing fire and thunder and then to collapse. A talker, Billy, and not a worker. No pluck. Still, he could be driven to doing it, though he'd do it so clumsily that they'd have him in quod before he was home again. And in that event all our trouble would go for nothing."

"Exactly." Billy looked discontented. "Nosey, it's useless going on with this unless there's cash and a lot of it at the end. We must put Cheldon in possession of the property so that he can pay us our little share for our—er—help."

Nosey smiled to himself.

"He says it's worth ten thousand a year," he murmured. "And a quarter of that each, Billy, would suit us nicely."

"Two thousand five hundred a year!" Billy pronounced the words with a solemn hush. "Two thousand five hundred a year."

"But we've got to have him so fixed that he won't be able to wriggle out," said Nosey with unusual earnestness. "We're aiming high, Billy, very high, and everything will depend on our proof. Should it happen that Cheldon doesn't remove his uncle and we arrange for a substitute there must be written proof, or at any rate something in writing, that can guarantee Cheldon forking out. Personally I prefer a lump sum. No quarterly or half-yearly payments for me. You never can tell what may happen to upset an arrangement of that sort."

"It ought to be easy to raise money on the property." Billy laughed. "That young fool has talked so much of his rich uncle and of the property he must inherit when the uncle dies that although I've never seen it I seem to know every inch of it. Broadbridge Manor—that's the name of the place. It must be about the size of Buckingham Palace. And the way he's spouted to Nancy about his ancestors!" His expression darkened, and Nosey, watching him closely, saw disturbing signs.

"Billy." The voice was peremptory.

"What's the matter now?" The dancer's manner was embarrassed.

"First, last and always you've got to remember that Nancy is not for you—at least, not until we've received every shilling we'll be entitled to for keeping to ourselves the exact method by which Cheldon so unexpectedly inherited his uncle's estate."

"But you said yourself this evening that I was to make love to her," he protested weakly.

"Exactly, and only for the purpose of keeping Cheldon's jealousy at boiling point. He must be reminded every moment that Nancy is wanted by someone else. My little lie about a contract helped, but there must be a rival besides the continental tour, and you can be that."

Billy's expression cleared.

"It's the part of the scheme I like best." Then his face clouded again. "But somehow Nancy isn't the same to me as she used to be."

"Why should she? Here's a good-looking johnnie with ten thousand a year in prospect who is willing to lick her boots. What can you offer her? She knows too much about poverty to see any romance in it. Cheldon thinks poverty is wonderful. That's the difference between the three of you. But mind you, Billy, there's one other thing."

"Yes?" Billy yawned. Excitement was passing and there was nothing else to keep in subjection his physical exhaustion.

"Nancy must never be told of our plan."

"Do you take me for a fool?"

"Yes, I do," was the blunt retort. "You're in love with Nancy. It's because you're in love with her that you've kept her as your dancing partner. Don't I know that if you weren't so desperately hard up you wouldn't lift a finger to help Cheldon to marry her? But you want money more than you want her, and to get the money you've got to help me to make it possible for Cheldon to engage a church and parson."

"She's too good for him," he muttered.

"Does Nancy think so? But we're old enough, Billy, to be sensible—at least I am. Now listen to me before you biff off. I hinted to Cheldon that he could see me at any time, and that means he'll be looking for me before I'm a dozen hours older. When we do meet I'll drop a few more seeds." The simile always amused him. "And by the time he's starting for the mansion he'll be thinking only of the quickest way to arrange for his rich uncle's funeral."

"But how will you trick him into providing proof—the proof that we must have?"

"Leave that to me." Nosey looked excessively sly. "Billy, he'll go down to Broadway—"

"Broadbridge Manor," his companion corrected.

"To this whatever-you-call-it full of zeal for helping Uncle Tom—"

"That's not the name. It's Mally or—"

"What on earth does the name matter?" Nosey was almost testy. "And don't interrupt. As I was saying, he'll arrive at Broadway Mansion with a knife in one pocket and a packet of poison in the other, both birthday presents for Uncle Algy. But do you think he'll take 'em out of his pockets when he's welcomed to the ancestral halls? Not on your life. He'll be too frightened to do more than look a bigger fool than he actually is and keep awake all night thinking about the hangman."

"A fat lot of good that'll do us," Billy grumbled.

"My boy," said Nosey who from the neck downwards bore some resemblance to Napoleon and who now assumed a Napoleonic pose, "it's your profession to think with your feet—mine to think with my head. Leave the conduct of the campaign to me. I'll produce the goods if you'll promise to do as I tell you."

"I don't want any fireworks," the dancer protested.

"They burn your fingers if you're clumsy or unlucky."

"No one will be any the wiser except ourselves," was the re-assuring reply. "Can't you see that I'm rehearsing Cheldon for the weekend at Broadway—Broad Haven—Oh, never mind! I never was good at remembering names. I'll prime him up just for a trial run. He'll do nothing except eat and sleep at his uncle's house, but when he returns to us and to Nancy he'll have been readied. Savvy?"

Billy sought the sofa.

"I'll sleep here, Nosey," he said in a tired voice. "Dead beat."

A minute later his host was standing over him and watching his unconscious form, smiling to himself all the while as though he had just recalled a joke which had hitherto escaped his memory.

"If I had fifty quid it'ud be a certainty," he murmured as he wended his way to his bedroom.

They had a noonday breakfast of kippers and coffee, and Billy Bright, unshaven and unoiled, ate with the appetite of a healthy schoolboy.

"Wonder if Cheldon will phone you," he remarked, after removing the contents of a marmalade pot.

"Can't do it here," said Nosey drily, glancing sideways at the apparatus on the small table near the door. "Cut off three days ago. Matter of six quid." He laughed shortly. "And for hours I've been trying to think of a scheme for raising fifty."

"I don't believe there's so much money in London—at least not in the West End. But why fifty?"

"Want to lend young Cheldon most of it. Know why?"

"That's easy. He's hard up and he'll be grateful."

"Not exactly. He'll have to acknowledge the money and with a bit of finesse I can get him to refer to his uncle's early passing from a world of sorrow to a world of bliss."

"A hundred to one against that," said Billy, drawing his chair away from the table and searching his pockets for a cigarette.

"No, only about five to one." Nosey frowned. "You're forgetting that I'm in charge, Billy."

"You don't give me a chance to forget. But fire away. Any matches?"

"Fifty quid." Nosey relieved his pockets of their contents, eight shillings and ninepence chiefly in coins of contemptible value. "I can't remember a pal I don't owe money to. Fifty quid," he repeated.

A knock on the door startled him. Knocks on the door always had done so for nearly three weeks now.

"Another summons," muttered Nosey. The knock was repeated. "You open the door, Billy. I'm not here of course."

The dancer's laughter instantly banished the tension.

"It's only a note from Nancy," said Billy, tearing open the envelope. "She says—what does she say?" He glanced through the letter quickly. "Tell her Mr. Ruslin will be there," he called to the boy, and tossed the letter across the table to his fellow-conspirator.

"'Bobbie has just phoned to say he wants you to lunch with him at the Villafranche,'" Nosey read. "'I can't come, and Bobbie says don't be later than half-past one. Nancy.'"

"There you are, Billy, didn't I tell you?" he cried triumphantly. "I knew I'd made an impression."

"You're a regular wonder, Nosey," said Billy Bright admiringly. "This fellow Cheldon's been haughty all along with me and the other chaps at the 'Frozen Fang'. How did you manage it?"

"Ah, my boy, that's only to be explained by what I once heard a bloke call magnetic charm and personality." He laughed. "But that fifty quid, Billy. Fifty quid and it's a certainty. What's the time?" He went to the window and by straining his neck saw sufficient of a public house clock on the other side of the street to learn that it was a quarter to one. "I'll run along and try and tap Buddy Rogers," he murmured to himself. He disappeared into the bedroom and as one was striking somewhere reappeared dressed for the expedition.

"Don't hurry away, Billy, if it doesn't suit your book," he said genially "And if the brokers arrive while you're here don't let them grab your overcoat. I'm off to begin the campaign." With unexpected seriousness he seized Billy's right arm. "You promise you will back me up—take your orders from me?"

"Of course," said Billy, staring at him. "Two thousand five hundred a year of the best—after this." He shuddered, but he was alone now.

Chapter Four

"The matter with a chap like me," said Nosey Ruslin across the luncheon table in the Villafranche, "is that he has more money than education. Mind you, I don't say brains—education's the word. Now you have brains and education, but no money."

"I wish I had your ability to make money, Mr. Ruslin," said Bobbie, with a wistful earnestness that carried its own conviction.

"It can be useful." The tone was condescending. "But it isn't everything, Mr. Cheldon." He smiled knowingly. "It isn't Nancy, for example."

"Without money it won't be Nancy," the younger man rejoined uneasily.

The expansive form leaned heavily towards him and a fat hand patted his arm almost affectionately.

"Nancy knows you may come in for ten thousand a year any day," he said consolingly. "Haven't I told her that a score of times since she let me know she was keen on you."

Bobbie flushed with pleasure.

"She said that, did she?"

"A hundred times if once, Mr. Cheldon. Do you know what I said? 'Nancy, you can bank on the boy friend—he's a winner. I know how to spot 'em and I've never made a mistake yet'. That's what I said, Mr. Cheldon, when I'd only seen you in the 'Frozen Fang', and now that I know you personally I'm certain I didn't make a bloomer."

"Thank you, Mr. Ruslin, thank you," whispered the ardent lover.

"You won't have to work twelve hours a day as I have to, Mr. Cheldon. You're a gentleman of position—county and all that. You ought to be riding to hounds and fishing for salmon and playing polo and talking in Parliament." The hotch-potch of the social round which he composed impromptu had a flattering inference which compelled his hearer to accept it seriously. "Who's this uncle of yours to keep you out of your fortune?"

It was so inaccurate a statement of the position that even in his present state of mind Bobbie could not accept it without experiencing a pang of conscience. But he offered no correction.

"He's an old man—nearly fifty-four—and lives as if he was going to lose every penny next week." Bobbie took a sip of wine and glanced around.

"Pity you can't give him a push over a precipice," Mr. Ruslin was remarking when Bobbie returned to consciousness of his companion's existence. "But, of course, there are no precipices in London that I've heard of." It was noticeable that whenever Nosey introduced, however obliquely, the subject of murder, he instantly annotated it with a selection from his stock of humour. But Bobbie did not discern that.

"Uncle sometimes talks as if he were dying, Mr. Ruslin, but as a matter of fact he's as strong as a horse." Bobbie gripped his wineglass again. "What could I not do with ten thousand a year!"

"You could marry Nancy," whispered the tempter across the table. "You could put your mother in the position she ought to have been in years ago. Fancy her, the widow of a colonel, having to live with common people. Just think of it, Mr. Cheldon, here I am living on the fat of the land, and your mother—well, there." He sighed. "You see, Nancy's told me a lot about her. People like her ought not to be poor. Look at this little lunch of ours. It'll cost a matter of a couple of quid, and that's less than I spend as a rule. It's a party of four generally, for I've got to entertain theatrical managers and film people a lot. It's the only way to do business." He caught a glimpse of the face opposite that intimated merely polite interest. Instantly he turned on the Nancy tap. "She's a peach, is that girl of yours, and I'm proud to take her out to lunch whenever she'll let me. Not that she's too fond of the Villafranche. It's the Ritz or the Berkeley with her if it isn't the Carlton. I don't often go to those places myself, Mr. Cheldon, because I feel a bit out of it with the nobs, but Nancy—Good lord!" He smiled all over his extensive face. "She's got the manner. You'd think she was like yourself—born to it. And how she loves the life!"

Bobbie's face clouded.

"Don't be depressed, Mr. Cheldon," said Nosey gently. "It's not as if you hadn't any prospects. You're heir to a fortune and when you've got it Nancy will drag you into St. George's, Hanover Square."

"When I get it," muttered Bobbie gloomily.

"You've got to get it and Nancy, too," said Ruslin earnestly. "That's the ticket, Mr. Cheldon, and damme, I'm going to stand by you and help you. I've never met a young chap to whom I've taken such a fancy as you. Now listen and don't let that aristocratic pride make you act foolish. Mr. Cheldon, it's no disgrace to be hard up. Most young men are and I was hard up all the time when I was your age." He jerked the pocket-book into action and held it in such a position that the wad of notes nearly concealed it. "Help yourself, Mr. Cheldon, and pay me back when you're the squire and Nancy is your lady."

"Oh, I say!" Bobbie's emotion was almost tearful as he stared at his friend, his cheeks red and his eyes watering.

"Go on. Help yourself. Twenty or even fifty quid." There was only forty in the collection, but exaggeration entailed no liability. "It's like lending to the Bank of England. You'll be a rich man soon."

Since he had been fined ten pounds and had his driving licence suspended Bobbie's finances had been in a chaotic condition, Uncle Massy having insultingly declined to subscribe to the fine. The consequence had been that the culprit's daily portion of cash had been reduced to a shilling or two, eked out by such credit as his association with Nancy Curzon secured for him at the 'Frozen Fang', and now there were dangerous debts unknown to his mother which clamoured for immediate settlement.

"Well, if I might—five pounds," he began nervously. Mr. Ruslin's effervescent generosity and friendliness were not to be damped. Clutching as many of the notes as he could he thrust them towards his guest.

"There's about twenty there, Mr. Bobbie."

"I make it twenty-three," said the grateful recipient.

"Then here's two more to make up the round sum." Before Bobbie could speak the waiter was approaching at the usual signal.

"Two six four. Right." Mr. Ruslin's recital was low but distinct. "Keep the balance for yourself, waiter."

Fifty shillings parted company, and Bobbie, sharing in the honours of the waiter's processional obeisance, walked into Wardour Street with the air of a man who has achieved all his ambitions.

"The office is round the corner," said Nosey, lighting the size of cigar he considered consistent with prosperity. "Only a temporary affair until the new building in the Haymarket is ready."

It was, indeed, a small affair, in a ramshackle building but as Nosey had merely borrowed it for the occasion he did not trouble to apologise further.

"I've sent my principal papers to the bank," Nosey disclosed when they were in the dingy room. "Too important to leave lying about here." He pulled open the top drawer in the desk and Bobbie heard him laugh. "I'd forgotten this." A small, silver-plated revolver glistened in the sunlight. "That reminds me, I haven't taken out a licence. I wonder what I can do with it. The police are pretty tough about weapons. They think everybody who's got one will be tempted to turn bandit." He glanced meaningly at Bobbie. "I wonder Mr. Cheldon...."

Bobbie was beside him in a couple of strides.

"Certainly I'll mind it for you, Mr. Ruslin," he said eagerly. "It's a small service for all you've done for me." He laughed. "Money does make a difference, and with your twenty-five pounds in my pocket I don't fear anyone or anything."

"There ought to be ten thousand a year in that pocket," said Ruslin humorously as he parted with the weapon. "But be careful, Mr. Cheldon, it's fully loaded. Slip it into your hip pocket. Good." He picked up an official-looking document. "Ta-ta for the present."

Bobbie was still thinking of his unexpected and unconventional ally when on the Friday afternoon he carefully packed his bag and travelled cheaply until at Broadbridge station luxury awaited him in the shape of a perfect Daimler and a magazine artist's conception of the ideal chauffeur. From that moment he had nothing to do except breathe and be a gentleman of leisure, and so far from having to handle the Gladstone bag he did not see it again until seven o'clock when he climbed the gorgeously spacious staircase at the

Manor with its portrait lined walls, assuring himself as he experienced a sensation of utter ease that luxury was something only to be appreciated by those who were born to it.

He had arrived at Broadbridge Manor at a quarter past six to find Uncle Massy before a big fire in the drawing-room which had its traditions, royal and noble.

The first Duke of Weybridge had received the second Charles there—an item of family history which the Cheldons had taken over with the title-deeds—and two of the Georges were reputed to have admired its ceiling.

"The train must have been punctual," was Massy Cheldon's conversational gambit, but the tone was friendly enough.

"I suppose so." A movement behind him enabled him to time the approach of a footman with a tray. "Thanks." He was facing his uncle again. "I needed that." He smacked his lips and surrendered the empty glass. "You haven't altered the room since I was here last."

It was the sort of remark that provides the hearer with opportunities according to his mental equipment for sarcasm or humour or a whine. Massy Cheldon naturally whined.

"The furniture's decaying but I'm not having it replaced," he explained to his nephew's surprise. "Costs too much, and I'm having a fight with the income tax people."

"But I love the room as it is, uncle," he protested. "There's something of English history about it." He went across to inspect an engraving of the Marquess Wellesley who as patron of Jonathan Cheldon had earned a niche in the Cheldon portrait gallery and also its archives.

"You don't have to pay for it," was the growling answer.

Bobbie, although not a tactician, had sufficient sense to refrain from reminding the tenant for life of the estate that the upkeep was amply provided for out of its revenues.

"Sit down and tell me how your mother is." They took opposite armchairs, the reigning monarch and his crown prince.

"She's putting up Mrs. Carmichael or Mrs. Elmers while I'm away so she'll not be lonely," Bobbie explained carelessly.

"Putting up Mrs. Carmichael means putting up with her." The nephew, for once anxious to please, used laughter to applaud this choice specimen of the Massy Cheldon Brand of Humour. "Women are curious creatures, Bobbie, and I know them…. There was…"

Bobbie was listening in a condition of welcome physical tiredness when the recital was stopped by the entrance of West, the butler, a replica of his employer without the latter's loquacity or self-esteem. He was quiet, efficient, thorough and intelligent, and he would have been quite useless to a dramatist, for he never took liberties with the aspirate.

"Excuse me, sir," he said in a voice which annoyed Bobbie who liked a butler to be butleresque, "but you are wanted in the library."

Massy Cheldon rose with a jerk. "Wanted in the library" was an agreed code message between himself and West for "I wish to impart something of immediate importance, sir."

"We don't get an evening paper here, Bobbie," he said at the door, "but you'll find *The Times* and the *Morning Post* and *Telegraph* behind you." Bobbie, as soon as he was alone, stretched out a lazy hand to retrieve the newspapers.

Massy Cheldon preceded his butler to the library on the first floor and did not speak or even glance at him until they were safe from interruption.

"What is it?" he asked, trying to smother his nervousness.

"This, sir."

West held towards him the revolver which Nosey Ruslin had entrusted to his new friend, Bobbie Cheldon, for safe keeping.

"Peters found it in Mr. Robert's Gladstone bag when he unpacked it to lay out his dress clothes, sir."

With an exclamation that was a mixture of an imprecation and a gasp of fear Massy Cheldon grasped it.

"Loaded—fully loaded, West," he muttered.

"Yes, sir. Exactly, sir." West was judicially impartial.

"Fully loaded and evidently specially brought down here." He shivered. He examined it again. "What do you think, West?"

"Well, sir, it's hardly my place to criticise Mr. Robert," he began.

"It's your place to do it when I order you," snapped his master.

"Well, sir, it occurred to me that Mr. Robert might be thinking of suicide. He lives in London and does nothing—hasn't a situation, I mean. I read in the papers how he'd been fined and his licence suspended. Or it may be that a love affair..."

Massy Cheldon seemed to wake up suddenly.

"A love affair and suicide." He did some quick thinking. "West, I hope Peters won't blab?" He looked anxiously at his butler.

"It was the first thing I thought of, sir. I warned Peters that he must keep it to himself or he'd have to seek another place."

"You can trust him?"

"I took care not to make too much of it, sir. Simply mentioned that it wouldn't do to talk about it in case Mr. Robert hadn't a licence for firearms. Said you'd be sure not to wish to have gossip about it in the servants' hall. He understood, sir."

"Thank you, West." Massy mused again. "I know what I'll do. West, the revolver is my nephew's property and I've no right to deprive him of it. But I can render it harmless—that is, unless he has brought a supply of ammunition with him."

West smiled dutifully.

"I examined the contents of the bag carefully, sir," he said, returning to solemnity, "and I could find no ammunition."

"Very well. Replace it." He handed it back. "And let Peters know my opinion that you were a fool to worry me about it. Why shouldn't my guests bring an arsenal with them if they wish?" He nearly winked. "But thank you, West, thank you very much."

He had the library to himself and kept it for ten minutes while he walked up and down as if his feet were on invisible wires.

"That revolver was meant for me," he muttered again and again, and with each repetition a renewal of fear added fuel to his fiery anger. He had grown to despise his nephew and heir. "His desperation won't run to anything more desperate than making an apple-pie bed for me."

The contemptuous testimonial to the innocuousness of Bobbie recurred with mocking deliberation. Yet he could not convince himself that he had been mistaken. Massy Cheldon was a student of human nature with a wide and a deep knowledge of his fellows. He paid himself that tribute once more and declined to modify it even with his pocket sheltering the ammunition removed from his guest's murderous-looking weapon.

"Could it be that woman?" The question brought him to a standstill. He recalled his own love affairs, and he had had several. But could Bobbie have been driven to murder by a pretty face? Yet these dancers, and the youth of today! What could you expect?

He was bemoaning the alleged vices of the youth of today when the first gong warned him that he must change his attire for the ritual of doing homage to the concoctions of his favourite employee. Bobbie, hearing that gong, uttered a curse on himself and raced to the room he always occupied when at the Manor. What an ass he had been to forget! What a complete prize idiot he had been not to have remembered his resolution to let no one open his bag! Was it possible he could have been so mad as to hand the key unthinkingly to Peters and never give a thought to danger until this moment!

He was flushed and his heart was beating so fast that he was in a condition of physical pain when he sprang at the bag and searched for the revolver beneath a layer of shirts and collars. A great breath of relief escaped him. Nosey Ruslin's property lay exactly where he had placed it. Evidently Peters, that prince of footmen, had done no more than his duty demanded. Peters had not been curious and had gone no further down than the layer of dress clothes. It was all right. He sank on to the bed to recover from the reaction. One thing was certain. Peters should be promoted and his salary doubled. Wages, he meant. The correction was pure Cheldonism. A servant who knew his place deserved reward in these days when Jack pretended to be as good as his master even when that master belonged to an ancient family.

He dressed to the accompaniment of toneless excerpts from the Cheldon saga.

Uncle Massy was already seated at the head of the oak table when he took the chair on his right with his back to the fireplace.

"Thought it better to have dinner alone tonight," he heard him mumble as his own eyes wandered in a lazy review of the contents of the room, particularly the portraits.

Everything he saw generated temptation. The spacious luxury of the room, the panelled walls with their impressive family portraits, the massive silver adornments of the table, and the noiseless butler with something of the dignity of a High Priest ministering to the comfort and pride of the choicer members of the Cheldon family.

It was impossible for him to avoid contrasting his surroundings with what five years of Galahad Mansions had brought him. The humiliating economies, the revolting evidences all around him of the struggle for existence, the contemptible substitutes for pleasure, and the third-rate people with whom he was compelled to associate.

His rightful place in the scheme of things was here. He ought to be in that chair with Nancy facing him. Uncle Massy was undoubtedly a Cheldon, but he had not inherited the imposing figure, handsome features and determined expression of old Jonathan, whose portrait by Lawrence was just behind him. Uncle Massy should have been a younger son and in that event would probably have done quite well as a solicitor. He, Bobbie, would, of course, give him his legal business to do and there would be a considerable amount arising out of the manifold duties and responsibilities the ownership of Broadbridge Manor must entail.

He ate mechanically as he found solace in his thoughts. Meanwhile Uncle Massy meandered through a story in which apparently a colonel and a club servant figured together with an exciting interlude about a forgotten whisky and soda.

"We'll have some one to join us tomorrow night, Bobbie." On hearing his name the guest sat up and tried to escape from his thoughts to his environment. West was filling his glass.

"That'll be fine." He went a trifle red as he struggled to recall the remark which had evoked his commonplace rejoinder.

"General Maltby and his daughter, Lady Kester, have returned from the south of France. I'll ask them. And the Bellamys if they're at home."

Bobbie smiled, grateful for the Bellamy cue.

"Is the girl married yet?" he asked without any interest.

Uncle Massy began to talk about the girl of today, and the dinner proceeded to the coffee stage. Bobbie was cracking his fifth walnut when his uncle arrived at what he considered the point of an illuminating anecdote, and having waited for the applause drew his chair closer to the table.

"Now we can talk undisturbed about your position," he said, and there seemed to be so much feeling in his tone that Bobbie experienced a twinge of remorse.

"You must put your shoulder to the wheel." The opening was ominous, but beggars cannot be critics. "The bottom rung of the ladder, my boy, to start with."

"What does the bottom rung mean in this case, uncle?"

A frown was the first answer. Then Massy Cheldon reverted to his original plan, that of a cat playing with a mouse, and he stifled his annoyance.

"A stool in an office," he said, and the younger man, aware that two small reddish eyes were fixed on him, defeated the attempt of his features to betray his thoughts.

"Will it be a—a—er—valuable stool, uncle?"

"Fifty shillings a week and you'll be lucky to get it."

Bobbie's sense of humour had yet to develop, but when he tried to picture Nancy Curzon's expression when she heard of his "prospects" laughter would have been loud and prolonged had he not been well rehearsed in the art of self-control under difficulties.

"Fifty shillings isn't much," his uncle resumed, "but it'll mean a great deal to you and your mother. For one thing it'll be as good as living rent free. Bobbie, you must from now onwards take a business view of things in general. Life isn't all loafing. The man with a purpose, with backbone, initiative..."

He knew the lay sermon by heart.

"...and within five years you ought to be earning at least four hundred a year. You have the advantage of being a Cheldon. A business training—a business career will be the best preparation for the day when you succeed me at Broadbridge..."

Bobbie surveyed the regiment of portraits again. They were meat and drink to his vanity and spurs to his ambition, but he differed from his uncle as to the meaning of ambition.

Nearly an hour passed before they rose and sauntered leisurely into the drawing room, and there in two enveloping armchairs they passed the time until somewhere between eleven and midnight the owner of Broadbridge Manor signalled his desire for sleep by a series of yawns and then departed abruptly to the upper regions of the old building.

When his own door closed behind him, Bobbie turned the key in the lock and flung himself on the bed. He was tired mentally rather than physically, and although West had been more than usually sparing with the wine, what he had drunk had produced a mellowness which left him limp. But he was determined not to sleep, persuaded that he had an immense amount of thinking to do.

He opened his eyes and was astonished to be informed by the clock on the mantelpiece that he had been asleep for hours. It was actually a quarter to two.

With the agitated, spasmodic movements of a man in a hurry he opened his bag and fumbled for the revolver. This he thrust into the right hand pocket of his dinner jacket, and almost in the same movement reached the door and unlocked it. Outside in the landing there was a silence consistent with the darkness that prevailed.

In his state of mind he really did not know what he was doing, though at the back of his brain there was a glimmering idea as to why he was doing it. He seemed to be under the control of a spirit alien to his weak, foolish character;

it was as if he was suffering from daydream somnambulism and had become a creature taken captive by thoughts too dangerous to be expressed in words. But had he been able to think he must have rushed back to his room and barricaded himself against the terrors of the temptation assailing him. As it happened he actually crept to the door of his uncle's room, pushed it open slightly, and with his hand gripping the revolver, entered.

From where he stood the bed was indistinct, for the room was nearly equal to the entire floor space of 15, Galahad Mansions, or at least Bobbie had once remarked on this comparison between the genuine mansion and the imitation. Not a sound worried him except his own breathing, and it was because of this too audible evidence of his own existence that he took the revolver from his pocket. As he did so he thought he heard a shuffling sound to his left and wheeling round he presented the revolver at a shadow in true conventional style.

"What's that?" he gasped, terrified.

The shadow gave him no time even to try and answer his own question, for it materialised into a pyjama-clad figure, and as a hand stretched out towards the weapon a well known voice said, "Give me that." The next moment the room was flooded with electric light, and Massy Cheldon, holding the weapon which he alone knew to be unloaded, gazed contemptuously at the form of his nephew stretched on the floor.

"You fainted," he said five minutes later. "But finish your drink first. It'll be a tonic."

"Uncle," the penitent began and stopped to hide his face in his hands.

"Feeling better?" Massy Cheldon, glowing with triumph, stretched out a hand to the soda siphon on the table between his own and his nephew's chair. That it had contained glasses for two and an assortment of drinks might have given Bobbie occasion for an essay in the art of deduction had he been in a normal condition of mind, but it was not his uncle's intention to admit that he had been expecting him. That would have been a foolish weakening of his own position and would of a certainty have lessened the effect of his confrontation in the darkness of an intruder with a harmless weapon.

"I don't know what to say—I must have been mad," Bobbie groaned.

"Of course, you were mad." The tone was extraordinarily good-humoured in the circumstances. And Uncle Massy had never shown a predilection for good humour even in the most favourable conditions.

"I've behaved like a cad, uncle."

"You've behaved like a fool. You forgot the Cheldon motto, 'Courage and Loyalty.'" He purred a chorus to his self-esteem.

"You certainly showed courage, uncle." Bobbie raised his head and disclosed scarlet cheeks. "It was the pluckiest act I've known or heard of. I couldn't have done it. But I shouldn't have harmed you. I swear I wouldn't. I was only bluffing."

"Would a bench of magistrates believe that?" The voice was for the first time harsh, even threatening. "Would a judge and jury at the Sussex Assizes accept that explanation?" He rose and stood over him, all the mean little soul of the man palpitating with triumph. "Had I been one of the nervy sort the shock might have killed me, but I think I proved that all the courage of the Cheldons isn't expended on the battlefield, that even a food controller can be brave."

"I'm sorry. I don't know what else to say. I must have been in a dream. Uncle, I swear, I didn't mean it. I was just pretending." The boyish apology came in detached sentences, and Massy Cheldon knew that every word was true.

"You see, Bobbie, you made the mistake of measuring me by your own standard. You naturally judged me as a coward. It never dawned on you that a loaded revolver pointed at me at a distance of a couple of feet would have no more effect on me than the threat of a blow from a toy balloon. Men of my calibre do not parade their courage. They conceal it. But, damme, why am I talking like this when I ought to be rousing West and telephoning for the police?"

Bobbie turned to stone.

"Uncle!" he gasped weakly.

"Oh, I know what that whine means. You were going to remind me that you had a mother and that I am fond of her. Well, you would have been right. I am fond of your mother, Bobbie. She's a woman in a million, and her husband, my brother, was a man in a million. For the sake of both of them I will forgive."

A delicate hand was stretched out and as hastily withdrawn when it failed to find a companion.

"Now don't talk until I give you permission." The lord of Broadbridge Manor began to strut. "The problem is one which must be solved here and now, Bobbie. For your mother's sake I shall forgive. It will depend on your future conduct whether I forget." He pursed his lips and looked profound, rather taken aback by his own eloquence.

All the fight had gone out of Bobbie, supposing any had ever been in him. But certainly all his powers of retort, anger, sarcasm and even resentment were banished too. He could only be conscious of the enormity of his stupidity.

"You idiot!" Uncle Massy cried, suddenly gripping him by the shoulders and shaking him. "What do you think you'd have got out of my murder except a rope around your neck? It is possible that it never occurred to you that if I were found dead in suspicious circumstances the only man who could profit by my death would be the first to be suspected?

Didn't it cross what you are pleased to call your mind that had I died a few minutes ago you would have been arrested before breakfast? Faugh!" He sought the consolation of his armchair and the assistance of another whisky and soda to restore his composure.

"Damn you, I must have a few hours' sleep before Peters comes in with the morning tea." There was a mask of evil which a return of his sense of triumph banished before Bobbie could look him in the face for a second or two. "Now listen to me, and answer my questions. First, who gave you that murderous weapon?" The adjective was introduced to minister to vanity.

"Chap of the name of Ruslin!"

"Any Christian name?"

"I don't know. His friends call him Nosey." Bobbie didn't smile.

"And did Mr. Nosey Ruslin—if I may be familiar—lend you the loaded revolver so that you might shoot me?"

"Of course not." Bobbie looked scared as though afraid his tone would provoke his uncle. "I mean, he hadn't the faintest notion. Mr. Ruslin was talking to me in his office when he opened a drawer in his desk to look for something and found the revolver. He'd forgotten all about it and hadn't a licence. As I have—shooting down here, you know—I offered to take care of it until he'd moved to his new offices. That's all, uncle, and it's the truth."

Massy Cheldon knew it was, but he would not surrender an inch of his highly moral position.

"Sounds dangerously akin to a conspiracy," he muttered, "but I'll accept your explanation. Where does this person exist?"

"I really don't know, uncle. I hardly know him at all."

"But you must have met him somewhere." The reproof was conveyed in a bark of irritation.

"Oh, yes, of course. The 'Frozen Fang', a new night club in Wardour Street. Mr. Ruslin is a well-known theatrical agent."

"Money?"

Bobbie's smile was genuine.

"Rolling in it." Memories of the lunch and the loan of twenty-five pounds comforted him now.

"Very well. I suppose if I address the weapon to Mr. Ruslin at the 'Frozen Fang' it will reach him. I can't allow you to handle it again. I shall remove the ammunition first." A handy tumbler served to conceal that part of his face which smiled knowingly.

"You won't—"

"Don't give another exhibition of your more obvious asinine qualities," was the swift retort. "Good night."

Bobbie rose obediently.

"I will see you after breakfast. Go for a stroll in the rose gardens and wait there for me." He yawned. "I must have rest," he added, in a natural and therefore complaining tone. "After the nerve-wracking experience I have gone through I shouldn't be surprised if I collapsed altogether. I am of a sensitive nature. There's poetry in my composition, but no one believes it. Because they think I am rich they think me incapable of anything which cannot be expressed in money. Clear off."

When Bobbie flung himself on the bed for the second time that night his whole frame was shivering and his state of mind that of a man who has had an even narrower escape from death than his uncle had had. The fabric of his glorious dreams had vanished and had been replaced by something too hideous, revolting and dangerous for contemplation. Ugly thoughts clamoured for expression. He fought to repel them and cried aloud when he heard his own tongue mumbling some of them.

Uncle Massy might change his mind. Uncle Massy was mean and cruel. Uncle Massy hated him. Uncle Massy.... It was Uncle Massy a thousand times until the moment the door opened and a footman brought in a tray.

"Why, sir!" he gasped, staring at the recumbent figure he had awakened out of a prolonged nightmare.

"Too tired to undress," Bobbie murmured sleepily. "Pour me out a cup of tea and get the bath ready."

The well-trained servant worked with speed.

"He is having breakfast in his own room, sir," West, the butler, explained in reply to a natural question, an hour later. "The master told me he had had a most disturbing night."

Bobbie bent well over his plate of bacon and eggs, but the food had not been more than prodded when he rose and lighted a cigarette. When West turned his back he beat a strategic retreat to the gardens.

Had he been in the mood to appreciate the glories of antiquity decorated by the skill of a scientific gardener with a regiment of assistants Bobbie must have enjoyed the hour and three-quarters available to him for an outside inspection of Broadbridge Manor and a tour of the beautiful grounds. The sweeping carriage drive entrance from the ancient gateway had been a source of gratification and pride on former occasions. Now he paced it moodily and never troubled to raise his eyes to the old world building which had been a ducal mansion for nearly two centuries until the all-conquering Jonathan Cheldon arrived from India with a bankful of gold coins and a boxful of jewels with which to displace the last Duke of Weybridge who had tempted his luck a hundred times too often at Crockford's. But the nervous, frightened guest had no heart for the noble façade, the artistic gables, mullioned windows and intricacies of wood and stone such as delight the architect. He was conscious that at that very moment Uncle Massy was deciding his fate, and Bobbie could guess that that fate would not be a pleasant or a comfortable one.

In due course he wandered to the rose gardens which were perfect, although the roses had yet to arrive, and he was lingering between two expansive beds when the atmosphere seemed to become thick with the approach of the master of Broadbridge Manor.

"So you're there!" was his substitute for a greeting. "Bobbie, I've been thinking things over and I've made up my mind." He spoke incisively after the manner of an imitation dictator.

"Yes, uncle." The tone was diplomatically submissive.

"I've already made a parcel of the weapon and dispatched it from the post office. I took it myself to prevent the servants talking. Your friend with the curious name will receive it tomorrow. Pity it won't be so easy to dispose of you." He looked careworn. "But one must face one's problems and difficulties, however undeserved they may be. Bobbie, I cannot undertake to settle the date when you start work, but as soon as I can see Sir James Honkin, who is one of my fellow-directors on the board of the rubber company, I will fix up everything. He is sure to let me have my own way. You are, of course, prepared to start work in the office at a day's notice?"

"Certainly, uncle."

"I will try and get you a commencing salary of fifty shillings a week, but the manager may raise objections. I know he usually pays only thirty shillings to beginners until they prove their worth. But as you're my nephew he will understand and make allowances." He left the sense incomplete, but Bobbie was not especially interested now.

"Hard work will make a man of you," Uncle Massy continued with a pretentious solemnity that suited his mean soul. "You won't know yourself in six months' time."

He struggled with a reluctant laugh. "Why, I shouldn't be surprised if you'll soon be refusing to let me continue the allowance I make your mother. A miracle is always possible."

"And do I remain for the weekend, uncle?"

"Of course. If you left you'd only alarm your mother and the servants would talk. Besides, I've asked some mutual friends in tonight and it would look odd if you didn't turn up. But I suppose you have no more death-dealing weapons in your possession?" The tone was facetious and Bobbie stared at him in amazement. "Ha! ha! You little thought that your uncle Massy had the courage of a lion. 'Courage and Loyalty', the old Cheldon motto. 'Courage and Loyalty'." Another chuckle and he retraced the path back to the house.

Bobbie stood with his hands behind his back to hide his clenched fists and in his heart a hatred a thousand times more murderous than that which had sent him creeping on tip-toe to his uncle's bedroom the night before.

"I hope I won't fail next time," he muttered, but the voice was weak and almost passionless.

Chapter Five

Nosey Ruslin stopped at the doorstep of the ham and beef shop, below which the premises of the "Frozen Fang" lay bathed that moment in stale tobacco smoke and neutral exhalations. There was no sign of life anywhere until he had opened and closed a second door and then a solitary specimen of humanity revealed himself in a touzled-haired young man with his body enshrouded in a sheet of green baize and his hands lazily attempting to control the epileptic movements of a veteran and wounded carpet-sweeper.

"Oh, it's you, Mr. Ruslin! Good afternoon, sir." The speaker readily paused to draw a hand across his mouth.

"Looked in as I was passing, Tom," said Nosey, his comparative freshness and animation enhanced by his surroundings. "Case there was anything for me—message or anything, you know."

The slow-motion human transferred his hand to his hair, and memory and intelligence being thus tickled into activity, he uttered an exclamaton which Nosey did not trouble to translate.

"Why, yes, of course, Mr. Ruslin! Funny you should call now. There's a registered parcel for you." He shuffled into outer darkness and returned with the parcel. With a nod that concealed his surprise Nosey reduced his capital to three shillings and a halfpenny.

"Thanks, Tom, see you later, I expect," He sauntered out, unperturbed if his demeanour could be accepted as a guide, but actually puzzled and even suspicious, and for a moment or two even frightened.

What could the parcel contain? Not money. He was sure of that. Not an infernal weapon? He was none too sure now.

Perhaps as a precautionary measure he ought to immerse it in a bucketful of water. Bombs had been sent by registered post before now and a man who had scored the successes he had must expect to have enemies.

He sought an unfrequented offshoot of Shaftesbury Avenue and examined the outside closely. Then he shook the parcel but not a sound came to suggest a clue to the mystery.

"I'll chance it," he muttered, and strength reinforced by curiosity he burst the string with one wrench. The paper parted in his fat fingers and he saw the revolver he had entrusted to Bobbie Cheldon.

"The fool!" he spluttered, in his reaction from fear. That quickly passed and he smiled. "Frightened him a bit, I guess. He's that kind. Mother's darling and no guts. What's this? Oh, a letter from Little Lord Fauntleroy. Love and kisses, I suppose."

The smiling contempt vanished when he had read the letter, and his smile rose to triumphant heights when he had grasped the meaning of the signature.

> "*Dear Sir*," wrote Massy Cheldon in his clear, classical handwriting,
>
> "*I am returning the revolver you lent my nephew and in doing so may I be permitted to point out that to entrust a deadly weapon to a young man on a visit to an uncle whose corpse is worth ten*

thousand a year to him is to subject him to severe temptation. He yielded to that temptation last night, but the Cheldon motto is 'Courage and Loyalty,' and I proved that I lived up to the first part at any rate. May I suggest that in future you look after your armoury yourself?

Yours faithfully,
Massy Cheldon."

The writer's reluctance to miss a chance of boasting of his courage was responsible for a letter which only a fool and a cad could have written without thinking of the danger. Not that Massy Cheldon would have been distressed by a suggestion that it might have an unpleasant sequel for his nephew if he put a statement of his guilt in writing. "He deserves it," he would have retorted, and at a hint of blackmail would have laughed. "You can't blackmail a pauper," would have ended the argument.

But now Nosey Ruslin stood on the pavement close to one of Shaftesbury Avenue's poor relations and gazed rapturously at the sheet of notepaper which took all the bitterness out of the wind and filled the air with the gracious warmth of desired companionship.

"Nosey's luck holds good," he murmured with a smile in which the whole of his face participated. "Properly used that letter is worth a fortune. I'll be able to retire sooner than I expected."

Fresh plans formed themselves with the minimum of assistance of his mind, and under their influence he returned to his lodgings off Oxford Street and buried the revolver under the floor of his neighbour's room, the weapon deriving its danger not from the absence of a licence, but solely from the fact that it had been stolen.

From his lodgings he came forth in search of Billy Bright and he found him within half an hour of dinner time.

"Borrow a quid off Nancy," Nosey ordered with some acerbity when the dancer had wasted minutes voicing his depression. "Hurry up, Billy. You don't suppose it's only to look at you that I want you to dine with me?"

It was a one-sided and inaccurate summary of their arrangements, but Nosey had a habit of assuming the pose of host even when the waiter did not bring the bill to him. But anyhow Billy was indebted to him for scores of meals and for much real cash, and so the dancer had no option but to waylay his partner and coax the pound note which was Nosey's minimum for a dinner for two in his present frame of mind.

They were the earliest arrivals at a small and not too popular restaurant within sound of Piccadilly, where Nosey had his usual flattering reception and a choice of tables which befitted a generous patron. In the fewest words he sketched the menu, ordered a couple of cocktails, and as he sipped his, surveyed the ground and estimated the hearing distance of their scattered fellow lunchers.

"Billy," he said suddenly, with his eyes on the table to the left, "you're not going to be a success as a dancer. Your day is over. Isn't that the reason for the face?"

"I've been to nine agents since I saw you last," Billy said, sourly. "And not a date."

"What about the films?"

"No good either. They say it'ud be only crowd work for me, and I couldn't come down to that."

"Nancy is very pretty," Nosey said gravely. "Pity she can't act."

Billy emitted a sound which might have been contempt.

"I wish I were not so fond of Nancy," he said, and he meant it. "It's been my professional ruin. Oh, yes, I know what you'd say, Nosey, and I'd agree with every word. She's a real peach and no mistake about it. She has personality and pep, but she's not a dancer. Good enough up to a point, but after that." He shrugged his shoulders.

"Why not get another partner then?"

"And let Nancy go to some fellow who'd kid her into marrying him!" The tone was a whine of contempt. "That's not my game, Nosey. I want Nancy and I'm going to have her."

"But what about this young Cheldon? She's rather keen on him, isn't she? Wants to be a lady, you know."

The sneer on the younger man's face amounted to distortion.

"He's only a half-wit; perhaps not even half. He'll never be able to marry Nancy, and she'll chuck him when she wakes up."

"But what can you give her, Billy? It won't be long before you'll have to tell her the truth, the whole truth and nothing but the truth." Billy shuddered.

"I wish you wouldn't talk like that," he complained. "It reminds me."

"Never mind, here's the fish."

The interlude proved comforting and when the dishes ceased and Billy was sipping the coffee he used as a minor drug he was in the best of good tempers.

"You were saying, Nosey?" he urged gently.

"That it was time you and me thought about settling down. Me for a quiet life in the country with a valet and a chicken farm. You with Nancy as Mrs. Billy Bright and a honeymoon at Monte Carlo and a racehorse or two of your own." It was his way of touching lightly on the more obvious features of the life genteel as understood by both of them.

The small eyes glistened feebly.

"No more looking for engagements—no more insults from agents—no more smelly night clubs with chaps throwing things at you because they're too drunk to see genius in two feet," the ex-pugilist whispered lyrically.

"That's it, Nosey, that's it," Billy breathed.

"Plenty of money in the bank with real ladies and gents anxious for to make your acquaintance and the county crowding round your beautiful wife." Nosey was working himself up into an hysteria of bad poetry. "The police touching their helmets to you."

The master-stroke dazzled Billy, who was more accustomed to police regarding him from under their helmets with an acquisitive expression.

"You'll be able to draw your cheque for a thousand quid and more and not think nothing of it either." Nosey once had had that blissful experience during the brief period when he had given promise of contesting the heavyweight championship of England.

"No more shaking hands when you'd rather be shaking fists," the ex-pugilist continued excitedly, but never once allowing his excitement to control his voice. "No more of dirty London streets, but the London you and me ought to be in now, Billy."

They both leaned back in their chairs to enjoy for as long as they were permitted the rapture of anticipation.

"But how are we to bring it off, Nosey?" asked Billy when he touched his empty glass and it symbolised to him the finish of the feast.

"Read that." The letter from Massy Cheldon changed hands. "Understand? Well, listen." The voice that annotated the letter and supplied explanatory notes never rose above a pawnshop whisper, but not a word escaped the dancer, whose sallow countenance deepened or lightened as hope or fear held sway. The powerful and penetrating optimism of his companion was not always able to prevent Fear rearing its head, but when at last there was nothing left even for the imagination his thoughts rose to the earthly paradise for two which Nosey had presented for his delectation and he pledged his enthusiastic co-operation in the achieving of it.

"But fancy Algy the Ass going in for that strong arm stuff!" he said with genuine admiration. "It only shows you that you never know."

Nosey rested both his elbows on the table.

"Billy, I've been thinking a lot of late about this here crime wave and do you know the conclusion I've come to?"

Billy waited for the exposition in silence.

"That to commit murder in a crowd is the only safe way of doing it." He laughed. "Not that you and me are thinking of that. Oh, no. That's someone else's job."

"Young Cheldon's?"

Nosey winked.

"Look at all them unsolved murder mysteries. I've counted fifteen of them in the last few years, and not an arrest, in some cases not even a clue. And, Billy." He paused impressively. "All of them was murders committed in crowded streets. There was that chap Creed, I think his name was, murdered in a shop with hundreds of people passing. There was the landlady of a Chelsea pub and we know Chelsea ain't exactly a desert isle. The girl, Vera Page, murdered in Kensington with thousands of people swarming round. And many others. Now take the country. Not many unsolved murder mysteries there. And why? I'll tell you. A chap kills someone in a lonely village where everybody knows him and he's missed if he doesn't turn out for his beer and a fag at the local pub. Supposing he's a stranger to the place? Well, everybody who sees him stares at him and remembers him. There's the difference between a village and London. You and me see thousands of men and women every day but we take no notice of 'em. Now if we lived in Sausage-cum-Chips we'd spend the evenings talking about a strange chap we saw standing outside the Pig and Whistle or inquiring the shortest cut to the farm where hours later the body was found. If he asked us a question or passed the time of day we'd make conversation out of it for a fortnight, and if there was a murder we'd be able to tell what the stranger looked like, and he'd be copped inside an hour. If he wasn't a stranger we'd know all about his quarrel with his wife's sister-in-law's uncle and the whole village would turn out to give evidence about the knife he sharpened on the stone above the river near the church. No, Billy, if you want to do a chap in do it in London where nobody takes no notice of nobody and it ain't anyone's business to talk about everybody's. If I wanted to commit murder," the articulation was barely audible. "I'd do it in the middle of Piccadilly when there was a big traffic jam worrying the peelers. I wouldn't go down to Muck-on-the-Ridge and have the fifty inhabitants talking of nothing else but my visit. London has always been good enough for me, and don't you forget it."

"I see your point," said Billy, nervously. "But where does young Cheldon come in?"

"We've got first to bring him in before he can come in," was the reply. "This letter's good enough but another one from him on top of it would be much better. I want my little plan to be fool proof and police proof. I want no mistakes. It's a scheme in a thousand with a bit of a risk that isn't a risk at all if you look at it the right way. But Billy, there's a fortune for us, and Mr. Bobbie Cheldon will hand that fortune out when we call on him at Broadbridge Manor and he's just finished paying the death duties on his uncle's—er—death." He smiled, and for the first time in their acquaintance Billy discovered that Nosey Ruslin could smile horribly.

"You can rely on me," he whispered.

"That's a certainty," said Nosey with a grimness that his companion resented but refrained from revealing.

"How much do you think it ought to be, Nosey?" The tone was most conciliatory.

"Share and share alike—you and me, and me and you, it'll be a matter of at least three thousand a year—I'm hoping it may be five. At least, that's how I reckon it. We're going to help Cheldon to inherit the family estate before he's too old to enjoy it, and he'll have to agree that it is worth dividing the money in equal shares."

"You're a marvel, Nosey, a right down, hundred per cent marvel, and no mistake," exclaimed his audience.

"I have a head on my shoulders," was the response. "Billy, you can leave the details to me. First of all I'll get Cheldon to write to me agreeing to a reward—yes, a reward for our assistance."

"Will he go as high as five thousand a year between us?"

"He won't be asked to. A thousand pounds payable in instalments of a hundred quid is what I'm thinking of."

Billy looked concerned.

"That's a come-down, isn't it?" he ventured.

Nosey's grin was born of superiority of intellect.

"Don't you see that all we want is something in his hand-writing that'd be good enough for Scotland Yard if they saw it?" he whispered, not really angry because it was flattering to self-esteem to be the explainer and not the explainee. "He'll write me agreeing to the terms and think himself lucky to have such a pal as your humble servant."

The dancer's face lighted up.

"Of course, what a fool I've been! I see it now, Nosey." He stopped, fearful lest his excitement should have rendered his voice louder than he intended. "It won't matter what the sum is, we can raise it sky-high when we have him in our power."

"That's it." Nosey let his napkin slide to the floor. "I'm going to make contact with young Cheldon again. He owes me twenty-five quid already, and he's going to owe me more.

Meanwhile, Billy, get busy and borrow another quid if you can. I must take Cheldon out to lunch or dinner immediately he returns home, and I'm broke. What's the bill? Eleven and tenpence. Give the waiter a couple of bob and I'll take what's left in case."

They walked out together smoking cigars.

"Nancy's dancing solo at the 'Frozen Fang' tonight," said Billy when they arrived at the corner which parted them.

"Righto. I'll bring Cheldon along if I can get hold of him. When I've got a job of work to do, Billy, I prefer to do it neatly and, if possible, swiftly." He patted his friend on the back. "There's an absolute money famine, and if we don't hurry up it'll get worse. And the worse it is the harder it will be to—er—to survive." He smiled in a lazy, effortless way.

The dancer smiled in unison, and then suddenly became grave again.

"But, Nosey," he said hesitatingly, "who's going to do the job?" He was so nervous that his legs moved convulsively as if on wires.

"Leave that to me, my boy," was the cheering reply. "Don't I know exactly which of the lads of the village will be equal to a job that'll be worth at least ten quid a second?"

The return of colour to Billy's usually pallid countenance was interrupted by another doubt.

"That's all right, Nosey," he said, trying to appear hearty, "but if you make the plans and one of the boys does the—what you called it, where exactly do I come in?"

"You will be standing by when I want you," said Mr. Ruslin, grave to the uttermost boundary of his lower chin. "You have promised to take orders from me, Billy, and you know what success will mean to both of us. You want a fortune. Well, did you ever hear of a fortune being made easily except in a sweepstake, and—" he paused impressively, "I ain't goin' to take no chances so this'll not be a blooming sweepstake. So long."

He sauntered away, a heavy figure of geniality, ease and good nature. Shaftesbury Avenue was thronged with pedestrians and loafers, but Nosey passed on his way as if he was a ghost who was invisible to them. Great and significant events were toward and he had to keep his thinking faculties in a condition of constant exercise. He had realised exactly the extent of the risks he was facing, the dangers lurking around him, and under and above him, but they dwindled into insignificance whenever he pondered on the rich monetary rewards that would await him when it was in his power to offer Bobbie Cheldon an undisturbed tenancy of the Cheldon estate but also a tenancy of this world for as long as it pleased Providence to grant him health sufficient to sustain life. Robert Cheldon, Esquire—the muser's formal rendering of Bobbie's full name and honorary suffix afforded him considerable consolation—might object. There was every reason to anticipate that he would "kick"—a term which summed up satisfactorily every possible argument and attitude Massy Cheldon's nephew could evolve or assume when he was presented with a demand for the relinquishment of half or two-thirds of his tragically-acquired income. Nosey Ruslin smiled under his lips at the surprise in store for the young gentleman and in the smile was all the savagery and cruelty of which the easy-going, gentle ex-pugilist was capable.

Seven of his friends were privately interviewed by him before midnight, but not one of them would disgorge any portion of the cash with which they were fighting the famine, as Nosey styled the general shortage before jokingly introducing the reason for the conference. He was accordingly still famine-stricken when at five minutes past twelve he entered the "Frozen Fang" and joined Billy Bright at a table in a corner some distance from the small platform on which Nancy Curzon was scheduled to dance for the second time.

"He's not here," said Billy, in front of whom was a glass which emitted a faint odour signifying that it had recently contained whisky.

"How did Nancy's turn go?"

The young man strangled at birth a look of satisfaction.

"Rotten," he answered, and as if appreciating what Nancy's failure could mean to him he added with feeling, "They were too sober to give her a chance, the curs! Nosey, unless she picks up when she dances at half-past it'll be all up with our partnership and I'll simply have to chuck her!"

"And if I know Miss Nancy," said Mr. Ruslin carelessly, "she'll express her opinion of you with her fists as well as with her tongue."

Billy shivered.

"She has the devil's own temper," he muttered. "But it isn't that, Nosey, it isn't that."

"Of course, it isn't that. It's your love for her, eh? The love that makes the world go round and round until you don't know what you are doing and soon regret what you have done." He called for a whisky to wash the taste out of his mouth. "Billy," he resumed when the band—a piano and a violinist—was helping the thirty or forty gravely-miened revellers to believe that they were receiving value for money, "there'll be no Nancy for you unless you—"

"Don't I know it?" he groaned. "It's money she wants. Nosey, she's beginning to suspect. I wish you hadn't made me keep her in ignorance."

"Her ignorance will be valuable to me—to us," he said quickly.

"Oh, well, I suppose you have a good reason. But she's beginning to suspect, Nosey."

"You said that before."

"And I'll say it again. Why shouldn't I?"

"I'm always glad to hear the latest news, Billy, but not more than six times. You see, it becomes a trifle stale then."

Billy Bright passed a nearly clean hand across his forehead.

"I suppose you're right, Nosey. For that matter when it comes to money you always are. But I don't care for Nancy's suspicious ways. She's a habit of asking questions, the sort that a woman answers herself and then tells you you are lying."

"I'm waiting for Cheldon," said Nosey, desirous of changing the conversation. "Can't you see, Billy, that Cheldon is the answer to all our puzzles and difficulties? You want to marry Nancy, and Nancy won't look at you unless you have money. Well, do as I tell you and I'll guarantee Nancy and the money, but you must remember it's—" He paused. "Here he is," he muttered. "Clear off. I want to be alone with him."

The voice of Bobbie thanking the obsequious attendant for some small service had drifted into the room and through the smoke before he appeared, looking anxious and almost disreputable in the old grey flannel suit he had donned on his return to Galahad Mansions from Broadbridge Manor. But there was every reason for his frayed and careworn ensemble. Mr. Ruslin attributed it to his passion for Nancy. The truth was that for two nights Bobbie had not slept. But then no one could have slept while playing the part of the mouse with Massy Cheldon in the role of the cat.

He paused to stare about the cellar which a few rugs, an elaborate bar and a number of tables and chairs around a dancing space of not many square feet, entitled its proprietor to style it a night club, but as soon as he saw his friend, Nosey Ruslin, something not unlike delight improved his expression.

The ex-pugilist, ex-theatrical agent, but not yet ex-convict, rose with hearty noisiness to shake hands.

"Didn't expect to see you tonight, Mr. Cheldon," he said, placing a chair for him. "Waiter, your best whisky and soda for my friend."

"Thanks," said Bobbie gratefully. It was revivifying to be with someone who appreciated one's social and intellectual importance.

"Come to see Nancy? Not much of a crowd here tonight. Wonder why Battray puts her on it. Ought to wait for Saturday when she'd have an audience."

He spoke to the accompaniment of the gurgles that indicated the emptying of his guest's glass.

"She's too good for a hole like this," said Bobbie, with angry good nature. "She ought to have the finest theatre in London."

"And when you get your rights, too, Mr. Cheldon," whispered the tempter with his customary flattering deference of tone and attitude, "she'll have it. You'll rent the theatre and Nancy's name will dazzle Piccadilly in electric light. She'll become world famous."

"Yes, world famous." Bobbie was so excited that he could scarcely speak. The band renewed its excruciating efforts.

"She'll be the luckiest girl in London when she marries you, Mr. Cheldon," Nosey said with that insinuating assurance that seldom failed to achieve the effect it aimed at. "Look at them." He waggled a hand towards the dancing couples. "What a crowd! What a crowd! And to think that Nancy has to try and amuse these swine. Mr. Cheldon, as I asked you before, for God's sake get that pure-minded girl out of this."

"But how can I?" Bobbie's voice was a wail. "She won't listen to me at present. Calls me a pauper. And I am one, worse luck." He stared at his empty glass and Nosey noticed the stare and misunderstood it. But he could not order a refill, for previous orders had carried away the last of his

coins and he was now penniless. And by special arrangement with Mr. Battray, the owner of the "Frozen Fang",
he paid cash for everything until it was possible for him to
wipe out a debit balance of about fifteen pounds, incurred
the previous month.

"How can you?" he asked with a degree of anger which
was not without a note of affectionate interest. "Do you
know how I'd do it, Mr. Cheldon? I'd take steps to remove
that interfering old uncle of yours and step into the estate
myself. Yes, I've heard about him. Of course, from Nancy.
You should see her imitate him. A.I. at Lloyds. Yes, sir. That
girl's a marvel. Ought to go on the halls if there are any halls
left to go on. A genius."

The band desisted and by contrast the half silence that
ensued was refreshing and comforting. The two waiters
rushed hither and thither, and Billy Bright was not to be seen.

"Miss Nancy Curzon, the famous dancer, of Bright &
Curzon." Mr. Battray was in the centre of the floor, his keen
observation having revealed the fact that no more orders for
drinks were to be expected for at least half an hour.

They switched off the lights save the one over the piece
of wood which was the platform for the occasion, and to
a rumble from the piano Nancy stepped out of nowhere.
Bobbie swooned into a condition of ecstatic admiration and
did not at once revive from it when an intoxicated patron
of the "Frozen Fang" uttered an exclamation of contempt
and flung an empty champagne bottle in her direction.
Fortunately the aim was also drunk and nothing was hit
except the floor, but it was well for the middle-aged scion of
a garage-owning family in outer suburbia that Mr. Battray
and his scullions closed in on the aggressor with the intention
of ejecting him before Bobbie flung himself from his chair
to the seat of the disturbance with fire and murder in his
heart and brain. Mr. Battray, however, had been dealing with

crises of this nature for years, and the offender's bi-monthly expedition in search of Bohemia ended with an assisted passage to the cool and unclean pavement and an addition to his small stock of stories for use in a local public house.

"That's all right, sir," said the proprietor of the "Frozen Fang" to the palpitating champion of insulted womanhood. "The artiste was never in any danger. Mr. Nooch is quite harmless. Have a drink with me, sir. Hello, Nosey, you must join us."

A backward glance at the piano, and the band was soon in full swing. Bobbie absorbing his second whisky and soda, was unaware of Nancy's close proximity until she spoke to Nosey.

"What can you expect?" she asked sarcastically. "Haven't I told you a thousand times they don't know what real art is?"

"You were wonderful, Nancy," said Bobbie, holding out both hands.

"Oh, shut up!" she retorted to his complete discomfiture. "I'm sick of that sort of talk. Give me something to drink, Nosey, or I'll scream." Bobbie, unaware that she knew her act had been a failure, could not find an excuse or a reason for her temper, certain he had done nothing to offend her.

"Nancy." He stopped when he noted the expression of her face. Never before had she displayed such ferocity of rebellion against life.

"Billy was right," he heard her say to Nosey, to whom she seemed to be exclusively devoted. "I'm wasting my time and talents here. I ought to make that continental tour and return with a reputation."

"What about America, Nancy? They'd eat your act there." Nosey had never been out of England in his life, hardly ever out of London, but there was pure cosmopolitanism in a tone which in a moment carried Bobbie at least to a crowded New York theatre.

"That's what everybody says," Nancy remarked with more complacence and therefore less temper. "I'm to blame, though," she added, lapsing into normality, "I've been thinking of other things besides my profession and my art, and I'm paying the penalty."

"Nancy," said Bobbie pleadingly.

She turned and established his existence at the table by according him a faint smile.

"You've done me no good by asking me to marry you," she said with an astonishing return to good temper. "I'm fond of you, Bobbie." His hand was on hers in an instant and she did not withdraw it.

"That dancing of yours was marvellous," he whispered. "It simply stunned them with its perfection."

She stared at him, suspecting ill-timed humour, but to her unspoken amazement she saw that he was sincere. Actually he was the only person in the club who did not know that she had been a failure.

"You're a lamb," she said impulsively.

"And I'm a wolf, I suppose," interposed Nosey Ruslin humorously.

"No, you're a bear," Nancy corrected prettily. "But I don't want to live in a zoo." To Bobbie's delight she caught him by the arm and brought her lips on a level with his right ear. "You're a dear, and I'll wait a month. If you can afford to marry me then…"

Nosey discerned an acquaintance at the other side of the room who was good for a drink, but when he returned refreshed, Bobbie was alone.

"She's dancing at a party with Billy Bright," he explained sulkily.

"I suppose what she whispered was a secret?" Nosey was almost playful.

"I wanted to tell you that, Mr. Ruslin," said Bobbie, eagerly. "She promised to wait a month and—"

Nosey uttered a cry of astonishment.

"You must have made a hit with her!" he said, enviously. "That means she'll chuck the contract I offered her. And all for your sake. You're a lucky chap, Mr. Cheldon."

"Lucky? How?" The voice was harsh, even hostile.

"Because there isn't another man in London Nancy'd do that for," he retorted with emphasis. "Can't you see she's an artiste with the soul of an artiste and that her profession means everything to her? If she's willing to give it all up for you—to share your lot—" the sentimental note was choked before it could rise to pathos.

"I know she won't marry me unless I'm rich," he blurted out.

"Well, why not be rich?" He surveyed the room. "Mr. Cheldon, we can't talk here. Come to my flat and we'll see if I can't think of some scheme to help you. I want Nancy and you to be happy."

Bobbie was muttering his gratitude when they reached the street, but his companion did not speak until the door of his flat was closed and locked.

"Nothing more to drink, Mr. Cheldon," he said, when his guest was filling the armchair on the other side of the fireless grate. "We've got business to do and we must have clear heads."

Something about the room reminded Bobbie of his debt.

"Oh, by the way, Mr. Ruslin, that twenty-five pounds. I'll—"

"You'll get a thick ear," said Mr. Ruslin facetiously, "if you ever refer to it again. I'm not a millionaire, but I've got all I want and a bit over. Any time you're in a fix for a little of the ready I'll be waiting with both hands full of quids." He smiled.

"You're my best friend, Mr. Ruslin!" Bobbie cried uncontrollably.

"You're not the first chap who's said that," Nosey rejoined placidly. "But let me begin with a question, Mr. Cheldon. Why did you send me back the barker?"

As he instantaneously translated the last word Bobbie sat up in a fluster. "I didn't return it," he gasped. "It was uncle."

Mr. Nosey Ruslin affected the politeness of inattention.

"You don't mean to say so!" His back was towards Bobbie and he appeared to be busy with a cigarette-box. "Suppose he thought it rather dangerous, Mr. Cheldon. Perhaps he suspected something was wrong." He was ambling towards the other chair now. "I don't know this uncle of yours, and if I did I can't say I'd want to kiss him." He laughed.

"Neither would anyone else." Bobbie grunted to himself. "But he's got pluck, Mr. Ruslin. I shouldn't have had the nerve to do it myself."

"Do what?"

Bobbie forced a laugh.

"I don't know how to put it."

"Can't you trust a pal?" The note was almost plaintive. "You called me your best friend a little while ago. Doesn't that go for something?"

"Yes, of course it does. I'm sorry, Mr. Ruslin." Bobbie laughed again. "I was worked up at dinner the first night and he said things that made me feel I wanted to choke him. When I began to think about the revolver I was minding for you—" he stopped as if thought had failed.

"You planned a little expedition to his room at night with some idea of removing uncle from this vale of tears?" It was all so very obvious to Nosey that he never imagined for a moment he was being clever. "But what happened then?" he asked abruptly.

"He walked straight up to the revolver and took it away from me," the culprit confessed. "Of course, Mr. Ruslin, it was just a try-on of mine—a little joke. I didn't mean anything serious. I was fuddled, perhaps, drunk."

"But it might have gone off. It was fully loaded. When it was returned to me the ammunition had been removed."

"Uncle did that. I'd never have thought he had so much courage. I really almost expected him to die of fright when he saw the weapon close to his cracking bones. As long as I've known him he's been whining about his health, and I well remember when I was a kid I exploded a paper bag behind him and he nearly had hysterics."

"It may be that he couldn't fancy you shooting him," Nosey suggested. It was a polite way of conveying the opinion that Massy Cheldon did not regard his nephew as anything better than an invertebrate loafer.

"But never mind, Mr. Cheldon," Nosey added, the moment he detected anger in the boyish face opposite him. "You and I are friends, and I'm going to stand by you no matter what happens. No, don't thank me. I want no thanks except your marriage with Nancy. That's all that matters to me. Money doesn't interest me and I'm too old to bother about mixing with the nobs. Give me Shaftesbury Avenue, winter or summer, and I'm happy. I may not be a gentleman of your sort, but fifty quid a week and reasonable health and Nosey Ruslin looks the whole world in the face, Scotland Yard and all." He was relieved that his impulsive indiscretion brought only a chuckle from his young friend.

"I can marry Nancy only when I'm master of Broadbridge Manor and the Cheldon estate," said Bobbie, returning to moodiness.

"Exactly. And now, Mr. Cheldon, keep your wits about you while we think out a plan to make you master of Broadbridge Manor and the husband of the finest little girlie in all London. First of all, your uncle knows you want him out of the way."

"That couldn't have cost him much thinking."

"No. But the revolver helped a bit. Mr. Cheldon, your uncle took the weapon from you and returned it to me. Has he told you that for the sake of the family he'll keep what happened a secret?"

"Yes. But he'd have to anyhow."

"Are you sure you can trust him? Mr. Cheldon, you're no fool. You're a man of the world. Tell me." Nosey thrust himself to the edge of his armchair. "Can you guarantee that he'll never lose his temper and give you away? Mr. Cheldon, your uncle has you in his power. Will you do nothing to get out of it?"

"How can I?" The quaver in his voice was not due to Nosey's question but to the influence of his melodramatic, rhetorical style.

"That's why I asked you here," said Mr. Ruslin with appropriate gravity. "And before we part, Mr. Cheldon, we've got to find the solution of the riddle."

"What riddle?"

"Getting out of your uncle's power and getting into the family property," was the earnest reply. "Then you will be able to marry Nancy and save her from the clutches of that dago, Billy Bright."

Bobbie winced at the mention of the dancer's name.

"An appalling bounder," he muttered, summoning to his aid all the puny anger of which he was capable.

"Mind you, Mr. Cheldon," the tempter resumed, "I don't agree with Nancy and I've told her so a dozen times. 'You're a fool,' I said to her only a few minutes before you arrived at the 'Frozen Fang.' You're a fool not to marry on any terms a young gentleman like Mr. Cheldon. He's good-looking, intelligent and straight. What more do you want, my girl? If it's money, that'll come sooner than you expect.' I think my words impressed her, but she's afraid of poverty, Mr. Cheldon, and in a way I can't blame her, for she's known it, and the Whitechapel brand fairly sizzles the soul, believe me."

Bobbie closed his eyes and drank in the flattery.

"I don't know what I'd do without you, Mr. Ruslin," he said in a nervous whisper. "It's worrying, though. I can't sleep for thinking of Nancy. I hadn't the pluck to tell her tonight that uncle had promised to get me a job."

"What sort of job?" asked Nosey, almost curt of tone.

"Oh, something in a rubber firm's office."

Nosey's exclamation was one of shrill contempt.

"Five quid a week, I suppose, and touch your hat to the boss." He laughed derisively, and Bobbie had not the courage to halve the estimate and turn it into fact. "You, Mr. Cheldon, a city clerk! Your uncle must think you're a fool. You're a county gentleman, that's what you are. You ought to be standin' for Parliament and makin' speeches an' taking Nancy to Court. A city clerk, indeed!"

"But what can I do?" The tone was plaintive.

"Look here, Mr. Cheldon, for your own sake I'll speak plainlike and put all my cards on the table. What you do really doesn't matter a curse to me. I have all the money I want and I'm quite happy to be what I am. At my age Love's young dream is something that don't exist. But there's yourself and there's Nancy." He dropped into a whisper. "Unless you're not the man I take you for you should get the Cheldon money as quickly as possible. You failed the other night—don't fail next time."

Bobbie went white as dread rendered his expression lifeless.

"I—I—how could—" he clutched at his throat as if attempting to wrench coherent speech from it.

"Your uncle alive means no Nancy. Understand? Well, it's got to be uncle dead, eh?" He leered. "You don't suppose you could do it yourself? Of course not. That's a job for someone else. Now let's come to terms, and, mind, there must never be no present for me. I want nothin'." He paused, but Bobbie remained silent. "Supposing I found a chap who could do it neatly and without danger to anyone, includin' himself, what would you say to paying him a thousand quid in four instalments of two hundred and fifty each? You'd know nothin' about it until the family solicitor was reading the will to you." Mr. Ruslin winked expressively. "You and me would be in the background. No danger, no nothin'."

The little that was left of Bobbie's conscience turned sick.

"It would be horrible," he gasped.

Nosey Ruslin shrugged his shoulders.

"Seeing that it don't make no difference to me either way I'll not argue about it," he said, advancing towards the sideboard. "But it's the Continent and Billy Bright for Nancy and a city clerkship for you. And won't Nancy laugh, and Billy, too, when they hear what you're doin'!" He laughed as if to provide Bobbie with a sample of the derision to which he was to be subjected.

"Nancy," Bobbie repeated, speaking to himself, "Nancy." With a sudden movement he was on his feet.

"I have no choice, Mr. Ruslin," he said, nervously, "and I'm grateful to you. I haven't thanked you before, but—"

"Don't you worry about that," said Nosey good-naturedly. He tapped him on the arm. "If you want another little loan you know where to come for it." He laid a hand on his own extensive mouth to indicate that he objected to any expression of thanks. "Now, Mr. Cheldon, let's draw up a plan of campaign. I don't know your uncle by sight, and so you must arrange to point him out to me. Is he often in London?"

"He comes up about twice a week. He's very fond of London," said Bobbie, rather surprised at the ease with which he had dropped into his friend's suggestion. "Once you saw him you'd easily spot him again. He's about three inches shorter than I am and very thin. Looks a lot older than fifty-three, and is fond of talking about his internal organs. Has two small, deepset eyes and a weak, sneering sort of mouth."

Nosey listened with apparent intentness and Bobbie saw his lips move as though he was memorising at least some of the description.

"When is he coming to London again?"

"Tomorrow. I am lunching with him at his club—299 Piccadilly—afterwards we're motoring into the city to see a friend of his who manages the rubber firm I spoke of."

"You'll leave the club between half-past two and three?" said Nosey.

"Nearer three. Uncle is a good luncher and never hurries." Bobbie smiled faintly. "Say ten minutes to three, Mr. Ruslin."

"Good. I'll be there, and with a pal, and if it's Billy Bright don't you worry. This is none of your business and never will be. You don't know nothing about it and that's all there is so far as you are concerned, Mr. Cheldon. But there's one little bit of business that's got to be done now."

"Yes?" Bobbie was feeling overwrought. Had his imagination been more powerful he must have rushed out of the flat.

"Just scribble a few lines to say you'll pay that thousand quid when you come into the property. Say it's for services rendered. No one will guess what the services are." He spoke jauntily and as carelessly he produced a writing pad, bottle of ink and pen. "Use whatever words you think will protect you. When the money is paid you will have the bit of paper back to burn or to keep as a souvenir."

As if under the influence of a drug Bobbie wrote with almost mechanical precision, "I promise to pay the sum of one thousand pounds in four agreed instalments of two hundred and fifty pounds within a year of my succeeding to the Cheldon estate. The payment to be made for services rendered by the holder of this document. Robert Cheldon."

"Thank you," said Nosey, carefully placing it within the folds of his pocket-book. "And now, Mr. Cheldon, another bit of advice. Be friends with your uncle from now onwards. Take that job and thank him with tears in your eyes for it." He laughed. "Or if tears won't come into your eyes put 'em in your voice. It must be 'Yes, uncle' and 'Thank you, uncle' and 'God bless you, uncle'. And as for Nosey Ruslin, well, you've never even heard of him. Twiggy-vous? as they say in Southend."

For some reason obscure to himself Bobbie experienced a feeling of relief. It may have been that the noisome atmosphere, the unlovely exterior of Nosey Ruslin and the general appearance of poverty and decrepitude that the room and its furnishings presented helped to banish reality. Actually it was due to the knowledge that in the dread and ghastly adventure that would be the prelude to his accelerated transition from poverty to riches he would not be compelled to associate with his confederate.

"And now you're thinking of beddy-byes," said Mr. Ruslin facetiously, "and a few hours between the sheets won't do me no harm. Ta-ta."

When he had the room to himself Nosey unearthed the document which henceforth he was to style "young Cheldon's autograph" and read and re-read it until fairy gold danced before his eyes. Once he walked up and down the room holding it before him, and once he read it aloud.

"A thousand quid!" he exclaimed in a sarcastic tone. "Ten thousand—twenty thousand—fifty thousand."

He fell asleep dreaming of a palace and he awoke to a rattle on the outer door of his flat and found that Billy Bright had arrived with noonday. For a man of his weight he leapt out of bed with amazing agility and the joy which grease and dirt and hairs could not conceal was instantly reflected in the dancer's expression.

"You've done it, Nosey?" he whispered, excitedly.

"As easy as winking," was the triumphant reply. "Got it in black and white. Billy, it's a cinch—money for nothing. Robbing a kid's moneybox is a right down regular feat compared with this certainty."

Billy read the slip of paper to the accompaniment of an increasing grin. Then, as usual, he had a doubt.

"Supposing you don't bring it off?" he asked nervously. "By the way, who were you thinking of?"

"Italian Charlie. It's his job," said Nosey promptly.

"Yes, of course. It's Charlie's when it's got to be done without a noise. But supposing, Nosey."

"Another supposing?" exclaimed Nosey angrily. "Well, out with it."

"Supposing for instance—mind you, I'm only saying supposing—something happened such as—" he paused while he grappled with his powers of intelligent anticipation—conscious that his friend was staring unpleasantly at him.

"Go on, will you?"

"Supposing Italian Charlie lost his nerve or refused. Supposing nothing at all happened, or something did happen and the police got Charlie before he could do the job at all or complete it?"

Nosey Ruslin deposited most of himself on the sofa and with the back of his head supported by his hands looked up at the ceiling.

"You're a dancer, Billy," he began in a tone of measured irony and insult, "and I suppose that's the reason why all your brains are in your feet. Do you think I haven't thought of everything? Do you think you have? Of course, you haven't, and that's the answer to all your questions. There's a lot more in this than'll ever meet your eye, Billy, and one of 'em is that we've got the uncle as well as the nephew. I don't say the uncle would pay as much as the nephew—there isn't so much at stake. But do you think he'd like to have a scandal in the papers about his high and mighty family?" He grunted. "The letter from the uncle is worth a thousand quid or so if the worst happens and we can't do him in." He resolved himself into a standing posture. "Got any dough, Billy?" The dancer produced a pound note and some silver. "I'll borrow the quid. Must have some breakfast. It'll be a busy day for me. And while I think of it, Billy, you might see Italian Charlie and tell him I'll be having supper at Toriano's tonight at eleven. He'll know what that means. If he doesn't or won't, we'll have to find an understudy. I'm in a hurry to make some provision for my old age, and I'm beginning in Piccadilly at five minutes to three today." He winked.

"All right, Nosey," said Billy grinning. "I'll tell Charlie, and you can expect me, too, for the conference."

"Attaboy!" exclaimed Nosey, waving a fat hand.

His enthusiastic confidence was infectious and yet at the same time a source of doubt and uncertainty to Billy.

"I don't seem to be doing much," he said suggestively.

"When the time comes I'll find plenty of work for you," his friend answered with a meaning laugh. "Billy, if you want to share in the golden harvest you must do some of the sowing as well as the reaping. That's only proper and right."

"Of course." The tone, however, was mechanical. Billy Bright belonged to the school which prefers to back a horse after it has passed the post. "How much do you think there's in it, Nosey?" He was ingratiating now or attempting to be.

"Ten thousand apiece for me and my partner—whoever he happens to be," said Nosey complacently. "It'll be a big job and a ticklish one, as I've mentioned before, but you can't make a fortune by betting in half-crowns, and it's the same with an—an enterprise of this sort. But don't forget to see Italian Charlie and don't forget to turn up. Should it happen that I can't come tell Charlie to drop in here tonight after you've given him my message. And if I were you I'd come with him or without him."

The door closed, and Billy walked away feeling as if he was propelled by air charged with dynamite. But the prospect of wealth was sufficient to keep his particular brand of cowardice which he called the artistic temperament, in check, and before another midnight took its place in the records the first of many conferences opened which had for its subject the safety and prosperity of two blackguards planning a murderous crime in the very heart of London, but Italian Charlie took part in one only.

Bobbie Cheldon knew nothing of these conferences, though occasionally he had telephonic conversations with the amiable Nosey, who was careful to promise him that in a very short time he would be released from the servitude of the rubber company's office and the fiver a week—it was actually fifty shillings but the Cheldon pride forbade the admission—and promoted to £10,000 a year.

Chapter Six

The last day in the life of a man about to be murdered would lack nothing of pity and terror were it possible to endow him and his acquaintances with foreknowledge of his doom. But when Massy Cheldon was called by his valet at three minutes to eight on the morning of June 8th, the temperate sunshine that streamed through the open window seemed to radiate health and invite happiness. Left to himself whilst he sipped an early morning cup of tea, the master of Broadbridge Manor pondered in succession on the weather, his investments, the eccentricities of the League of Nations, the mistakes of the Conservative leaders, and the lunch to which he had invited his neighbours, Viscount Firmin and Sir Beckwith Dent. To a self-important person every moment is important, and Massy Cheldon from the first splash in the bath to the careful brushing of his coat by the valet concentrated his mind on each act and accompanied each with an inward running commentary on its relation to his appearance and his affairs. So far the day promised well and there was nothing to disturb the smoothness of his satisfaction. It was good to be the head of the Cheldon family at any time—it was magnificent to be head of it on a day like this with nothing from the financial markets to disturb his serene enjoyment of the old mansion and the comparatively new income with which it was endowed.

The postman was a little late and Massy indulged in some pungent criticisms of the Postmaster-General before he began a cursory examination of the pile of letters and circulars. The circulars and the requests for loans and donations were carted off by West midway between the fish and the marmalade, and by the time he was smoking a cigarette he had only three letters lying before him on the table. One was from his broker and informed him that by taking advantage of the market at once he could realise a profit of eleven hundred pounds or thereabouts on certain gold shares; the second was from Ruby Cheldon reporting that Bobbie "simply loves his work and never mentions that night club girl," and the third was from the private secretary to the Lord Lieutenant of Sussex inviting him to accept the dignity of Justice of the Peace.

Profit, Gratitude, Honour.

Massy Cheldon's smile surprised the watchful butler by reason of its almost youthful quality and obvious sincerity.

"A lovely day, West," he said with a too emphatic condescension.

"It is indeed, sir." West was grateful for the opening. "You have not forgotten that Lord Firmin and Sir Beckwith are lunching here today, sir?"

"Oh, of course. Yes. I'd nearly forgotten." Massy Cheldon liked the society of viscounts on principle. Baronets, too, were always welcome at Broadbridge Manor, even if they happened to be, as in the case of the former Governor of Burmah, the first of the line. "By the way, West, tell Waterhouse to be ready to drive me to Lewes to catch the three ten to London. I've decided to remain in town overnight."

The butler nodded. It was a new economy of the wealthy master of the Cheldon estate to dispense with the services of chauffeur and car at the nearest convenient railway station. There was a time when he overworked both. Now, in West's opinion, both were underworked.

After breakfast Massy retired to the library to compose the letter to the Lord Lieutenant accepting the dignity of J.P. "I promise you that I will devote as much of my time as I can to the duties," he wrote. "I have always been a severe critic of magistrates who shirk their duties and responsibilities, and I am determined to avoid the obvious *tu quoque*." He pondered here, admiring what he considered a neat turn of phrase but not too confident of the Lord Lieutenant's perception of its beauties. "I ought to be chairman of the Bench in five years," he said to himself. "Firmin doesn't want it and Dent doesn't care for the work. As for Salmon and Weatherby they're just waiting for the grave."

At half-past ten he was on the telephone to his broker, and at twenty minutes past twelve he was convinced that this was the very best of all possible worlds, for had not his broker's anticipations been exceeded and was he not richer by the delicious sum of thirteen hundred and eighty-six pounds ten shillings! As he stood at a window and surveyed his domains he was more than once on the point of admitting that there must be a Providence greater than himself working miracles on his behalf.

"Never felt better in my life," he exclaimed with more truth than he was capable of realising, when Viscount Firmin, tall and portly, shook hands with his customary stiffness in the old world drawing-room and simultaneously made the conventional inquiry.

"Dent won't be long. He 'phoned to say he was engaged with someone from Whitehall," said his host.

"They can't be thinking of offering him another governorship!" exclaimed Lord Firmin with pompous irritability. No one had ever thought of offering him anything outside the liability of his cheque-book and he resented any increase in the importance of his neighbours.

"You can ask him," said Massy Cheldon, proffering the cigarette box that decorated the small table behind them. "I wonder, Firmin, if you ever thought of dabbling in Fermanagh Gold. I've been—"

The tribute to his own astuteness as a speculator lasted until West announced the baronet and was only resumed when Viscount Firmin, having delivered his opinion of the excellence of the sole, yielded without undue pressure to an invitation to taste it again.

"We're not going to lose you, I hope, Dent?" said Massy Cheldon with more inquisitiveness than politeness.

The baronet, who was as tall as the peer and about half his weight, smiled languidly until he had uncovered most of his teeth. He was very thin and inclined to sallowness of skin, and from the east he had brought a taciturnity which in contrast to the viscount's disjointed verbosity could assume the dimensions of wisdom.

"I am sixty-seven," he confessed lazily, "and that's well past the age limit. Firmin there is seventy and—"

"Sixty-nine—not seventy until August," was the indignant correction. "I am surprised, Dent, that a Civil Servant shouldn't be more accurate. When I was…"

"We'll take the rest for granted, Firmin," said Dent with a burst of loquacity. "We were talking about ages." He sighed. "Cheldon is only fifty. Fifty-three, you say? Thanks. Fifty-three." He repeated the number of years with a melancholy emphasis. "He'll be coming to our funerals, Firmin, and perhaps he may subscribe to memorials to us in the village churchyard."

"For heaven's sake, don't start talking about funerals and memorials and village churchyards!" protested Viscount

Firmin, gesticulating with his head. "I'm not too well just now. Had to have the doctor yesterday."

"Do you think you can spend nearly forty years in the east and not feel the effects?" asked the baronet with a measure of contempt.

Their host simmered with good humour. The company of Bobbie and fellows of that age gave him an odd feeling that he was rapidly approaching the centenarian stage, but with these two veterans for society he glowed with juvenility and careless good spirits.

"Don't worry, Firmin," he said, cheerfully patronising, "you may top the century yet. Anyhow, look at old Mrs. Ellis-Wood. Given up by the doctors eleven years ago and next Saturday she's opening the flower show and I'm to propose her health at the lunch."

"I'll be there, too," said Sir Beckwith Dent, drawing his wineglass to within a more convenient latitude. He yawned. "Awful bore these village functions, but they expect it of people in our position."

"I only hope it won't be too hot," said Viscount Firmin, breathing heavily. "It's all very well for youngsters of your age, Cheldon." He drained the glass of Beaune which was his favourite wine.

Massy Cheldon returned to the subject of the gold mining market. He was a recognised expert on money greed, and the peer and the baronet listened with respectful attention to his dissertation on the art of turning sufficient into superfluity. All that was needed, he reminded them, was cleverness, astuteness, mental poise, vision and a *savoir faire* which to the multitude must ever be an unknown quantity. Anyone, however, fortunate enough to possess these attributes, which in rare, very rare instances, could be found allied with genius, might be certain of triumphing over the difficulties and obstacles which beset ordinary persons in their efforts to tempt Dame Fortune successfully.

At the coffee stage Sir Beckwith Dent was giving his opinion of recent events in Burmah, and Viscount Firmin was listening with his eyes closed and his mouth open. He revived, however, when his opportunity came and he demanded of his audience why the Conservative Party tolerated Mr. Baldwin?

Massy Cheldon interrupted the diatribe to explain with suitable apologies that he was catching the three ten at Lewes with the intention of spending the night in London.

"I wonder if you'd take me along with you?" said the baronet.

"Delighted, my dear fellow."

Viscount Firmin rose and, not to give his departure too abrupt an appearance, began to stare in turn at the portraits.

"I envy you this place, Cheldon," he said, and he meant it. "What a clever notion that was of your ancestor to keep most of the Cheldon estate in a strong room in a bank! I wish mine had. Land's a curse."

Had they had time the trio would have discoursed long and complainingly of the worries of landlords, but the information that Waterhouse was waiting to start the car broke up the debate.

"Poor old chap," said Sir Beckwith Dent as he and Massy Cheldon were racing towards Lewes, "as he gets older he simply can't stop talking about himself." He laughed under his breath.

Massy Cheldon, unaware of the fact that all three of them had done nothing else, was moodily sympathetic.

"We'll be attending his funeral soon," he said, mercifully unconscious of his own impending doom, a doom which was to bring to Viscount Firmin the role of reader of the lesson at the funeral of the murdered owner of Broadbridge Manor. "But here we are."

They parted at Victoria Station, and Massy Cheldon at once took the Underground to his sister-in-law's flat. A man who had cleared some hundreds of pounds with no more trouble than two telephone calls could not afford a taxi all that way. Now had it been thousands instead of hundreds…

"This is a delightful surprise, Massy," said Ruby Cheldon, the flush in her cheeks bringing to her face something better than youth. "Bobbie will be back from his office soon."

"I thought I'd call to have a chat about him," he said from his chair, the most comfortable in the room, "but somehow, Ruby, whenever I see you I forget Bobbie."

She flushed again.

"I suppose it's because it's impossible to imagine you have a grown up son." He spoke in level, measured tones, without any note in his voice suggestive of attempt at flattery. "How you keep young beats me. Lord Firmin and Sir Beckwith Dent were envying me my youth at lunch today, but they're a couple of old fogies, one with his third wife and second mistake, and the other with his liver and his politics. But you are young, Ruby." He sighed.

"I believe you're making love to me," she began gaily, and stopped when she observed his frame quiver.

"I wish I could, Ruby." He looked across at her. "But things are difficult." He stood up, looked about him and sat down again. "Tell me about Bobbie. Is he keeping regular hours?"

It was Ruby Cheldon's favourite subject and without any effort of memory or imagination she kept it going until Bobbie, looking a little wan and tired, entered on the scene.

"Yes, uncle, I know something about rubber," he said in answer to a polite question. A little later he excused himself on the plea that he had to make a telephone call. They heard the door close before either of them spoke.

"It's to that girl," said Massy Cheldon angrily.

"I don't think so," Ruby ventured, but her face betrayed her. "He hasn't mentioned her name for days now."

"A bad sign," he muttered. Then he stood up again. Ruby thought he was remarkably restless and ill at ease that afternoon. Could it be true that he was really in love with her? It was notorious in the family that Massy Cheldon had been in love with himself for years. Still, she was a woman and he was a man.

"Ruby." The new note in his pronunciation of her name startled her. "It's a funny world, Ruby, for just when one believes one has everything something happens and you realise you have nothing. I would like to help you more. You've been a wonderful mother, and Bobbie isn't worthy to touch the hem of your garment."

"Old Weller would have called that 'werging on poetry'," she exclaimed, seeking in a well assumed extravagant delight relief from her embarrassment. Yet to be mistress of Broadbridge Manor!

"I wish I could do something."

She smiled, thinking he was about to plead poverty.

"Ruby, it's a wonderful world when you think you are on top of it, and I thought so until I came into your presence. Now I feel I'm completely under it and that it's crushing me."

"What's happened? Have you lost money?" she asked innocently.

He smiled in compliment to his possession of that regiment of qualities which at lunchtime he had outlined as essential to success.

"For the moment money isn't worrying me." Then he hastened to hedge. "But, of course, one never knows from minute to minute what may happen." A familiar moan escaped him.

"Let me make you a cup of tea," she pleaded. "I'm so grateful to you, Massy, for having got Bobbie out of the rut.

It doesn't matter that the salary is so small. It's something to know that he's doing work that will make a man of him. I was terribly afraid he was sinking into the night club morass and would never get out of it."

"Ah, Ruby, you forget he's a Cheldon. The boy will be worthy of the name yet." He was flattering her now and she knew it, and a curious dread seized her mind and limbs.

"Don't bother about the tea, Ruby. It's rather late, and I've something else to say. I'm in rather a fix and I want your help."

She turned on him with the celerity of an acrobat.

"Is it a woman, Massy?" She was looking scared.

For a moment he was tempted to be truthful, but the habit of a lifetime overwhelmed him.

"If it's a woman that woman is you," he answered with a gallantry that sounded as false as it actually was. "Ruby, I'm staying in town overnight and the reason is that I want to see you alone when we won't be interrupted. Will you lunch with me at the Berkeley tomorrow at half-past one?"

"Won't I? I'll do that easier than a duck takes to water." Her face was alive with delight. "Why, Massy, it's years since I've been in the Berkeley or it seems years—a hundred of them. You don't know what it means to escape from a three-day joint existence."

"I'll see if I can't change that," he said significantly, and added a curse to himself when Bobbie reappeared.

When Massy Cheldon departed with the expressed intention of interviewing an old acquaintance who had written offering his services as private secretary—"I'm thinking of having one," he explained—Ruby waited nearly three minutes for Bobbie to answer the question that was troubling her. It was only when his silence exasperated her that she gave voice to it.

"No, it wasn't Nancy," he answered moodily, "I couldn't telephone to her even if I wanted to, for she's not on the phone. It was to a chap I saw in the city today." It was the truth, for Nosey Ruslin had waylaid him as he was leaving the office for a teashop lunch and had shared it with him. But it was also more dangerous than a lie because of what it was intended to conceal and did conceal.

"I'm glad of that." His mother's tone was, he thought, censorious, and he nearly flared up, but he recalled something exhilarating Mr. Ruslin had said to him and it rendered his temper foolish-proof.

"I'll be a bit late tonight," he remarked when another pause had reached its limit of endurance. "No, you're wrong again, mother. It's not Nancy. She'll be elsewhere earning in half an hour four times what I get in a week from the bald-headed pleb who runs the office."

She would have inaugurated one of their bickering duo-logues had it not been for memories of her brother-in-law's invitation. Remorse animated her when she compared her lunch of tomorrow's with Bobbie's. It would not be finished by the time Bobbie was back at the office poring over unin-teresting ledgers.

"I'm lunching with your uncle tomorrow," she said suddenly.

Bobbie emitted a whistle of surprise.

"And at the Berkeley!"

A gape expressed his astonishment now.

"What's happened to him? Has he inherited another for-tune or is he in love with you? Don't blush, mother. I don't want to dash your hopes, but when uncle discovers that a marriage licence can cost as much as seven and six, or so I've been told, he'll scratch the fixture. Still, a lunch for two at the Berkeley and uncle paying the bill! My hat, and my whole suit and wardrobe for that matter." He came to her side and kissed her. "Will you lay me five to one, mother, that you won't be married before me? I'll take you to all the money I've got. Come now, be a sport." His laughter filled the room pleasantly.

Not very far away Massy Cheldon was also laughing, for it was half-past seven, his appetite for dinner was rapidly improving, the profit of the day seemed to add to the beauty of that June evening, he had banished his cares, and he did not know that he had only four hours and fifteen minutes of life left.

When the Underground propelled him into the open and he found himself in Piccadilly his exhilaration was so intense that he had to mount guard over it. But the sight of pale faces and tired bodies hurrying home after the day's labours to suburban homes and equally unlovely incomes threw his own circumstances into such strong relief that he could have voiced his satisfaction aloud. He was a free man—the others were slaves. He had the key to all the desirable and lovely things which the world produced—they had nothing except the struggle and the certainty that the struggle would avail nought.

A shadow crossed his path and materialised into Colonel Crabb, red-faced, dapper, simply impetuous when not explosive.

"Why the devil, Cheldon, do you cut your friends?" he demanded with a friendly ferocity of manner that he mistook for humour.

"Sorry, Crabb," said the day-dreamer, smiling. "On the way to the club or is it the Carlton?"

"I never dine at the club now," the colonel answered, falling into step. "But I don't mind being seen with you in Piccadilly, Cheldon. You look so damned prosperous that it will do my credit good."

Massy smiled again. It was perfectly true what Crabb was saying. The old and impecunious bore with a pension, a liver and a termagant of a wife did require some shoring up of his credit.

"I was thinking of the Berkeley," he remarked, pensively. "They have an excellent grill room there."

"Good. I'll join you." The colonel laughed boisterously. "But don't worry, Cheldon, I'll pay my own account."

Cheldon took the safe and cheapest course of passing the pleasantry by, but at the same time he did some mental juggling during which he arrived at the conclusion that it would cost him at least twenty-five shillings to feed the colonel with solids and liquids.

"Can't afford it," he muttered unthinkingly.

"Can't afford what?" barked his companion.

"Sorry, Crabb, thinking of something else. Ah, you may well pretend to envy me, but I'm not so well off as you think. Heavy taxation—"

In self-defence the colonel put on for a run of eleven minutes the story of a tiger he shot between tiffin and dinner at Simla just before the war. The animal was well and truly slain by the time they sat down at a table in the grill room of the Berkeley, which Massy Cheldon had thought of only because he had been thinking most of the time of his invitation to Ruby for the morrow.

As he was not a guest and therefore considered he was under no obligation to be polite the colonel departed before the coffee stage, having espied a fellow-campaigner of his Indian days in solitary greediness at a neighbouring table. Massy Cheldon, muttering the relief which he felt, wandered out of the building and sauntered in the direction of his club. It was only half-past eight, and he had three hours and fifteen minutes left of life, but his only worry was inability to decide whether to "see a picture" or drop in at one of the revue theatres before retiring to his hotel. On second thoughts he voted against the "pictures" and with it banished the idea of patronising any part of a theatre where a lounge suit was permissible. The gentility of the Cheldons was over one hundred years old, but it had not lost its veneer yet.

His club, situated in the most virtuous part of Piccadilly, afforded him for more than two hours the undisturbed solitude which his internal organs craved after the recent assault on them, but when at twenty minutes past eleven he left it he was feeling sleepy. The heavy air of a warm night increased his tendency to unconsciousness, but with a supreme effort he mastered himself and when the proximity of Piccadilly Circus revealed proof positive of London's teeming millions he began to take an interest in life again. He was within twenty minutes of death at that moment, but to him there appeared to be no such thing. Others might die or be dying. He had fortune in his grasp and happiness within beck.

In the Circus he stopped and watched the crowd again. It was one of his favourite hobbies, far more interesting to a thinker and philosopher, as he was wont to phrase it, and also as cheap as nothing. A pretty girl without paint attracted his attention. He recalled a girl like her he had been introduced to by Gleeson of St. John's. Poor Gleeson. A war casualty. Fine scholar. That reminded him. The international outlook was threatening and the stock markets might collapse if there was more war talk from Rome and Berlin.

Someone brushed against him and murmured an apology. Massy Cheldon looked across at the clock with the moving seconds-hand and saw that it was forty-one minutes past eleven.

"I'd better be moving," he said to himself, and advanced down the steps leading to Piccadilly's vast Underground station. He walked rapidly through a stone-paved corridor towards beacons of light and masses of moving humanity, observing no one in particular, and in the crowd no one took any notice of him, everyone intent on getting home as quickly as possible, hope and enjoyment apparently satiated for the time being.

When Massy Cheldon left the corridor behind him he came abreast of a telephone kiosk. At the same moment another man stepped into line with him and about half a minute later a woman's scream startled the crowd, but not Massy Cheldon, who lay huddled on the ground with a knife in his heart, amid the stillness of death that is not quiet.

At the very instant of the murder of Massy Cheldon the Piccadilly Underground was a microcosm of London. At the various descents to the trains, the ticket offices and machines, the illuminated shop windows and other temporary aids to the loafer and the prowler, there were groups of men and women, small and large groups, and scattered through the arena of light and movement were hundreds of persons, any one of whom might have been an actual spectator of the deed.

But the first signal that anything unusual had happened came from a portly dame awaiting her husband's return with the tickets. She happened to be glancing towards the entrance which Massy Cheldon had just used and he came into her line of vision. There was nothing about him to attract her and she was barely cognisant of his existence, disinclined to single him out from the other human automata until he swayed to the left and fell headlong to the ground. She was positive ever afterward that the scream came before and not after the stranger's collapse, but no one believed her.

"Oh!" she exclaimed involuntarily, and for the benefit of an unaccompanied girl of artificial prettiness added, "Drunk."

"Rather," said the girl, and began to walk towards the group which could do nothing except surround the body.

Then there came another scream, a woman uttered a wail and tottered away, someone pointed to a streak of blood and there was a rush to satisfy excruciating curiosity.

"The police. Is there a doctor here?" The voice was impersonal.

A doctor was not required, and there was, as it happened, none. But presently a policeman forced his way through, and after him another, and as the crowd grew into a mob and the mob into a nuisance more police came, a stretcher was produced, and all that was mortal of Massy Cheldon was carried away into decent privacy.

For nearly a quarter of an hour London seemed to have stopped still. For fifteen minutes homes were forgotten, petty troubles banished, cares and difficulties ignored. Scores of men and women died daily in London, but on this day of days one of them had died in the very midst of a crowd and the cause of his death was a dagger piercing his heart. Death had become something very real.

Chief Inspector Wake, hastily summoned from his home in Chelsea, listened without emotion to a bare recital of the facts by Police Constable Sibon, who had been first on the scene.

"We have identified him, sir," he concluded. "Name of Massy Cheldon and lived at Broadbridge Manor, near Lewes. From papers found on him, sir."

"He was stabbed to the heart at a moment when the Piccadilly Underground was crowded and no one saw the murder or the murderer?" Chief Inspector Wake's tone was merely one of inquisitiveness. There was no surprise or anger or resentment of alleged stupidity in it.

"That's how it looks, sir," said the constable. "Davidson, Houston and Cooper helped me to get names and addresses of men and women likely to be of use, but they all swore they had seen nothing."

"Of course, they didn't see anything," said Wake, quietly. "Did you ever know a London crowd that saw anything except a fallen horse or a Punch and Judy show? But it was clever, Sibon, damned clever. Somebody's discovered the art of getting away with a murder, and I didn't think anyone knew it except myself. But we can do nothing much now, Sibon. I'll see the inspector on duty." They were in the Chief Inspectors' room in Scotland Yard. "The divisional officer will do all the needful, but it's not going to be easy. A carefully and cleverly planned murder."

He repeated the opinion to Chief Inspector Hance, a tall, gloomy person with almost as poor an opinion of the unhanged as he had of the hanged.

"Hance, this is a teaser," he said, breathing heavily. "Fancy, knifing a man in a crowd of at least a thousand and with a score of persons within a few feet! That's courage if you like."

"Daring, not courage," Inspector Hance corrected in his slow manner. "Murderers have no courage—at least, I've not met one built that way. They're cowards, all of them."

"Well, we're up against a clever thinker this time, Hance," said Wake in his heaviest and yet quietest manner. "It'll be a pleasure to catch him."

"If you can," said his colleague with the outline of a smile somewhere in the region of his lower lip.

"Only a genius could have committed such a crime." Chief Inspector Wake was a skilled craftsman who recognised skill in others without confessing by jealousy that it was superior to his own. "Think of it, Hance, someone followed this fellow, Cheldon, until he got him in a crowd. Then he killed him, knowing that one thousand or two thousand witnesses can see nothing. I suppose they get in each other's way or something." He yawned. "I'm going home. Can't do anything until the morning. The murderer must help us to find him or we're beaten. Good night."

In Whitehall a plainclothes man came up to him.

"We've collected quite a bit of information about Mr. Massy Cheldon," he said, taking a small sheet of paper from his pocket. "He left Lewes at three ten this afternoon; called to see his sister-in-law at Galahad Mansions, Fulham, about six, and dined at the Berkeley with Colonel Crabb, a member of his club. I've seen the colonel and he told me about the visit to the sister-in-law. He said that Mr. Cheldon referred to it more than once."

"All very interesting, Davidson," was Chief Inspector Wake's comment, "but I've had a hard day on the Pimlico blackmail case and I can't work right round the clock. What's your opinion of the murder?"

The subordinate smiled his pleasure at the compliment.

"A vendetta, sir," he answered promptly. "You always find foreigners mixed up in a job where a knife is used. You've seen it, sir?"

"I have it in my pocket," said Chief Inspector Wake carelessly. "I am hoping it's going to prove of use. A vendetta." He smiled. "Somehow I can't picture a vendetta in the Piccadilly Underground. Too English, you know, Davidson, much too English. Good night."

Chapter Seven

Ever since Bobbie had so surprisingly consented to occupy a stool in a city office his mother had accustomed herself to rising at seven and preparing the breakfast she considered essential for the maintenance of her son's not too robust strength. On the morning of June 9th she followed her customary programme, and as Bobbie had been rather late the previous night she decided not to rouse him until the last moment. She was thus enabled to give the sitting-room a semblance of cleanliness and tidiness which reached heights to which Florence never attempted to rise, and also to rearrange the furniture before she opened the front door and captured the morning portion of milk and the two daily newspapers, Daily Mail and Daily Express, which ministered to their respective spheres of thought. It happened that the Daily Mail first attracted her attention by its front page advertisements of intimate garments, but as she placed the milk bottle on the kitchen table the Daily Express came under review and she read with filmlike breathlessness because she could not help it,

MURDER IN PICCADILLY.
UNDERGROUND TRAGEDY.
WELL KNOWN LONDON CLUBMAN'S TRAGIC DEATH.

Three times at least she read, and was beginning to ask herself if this was not another "stunt" when she caught sight of the most familiar of all names to her, Cheldon. Instantaneously her heart became as stone, her fingers convulsively clutched the paper and her eyes assumed rigidity. A sort of frozen dread enveloped her, a dread of a horrible surprise, and yet at the first glimpse of the name she had persuaded herself that it could be only her brother-in-law.

"Massy. Stabbed to the heart." She uttered a moan that embodied misery and horror. "Oh, my God!"

The paper slipped from her fingers and she found herself staring in the direction of Bobbie's room.

The murder had been committed at forty-five minutes past eleven and Bobbie had not returned home until half-past twelve. She remembered that, for she had heard him enter and close his bedroom door, and a glance at her luminous clock had told her the time.

Rigidity left her as her terror increased.

"Bobbie," she screamed, "Bobbie."

She covered her mouth with her right hand, frightened by the sound of her hysterical voice.

"What is it?" Bobbie in trousers and pyjama coat was standing in the doorway of his room. "What's the matter, mother?" He was irritable as though she had disturbed his sleep.

"Your uncle. Oh, Bobbie." She burst into tears.

He sprang the distance between them and picked up the paper.

"My God!" she heard him gasp. "Uncle Massy—murdered. I can't believe it." He looked from the paper to his mother. "But you were to have lunched with him today! What can it mean?" He paused to try and answer his own question, and the silent answer came pat, "The Cheldon estate for you. You are rich now and Nancy is yours." But it only added to his confusion.

"What's that?" Ruby Cheldon ran into the the little hall and listened. Footfalls could be heard, many of them, but they all stopped when they reached the landing.

"Perhaps it's the newspapers," Bobbie whispered. "Come back."

They closed the door and listened as though they were in midnight darkness and a ghost might be expected at any moment.

Knocks, rings, murmuring voices, more knocks and rings. Half an hour of breathless expectancy passed slowly.

"You'll be late for the office," Ruby whispered, and only the seriousness of the situation prevented him laughing at her inanity.

"I'll not have to go to the office again," he said, speaking out of the reverie into which he had fallen.

"I think they've gone," she said in a husky voice, not having heard him. They had not moved for ten minutes, and limbs and necks were stiff.

He stole on tiptoe to the door and listened.

"Poor uncle," she heard him murmur, and for some reason it brought her immense comfort. "Poor old Uncle Massy! He didn't deserve this."

"You'd better have breakfast," she said, anxious to create a diversion. "I must do something—we must both do something. It's horrible having to think about it at all. I'll go mad." She pressed her forehead. "I'm sorry, Bobbie, but the shock."

Before he could speak words of comfort the bell went noisily and they looked at each other.

"Might be a friend," said Bobbie nervously. "I—I think I'll answer it. In any case we can't remain prisoners here for ever."

A stout, middle-aged man with an umbrella, and a dark blue suit that seemed lonely without an overcoat with a velvet collar, met his gaze of inquiry with a look of bland neutrality.

"Are you Mr. Robert Cheldon?" he asked politely.

"Yes. Who are you?" Bobbie wished he had nodded and not spoken as soon as he understood the note in his voice.

"I am Chief Inspector Wake of Scotland Yard and I've called to ask you if you'd be so kind as to tell me something about your uncle. Of course, you've read the morning papers and——?"

"Come in," said Bobbie, suspecting that the invitation was unnecessary and that his visitor was quite equal to forcing his way in. "I'll just slip on a coat and join you in a moment."

As he passed the kitchen he breathed to his mother, "Scotland Yard man. Don't worry. I'll tackle him."

To his annoyance his mother was speaking to their caller when he returned, speaking words of sympathy to which the inspector nodded with apparent understanding and appreciation.

"We'll get the murderer, madam," he was assuring Ruby when Bobbie, white and shaky, took the chair opposite his mother. "But not without the help of Mr. Cheldon's relations."

"Any clues?" said Bobbie, wondering why it was necessary for him to pretend to be interested when as a matter of fact he was only frightened.

"None except the dagger." Chief Inspector Wake looked over Bobbie's head at an enlarged photograph of Colonel Cheldon, and throughout the interview hardly ever lowered his gaze.

"I don't think we can help," said Ruby, nervously, her fine features almost disfigured by their dead white pallor. "My son and I have always lived very quietly and——"

"Mr. Cheldon called here at soon after six yesterday. Did he say anything or hint at anything likely to indicate an attack on his life?" The suddenness of a question which was also a disclosure was the first shot in the campaign and the middle-aged woman and the young man both experienced an involuntary terror which reduced their bones to sawdust.

"I had never seen him so happy," said Ruby, after a pause. "Once he remarked that he was feeling on top of the world. On top of the world. That was his exact expression."

Chief Inspector Wake smiled blandly.

"Mrs. Cheldon," he said, in a paternal voice, "I've nearly forgotten that I'm a policeman on duty. But there's no danger to you, madam, none at all. Yet they'll rap me over the fingers at the Yard if I don't warn you that—"

"Warn me?" she cried, shrivelling up.

"What do you mean?" Bobbie's effort at thunder resulted in a squeak.

"I'm sorry. It's only a formality. Of course, you will help. There's no need to warn you or to talk of taking down what you say. Naturally you're even more anxious than I am to know why Mr. Massy Cheldon should be on top of the world at six and murdered at a quarter to twelve. You're determined, as I am, to bring the murderer to justice. Mrs. Cheldon, and you, Mr. Cheldon, you are willing to help me?"

They had no option—that was what Bobbie thought—as his mother eagerly embraced the offer of an unofficial partnership.

"We will do all we can to help you, inspector," said Bobbie with a gravity that lost its dignity mainly because of the twitching of his cheeks.

"Thank you very much, Mr. Cheldon," said Chief Inspector Wake in a voice husky for moisture. "When I was given charge of the case I knew at once that I would fail unless the family helped, especially the head of the family now that Mr. Massy Cheldon is dead."

"The head?" Bobbie gasped, and trembled for no reason.

"You succeed to the family property, don't you?" Chief Inspector Wake lifted his chin a little higher and appeared to be absorbed again in the photograph of the late Colonel Cheldon.

"How did you know that?" The voice was weak and querulous, but there was fright in it, too.

"If it's true what does it matter, Mr. Cheldon?" was the polite rejoinder. "You see," he lapsed into the confidential, "you see, Mr. Cheldon, when I had all the known facts about the Piccadilly murder, as they're calling it already in the newspapers, I remarked to the superintendent 'In my opinion, sir, if it's not the man who benefits most by the murder of this wealthy squire and clubman we must rope him in to help us, and if he does we'll not add this to our so-called failures.' That's what I said to him, Mr. Cheldon, and as you'll have no trouble in proving where you were last night it stands to reason that you'll be only too anxious to do all you can for us."

The speech was long enough to restore Bobbie's confidence by giving him time to think, but could he have guessed that that was the inspector's only object in indulging in loquacity he might have failed to recover his grip on his tongue and heart.

"You can rely on my co-operation, inspector," he said after the manner of the new squire of Broadbridge and narrowly missing "my man."

Ruby Cheldon stared at her son and instantly thought of her own complexion. She had never seen Bobbie so white, so yellow about the eyes. But was it yellow? The silly question persisted until a repetition of the earlier attack on the flat was presaged by the sound of footfalls.

"It's all right," said Chief Inspector Wake, remaining seated as both of them jumped up. "Don't worry. They'll not disturb us. I have two of my men on guard."

"Two men on guard?" Ruby's repetition of what she considered a sinister phrase reached its apex in a weak scream.

"It's only to help us, mother," said Bobbie, but there was no comfort in a voice that shook. "Do sit down and let's talk quietly. You know we must help to avenge Uncle Massy's cowardly murder."

"You ought to be proud of your son, madam," said the man from Scotland Yard. "I am sure you can trust him to protect you."

As there was no obvious answer to this remark they listened for a couple of minutes and two of them found no comfort in the silence that to Bobbie at any rate had the quality of prison solitude in it.

"Now, Mrs. Cheldon," said Chief Inspector Wake, turning to her and thereby arousing fresh suspicions in Bobbie's elastic, fluid and fluent mind, "if you do not object I will begin business. Please remember that in investigating a case of this kind a man in my official position has to do a lot of things that seem unnecessary and even stupid, but I have a method—a famous detective taught it to me—of first getting rid of everybody from the case who could be suspected of a connection with it and then concentrating on those who are left. When I am lucky I have only one person left and he says good-bye to me at the Old Bailey."

Bobbie shuddered again.

"And how do you get rid of them?" Ruby was clutching her handkerchief now.

"By patient and, whenever possible, friendly investigation," he answered, showing no interest in her emotion. "It is, as I think I have mentioned, routine and nothing more. We all have our own methods, and, of course, I have mine." Although he never moved he seemed to wheel round on Bobbie as he put the question, "Where were you at a quarter to twelve last night?" He breathed heavily as if the effort had cost him something.

"On my way home," said Bobbie, with an emphasis that angered him because it was born of his dreadful fancies.

Chief Inspector Wake smiled.

"You didn't murder your uncle. Gentlemen like you don't use stilettos anyway. But I must account for your movements."

"It was about midnight when I reached home," and Ruby nearly screamed again. "I was later than usual. Don't often dine out these days when I have to be early at the office."

"Dine alone?" The manner of the question was cheerful.

"No." Bobbie laughed sketchily. "It would have been a bit of bad luck if I'd had to pay the bill. Funds are low."

"You have succeeded to a fortune, I'm told."

Again Ruby squirmed. The inspector's utter lack of hostility, his unruffled suavity and his very unimportance all conjured up in her mind the picture of a Machiavelli such as only the craftiest and most cunning brains of Scotland Yard could have created. She saw a trap in every sentence and a threat in every movement.

"Your friend, eh? No objection to mentioning his name, I suppose?"

"Of course not. He was Mr. Ruslin." Bobbie was on firm ground now, but the next remark of the detective's had the effect of an earthquake.

"You don't mean Nosey Ruslin, by any chance?"

Bobbie half rose and sank back again, tried to laugh and failed even to grin, and finally bleated something that sounded like an invitation to drink.

"So you know Nosey Ruslin, do you?" Chief Inspector Wake gazed up at the ceiling.

"Well, know him is hardly correct. I met him first only a short time ago." While Bobbie was telling himself he was an ass to be apologising when no apology was needed or might even be dangerous, his mother was on the brink of collapse.

She read more into the conversation than either of the two men, but then she alone knew, or thought she knew, the significance of Bobbie's lie, and fearful that other lies were on the way she was palpitating with terror.

"An interesting chap, Nosey Ruslin," the inspector said musingly. "I remember him when he was tipped for the heavy-weight championship. Drink finished him then and he gave it up. Never been drunk since." He laughed shortly. "London's full of funny people, and Nosey is one of the funniest." He laughed again, but not the sort of laugh one is invited to share.

Ruby was trying to find the exact meaning of the word "funny" according to the lexicon of Scotland Yard detectives when another question frightened her back to realities.

"Where did you and Nosey dine?"

"The Greville in Gerrard Street," said Bobbie.

"And he paid the bill? That's curious. My information was that Nosey's been hard up for months. Quite recently his telephone was cut off because he couldn't pay a small amount he owed."

"While I've known Mr. Ruslin he's always been in funds," said Bobbie innocently. "He's a generous man." The tribute was delivered in an angry voice. "A rough diamond, and unconventional, but straight."

Chief Inspector Wake was lost in thought for nearly a minute.

"When did you leave the restaurant?"

"About half-past ten."

For the first time the inspector made a note. It was only on the back of an envelope, but to Ruby it had all the suggestiveness of a warrant.

"You parted shortly afterwards, I suppose?"

"Yes."

"Did it take you over an hour to reach home?"

"It was a lovely night and I walked." Bobbie's nervous restlessness was evident from the sharpness of his tone.

Ruby would have sacrificed the Cheldon inheritance for the courage to bring the terrifying questions and equally terrifying answers to an end, but she felt that to intervene would be to create the impression that she was trying to protect Bobbie from danger. And what danger could he be in if he were innocent?

"Do you know much about Nosey Ruslin, Mr. Cheldon?"

"Very little except that he's one of the best."

"That does credit to your loyalty, Mr. Cheldon," said the detective, drily. "If I pretended to be smart I might ask you one of the best what? I've dealt with some of the best rogues in London, speaking of course, from the point of view of skill. But Nosey interests me. Somehow I never thought he would get into fashionable circles."

"This is hardly fashionable," said Bobbie, trying to be grim but too much under the influence of a compliment that was balm to his pride to succeed.

"The death of your uncle has made you a rich man," the detective reminded him. Then he smiled. "Forgive me, Mr. Cheldon, but I'm apt to forget that the world is not peopled with detectives and criminals. I asked you to help me and—"

"I'm afraid we've been unable to do anything," said Ruby, forcing herself to speak for fear Bobbie's silence might be misinterpreted.

"On the contrary, madam, you've helped me a lot, and I must thank you for your courtesy and patience." How they would have laughed at the Yard had they heard him! "It must be extremely annoying to you to be associated in any way with a brutal murder, but you understand I have my duty to do, and often it's an unpleasant duty."

"I understand." Ruby's heart warmed to him. "The shock of my brother-in-law's death has numbed me. I was to have lunched with him today." Tears came into her eyes.

"Is there anyone you suspect?" asked Bobbie, relieved that a general discussion had replaced the question and answer ordeal.

"It's too soon to know anything about it except that Mr. Cheldon was murdered." Chief Inspector Wake stood up and, as Bobbie subsequently observed sarcastically, examined the room in the style of a broker's man estimating the auction value of its contents. "Have you any ideas about it, Mrs. Cheldon?" The suddenness of the question as much as its nature startled Ruby into a pallor that was instantly succeeded by a dull flush.

"I—er—no." She thought a slight smile might help, but was sure she had merely twisted her mouth. "My brother-in-law couldn't have had an enemy. He was reserved and self-opinionated, but not quarrelsome."

"Most of us are built that way," the detective commented.

"He was a rich man who lived mostly in the country." She stopped and searched her mind for something else to say, and was amazed that when it came to the point she knew so little, so very little, about her late husband's brother.

"I suppose you often saw him?"

"Yes, I think so." Her expression was thoughtful.

"Was he generous—free with his money?"

"Why do you wish to know?" asked Bobbie.

The heavy frame moved slowly round on two obvious feet.

"Why shouldn't I?" Chief Inspector Wake smiled. He could smile better than either of them, and Ruby, a quick thinker, decided at once that it was because he was the only person in that room who had nothing to fear. Her heart became heavier.

"Oh, well, if you want to know he wasn't exactly a spendthrift," said Bobbie, and the detective, quick to notice trivialities which promised to grow in importance, commented inwardly on the complete detachment with which he criticised a near relation murdered the night before. There had even been a streak of humour in the tone.

"But that wouldn't create enemies," he said, carelessly. "He was a man of honour, of high principles?"

Bobbie thought the detective was paying a tribute to the century old eminence of the Cheldons, but his mother knew it was a question, and resented its implications.

"My brother-in-law never failed to meet his obligations," she said with something of the pride with which the Cheldons had infected her. "I've heard him say more than once that he hated owing a penny to anyone. It's quite true that he was not lavishly generous, but he was a bachelor and apt to think a little too much of himself."

It was a blow in favour of matrimony, and Chief Inspector Wake, who had a wife who regarded all bachelors as blacklegs, nodded agreement.

"That's a help anyhow, Mrs. Cheldon," he said gratefully. "You are surprised, but if Mr. Cheldon wasn't murdered for revenge it's obvious his murderer expects to benefit by his death."

Ruby's heart sank. She wished she could have flared up and demanded with all the heat she could generate at a moment's notice if Chief Inspector Wake meant to infer that her son...Her son....

She went to the window and looked down into the street. Some flies on the panes attracted her eyes, but her thoughts were confined to the room.

"There's always a motive for murder unless the murderer is a lunatic," said the detective in his quiet, rather wheezy voice. "At first sight it seemed to me that this might be one of those rare instances of a lunatic running amok with a dagger of Italian origin," he was watching Bobbie, but the face before him was a blank. "Though if you think it over as I did for hours this morning you'll see that such a theory is impossible. The murder was most carefully planned."

"Carefully planned?" Bobbie repeated in a sceptical tone.

Chief Inspector Wake smiled vaguely.

"You're thinking of the scene—one of the most crowded Underground stations in London. A mere amateur would never have thought of killing anyone there. Too many witnesses, he would decide. But a professional would know that a crowd can be a safeguard, that a crowd never has eyes."

Bobbie, suddenly confronted by a vision of his uncle lying dead amid the glare of lights and the blare of noise, felt sick.

"I'd better dress," he mumbled. "I expect you'll want to get back to the Yard, inspector?"

Ruby admired his courage in walking to the door and opening it.

"Yes, I must be going," said the detective calmly, "but it'll be a few hours before I return to the Yard. Thank you, sir, and you, too, madam. I know I can rely on your help."

"We'll do anything to hang the murderer," said Bobbie, and meant it.

When he had gone Ruby burst into tears which had been waiting to be shed since she had read of her brother-in-law's death. Bobbie, distressed and ill at ease with his conscience, watched her helplessly.

"What will happen now?" he heard her murmur between sobs. "Poor Massy! With all his faults he was a good friend to us."

He ventured to lay a hand on her shoulder. Something told him that he ought to take her in his arms, but he was afraid of her, afraid of the only person capable of looking below the surface of his mind and discovering its unpleasant secrets.

"It's all right, mother," he whispered, and the banality irritated him.

He knew that even if the best happened they were to pass through the scorching ordeal of blood-red publicity. Chief Inspector Wake had protected them that morning, but they would be at the mercy of newspapers and anonymous letter-writers, gossip-mongers, slanderers, and their own capacity to breed fresh fears with every passing moment. London had not had such a sensational murder for years. It was true that Soho had had some mysteries, but the victims had been women of the underworld who had lived dangerously and had died as mysteriously as they had existed. But Massy Cheldon was the head of a county family, a rich man, known in many clubs; precise and pompous, a hundred per cent snob with a passion for gentility in himself and in his society. That the place of his death should have been Piccadilly's Underground station made the tragedy as bizarre as it was dramatic and challenging.

"I hope they arrest the murderer," said Ruby, wiping her eyes.

"Of course, they will," said Bobbie hurriedly. "Chief Inspector Wake never fails. Don't you remember how the papers talked about that murder on the beach at Brighton and how just when they were saying nasty things about Scotland Yard Wake came along with the murderer and secured his conviction?" He paused and then went to his bedroom. "Mother," he called out, "when do you think I ought to see Mr. Parker?"

The reference to the senior partner in the firm of Parker, Mellish & Parker, the solicitors acting for the Cheldon estate trustees, had the effect on Ruby of a cold douche.

"I—I don't know," she answered. She had fallen into a voiceless discussion of Bobbie's lie about the time of his return home overnight and she could not persuade herself that out of all the welter of blood and terror and danger there could be Broadbridge Manor and its extensive income for her son. Her imagination was not powerful enough to transform in the course of an hour or two Galahad Mansions into the old Sussex mansion which was the outward and too often the only visible sign of the Cheldon gentility. She wished she could question Bobbie about last night's doings and elicit from him a minute to minute account of his actions that would relieve her mind. But the lie was responsible for a terror that subdued her anxiety to banish it.

She never stirred until Bobbie returned shaved and dressed. She shivered a little at the dark suit and the black tie. In mourning already!

"This friend of yours," she began, weakly, "the man with the curious name. Nosey something." She did not even smile.

"Oh, Mr. Ruslin's all right," said Bobbie. Now that he was fully clothed he was confident and authoritative. After all, he was the head of the family, and to be head of the Cheldons was something in a democratic age when the parvenu was too much with us.

"You don't think—"

"My dear mother," he said, pityingly, "you mustn't allow this affair to get on your nerves. It's horrible to think that Uncle Massy has been murdered, but it's not our fault. I can't say I was fond of him and he did me no good by turning me into a city clerk. Thank—" he stopped in time, for thanking the Deity at that moment for having rescued him from slavery by means of a timely murder would have been incongruous, if not bad taste, and the Cheldons prided themselves on their good taste. He had to bear that in mind now that he was head of the family.

"It's the lottery of life," he resumed, determined to control his natural satisfaction at his own good fortune. He was genuinely sorry for his uncle, but £10,000 a year and Broadbridge Manor!

"Why is it that the Inspector was so interested in your friend Ruslin? Do you think he suspects him?"

Bobbie laughed ironically.

"Really, mother, you'll be saying next he suspects me!" he protested.

"He'll suspect everybody—it's his business to—and it's easy to suspect with or without a reason. But Mr. Ruslin—"

"My dear mother, if necessary I could prove that Ruslin couldn't have done it. I was with him until nearly twelve. I mean to say, it must have been until after the murder."

"Then it wasn't true you parted at the restaurant?" The scared eyes had blood-red rims to them.

"I wasn't thinking when I said that," he answered, struggling to assume the indifference of perfect innocence.

"But supposing the inspector discovers that?"

The master of Broadbridge Manor smiled tolerantly.

"Get it into your head, mother, and keep it there, that if I didn't murder uncle Mr. Ruslin didn't."

"It's all so horrible," she covered her face again. "Poor Massy!" The tears flowed again.

"You must be more courageous, mother," said Bobbie fussily. It was a Cheldon trait. "Our position." He stopped short and listened. "I thought I heard the bell," he murmured, and went to the front door.

It required all his power of self-control not to utter an exclamation of terror when he saw Chief Inspector Wake, heavy, expressionless, sinister.

"Sorry to trouble you, Mr. Cheldon," he said with a carelessness which did not suit him, "but I have an idea I left my umbrella behind."

"I—I don't think you did," said Bobbie nervously, holding on to the handle of the door and uncertain whether to invite him in or not. What would a perfectly innocent person do in the circumstances? He asked himself the question and at once was angry. "Come in, Mr. Wake, come in." It was an effort to appear consistent with the new dignity conferred by the tragic death of the tenant for life of the Cheldon estate.

The heavy footfalls pounded into Ruby's brain, and her half-laughter, half-exclamation produced a mixture dangerously akin to hysteria.

"I thought so. Here it is. Sorry to trouble you, Mrs. Cheldon. Good morning." He passed out to the accompaniment of his own voice, though it was not his usual one. Bobbie discovered that for himself as he clutched the handle of the hall door again.

"Oh, by the way, Mr. Cheldon, what did your uncle think of your friend, Nosey Ruslin?"

"He never met him or saw him in his life," Bobbie answered, unable to resist a smile at the bare idea of the ex-pugilist hobnobbing with Uncle Massy, prince of snobs.

"You are sure of that?"

Bobbie smiled.

"You can take it from me that they didn't know each other and couldn't have. Mr. Ruslin never wished to meet him, and my uncle would have had a fit had I suggested it."

"Thank you, Mr. Cheldon," said Chief Inspector Wake, following his umbrella to the stairs. "Thank you. Good morning. A most useful item of information." Bobbie caught the last words and stood rigid, puzzled.

Chapter Eight

Chief Inspector Wake passed unnoticed through the crowds forming irregular queues at the numerous entrances to the Piccadilly Underground and in a general way scrutinised with his large and lazy eyes the latest exhibition of London's fascination for the tragic and horrible. The papers had already recorded that the scene of Massy Cheldon's death had become a resort of pilgrims and that in an effort to discourage the morbid, a cordon of police directed with suggestive curtness the lingering travellers who came to pay a visit to the scene and who qualified for admission to the catacomb by purchasing a penny ticket to anywhere, meaning nowhere.

Yet it was all understandable and pardonable. To the majority of the city's millions murder was something that did not exist outside a novel or a newspaper, and when it was actually brought to their doorsteps they were aroused to a pitch of excitement and curiosity that affected the nervous system and clamoured for satiation. It was the crime of the year, something peculiar to London itself, something that seemed to strike at London's very heart. None of your Hammersmith or Whitechapel now. This was London, real London, Piccadilly. And to the hysteria of horror was added the wonder of its daring.

The newspapers concentrated on it and left no rumour untested and no surmise unexploited. Pictures of Massy Cheldon and his mansion in the country appeared everywhere. Mortals think in terms of money, and in the case of Massy Cheldon mental arithmetic centred on the fact that the assassin's knife had deprived a country squire of an income estimated at not less than ten thousand a year.

"Soho Underworld Combed." "Scotland Yard looking for an Italian." "Latest developments." "The Underground Murder Must be solved." "Another Murder Mystery." Chief Inspector Wake read them without comment. His colleagues were fond of dismissing the press with the remark that "them damned papers meant next to nothing," but he was of the opinion that that "next to nothing" might mean all the difference between success and failure if tacked on to their own discoveries and special knowledge.

At the moment he was of all men in the case the least perturbed and hurried so far as externals went. But then he never moved and never thought rapidly. In his early days in the force he had nearly ruined his career by thinking quickly, having been foolish enough to allow himself to imitate the infallibility of the detective of fiction. Wise and dapper Superintendent Melville had taught him then a needed lesson by pointing out that in a real life mystery the key had to be made to fit the lock, whereas in fiction it was the key that was first manufactured. Now he thought over every line of inquiry and every word and deduction arising out of it. He took his time because he had at his command fifty, a hundred, a thousand men if necessary, to hurry and scurry. Londoners might crowd the Piccadilly Underground and the newspapers give the impression that the rest of the world had been swallowed up in an earthquake together with all its problems and dictators and peace conferences; Chief Inspector Wake knew that one man had stabbed Massy

Cheldon to the heart and that if he could only find the man or the motive his own work would be well and truly done and he would have earned his wages.

So he passed the crowds and wandered into Shaftesbury Avenue, apparently unconscious of his fellow pedestrians and yet carefully noting any of them inclining to the generous proportions of Nosey Ruslin. It was half-past twelve and he was confident that before half-past one he would meet Nosey in Shaftesbury Avenue or in one of its side streets. The ex-pugilist was a man with no regular work and therefore having nothing to do had by force of habit fashioned for himself a routine as regular as that of a bank clerk. He was not aware of it, and doubtless believed that he had none of those habits which mark the more conventional portion of the population.

"Hello, Nosey!"

"Why, it's the inspector!" exclaimed Nosey, stretching out a hand. "It's a pleasure to see you on this lovely morning."

The detective tapped him familiarly on the chest.

"It's all very well *you* talking like that," he remarked, and his brow was furrowed. "*You* haven't got to solve a mystery without a clue. *You* have no reason to worry, and I have."

"A weird affair, inspector." Nosey had picked up the phrase from Bobbie Cheldon. He was a collector of phrases, chiefly worthless ones, but not having even a bowing acquaintance with an English dictionary he was easily impressed and surprised by what others regarded as commonplace language.

"I wish I could meet someone who knew Mr. Cheldon," the inspector said, and offered his cigarette case. Nosey languidly made his choice and lighted up. "I've been to see Mr. Robert Cheldon, but he knows nothing."

"You bet he doesn't." Nosey sniffed. "The old man wasn't half good enough for his nephew. Mr. Robert Cheldon is a gentleman."

"That's my impression, too, Nosey. He did what he could and told me everything. He seems to be fond of you."

The ex-pugilist had a passing vision of a weekend, complete with valet, at Broadbridge Manor, and threw out his chest.

"I've given him good advice, inspector, and the boy's been grateful. I wish now though he'd introduced me to his uncle. I know the world and I might have heard something which would give you a line on the present little bit of business." He shook his cigarette. "But what a nerve the fellow had! Piccadilly Underground, of all places, and just when it was most crowded, of all times!"

Chief Inspector Wake tapped him on the arm.

"You know the West End better than anyone at the Yard," he said, with flattery aforethought. "That's why I came along here hoping to run into you. Now, Nosey, where can we go and have a chat without exciting suspicion. The Monico and the Trocadero are no use—I'm too well known in both places."

"Come back to my flat. Only a minute in the bus."

"Let's walk," said the detective cordially. "We can't talk in the bus."

They walked side by side, and every other pedestrian glanced at the abbreviated nasal appendage of the stouter man, and those who were pure Cockney grinned unashamedly. The others grinned after they had passed.

"Have you any idea why anyone should have murdered Massy Cheldon?" the inspector asked.

"If I hadn't seen so much of Mr. Robert Cheldon," Nosey answered, lulled into a state of equal candour and ingenuousness, "I'd have said, look for the chap who's making money out of it and introduce him to the darbies. But the nephew didn't do it."

"I know that."

Nosey glanced sideways at him.

"Why are you so sure?"

The inspector looked straight ahead.

"Because he spent last night with you, and if he did it you'd have been in with him." He assumed a more jocular tone, but his audience of one was not deceived. "Murder is not in your line, Nosey, and don't I know it! Why, if I found you stooping over the body with the dripping knife I'd suspect you were doing it for a film."

Nosey Ruslin floundered as he tried to interpret his companion's pleasantry in accordance with his wishes.

"Here we are," he said, relieved to have an excuse for a temporary diversion. "I think there's some whisky in the decanter."

Chief Inspector Wake settled down in the armchair as if with the intention of remaining to lunch and the meal after that.

"No, I won't drink," he said, cheerfully. "Too early. By the way, you and Mr. Robert Cheldon left the Greville about half-past ten, wasn't it?"

"I should have thought later," said Nosey, balancing his body on a chair.

"I was told half-past ten, but it doesn't matter."

"Why should it?" Nosey was a trifle testy. "The chap whose time-table you should compile is the murderer of Massy Cheldon."

"At the moment it's Robert Cheldon's time-table I'm interested in, and you come into it only because you can help to fix the time. I don't suspect Robert Cheldon. You've only got to look at him and talk to him to see he wouldn't kill a rabbit."

"That's what I said about him the other day, and Nancy didn't half like it, and threatened me with a thick ear."

"Who is Nancy?"

"Girl young Cheldon's keen on. Dances at the 'Frozen Fang' and other night clubs. You must have seen her. Looks like a doll but is a bit fresher than those you see in a shop window." Nosey gazed in astonishment at his companion's blank expression and could not resist the temptation to enlighten him further. "Nancy's partner is Billy Bright."

"Oh, of course, I remember now. When Clarke took Bright to Vine Street in connection with the Savile Hotel jewel robbery he proved an alibi through producing this girl, Nancy. If it had been my case I'd have remembered her right enough. But one sees lots of new dancers at the 'Frozen Fang.' They don't keep them long there."

"Nancy's lasted longer than any of them," said Nosey.

"And young Cheldon is in love with her?"

"Crazy. Cottoned on to me as soon as he heard I was one of her pals. Won't rest until he's made her Mrs. Robert Cheldon of Broadbridge Manor. And a manor it is too, inspector. Did you see the picture of it in the *News Chronicle*? Nancy will scream with delight at the prospect of having that little hut to rehearse in."

"Will he marry her now?"

"Will a copper accept a drink?" Nosey emitted one of his favourite whistles to indicate the limit of amazement at the stupidity of the question. "He's madly in love with her and no mistake."

"When you were dining at Greville's last night did he talk about her?"

"From the fish to the chips and all the rest of the time," was the humorous answer delivered with something of the sharpness of a retort. "It was Nancy with every course. I'm a good-natured chap and I hate rows, inspector, but there were moments when I felt as though I wanted to land him one on his kisser. I couldn't do it—simply couldn't. Young and in love. We were both once, inspector." There was a tenderness in the husky voice.

"He worried about her, of course." The detective was not asking a question now. "They all do. The girl wouldn't care to give up her dancing and her friends to be the wife of a poor man. I've known many cases."

Nosey Ruslin, the astutest professional crook in all London, fell headlong into the pit which had been specially dug for him.

"Nancy isn't a fool," he said, almost roughly. "And she wasn't going to be no servant to any man with five quid a week even if she wasn't called a slavey and could hang her marriage lines over the sink."

Chief Inspector Wake could not at the moment add that to the scribbled records of the Piccadilly murder, but he carefully memorised it.

"I don't blame her," he said warmly. "A pretty girl with her talent."

Nosey beamed on him.

"Naturally. But then, inspector, you're the only man at the Yard who knows men and women and their troubles. You're not a machine. Would you let a daughter of yours marry a chap with uncertain prospects for twenty or thirty years? I know you wouldn't. How could you tell that the rich uncle was going to be poleaxed just when you wanted his money?"

"That's plain commonsense," said the detective placidly. The interview had been amazingly fruitful so far, and he had not expected much more than the opportunity of a close study of Nosey Ruslin at home. "One man's misfortune is another's fortune. Massy Cheldon is murdered at a quarter to twelve at night, and his nephew, Robert, a city clerk, wakes up to find himself rich and in a position to marry the girl he loves."

For some inscrutable reason Nosey smiled to himself.

"So you see, Nosey," continued Wake, almost carelessly, "why I have to compile the Robert Cheldon time-table for the night of June the eighth. He didn't murder his uncle, and you and I know it—*you* particularly."

His host quivered with sudden apprehension.

"Why are you so sure about that?" he demanded, but the demand lost its force because it was delivered in an involuntary whisper.

Chief Inspector Wake smiled gently.

"Because you were with him last night," he said. "You seem to have forgotten that. You're his alibi and—"

"He's mine." There was the weakness of fear in the usually well controlled voice of the ex-pugilist.

"You took the words out of my mouth, Nosey. Naturally, he's your alibi if you wanted one. But if it's of any use to you I'll be prepared to guarantee that you did not stab Massy Cheldon."

Again, in spite of the words, fear haunted Nosey to his extreme discomfort.

"I might ask why that should be necessary," he remarked shakily.

"Everybody who is in any way connected by blood or acquaintance with the murdered man may be suspected. It's a habit of ours which is often of the greatest help."

"And you're sure I didn't do it? Why?" He raised himself on to his feet and stared down at his visitor.

"Because, Nosey, with all your faults you're an English-man and Englishmen don't use Italian poignards or daggers. If you'd any reason for ordering Massy Cheldon's coffin you'd help him into the next world with a revolver. It's un-English, isn't it, this murder? and yet it's brought a large fortune to a young man in love with one of Soho's loveliest dancers. That's the point where the real mystery comes in."

"It's all mystery to me," said Nosey, not anxious to discuss Nancy and her lover. "Still, if I were you I'd not be so sure about the foreigner doing it. It's easy to learn to use a dagger."

"Only a master could have used it in the way it was used last night," said Wake confidently. "Come, Nosey, give me the benefit of your knowledge and experience. Do you know anyone—not a friend, of course, for you don't mix with foreigners much—but do you know or have you heard of anyone likely to commit murder with a dagger?"

Nosey tried his hardest not to think before shaking his head.

"That must be the third or fourth lie he's told me," said Chief Inspector Wake to himself. Aloud he remarked, "I'm sorry." Then he decided to give him a clue. "What about that little thin chap who used to be a smasher and got into trouble over the Hoxton fire-raising case?"

"Oh, you mean Carlo Vazetti—Lucky Car we used to call him. Why, he went back to Italy six months ago."

"No one else?"

Again Nosey shook his head.

"Now if you wanted some real out and out Londoners, tough guys from birth and ready to do a job for half a quid, I could give you a list."

"That must be the fifth or sixth lie," the Inspector mentally recorded. "No, thanks," he said politely. "We have the best list at the Yard already." He stood up and casually inventoried the contents of the mantelpiece and a table near the window. "I'll be going, Nosey, but you might bear in mind what I've said and give me a ring if anything happens that you think might be of use to me. I shall be grateful for anything."

"You can rely on me." Nosey laughed outright. "Pity for the sake of your reputation that young Cheldon didn't do it. That would have given you an easy score." He laughed again.

"My only regret is that he doesn't seem to know who did it, and that really puzzles me, Nosey, if you want to know. Here's a murder which apparently benefits only one person, and that person not the murderer. Was it the work of a lunatic anxious to let the hangman spare him the trouble of committing suicide? In that case he wouldn't have run away. Was it the result of a cleverly planned crime on the part of a syndicate acting in concert with the heir to the estates? That's too far-fetched for serious consideration. Yet we must assume that there is a link between the murderer and the money."

Nosey Ruslin almost betrayed himself with a snort.

"You'll be wasting your time and making trouble for yourself, inspector," he said, trying to speak as a friend, "if you worry young Cheldon. He's absolutely innocent—you've just admitted it."

"I'll admit it again. But, Nosey, the man who murdered Massy Cheldon did it to help Robert Cheldon to inherit the property. I'll swear to that, and one day I'll be able to prove it. I talk freely to you because you're no fool and you can look at the problem fairly and without bias."

"But why should anyone kill at random, if that's the word I want."

"It isn't, but never mind." Chief Inspector Wake smiled. "As I see it the murderer will wait until the storm's blown over— supposing we don't get him— and then he'll approach young Cheldon hoping to receive payment for services rendered."

Nosey Ruslin's blood chilled.

"But that's practically saying that young Cheldon had a hand in it," he protested.

"You can put what construction you wish on my words," said the detective with lazy tolerance, "but that's my view and I'll stick to it." He picked up his umbrella and his bowler hat. "Nosey, the inquest opens tomorrow and we'll ask for an adjournment for eight days. Now you're a betting man. What odds will you give me that when the inquest is resumed I'll have the murderer under lock and key?"

The ex-pugilist turned on him the full broadside of an expansive smile.

"A thousand to one—a million to one," he said, and bulged visibly with laughter.

"Give me five to one in pounds?" The inspector was serious.

"That's a bet," said Nosey, suddenly serious too.

"I'll stand you the best dinner Greville's can do when I win," said the detective, still without a smile.

Nosey Ruslin started as if something important and dangerous had at that moment dawned on him.

"I hope you don't think that I want the murderer to escape?" he exclaimed, exhibiting palpable nervousness.

"Why should I? Five pounds won't hurt you." Chief Inspector Wake glanced at him in his friendliest manner. "If you managed to put me on the right track it would be worth a lot more than five pounds," he added suggestively.

"You want me to be a police spy—a copper's nark?" The question was involuntary and immediately regretted.

"Surely, not. This is murder and murder is different." The detective's expression was one of bland surprise.

"Murder is different," Nosey repeated huskily. He took out a whitish handkerchief and wiped his forehead. The atmosphere had turned uncomfortably close and heated.

"Massy Cheldon was murdered because he was rich and for no other reason," said Chief Inspector Wake, stopping at the door and turning his back to it. "The murderer knows his London and Londoners. He is probably a foreigner or of foreign extraction. And his friends?"

Nosey sought distraction in moving the empty decanter from one end of the sideboard to the other, and the hand he used shook violently.

"Well, who are his friends?" he asked, unable to control his anxiety and curiosity. He was on the verge of a sneer when he realised the danger of offending the placid, unruffled man from Scotland Yard who never lost his temper and therefore seldom lost an argument or a case.

"His friends are likely to be night club frequenters. I mean the sort that live in the neighbourhood of night clubs—not the dupes who provide the profits." He looked at his umbrella. "I don't mind taking you into my confidence, Nosey, and so I'll tell you in the strictest confidence that I mean to get the murderer through his friends."

"Isn't it usual to get a clue from the—the—er—the history of the victim?" said Nosey, whose nervous curiosity was in control of his thinking faculties. "The man who murdered Massy Cheldon must have been known to him or at any rate he—"

Chief Inspector Wake shook his head.

"There is no such thing as an original murder, Nosey, but each murder has its original points, and its peculiarities. Of course, to a certain extent I'm only guessing, but from what I've seen and learnt myself, added to what my assistants have told me, I should say that the man who murdered Massy Cheldon last night never knew him."

"That sounds rubbish to me."

"Let me explain. When Massy Cheldon descended into the Underground by the steps near the London Pavilion he was walking leisurely and we may assume looking about him. Now in a London crowd a murderer can't follow his intended victim stealthily or go in for any of those antics which would ensure someone taking notice. The essence of success from his point of view depended on natural behaviour. Then the chances of success would be lessened considerably if there was a danger of Massy Cheldon turning round or looking sideways and recognising him. For these reasons and because of the astonishing luck of the murderer I believe that while he knew Massy Cheldon by sight Massy Cheldon did not know him. But I must be off, Nosey. Don't forget your promise to help me and don't forget that if I win with your aid our little bet you'll be able to look your bank manager straight between the eyes for months to come."

He wandered out as stolidly and as unthinkingly as appearances could suggest, and in Piccadilly was joined by his favourite aide-de-camp, Detective-Sergeant Clarke.

"We'll have a taxi to the Yard," he said, and as he never opened his mouth throughout the journey the sergeant, also a lover of prolonged silences, remained mute and at his ease.

In the Chief Inspectors' room a bundle of documents awaited his attention and he rapidly and yet thoroughly examined each one.

"Nothing here at present, but they may be useful," he said across the desk to his assistant. "Thirty-seven statements taken from persons who were within a few feet of Massy Cheldon at the moment of his death last night and not two of them agree as to what actually happened."

"If you'll remember, sir, Professor Munsterberg, in his lecture—"

"Oh, yes, I tried to read that book you lent me, Clarke, but I prefer my psychology in the raw and I can get that any time in the London streets. I don't want a professor or a book to tell me that people never see what they are look- ing at. I know it. There must have been a thousand persons in the Underground last night when Massy Cheldon was stabbed and here we are without a single important witness to attend the inquest tomorrow."

"That's true, sir, though we have warned six to be prepared for the adjourned hearing."

"We'll have to work on our own as usual, unless our old friend Inspector Luck comes to our aid. But I've not wasted my time, Clarke." He nearly rubbed his two ponderous hands together but stopped at the approach to a clasp. "I've made some progress." He smiled knowingly. "Clarke, I've come back with a nice collection of lies."

"You don't mean it, sir?" exclaimed the sergeant, a lean, lithe and cadaverous person of forty with deepset eyes and a heavy black moustache.

"Yes, a nice little collection. First of all, the nephew and heir lied, and that's very important."

"I hear he comes into ten thousand a year owing to his uncle's death," Sergeant Clarke interposed. "A tidy income that."

"Exactly. He benefits more than anyone—in fact, he is the only person who benefits at all, and when I ask him a few friendly questions he lies to me. It isn't a major lie, Clarke." The tone expressed disappointment. "But it indicates the way—a sort of road sign, in fact." He chuckled. "You know how keen I am on lies when I'm on a big case?"

The only reply needed was the sergeant's reminiscent smile.

"I went on to see my old acquaintance, Nosey Ruslin, and he added one or two gems to the collection."

"Nosey Ruslin, sir!" The sergeant was plainly astonished. "How did you know he came into it?"

"Young Cheldon, the heir, mentioned that last night he dined at Greville's with Nosey and that Nosey paid the bill. I thought that would surprise you. The dinner was important, as you will guess."

"Fixing an alibi for both of them, sir?"

"Exactly. And they lied about the time they left Greville's. I knew it, for after seeing young Cheldon I called at Greville's. Adler is an old friend of mine and to be trusted. He was positive that Nosey and his friend left at a quarter to eleven or even later and that they walked in the direction of Piccadilly. Clarke, you must spend a few hours trying to find evidence that they were in the Underground at the moment of the murder. I want such evidence badly."

"You think they had a hand in it?"

"One hand struck Massy Cheldon down, but other hands may have provided the temptation—a golden temptation, Clarke. Yes, it's a most unusual case and full of possibilities. But I've got Nosey worried and guessing. You heard me give orders he was to be watched. And young Cheldon, too. But it's Nosey I want."

"Because he'll lead you to the murderer?" Clarke smiled darkly. "It wasn't Nosey's work—not in his line."

"I admitted that, and he looked so happy about it that I suspected he knew something. But the person from whose looks I derived most information was young Cheldon's mother. She has a face that dials lies like a clock that registers arrivals and departures. I was watching her when her son said he had come home about midnight and her eyes simply shouted at me that it was a lie. She was frightened, Clarke, terrified and numbed. She is trying not to believe the worst."

"She can't suspect her son did it to get the money."

"Terror can persuade a woman to believe anything," said Chief Inspector Wake quietly. "But for the moment we'll forget Mrs. Cheldon. She was really upset by her brother-in-law's death and said so, but I could see that for myself. It's Nosey we've got to concentrate on. You know the sort of life he leads?"

"Gets up at noon, parades Shaftesbury Avenue and Wardour Street, calls on agents and tries to borrow, dines expensively as a rule and finishes up at a night club. Never leaves his usual haunts even for a race meeting." Detective-Sergeant Clarke recited his piece without attempting to introduce humour into it.

"Exactly. Well, I'll bet you five pounds to sixpence, Clarke, that for the next few weeks Nosey Ruslin will not enter a night club, will avoid his favourite restaurants and will hardly ever be seen in Shaftesbury Avenue. Is it a bet?"

Detective-Sergeant Clarke had an official sense of humour and plenty of tact.

"No, sir," he said. "I've never yet known you lose a bet. All the same I'd like to know why you are so confident. Did he promise to move back to the East End?" There was a smile now.

"He promised nothing, but I talked, Clarke, and talked until he had the idea that I was laying all my cards on the table. I told him I believed that the murderer was a foreigner, preferably an Italian, and I asked him if he knew any Italians, and he lied."

"What! Why, there's several of them still about who backed him when he lost the big fight with Slasher George!"

"I could have named at least three of his pals whose parents came from Italy," said Wake, selecting a cigarette. "Following up his lie I invited him to help me, and he agreed. You can judge for yourself if he was not lying then. After that I induced him to make a bet." He laughed. "I'm gambling today, Clarke. Five pounds to a pound that I don't find the murderer of Massy Cheldon by the time the adjourned inquest opens. He didn't wish to do it, but evidently suspecting that it would seem odd if he didn't he pretended to be quite jolly about it. So you see, Clarke, I've got him on the jumps. Sooner or later he'll give himself away by doing none of the things he ought to do. He'll make clues by avoiding the danger of making them. Mark my words, the first report will say that Nosey Ruslin kept indoors most of the day and when he came out took a tram or a train into the country. The 'Frozen Fang' won't see him again until we've forgotten the Underground murder."

"And will that tell you anything?"

"Yes, and a lot, too. It will tell me amongst other things that he knows who the murderer is. He didn't stab Massy

Cheldon, but I suspect he was in the plot. Aye, and I suspect the blameless young nephew too, for all his devoted mother and weak-kneed flounderings. He's not a murderer, Clarke, and never could be, but he's a spoilt, self-important and lazy young man. I know the type. And so do you. You remember young Lofthouse?"

Detective-Sergeant Clarke nodded. That had been a famous case in its way and had begun with an empty mustard tin in a Stepney warehouse and had ended in a sentence of death at the Old Bailey.

"There were other lies, Clarke, but I'll keep them to myself for the moment and let them grow in importance." He shuffled from his chair and walked up and down the room. "It won't be one of our failures, Clarke, it mustn't be. The murder is a challenge. I suppose I'm a fool to take it so much to heart, but I can't help it. These peculiar murders are generally the easiest to deal with. It's your revolver or your hammer that gets away with it. But I'll win, Clarke, and when I do I'll not be too proud to admit that the credit will be Nosey Ruslin's. Come in."

The knock and the invitation produced a plainclothes man with a typewritten document.

"Nancy Curzon, sir," he explained and departed.

For a long five minutes, according to the impatient estimate of the curious sergeant, Chief Inspector Wake devoted himself to the sheet of paper but never did the stolid face give a sign.

"That's something, Clarke," he said, at last. "She's one of those night birds who somehow keep themselves clear of the sticky adventures of their men friends. A dancer and keen on her work, but—" he paused and looked at his subordinate, "has been often in the society of Nosey Ruslin lately. Is very friendly with Robert Cheldon. Has told many persons that she was going to marry him when he had money. Dances with a former waiter who calls himself Billy Bright but whose father was deported to Italy in 1928 for keeping a gaming house. Billy Bright is a dancer who between engagements lives by his wits. Was supposed to be engaged to Nancy Curzon until Robert Cheldon appeared on the scene."

He tapped the document. "We're warm, Clarke, delightfully warm. Look at the sequence. Robert Cheldon in love with a mercenary little dancer; Nancy Curzon friendly with Nosey Ruslin who's been in our bad books for years and has kept out of our clutches very cleverly. Nosey pals up with Nancy's boy friend, the young heir." He tapped the paper again. "Whoever drew up this report should be promoted. I might have done it myself." It was the highest praise he could award anyone. "As I see it Nancy lets the boy friend understand that there'll be no wedding bells until he can afford to clothe her in diamonds. Young Cheldon thereupon becomes desperate. Nosey at once plays the part of benevolent and helpful friend, unofficial uncle and all that. He entertains young Cheldon and when money is scarce spends it on him. Why?"

"Exactly, sir. Why? How could Nosey benefit by young Cheldon having his uncle removed? Now if he were Nancy's father…"

"Clarke, you and I know that Nosey never did anything in his life unless there was the prospect of a lump sum for himself at the end of it. What he did exactly in this instance I don't know, but we'll arrive at the beginning by examining the end."

"And the end is, sir?"

"The murder last night in the Piccadilly Underground. We'll have to work backwards, as we always have to do in these cases, but for a change we'll think more of Nosey Ruslin, who didn't wield the dagger, than of anyone likely to have acted for him at his orders. You see, Clarke, the moment young Cheldon proved his alibi by dragging in the name of

Nosey Ruslin I knew that this was not a teaser. I knew I had the solution somewhere and that if I kept my eyes open I'd find it. But the staff work must be perfect. I don't want the murderer to escape. I must have him." His voice rose, and, half ashamed of anything approaching excitement, Chief Inspector Wake laughed apologetically. "It's spade work and not genius that has made the Yard famous," he added, indifferent to an audience. "Massy Cheldon died because he had money, and money's the best of clues when there isn't a woman in the case."

"But isn't there a woman here, sir?"

"Nancy Curzon? Of course. But only in a minor part, Clarke. You can bet your life she knew nothing about it. I may be wrong, but I won't admit I am until it's proved. Men of the Ruslin stamp don't take women into their confidence when they're planning murder. They know women who don't talk can be eloquent in terror. Look at that." He threw the report across the desk to him. "The third paragraph."

Detective-Sergeant Clarke read, "She was startled when she heard of the murder of Massy Cheldon and at once began to talk of knowing him. Seemed to be proud to have met him at Mrs. Cheldon's and remarked that he was kind to her. Said little about Robert Cheldon and never once referred to Nosey Ruslin. When the name of Billy Bright was introduced merely smiled and returned to the subject of the murder."

"That'll do. The report goes on to say that she could not have had prior knowledge, but that is obvious. Just file it with the other papers. What's the latest about the inquest proceedings?"

The conversation became purely technical.

"I'll lunch at Greville's," said Chief Inspector Wake, examining his watch. "It's nearly two and I haven't eaten anything since six."

As he had anticipated the little restaurant at the back of the Palace Theatre was only about one-third full when he entered and all those present were distinctly of a foreign type, Londoners by adoption whose day began in the afternoon and ended in the early hours of the morning. Some of them recognised the detective and pecked at imaginary crumbs while they estimated their chances of a reassuring nod if they smiled a welcome. The majority, however, continued their sleepy discussions, or where there was female company stared and gesticulated.

The proprietor hurried forward to serve the guest who was a danger to many of his clients and could be a danger to the business itself.

"A leetle fish, sare?" he began.

The meal was grateful and comforting, and Chief Inspector Wake derived rest as well as nourishment from it.

"I don't see any of my friends here," he remarked when he was paying his bill. "Not Nosey Ruslin or even Billy Bright."

The dark visage of Adler became darker.

"I wish Bright would see me," he said angrily. "I have ze bill—you call it, eh?"

"Oh, he'll pay it, I'm sure," said the inspector carelessly. "How's business these days—and nights?"

The proprietor answered with a preliminary shrug and an extension of both arms, but there was no change of expression.

"I suppose there's been a lot of talk about the Piccadilly murder?" It was a bow drawn at a venture.

"Nothing else, sare, absoluteetly. They talk an' talk. Dagger." His teeth gleamed and he muttered something in Italian. Chief Inspector Wake badly wanted a translation but did not ask for it.

"How much is Billy Bright's account?" he asked, abruptly changing the subject or appearing to do so.

"Three pounds eighteen shillings and eightpence, sare." There was anguish in the proprietor's voice.

"Three pounds eighteen shillings and eightpence." As he repeated the amount the inspector took out his pocket-book and counted the notes it contained. "Look here, Adler, I shall be passing this way at ten o'clock tomorrow morning and will drop in. If by then you have a list of the names of all your foreign customers—I mean those you happen to know by name and who are not English—I will settle Billy Bright's account. Is it a bargain?"

The lively eyes danced.

"Thank you, sare," he whispered, breathing all over the table.

It was a very tired but not a dissatisfied or irritable chief inspector who went to bed at half-past twelve that night, though it was an anxious one who breakfasted early and reached Scotland Yard before nine. A sheaf of reports awaited him and he had not studied them all when he had to keep his appointment with the proprietor of Greville's.

"Thank you," he said, producing the money and carefully pocketing the receipt along with the precious document. "No, nothing to drink, thanks." He waved a hand and ambled out to seek a taxicab.

Ten minutes later Billy Bright came through the swing door and cornered Adler in a corner of the dining-room.

"What about that account of mine?" he said cheerfully.

"That's all right. It's paid."

"Paid?" Billy thought of Nosey and smiled happily.

"Yes, paid. Settled." The proprietor grinned. "Inspector Wake gave me the money and took away the receipt."

The dancer, yellow to the ears, repeated the name dully.

"Inspector Wake! Inspector Wake!" he muttered and collapsed.

Chapter Nine

"So he fainted, did he, when he heard I'd paid his account at Greville's?" said Chief Inspector Wake, lolling in the corner of the first class carriage of the train which was taking him and Detective-Sergeant Clarke to Lewes and to Broadbridge Manor. "I thought I'd stir him up, Clarke, in fact, I've stirred them all up. Listen to this." He selected a newspaper from the untidy bundle beside him and spread it open. "Soho silent in Terror. No clue to the murder of Massy Cheldon. Inquest adjourned."

"That's more or less what they all say, sir," his colleague remarked. "But the West End is enjoying the murder as if it were a play."

"It won't have a long run, Clarke, not if I can help it." The fleshy face was further disfigured by a frown. "Wonder if I'm right to be bothering about Broadbridge Manor. We've had plenty of reports from there."

"You never know, sir." Detective-Sergeant Clarke's private opinion was that his chief was a fool, but even had the regulations and the circumstances permitted the enlarging of his thoughts into words he would have remained silent. Too often in the past had he been taught by experience that the foolishness of Harry Wake would have made the reputation of more than one of his subordinates.

"I think we'd have been wiser to come by car, sir," he ventured, for he was a lover of motoring and could never understand the contempt the chief inspector had for modern methods of speed.

"It's more comfortable this way," was the answer, "and it's easier to think and certainly easier to read. What do you think of the papers, Clarke? Are they going to score over us?"

The sergeant grinned as much as he could.

"It's the usual stuff," he said, "and it must be right some time or another, as it was in the Gerrard Street affair."

"Besley had charge of that," growled Wake, who had the sensitiveness of a prima donna and a faded professional beauty combined. "But I'll get the murderer of Massy Cheldon, Clarke, and I'll get him before we're a month older. I win five pounds from Nosey Ruslin if I solve the mystery by the time the coroner is on his feet again."

"Nosey Ruslin." The sergeant repeated the name with a gentle emphasis which indicated his estimate of its importance. "A wily bird, Nosey, sir. Wish I had his knowledge of Soho though."

"So do I. But I'll extract some of it from him very soon. Don't forget, Clarke, when you're dealing with a secretive crowd you must worry them into talking and doing things. Get on their nerves. Make them commit mistakes. I mean, keeping away from their usual haunts, getting scared at the least little incident. You see how Billy Bright fainted? Of course, he doesn't know he's being watched day and night."

The sergeant laughed.

"He'd have fainted again if he'd known that the chap who held the smelling salts to his nose was one of ours."

"They're a queer crowd, Clarke, a queer crowd, and Nosey Ruslin's the queerest and most dangerous of them all. I don't suppose he's ever done anything worse than cheat at cards or swindle a bookmaker, but he's been behind a few serious affairs which have interested us."

"And we can never get him." The tone was a sigh.

"We'll get him now, Clarke, and at once. Something in my bones tells me that. You know it's not my form to boast and that outside the office I don't talk except when I take the office with me in the shape of Detective-Sergeant Clarke."

There was no need for the younger man to endorse the testimonial. Besides, he knew his chief disliked sycophancy. It was one of the reasons he had chosen him for his A.D.C.

They read the newspapers in scraps and between intervals of comment throughout the remainder of the journey, and they seemed to know by heart all that had happened to the millions of Londoners outside the actual murderer when they stepped from the train at Lewes.

"There'll be a fairish crowd at the Manor today," said the inspector with a sour expression, "but tomorrow and Sunday the place will be in a state of siege."

"Didn't you see the picture in the *Daily Express* and the larger one in the *Daily Mail*?" asked the sergeant in surprise. "It says there were over three hundred cars outside Broadbridge Manor yesterday."

Chief Inspector Wake did not answer. He had by now identified the car which was to convey him and his assistant to the small Sussex village where only three days previously Massy Cheldon had been the squire and overlord. Only three days since he had bubbled with pride at the offer of a seat on the county bench, and now he was a corpse, a spectacle of sensation and tragedy, the centre of an absorbing and puzzling murder mystery. Life was like that and death also.

Six policemen saluted him when he descended into their midst, and standing afar off after the manner of the disciples on a famous occasion were several groups of curiosity-mongers complete with cars. It was nearly three in the afternoon and most of the spectators were munching sandwiches and staring at the low wall surrounding the manor grounds and apparently deriving satisfaction from the inspection.

"Anything new?" Wake asked of the sergeant who was in charge.

"Nothing, sir." He moved his heavy feet to the left and gave the onlookers the full benefit of a hostile stare.

"Never mind about them," said the chief inspector sharply. "I'm going into the house. There might be something there."

"We've been through it, and your colleague, Inspector Carlett, has almost scrubbed the floors." The essay in humour passed unrecognised.

"I have seen his reports. They leave nothing to the imagination or to hope. But all the same I wish to see for myself."

The mansion impressed him with its air of wealth, luxury and superiority over most of the other mansions he had entered in his professional capacity. The walls seemed to breathe ancient lineage, the furniture proclaim the eternity of the wealth and standing of the Cheldons. West and his underlings had obviously not permitted the gloom and the horror without to interfere with the daily ritual of maintaining the cleanliness of the mansion which even now did not convey an impression or suggestion of desolation and emptiness.

"There is a new heir, sir," he explained, a trifle condescendingly to the man from Scotland Yard. "There always is an heir. Just as the throne is never vacant so is Broadbridge Manor never without a master. The moment Mr. Massy Cheldon died Mr. Robert Cheldon became the squire."

"But he hasn't arrived yet?"

"No, sir. I understand that the etiquette is to keep away until after the funeral. In this case as the death of the late master was so tragic it is probable Mr. Robert will wait until the inquest is over and done with. The Cheldons are always sensitive. They could not bear to live at the Manor when it is surrounded by trippers and their cars."

Chief Inspector Wake listened with a patience which was only possible because he attached no importance to the speaker or his speech. He had never expected to be rewarded at Broadbridge Manor for his trouble in coming all the way from London to see it, but it was a duty which he had to perform as the chief of the squad responsible for bringing the murderer to justice. The house told him nothing, the butler and the other servants less. Whatever secrets, good, bad and indifferent, which the late Massy Cheldon had had they were not at home at Broadbridge Manor now.

"He was murdered in London and the whole explanation of the murder is there," he said later on to his assistant.

"Had Mr. Massy Cheldon many visitors during the last month or, perhaps, it would be easier to remember the last week of his life?" he asked West, who had taken a dislike to the unfashionable umbrella if not to its owner.

"Mr. Massy Cheldon's friends were not many, but I can show you the visitors' book which I keep myself."

"That would be a help," said the inspector.

The names suggested nothing and revealed nothing, and after another colloquy with the local sergeant Wake strolled unaccompanied down to the village of one street and five alleys. He was not a lover of the country although he had been trying for thirty years to convert his back yard in Chelsea into a flower garden, and he was too conscious of the fact that he was wasting his time. A few women and children with an occasional male constituted the representatives of the population at the moment, for the closed doors of the "Wheatsheaf" deprived the thirsty of any temptation to leave their work prematurely.

But when he could forget the mileage between himself and his beloved London he could be grateful for the opportunity to think, and soon he had once more completed a panorama of events and scenes since he had been called from his well earned rest to take charge of the Piccadilly Murder. It was satisfactory to know that he had electrified Nosey Ruslin, Billy Bright, Robert Cheldon and the last-named's mother. One of the four if not all of them, could supply the solution of the problem, or at the worst make a guess which would be more than half the truth. He dealt in half-truths and lies and everything appertaining to them, for out of them there often emerged the exact truth.

There was no Broadbridge Manor end to the mystery, however. That was certain. If the late Massy Cheldon cared to mingle in bohemian circles in London he did not permit his more or less disreputable acquaintances there to invade the aristocratic solemnity of his country mansion. It was useless looking to the servants or to the locals.

As he muttered this to himself he came to a standstill outside a shop window which from the variety of its contents might have been a London store in miniature. But he was not interested until he noticed a piece of cardboard bearing the legend "Post Office."

"A shillingsworth of threehalfpenny stamps and a packet of stamped postcards," he said to the plump, spacious and elderly woman who appeared before the door bell had ceased to tinkle.

"Yes, sir." She deducted he was from London by the simple process of remembering that she had had many customers from outside the village since the death of the owner of Broadbridge Manor. To Mrs. Chalk England consisted of Broadbridge and London.

"I suppose you've had crowds down here?" said the inspector, assuming that she was one of nature's talkers, the living local newspaper whose one accuracy could redeem a hundred inaccuracies.

"Trippers!" A sniff of contempt. "How they find the time puzzles me. Now on Saturday and Sunday one expects plenty of people."

Chief Inspector Wake leaned across the counter and examined a pair of men's socks which were cheap enough to warrant purchase as a prelude to a more friendly atmosphere.

"Thank you," he said, as he paid the half-crown. "I suppose you knew Mr. Massy Cheldon rather well?"

"Can't say that, sir." Mrs. Chalk had her pride and it forbade her to claim acquaintance with the great unless the claim could be substantiated. "The last time I saw him was some weeks before his murder when he surprised me by coming in here."

"Indeed! Was he looking well?"

"Looking well? Why, I never saw him so pleased with himself in his life. When he was in the temper he could be very pleasant, and he was very pleasant indeed, that morning."

She paused, and the detective, knowing how foolish it is to attempt to force a conversation into a desired channel, picked up a packet of scented soap and read the label.

"I hadn't seen him for nearly a month and it was the first time he'd been in the shop since I took it over eleven years ago."

"That was remarkable!" exclaimed Wake with flattering astonishment.

"It was, and I said so." She smiled. "Seeing that Mr. West or one of the other servants usually brought the parcels and letters that had to be registered it was a surprise when in he walked with a parcel of his own."

"Doing the work himself he paid others to do?" said Chief Inspector Wake with an encouraging smile. "That's not my idea of spending money."

"And it isn't mine. But he was that affable that I quite enjoyed our little chat. I remember how he laughed when I remarked that the parcel was heavy for its size, the heaviest I'd ever handled."

"Heavy was it?" The question was an articulate thought. "I suppose it was addressed to someone in London?"

To his astonishment Mrs. Chalk burst into the heartiest laughter he had heard for years.

"Addressed to London!" She laughed again. "I should think it was, and the funniest address I've ever known. I don't need to look at the book to remember it. Didn't I tell everyone about it?"

The detective could not hurry her, but his curiosity was developing at such a rate as to threaten to imperil his peace of mind.

"I come from London," he said suggestively, "and I know there are some funny names there, people and odd streets. There's one in the city which sounds as if it—"

"But this was in the West End—in Dean Street," she interrupted. "N. Ruslin, The Frozen Fang, Dean Street, London, W.1." She repeated the address with the readiness with which a child proclaims the only date it knows, that of the battle of Hastings.

Chief Inspector Wake was not naturally a stolid man and although he substituted for the daily dose the daily thought, "Never let your face or your tongue give you away," he was ever exposed to the danger of self-betrayal. He very nearly betrayed himself now when Mrs. Chalk, all her features animated by merriment, startled him by pronouncing the name and address of the last man he would have associated with this quiet backwater in Sussex. Had it not been for the gloom of the shop even on a sunny June day she must have noticed the sudden convulsion of his frame and the trembling of the stolid umbrella infected by the shakiness of his left hand. But to Mrs. Chalk he was merely an audience and her enjoyment of the rarest episode in her career was too vivid and intense to permit of any kind of deviation.

"The 'Frozen Fang' is a night club," he explained.

"Is it? I thought it was public house. But fancy your knowing it? A night club. I've heard of them. A niece of my late husband used to be a waitress in one at Birmingham."

"The 'Frozen Fang' is not one of the best in London," said her customer, determined to steer the conversation round to Nosey Ruslin. "I'm surprised Mr. Massy Cheldon ever heard of it."

"He was never in it. He told me that. Oh, he was affable that morning. Quite the free-spoken gentleman." Mrs. Chalk's pride was something which had to be encouraged and flattered.

"He probably saw you were a sensible and intelligent lady," said the detective, venturing into what he was afraid might prove to be a morass. "Men like to talk to women who have a sense of humour."

He was relieved when she smiled her appreciation.

"He laughed when I told him the postage would be one shilling," she resumed at a gallop. "But that included the reg-istration fee. Then he didn't want the receipt, but I insisted. We don't often have registered letters here. There was the big box with Milly Ellis's new hat in it which she was sending ahead of her to Derby and she registered it and claimed…."

The adventures of the hat continued for nearly five minutes.

"Could I see the duplicate receipt?" he asked suddenly. "I am rather interested in Mr. Massy Cheldon although I never met him when he was alive."

Mrs. Chalk, unable to detect anything sinister in the distinction between death and life, spared Chief Inspector

Wake the trouble of disclosing his identity by producing the book.

"Thank you," he said after giving it a glance. "And now I think I'll have that tie with the blue and green spots. It's taken my fancy. Four and six? Here it is. Oh, by the way, I suppose Mr. Cheldon didn't tell you what was in the parcel? I mean as he was in such an affable mood he might have asked you to guess."

Mrs. Chalk, pausing in the act of wrapping up the tie, stared at him in astonishment. Evidently he had scored with his guess.

"Why, you might have been in the shop at the time!" she exclaimed. "That was just what he did do. 'I'll give you three guesses, Mrs. Chalk,' and I said 'diamonds, clock and old iron'. How he did laugh to be sure! 'You're not so far off, Mrs. Chalk', he says, but he didn't tell me what it was."

Chief Inspector Wake made his exit on her last word of gratitude, for the tie had been written off as a dead loss eleven months previously, and once he was in the sunshine he walked as rapidly as he could back to the sophistication represented by Detective-Sergeant Clarke and a police car.

"We'll catch the next train from Lewes," he said without a sign of the feeling of triumph which he was mastering. "There's nothing here, Clarke, and yet I haven't wasted my time."

They were a mile out of Lewes station when he disclosed his discovery.

"Clarke, I nearly let myself be tricked by that young Cheldon. You remember I said I thought his part in the business was small if he had had any part in it at all?"

"Yes, sir." The sergeant showed his excitement by sitting bolt upright.

"I was wrong. He's been lying to me, and lying with intent. He told me again and again that Nosey Ruslin had

had nothing to do with his uncle, that they had never met; that his uncle didn't even know Nosey by sight."

"And it isn't true?" Clarke's question was put in an awed whisper.

"I know now it isn't. On April 9th, Massy Cheldon took a small parcel to the local post office, and that parcel was addressed to Mr. N. Ruslin, The Frozen Fang, Dean St., London, W.1. I inspected the entry in the registration book at the post office."

"But this is amazing!" his companion exclaimed. "It alters everything. You were so confident that they had never met."

"It's never too late to learn, Clarke," said his chief gravely. "Thank goodness, I've done nothing that'll have to be undone. This discovery of mine will only grease the wheels of the case and compel us to work faster. But it's all to the good. Fancy Nosey and the squire of Broadbridge Manor being acquaintances! Somehow I'd never imagined it. I did think of it at first, but knowing Nosey as I do I soon put it out of my mind. Clarke, we'll have to pay more attention to the young heir." He laughed throatily. "Ten thousand a year—that's what they say he's come in for by his uncle's death."

"Ten thousand a year." The voice had envy in it.

"It was the first time in his life Massy Cheldon ever took a parcel to the post office himself. One of his servants always attended to the letters and parcels. Mrs. Chalk, the postmistress, made an instant hit with the squire and they talked quite a lot. He asked her to guess what was inside the parcel. She voted for diamonds, clock and old iron, and he told her she wasn't so far out."

It was Detective-Sergeant Clarke's turn to smile knowingly.

"You didn't tell her, sir, that if she'd said 'revolver' she'd have very likely won his money?" he remarked.

"What would have been the use? I left her to guess further. What interested her, though, was the address, the 'Frozen Fang' took her fancy."

"Mr. Massy Cheldon evidently had nothing to hide or he wouldn't have taken the parcel to the centre of local gossip," said the sergeant.

"We must remember that." Chief Inspector Wake half closed his eyes. "Clarke, there'll be no rest for either of us until we find the answer to the question, why did Massy Cheldon send a registered parcel containing a revolver—we can bank on the contents—to one of the most dangerous men in London a few weeks before he was himself murdered."

The sergeant looked thoughtfully in the direction of the fields they were passing at forty miles an hour.

"He sent a revolver but he was stabbed to the heart," he murmured as if memorising a lesson. "Yet it may not have been a revolver. I suppose you have a reason for not inquiring about it at Broadbridge Manor?"

"You evidently understand me, Clarke," said Wake with a bare smile. "My first intention was to question the butler and the other servants, but I quickly saw that would be a mistake. For the time being only you and I know about the registered parcel."

His companion nodded.

"It's a rare piece of luck, Clarke, and if only it will hold all our troubles are over. I only hope one of the local men may not wander into the post office and hear how Mrs. Chalk broke a regulation. That's what I like about these country places though—they don't worry about red tape and rules and etiquette." He raised a leg on to the seat. "Of course, we are only guessing it was a revolver, and yet if it wasn't it won't really matter. It would be of great importance had Massy Cheldon been shot, but as the weapon was a dagger the actual contents of the parcel are of minor importance. I gathered from Mrs. Chalk's description it wasn't long enough to have held the dagger. What is important is the fact that it proves that Massy Cheldon and Nosey Ruslin were acquainted. I shouldn't be surprised to hear that they were intimate friends."

"That's what I think, sir. Mr. Cheldon wouldn't have bothered to act as his own messenger if that parcel wasn't important for some reason." Detective-Sergeant Clarke lapsed into profound thought.

"When I have cleaned up the London end of the parcel I may return to Broadbridge," said Wake thoughtfully. "But only if absolutely necessary. The murder took place in London and the murderer is most likely still there. If it's Billy Bright, Nosey Ruslin or young Cheldon they can't move fifty yards without our knowing it."

"You think one of the three is the man?"

"Don't you?"

"I'm not so sure, but if I had to pick I'd choose Billy Bright. Nosey never risks his own neck, and this young Cheldon couldn't be such a fool as to hang himself. Besides, there's the dagger. That's un-English."

"Young Cheldon gains a fortune by the murder of his uncle. He is the one person in the world who benefits by the crime. We know that he is desperately in love with a dancer who wouldn't marry him as long as he was poor. That's obvious, isn't it, Clarke?"

"Certainly, sir. But he wouldn't use a dagger, and he'd never have trailed his uncle to the busiest and most crowded spot in London and knife him there. No, I won't have young Cheldon at any price."

"Only as an accessory before the fact, eh?" Chief Inspector Wake was smiling paternally at his junior, who had had only sixteen years' experience compared with his own thirty odd.

"Possibly. But from what I've seen of him I should say that young Cheldon hasn't any nerve. He's a pampered specimen of mother's pet and no mistake. Never worked in his life."

"He was in a city office for a few weeks," his chief reminded him. "Fifty shillings a week, too."

They both laughed.

"And from fifty shillings a week to ten thousand pounds a year in a night—actually in a few moments—because some expert with a stiletto put finis to his uncle." Wake became grave again. "Clarke, every day has produced fresh clues linking the three men I have named, but especially Nosey Ruslin and Cheldon. We know that when Nosey hasn't been with young Cheldon he's been seen with Billy Bright. I'm positive there's something between them, something that binds them into a silence and a caution that are forced on them by danger. The parcel to the 'Frozen Fang' is the strongest link of all." He brought his flat hand down on the newspaper lying negligently across his knees. "Nosey is our man, and when we have him we'll have the murderer."

"How will you get him, sir?" There was a trace of scepticism in the sergeant's voice which his chief understood and appreciated.

"I know it won't be easy," he answered quickly. "But if I can't outwit Nosey I'll resign and enter an asylum. He's clever, Clarke, very clever in his own opinion and in mine, but I can work on his knowledge of the conspiracy that led up to Massy Cheldon's murder and I'll have him on it eventually. He can be as nervous as a kitten."

The sergeant interrupted him with a sound that might have been a snort, a laugh, a half-strangled cough or an ejaculation of contempt.

"We're dealing with three nervous men, sir," he said as if a new light had dawned on him. "You couldn't have anyone more nervous and more easily upset than Billy Bright. Look at the way he fainted simply because you paid his account at the Greville. And young Cheldon."

"You needn't try to tell me anything about him. He was in a blue funk all the time I was talking about his uncle's murder. And it wasn't caused by sorrow either, Clarke. I know the human face—been studying it for most of my lifetime. Too often it tells you nothing, but once in a while it's a regular talking-machine."

"And Nosey Ruslin?" The sergeant actually grinned. "No doubt about him, sir. I remember, now that you mention it, how nervous he was when he fought the Wapping Tiger."

"He was ten times the better boxer," said Chief Inspector Wake, his expression darkening, "and should have won in the first or second round. But he was so nervous that he threw the fight away. I was less experienced than I am now, and I had nearly a week's pay on Nosey." He leaned forward to choose a cigarette from the other's case. "Well, if I lost on his nervousness then, Clarke, I'm going to win on it now. He's prepared for me and he has an answer for every question. Has he?" He reclined back. "I'll play with him as a cat plays with a mouse and at the right moment I'll knock him flat with a little story about a registered parcel. But, remember, Clarke, not a word to anyone. When I am prepared to disclose it, it shall appear in my report. I regard the parcel as the luck of a lifetime."

Chapter Ten

To a sensitive and imaginative *dilettante*, such as Bobbie Cheldon was, the events following on the murder of his uncle were more horrible and disturbing than the murder itself. The flaunting headlines and the bouncing newspaper reports; the insurgent suspicions of himself which every day bred, the inability to detach himself completely from the crime and look only to the future, and the embarrassment of his acquaintance with Nosey Ruslin and the other night club habitués amalgamated to render his waking hours a torture and his sleeping ones a nightmare.

On top of his own self-conscious demeanour there was the unhappiness of stifling anger caused by his mother's attitude. She scarcely ever referred to the murder now unless compelled to by the course of their infrequent conversations or a particularly disturbing insinuation by an enterprising newspaper, but he could detect fear in her eyes, and in the circumstances such an emotion was tantamount to accusation.

Could his mother really suspect him? He did not ask her that question because he knew what her indignant, reproachful reply would be. But that she was on the verge of a nervous collapse because she deducted from every approaching footfall the minatory figure of Chief Inspector

Wake with a warrant in his pocket, required no extra intelligence to discern. He had implored her not to read the newspapers, but they fascinated her as the serpent does the rabbit. He declared and shouted in turn that they had nothing to fear or to be ashamed of, and she agreed with her tongue and contradicted herself with her eyes. And to add to his misery and threatening doubts was her decision that "for the present" he must make no move in the direction of Broadbridge Manor. The family lawyer, Mr. Parker, who was now watching his interests, had expressed the opinion that as soon as Massy Cheldon had been buried there could be no objection to Bobbie formally entering into possession of his estate, but she had over-ruled that opinion, and Bobbie, afraid of quarrelling with anyone, had no option but to acquiesce.

"Adjourned for eight days," Ruby read from her morning newspaper.

"That was in the paper last night," he reminded her with the faintest ebullition of irritation.

"And here's an exclusive interview with you." He saw her smile bitterly and ground his teeth in rage.

"I only told a reporter that I had seen my uncle a few hours before his death," he remarked with an effort to keep his temper. "That and I was not going down to Broadbridge Manor just yet."

His mother flung the paper from her.

"It's horrible, Bobbie, horrible." She stared pensively before her. "Poor Massy! He deserved a better fate." Her expression hardened. "I'll not be happy until they catch the murderer, the cowardly ruffian."

For a reason he would not have admitted to himself Bobbie was unable to resist retorting in a harsh and unfeeling voice.

"Let the police do their work, mother," he said. "It's no business of ours. We're not detectives and—"

"No business of ours?" she exclaimed in astonishment. "Bobbie, it's our business more than anyone else's. The murderer must be found and convicted before I can know another happy moment."

He went a trifle greyer in the face, but forced himself to confront her with a question that could not be suppressed.

"Are you afraid of—of me?"

"You!" She strangled the scream in time, but the horror remained in her large grey eyes. "Of course I'm not. What nonsense you talk, Bobbie! I know you couldn't have done it, but do the public and—and Inspector Wake?"

He contorted his shoulders to express his contempt for public opinion, and almost instantly was shaking with fright.

"There have been hints in the papers," he said kicking at the worn carpet. "It's beastly." He was nearly crying. "I had nothing to do with it. I swear I hadn't."

"For God's sake, don't deny it," his mother cried. "Don't speak of it at all. I won't have you defending yourself. No one has accused you, and you mustn't accuse yourself."

The conversation had taken such a curious turn that each became afraid of the other and for several minutes there was a silence that embarrassed them. Ruby, appalled by the indiscretion which had brought her to within a hair's breadth of betraying her worst fears, dared not trust to language again, and Bobbie had nothing to say which could be expressed in moderate language.

"Hadn't we better have lunch?" he remarked suddenly. A turn up and down the room and he took up a position before the fireplace. "Funny state of affairs, mother, isn't it? Here we are lunching on cold meat and cheese in a Fulham slum and yet I'm worth ten thousand a year. A rich man compelled to live as a pauper! It's the limit."

"That needn't worry us now," she said quietly. "It would be bad taste to begin spending when your uncle is—"

With a gesture of impatience he picked up a newspaper and ostentatiously devoted himself to the sporting pages, not because cricket or racing interested him, but because references to the Piccadilly murder could not be found there. He was still studying the cricket scores when his mother reminded him that lunch was ready. Half an hour later when she rose the food she had provided for both of them had not diminished in weight more than an ounce or two.

"I haven't any appetite," he said miserably. "Oh, if only we could get away from all this! If only we could go abroad!"

"You can't until the inquest is over," she reminded him unnecessarily, "and even then the papers and the public would think…" She stopped dead.

"That I was running away from arrest." He laughed loudly. "Oh, it's lovely to be suspected by one's own mother!"

She uttered a stricken cry of protest at his cruelty.

"Bobbie," she said, driven to anger by his indifference to her distress. "It's not you I'm frightened for, but it's you plus your queer friends from the night clubs. You couldn't hurt anyone. All the money in the world wouldn't have tempted you, but these others." She wiped her eyes with her hand-kerchief and he wondered why she was crying.

Before he could trouble his wits further for a way out of the impasse created by her avowal the bell rang.

"Another reporter or a policeman," he muttered, and was still muttering when he found Nancy, dainty in white and dainty of expression, standing before him.

"You're not to see Nosey yet," she whispered as they kissed. Then in her usual voice, "Just dropped in to see how you were, Bobbie."

To his relief the living-room was empty when they entered it, and at his suggestion Nancy took off her hat and having performed in front of a mirror threw herself into the armchair.

"Dead beat, Bobbie, and worried," she said, all her animation gone and in its stead the pallor of fear.

He stared in surprise until she had to smile.

"I was pretending, Bobbie, in case your mother opened the door. Can't be too careful. At least that's what Nosey says."

"Why does he say it?" he asked, irritably.

"You ought to know why," she retorted, suspecting that he was playing a game with her. "Nosey is your pal, isn't he?"

The sneer in his expression was obvious, and Nancy took umbrage at it.

"Oh, I see," she exclaimed, and if her arms were not akimbo they ought to have been if the picture was to be complete. "Now that you're the rich Johnny with thousands a year and an estate Nosey doesn't count!"

"Be careful," he whispered, imploringly. "Mother's in the next room. But you're wrong Nancy, about Nosey. He never has been a pal of mine."

"Never a pal, and he lent you money? Never a pal and he stood by you when no one else would? Never a pal—" Speech failed her and she stared contemptuously at his troubled countenance.

"If you'll let me speak I'll explain," he said.

"Explain what and how you like," she cried, still unappeased, "I suppose you'll be telling the world next that I'm not your pal?"

"I hope you're more than that," he answered quickly.

"Oh, you're a fool!" she cried, losing her temper. "I wish I hadn't come. I wouldn't have either only Nosey is that worried and upset that I couldn't refuse. You're not to see him or write him or ring him up. When he wants to talk he'll let you know. He wouldn't even write the message down, Bobbie, and he nearly bit my head off when I asked him to tell me what it meant. I suppose it's something to do with—"

"Don't," he gasped, "Nancy, don't. I hate even the barest reference to uncle's murder."

"So that's the effect it has on you, too, is it? Bobbie." There was alarm in her voice and the effect was to deepen his fear into terror. "You're behaving just like Nosey did. What's come over you all? There's Billy Bright hiding in Margate. Went off last night looking as though he was going to his own funeral. Bobbie, what's this between you and Nosey?" She rose and her voice culminated in a scream. "My God, it's not true—it's not true!" She started away from him as though the outstretched hands were covered with blood.

"I swear, Nancy, I had nothing to do with it. On my honour I swear it. Nosey and I were together when it happened."

She pushed him away.

"I'll not be dragged into this. I tell you I won't." She was now the vulgar, hysterical creature of the gutter fighting for a reputation that was always in peril. "You'll do your own dirty work without me. Nosey's a gentleman compared with you. Nosey wouldn't—"

It was not exhaustion that brought the tirade to an end, but the figure of Ruby Cheldon in the doorway.

"Chief Inspector Wake has called again, Bobbie," she said, without so much as a glance at the girl. "He wants to have another chat with you."

"If your son has no objection," said the familiar husky voice. The detective had followed Ruby in, an act of discourtesy which Bobbie would have resented had he noticed it, but as it was he was in such a condition of nervous uncertainty that he saw nothing and thought of nothing.

"Why, you must be Nancy Curzon, of Curzon & Bright, the famous dancers!" Wake exclaimed with an enthusiasm she mistook for the genuine article. "Remember seeing you at that charity matinee at the Hackney Empire."

Nancy giggled her pleasure at the compliment of his recognition, and he did not trouble to inform her that the reason for his presence at that particular show was a suspicion that her partner had taken part in the Chiselhurst jewel robbery. He could recall now his disappointment when he found that he had wasted two precious hours on a dull programme.

"I'll be off as you're wanting to see Bobbie—Mr. Cheldon," she said, adopting a set manner which suited her less than a crinoline would have done.

Chief Inspector Wake smiled again.

"I love satisfying a woman's curiosity—been married twenty-eight years myself—and I'd rather you stopped with us. It's nothing very important, Miss Curzon, and when I'm gone you can resume your tête-à-tête." He smiled for the third time because he thought his descent into the French language had been a success.

Nancy took a mental census of the room before deciding. That Bobbie's mother should refrain from supporting the inspector's invitation was natural. That Bobbie himself should say nothing was not surprising either. He was not a he-man according to the abbreviated and imported vocabulary of her little underworld.

"All right," she said, sitting down again. That she was not wanted by Mrs. Cheldon gave a spice to her decision; that Bobbie did not want her inflamed her curiosity. And yet when she had assumed what she had decided would be a comfortable position she began to tremble.

"Am I required?" The gentle, musical voice of Ruby Cheldon filled the room, banishing the shrill tone of the dancer, the gruffness of the detective and the mumbled politeness of the mystified and terrified Bobbie.

"I think it would be better if you rested, mother," was the only reply. Chief Inspector Wake plainly did not care what she did, and it was no concern of Nancy's.

"Yes, I am tired," she murmured, reading into his words an admission that he did not wish her to hear what the detective had to say to him.

"Wouldn't it be better, Nancy?" he began and hesitated.

"Let's sit down and have a quiet chat," said the detective, pulling forward a chair for himself. "And Miss Curzon may be of assistance to me. She knows the West End as well as I do."

The extravagant lie she accepted as normal flattery.

"I've been dancing for years," she said, as if that explained more than any of them had the right to expect.

"You're sharp-witted, Miss Curzon, and the sort of girl I prefer to deal with. Besides, I'm interested in the 'Frozen Fang' at the moment."

Her attack of nerves returned. He might have been accusing her of the murder of Massy Cheldon to judge by her reaction to his seemingly harmless words, fat forefinger, prominent umbrella and too, too easy assumption of command over all of them.

"There's not much that happens there that I don't hear of," she said, speaking at random because as a woman she had to attempt to obtain the last word.

"Exactly, and that's why I regard you as a valuable ally." She nearly demanded with severity such as a perfect lady could assume, if he regarded her as a coppers' nark, but that would have been vulgar and unladylike, and how she wished she could think of the slang term for coppers' nark! But she was so flustered she could not think of anything.

"You know Nosey Ruslin?"

The question nearly overwhelmed her and she was barely in time to reply before her embarrassment could become noticeable.

"Nosey Ruslin? Oh, yes. Everybody knows him. I often see him in the 'Frozen Fang'. Used to be keen on Alva Carleon, a Spanish girl."

"Italian," he corrected, and she moved slightly.

"You seem to know more about it than I do," she exclaimed with a laugh from which all the merriment was banished. "But there, I'm just an acquaintance of his. He's kind to everybody, I daresay."

Bobbie, who was conscious that he was not in the picture, could have smiled at her cool repudiation of the man whom she had been championing at the very moment of the inspector's entrance, but he was too absorbed in trying to prepare for the visitor's first question to himself to have any desire to analyse the motives and the conduct of another.

"Oh, Nosey is unique," said the inspector pleasantly. "I've never known another of his sort. Full of surprises, but clever in one respect at any rate, and an important one."

Nancy's curiosity overcame her growing nervousness.

"If you ask me I think he's a dear," she said defiantly, but the defiance was of her conscience. "But what is it you mean exactly?"

"I'll tell you, Miss Curzon." To her disquiet he moved his chair nearer to hers and it had been too near. From her earliest years Nancy had been brought up to fear and suspect the police, the natural enemies of the denizens of the alley in which she had been born, and all the music hall songs and jokes about them which had become familiar to her since had not eradicated that suspicion and fear.

"He is never more than a friend to any woman," was the surprising answer.

Nancy, who had never looked at Nosey Ruslin from this angle, was at once struck by its truth and accuracy. Nosey had always been so friendly with herself and other girls that somehow it had seemed his popularity was due to an amorous nature, but now that she had had her eyes opened she saw that for all his geniality, generosity and fondness of the society of her sex he never had an affair with any of them.

"I believe you're right," she exclaimed, carried away by the discovery. "I suppose that's why I've always felt safe with Nosey and why all of us girls treat him as a father."

"Of course." The inspector smiled again. "And that's why it's not easy to find out anything about him that he doesn't choose to tell himself. Now if only he had a wife or a—"

A sudden return of terror and of fear of this placid, homely-looking man, whose smiling confidence presaged dreadful possibilities to her, infected Nancy with a hysterical anxiety to rush from his presence.

"I—I must be off," she said, rising. "I'm dancing at the 'Frozen Fang'—"

"The 'Frozen Fang' is closed for a week," he said calmly and without any challenge or note of triumph. "For repairs, the proprietor says."

"I meant rehearsal," she gasped.

"Oh, that's different." He stood up to do the courtesies of farewell. "I hope the rehearsal will be a success."

Was he laughing at her or trying to entangle her still further? Before she could decide whether it would be too risky to retort after the manner of the school which had been her first environment he diverted her thoughts by an unexpected reference to Nosey Ruslin.

"Should you happen to see Nosey Ruslin tonight you might—"

"I shan't be seeing him," she began, flustering in an effort to lend an appearance of courage to her timid anger.

"You are having supper with him," he said with the same quietness that hurt her more than a denunciation of her lie would have done. "Just mention to him, will you, that I'm calling early tomorrow. Nosey promised to help me all he could although he stands to lose if I get the murderer."

Bobbie, unable to interpret correctly the mysterious reference to a loss by his most recent friend, uttered an exclamation which he could not stifle, but the others took no notice of him, and for that he was thankful.

"Oh, all right," said Nancy, pettishly, "I'll give him your message, but it's something new to me to hear of Nosey turning a bloom—"She stopped, looked embarrassed, and then, after the manner of her kind laughed a shrill apology. "I mean to say, it's queer—" she hesitated again.

Chief Inspector Wake gallantly came to her rescue.

"You won't have much time for that rehearsal," he reminded her, "and I expect Mr. Cheldon will want to escort you downstairs."

The lovers' eyes met in a simultaneous glance of inquiry, each reading into the drawing-room nonchalance of the detective a sinister meaning of an importance in proportion to the liveliness of their fears. The quicker-witted Nancy was the first to regain a semblance of self-control.

"Come along, Bobbie," she cried gaily, for the moment animated by Cockney wit and independence, "you can trust Inspector Wake with the family silver and he can't do a guy with the furniture."

She frowned at her lapse into the vulgar, but Bobbie was beside her now and there was no further opportunity for self-criticism. Her brain might not be of the highest quality but it was in good working order for a girl who had yet to celebrate her twentieth birthday.

"Bobbie," she said as they kissed on the landing, "Nosey." She paused when he made a gesture of annoyance. "It's no good doing that. You've got to play straight with Nosey."

"What do you know?" he gasped.

"Nothing. Nosey doesn't tell me anything. Only you're not to talk too much to Wake. He'll encourage you to chatter. That's what Nosey says. Good-bye. No, don't leave him alone for long. I know nothing—remember that. Nothing."

She ran to the top of the staircase and descended with something of the movements of one escaping from imminent danger.

"Good-bye," she called from the well below, but Bobbie did not hear her. He was worrying about Nosey's message and resentfully repeating his sense of disgust that this rather vulgar person should be trying to draw him into a partnership of conspiracy over the murder of his uncle.

In this mood he rejoined the detective and, still under the influence of a sense of superiority, lolled against the mantelpiece.

"I believe you have some information for me?" he asked with something of the affability of a politician and the dignity of a duke.

"Not information, Mr. Cheldon. I've come from Broadbridge Manor and what information I picked up there must be known to you."

"You'd probably be surprised to hear that there's very little I know about Broadbridge," he answered languidly. Languor suited him, and if only he could keep it up might prove his best defence.

"But you're the owner of the property now?" Chief Inspector Wake was content to sit and to make no attempt to assert himself. "You're the lord of Broadbridge Manor, thanks to the death of your uncle."

"I don't care for the word 'thanks'," said the youthful critic who prided himself on his sensitive ear. "An unfortunate accident, shall we term it, inspector?"

"Nosey Ruslin wouldn't call it unfortunate," Wake remarked with an assumption of ease and indifference which was a trifle too perfect to be convincing.

"The opinion of a person of his stamp," Bobbie said fussily.

"I know Nosey isn't your class, Mr. Cheldon, but he's proud of being your friend." He paused and gazed meditatively at his inseparable umbrella. "Perhaps he hopes to benefit by your accession to wealth. You never quite know what Nosey is thinking about. And that reminds me. Mr. Cheldon, didn't you assure me that Nosey was not acquainted with your uncle? If I remember right you said they'd never met and had never corresponded? You were most positive about it."

"And I'm equally positive now. Ruslin was more or less friendly with me. As Miss Curzon remarked he was kind to everybody and I was grateful to him for encouraging me when I was depressed."

"But you never introduced him to your uncle?"

"Excuse me laughing, inspector. Introduce Nosey Ruslin to my uncle! That would have been funny. I don't wish to speak ill of the dead, but Uncle Massy was England's Public Snob No. 1. He never associated with people he didn't consider his equals."

"He never wrote Nosey?"

The question was too direct and abrupt not to arouse suspicion, but Bobbie was not a comprehensive thinker and he founded his reply on his own narrow knowledge of the world and of men.

"Of course not. My late uncle was not fond of writing letters to anyone, and he certainly wouldn't have chosen Nosey as a correspondent."

"Then how can you account for the fact that on the ninth of April your uncle sent a parcel to Nosey at the 'Frozen Fang' and that for a special reason took the parcel himself to the post office to be registered?"

Chief Inspector Wake, who had no sense of the dramatic, stood up to emphasise the question which was an accusation.

"Good lord!" Bobbie exclaimed involuntarily, "I'd forgotten that."

"Forgotten what?" The fleshy face was thrust towards his own.

Bobbie tried to laugh lightly, groaned heavily instead, and flushed with an anger which the detective could trace to its origin without inflicting any strain on his brain.

"Forgotten what?" he repeated.

"Am I on trial?" Bobbie was floundering helplessly. He attempted to clutch at another straw. "What my uncle did is no concern of mine."

The inspector turned away to place his umbrella against the wall. He may also have desired from a sense of fairplay to allow his antagonist an opportunity for recovery.

"Look here, Mr. Cheldon," he said, without rancour or heat, "every little thing your uncle did concerns everybody who is in danger of being lugged into the ugly business of his murder."

"You don't suspect me?" came in a series of gasps.

"No, I don't, but what I do suspect is your motive for not being open and frank with me. It was a lie when you said Nosey never met your uncle."

"It was the absolute truth!"

"And the registered parcel containing what I suspect was a revolver?"

Bobbie's knees began to wobble and he took a seat with an exaggerated leisureliness which was not worth noting because it was too obvious.

"That you had better ask Ruslin about," he answered.

"I mean to, Mr. Cheldon." The inspector changed his tone. "I am your friend and I've been your friend although you mightn't care to admit it. Any other man would have clapped you and Nosey and one or two others into a cell before now."

"With the result that you'd be out of the force in a week," Bobbie found the courage to retort.

Chief Inspector Wake smiled gently.

"You're very young, Mr. Cheldon, and so you'll be surprised and perhaps disbelieving if I tell you that this year alone, and it's not half over yet, that's been said to me by at least twenty persons. Did you read of the trial of a James Carruthers for arson? A sensational affair. He was sent down for ten years. I see you did. Well, Jim—we're rather old acquaintances—guaranteed that I'd be kicked out of Scotland Yard when the country heard of the infamy of his arrest and of my blunder in imagining he had had anything to do with the city fires. Then there was young Mrs. Unwin." He smiled. "But that doesn't matter. I merely referred to them to convince you that almost daily I'm threatened with being kicked out of the force, as you put it." He moved slightly and his expression hardened. "Mr. Cheldon, you didn't murder your uncle."

Bobbie's lips moved but not a sound came to give articulation to the desire to say, "Thank you for nothing."

"You didn't murder your uncle," the inspector repeated, "but if you will only be candid you could help me a lot. Don't imagine it's a difficult case, for I don't. I'll have the man before the week passes, and then it won't be pleasant for those who are putting obstacles in my way."

"Is that a threat?" Bobbie was once more under the influence of ten thousand a year and Broadbridge Manor.

"That depends on your conscience, Mr. Cheldon," was the disturbing retort. "Come, be candid. Was it news when I told you just now that your uncle sent a registered parcel to Nosey Ruslin? You hesitate. That's the answer I wanted. Mr. Cheldon, what was in that parcel?"

"I—I refuse to answer. It wouldn't be fair to—to my uncle." He had nearly blurted out Nosey's name, and the last moment substitution of his uncle's was a stroke of genius, for you cannot cross-examine the dead.

"Oh, very well. You won't reply and so I must have a few words with my old friend, Nosey Ruslin." The heavy voice was heavier by a sneer. He reclaimed his umbrella, and to Bobbie's relief appeared to be intent on preparing to depart. "Oh, by the way, Mr. Cheldon, know much about Nosey? Anything of his past, eh?"

"I'm afraid not." The tone was patronising, but it was patronage of the absent and not of the present. "He introduced himself to me at the 'Frozen Fang' and I thought him a good sort. Free and easy, Bohemia and all that sort of thing."

"Did he attempt to borrow money?"

Bobbie's laughter was genuine.

"To be fair to Mr. Ruslin I must admit that I borrowed from him, or he insisted on lending me twenty-five pounds."

"Did he know you had no prospects of repaying unless you came into the family property?"

It was a silly question, and Bobbie very nearly said so, but another attack of nervousness silenced him.

"Nosey is generous, Mr. Cheldon, when he is in funds, but twenty-five pounds at a time when he's had to owe for his rent and couldn't pay his telephone account! I wonder—I wonder." He was eyeing Bobbie slyly. "Mr. Cheldon, Nosey has never been through our hands, but he's dangerous, very dangerous. Twice I thought I had him—once in connection with a murder and once for a cheque fraud—but he wriggled out. He is nearly the cleverest crook in London."

"Crook?" Bobbie breathed.

"Crooked and clever. He trades on his good nature and generosity, and uses men and women without scruple in his trade of crime. He's an organiser and not a doer; he hands the weapon to the stabber to do the dirty work for him. Mind you, I'm not saying he had anything to do with your uncle's murder—that is, I'm not saying it officially, for I've no proof that would satisfy an Old Bailey jury, but he's equal to murder by deputy. When your uncle was stabbed to the heart and—"

"For God's sake, don't," Bobbie cried, shuddering. "You've no right to torture me. You've admitted I'm innocent."

"But I haven't admitted that you've been lying to protect someone. Yes, lying, and lying deliberately. You're trying to protect Nosey Ruslin, and that means you believe he's behind the conspiracy that resulted in your uncle's death. Of course, he didn't do it—that isn't Nosey's line. He's the thinker, the planner, and by thinking and planning, Mr. Cheldon, he's brought you an income of ten thousand a year about twenty years before you'd have had it in the ordinary way. Isn't that it?"

"No, I swear it isn't. I know nothing about Ruslin. I hope never to see him again. I wish I'd never met him." The whine revealed to the full the weakness, indecision, supineness of the speaker.

"Someone's ringing and knocking," said Chief Inspector Wake, picking up his hat. "I'd better be going. It's late enough and I've plenty to do."

He remained in the doorway of the room as Bobbie went into the hall and ended the impatience of his visitor.

"Mr. Cheldon," said a voice that the inspector knew better than any other in all the expanse of London, "Italian Charlie's reached Florence."

Bobbie's state of mind involved slow thinking, and Ruslin's cryptic message sent his thoughts in the direction of the occasional "help." When, however, Chief Inspector Wake announced his presence with a cordial, "That you, Nosey?" he hastily substituted the Italian city and was angry and afraid.

Chapter Eleven

"Hello, inspector!" Nosey Ruslin was too astute to overdo it by adding to the cordiality of his tone an attempt at handshaking. "You're looking fine in spite of your troubles."

"Can't say the same of you, Nosey," was the genial response. "Seems to me you haven't had much sleep lately."

It was quite true, and the confident rogue visibly resented its exposure, for sleeplessness argued worry, and worry could be due to events arising out of the Piccadilly murder.

"Oh, I'm all right," he said, as sulkily as his super-optimistic temperament allowed.

"That's fine. Bit of luck seeing you, Nosey. I was going to look you up after you'd taken Miss Curzon to supper. Perhaps you'll let me walk back with you?"

Nosey Ruslin reverted to the roughness that denotes the bully.

"Why not do your business here?" he asked. "Mr. Cheldon won't object. He's a gentleman and—"

"It doesn't require detective ability to spot that, Nosey." The sly note of banter exasperated one of his hearers and upset the other.

"Come into the room—you may be disturbing my mother," said Bobbie in a whisper which was meant to be impressive.

Chief Inspector Wake placed his umbrella with meticulous care against the wall under an outsize picture of a herd of faded cows, and as carefully sat down, the only self-possessed person there.

"Perhaps, Nosey," he said, genially, "you want to have a word or two with Mr. Cheldon about this friend of yours, Abyssinian Charlie?"

He was laughing at them, and Chief Inspector Wake's laughter was never without a reason and a meaning.

"Italian Charlie," Nosey growled, compelled to come into the open. "A mutual acquaintance Mr. Cheldon was thinking of taking dancing lessons from."

"Then we can begin our little discussion, Nosey. We're all friendly here without being exactly friends, and I have a question or two that you might try and answer. Mr. Cheldon rather upset me by declaring that you had never met his uncle in his life."

"That wasn't a lie. I knew him only by sight and then not much."

"Did you ever write to him?" Nosey hesitated, and the inspector brought into play his powers of subtle suggestion. "That reminds me, I ought to warn you that you needn't answer any of my questions in case they tend to incriminate you and—"

"Incriminate me," exclaimed Nosey furious with fear. "How could they? Ask me what you like. Haven't I told you that I was willing to help you all I could?"

"Yes, of course. I'd nearly forgotten. But I was asking you just now if you had ever written to the late Massy Cheldon?"

"No." Nosey was struggling to regain his placidity. "I don't go in for writing letters and if I did I'd write only to my pals."

"Quite so. But did Mr. Massy Cheldon ever write to you?"

"Never, and that's a fact." The lie carried conviction.

"Did Mr. Massy Cheldon ever send you a registered parcel?"

Bobbie, watching Nosey Ruslin, could not detect the slightest change of expression or any other indication of unpleasant surprise.

"Yes. Some time in April he returned to me a revolver which I tried to sell him. I'd met Mr. Cheldon here"—he jerked a thumb in Bobbie's direction,—"and I thought it was a good chance to get rid of the weapon for which I hadn't a licence. So I asked Mr. Cheldon to take it with him to his uncle's house and try and do a deal."

"With the result that the uncle refused to buy it?"

"You know," said Nosey curtly.

"And Mr. Massy Cheldon was so anxious that you should receive your property intact that he made a parcel of it, took it himself to the local post office and registered it?"

"That's about the strength of it," said Nosey, humorously.

"It was too precious to entrust to his nephew to take back with him to London, Nosey?" The inspector's voice was too gentle to be genuine.

"That was his business—not mine." Nosey's verbal skill was astonishing, but the inspector at least knew that in the give and take of a contest of lying he was almost certain to be defeated.

"I can't ask him so I must ask you," he remarked, purposely ponderous and slow in order to discourage the speed of the other. "If Massy Cheldon returned the revolver direct to you he was unnecessarily particular, Nosey. I suppose you were surprised?"

"Clean knocked off my perch," said the ex-pugilist with an abandonment of caution which established his lapse into truthfulness.

"But there was no letter?"

"Why should there be? And if there was what would it have mattered?"

Chief Inspector Wake was cornered. Nosey had delivered one in his solar plexus, but he was only slightly winded.

"I wish you'd told me all this sooner," he said regretfully, but not with any reproach in his voice.

"As it had nothing to do with the murder or with you I didn't," was the swift reply. "I never met Massy Cheldon and had he lived to a hundred I never would and that's a fact."

"Still, Nosey, you must admit it was rather queer."

"What was queer?" The large face was hardening into a sinister and threatening aspect which became more evident to Bobbie when he noticed the clenched fists moving.

"Your sending that revolver to a man you didn't know. Why should the late Massy Cheldon want to buy a revolver? His life wasn't in danger." Only Bobbie moved. "And I expect he had firearms of his own."

"Plenty," said Bobbie, glad of an opportunity to speak. "But Mr. Ruslin wanted to be rid of the revolver and I was spending the weekend at Broadbridge Manor."

"It all fits in perfectly," said the inspector.

Nosey Ruslin smiled reassuringly to Bobbie, conscious that he had scored heavily and all along the line.

"Anything more, inspector?"

"Not at the moment." Wake rose and attached himself to his property. "Where is Billy Bright?" he asked suddenly.

"I don't know," Nosey barked back, taken unawares.

"Now, now, Nosey," said the inspector, playfully reproachful. "You really mustn't tell fibs. You know quite well that Billy the Dancer is at Margate, for you walked with him to the station, and there was no reason why you shouldn't have seen him off."

"You asked me where he was and I don't know his address," said the ex-pugilist calmly. "It wouldn't have helped you if I'd mentioned Margate. But if you know so much why not answer your own question?"

Chief Inspector Wake nodded.

"I'm lazy, Nosey, very lazy, and I'm fond of letting people think and act for me. I'll get Billy whenever I really want him. At present I don't believe he'd be of much use."

"None at all," said Nosey promptly, "but of course, you'll please yourself. I've no use for Billy. Simply because he met Massy Cheldon here he's been upset by the affair in the Underground. A nervous, thin-skinned chap who's frightened by a peeler's uniform, but that's the worst of not being an Englishman."

"Conscience makes cowards of us all," the inspector quoted from a repertory strictly limited through force of circumstances. "I hope Billy is enjoying the sea air. I wish I could have a holiday, but I can't even think of one until I've landed the murderer of Massy Cheldon."

"And when you do you'll have earned it."

The inspector glanced at him casually.

"That's true, Nosey, very true. How many days have I left? Five? Good." He brushed his bowler with his sleeve. "I'm always relieved when the end of the chase comes, but sometimes I wish the Underground murder was a little more difficult. There'll be no credit for me when I solve it. It's only hard work and nothing more."

Nosey Ruslin smiled again at Bobbie.

"I wish you luck, inspector. Pity for your sake there isn't a thumping reward."

"Such as ten thousand a year?"

Nosey's grin faded into nothingness.

"You'd be rich then!" he said, unable to think of anything less stupid and less banal at a moment when his thoughts were too dangerous for expression.

"But the police are not allowed to accept rewards," said the inspector cheerfully. "We work for small wages and the love of it. But I must run away. Got a lot to do, Nosey, and hundreds of reports to read. That's an attractive young friend of yours, Mr. Cheldon."

"Eh?" exclaimed Bobbie from out of the depths of a reverie.

"Miss Sylvia Brand," the inspector explained. "I took a statement from her last night. Far more sense in her pretty head than Mrs. Carmichael or Mrs. Elmers, and as for Miss Kitty—"

"Good lord, you don't mean to say you've been at all of them?"

"Every little helps." Really, Chief Inspector Wake was too human to be genuine! Nosey thought that as with the meagre and gaunt resources of his mind he attempted to pierce the armour of cheerfulness and good humour. "Miss Brand was most helpful. Her description of Billy Bright produced the biggest laugh the chief inspectors' room at the Yard has heard for twenty years." He went to the door and opened it. "Oh, I say, Nosey, don't you join Billy the Dancer at Margate. I may want to see you again, and I can't afford the time for travelling."

"Good old London is my happy home," Nosey sang croakingly. "You can have your Margate, your Paris and your Rome."

"Thanks," said Chief Inspector Wake, and when the door shut him out it also shut out all the cheerfulness and good humour.

The two men remained as lifeless as statues until the closing of a second door convinced Bobbie that they were really rid of the detective. But Nosey Ruslin was not as easily satisfied, and he crept out on tip-toe and returned to report safety before speaking.

"What do you think of it?" he asked in a conspiratorial whisper which sent a chill of fear through Bobbie's frame and left as an aftermath a feeling of anger at the familiarity and the assumption of this plebeian, this non-member of the house of Cheldon.

"Think of what?" he demanded testily.

Nosey nodded in the direction they could assume the inspector had taken.

"You heard him?" A friendly tap on the arm. "Me and you've got to be slick. He's dangerous when he's in that mood."

"I'm not afraid of him," said Bobbie, trying to infuse into his voice the authority of superior rank and wealth.

"Neither am I." Nosey winked expressively. "That was a little dodge of mine, as you guessed first time."

"What little dodge? I don't understand."

His companion winked.

"About Italian Charlie being in Florence."

The younger man started.

"He must have heard it," he gasped, and could have kicked himself for departing from his attitude of lofty and dignified contempt for the vulgar society to which Fate had unkindly consigned him.

"He was meant to hear it." The grin changed to a frown. "I wonder why he didn't show surprise. Never once referred to it. Bluff, eh?" The appeal to immaturity had a pathos of its own.

"A man of the Wake type always bluffs," said Bobbie, trying not to blink as he spoke. "But, Mr. Ruslin, you are unnecessarily concerned about the movements and notions of Inspector Wake. It may interest you to hear that he admitted to me that if I proved an alibi with your aid you proved an alibi with mine."

"Oh, did he? Well, that's the sort of thing Wideawake would say." The frown deepened into brooding fear. "Wake's most dangerous when most talkative—and he's been talking a lot."

"But how can he be dangerous to you or me, Mr. Ruslin?" Bobbie as he spoke was surveying his flannel trousers and thinking to himself that the cut was extremely poor, worse, in fact, than the ravages time had inflicted on them.

"Don't ask silly questions, me lad, or I'll lose me hair," was the totally unexpected answer.

The heavy jowl was thrust forward, the bleary eyes distended to their utmost limit, and the large simian lips revealed the aimless ferocity of the savage. Bobbie was having a glimpse of the Nosey Ruslin who had been the terror of the East End ring until drink and the devil had done their work and reduced him to the ranks of the cadgers from which his wits had in the nick of time rescued him.

"Don't ask silly questions, me lad," Nosey repeated sullenly. "We're alone, you and me, ain't we?"

Physical fear beset Bobbie and the sensation produced a feeling of nausea. He had never come so closely in contact with the primeval brutality of the human brute Nosey Ruslin represented, and he was afraid. He thought he saw murder in the red eyes and protuberant lips, murder more horrible than that which had ended the life of his uncle.

"Why don't you talk? Must I do all the shoutin'?" Nosey inquired. He looked back at the door. "Someone here?"

"Only my mother," said Bobbie in a faint voice.

"Your mother? That won't do. Look here, Mr. Bobbie Cheldon, of the Manor, Sussex, the whole blooming world, you and me's got to hammer things out right now."

"I'm afraid it's rather late. We'll be dining—mother."

"Just you tell the lady mother you're dining with me," said Nosey, in a threatening whisper. "You needn't say we're going into conference to save our bloomin' necks, but Wake is dangerous and I'll not carry you any longer. You must help me to hold up our corner. I tell you, Mr. Millionaire Cheldon, it's getting on my nerves, and I won't be alone any longer. Wake's watching me day and night." He laughed because he did not wish to swear. "I'll be waitin' for you outside. Don't be long."

Nosey the amiable, the tolerant and the philosopher, had gone berserk and did not know it, but ever since the murder of Massy Cheldon he had been in a state of fiery nervousness all the more excruciating because he had been afraid to relieve it by an explosion of temper even when alone. That had been a strain which had threatened to break his spirit, for Nosey was gregarious and his own society disturbed him.

He was muttering to himself when Bobbie, white of face and scared of expression, joined him on the littered pavement.

"Where are we going?" he asked, forcing into his voice a strength which had left his body entirely.

"Got the price of a taxi to my flat?" Nosey said curtly. "Right-ho." Nothing further was said until they were being driven towards the West End, but Bobbie's brain was thronged with questions and self-criticisms. Why had he not exerted himself and put this common person in his place? Why had he been such a fool as to be afraid of him? Why had he been afraid at all? He squirmed when he admitted that all these questions could only be answered in one way.

He was afraid of Nosey Ruslin, afraid of the gangster roughness and mercilessness of the ex-pugilist, but behind that fear was another and a more pregnant one, a more than faint suspicion that Nosey's sudden change from good temper to ferocity and his own tame surrender were based alike on the tragedy of his uncle's unexpected passing.

Chief Inspector Wake had hinted that there was more than mere coincidence in the timely death of the tenant for life of the Cheldon estate, that the heir had not owed his quick succession to mere luck and that, therefore, the murder of Massy Cheldon was the logical outcome of a cleverly planned conspiracy. Chief Inspector Wake had said all that and more in matter of fact, commonplace words and without any melodramatic display. Now as Bobbie tried to account for Nosey Ruslin's revelation of his ugly soul the only explanation that obtruded was that they were in some queer and inexplicable manner partners.

He began to perspire as recollections of stray words and sentences occurred to him. In the light of the tragedy in the Piccadilly Underground much that had been apparently ordinary and meaningless now became extraordinary and suggestive, even threatening. He wished he could laugh at a mental picture of the scene in his uncle's bedroom at Broadbridge Manor, but with Nosey Ruslin staring tight-lipped into vacancy it was impossible to see the humorous side of anything.

In silence they ascended to the second floor of the dilapidated block of flats and Bobbie, feeling that when the faded and paintless door opened to his companion's key he would be placed in a cell, had a fresh source of satisfaction in the recollection that he was now rich enough to forget that poverty of any sort existed.

"Nearly eight," said Nosey, picking up a cheap clock and shaking it. "Have to meet Nancy at half-past. But we can do a lot in half an hour, Mr. Cheldon. Sit down."

The voice was more conciliatory and the manner almost mild. Nosey wiped his forehead.

"'Fraid I was a bit off my head just now," he said, apologetically, "but Wake has got me guessing and my nerves ain't improving."

"Oh, that's all right, Mr. Ruslin," said Bobbie, too relieved at the return to what he thought was the normal Nosey to remember his worries. "It's rotten to be mixed up in—in—"

Nosey Ruslin stared at him.

"We're both mixed up in it," he said, grimly.

"Do you mean me?" Bobbie gasped.

"I mean you and me—that's the trouble." Nosey was actually smiling.

His guest did not express his astonishment and dare not reveal the full extent of his resentment.

"Look here, Mr. Cheldon, if I've been a bit too ready with the rough stuff just try and forget it. The position's too serious for us to quarrel. I knew Wake would be with you when I called. He's not the only person who has watchers." He chuckled without disturbing the gravity of his face. "But that was a jolt he gave us over the parcel," he added, gloomily. "That's the worst of Wake, you never know exactly what he's up to. Keeps you guessing all the time by telling you everything or pretending to. He's famous for it. But I never thought he'd find out about the revolver."

Bobbie's nervous horror was pitiful.

"Still, it's lucky he can't find out about the letter."

"Did uncle write to you?" Bobbie whispered.

"You bet he did, and the sort of letter I'd have expected if I'd known him, I daresay."

"Might I see it?" The voice was painful to hear. Nosey shook his head.

"It's not on the premises—'twould be too dangerous with that devil Wake on the prowl. I've hidden it along with one or two bits of paper from yourself. But Wake knows about the parcel and although I think I did a little expert lying he may worry us about it. Now, Mr. Cheldon, that's why I insisted on your coming here. We must have a plan, an agreement for the present and the future."

"You must tell me more, Mr. Ruslin," said his guest weakly. "Every time I try to think my brain seems to catch fire."

"I know that feeling," said Nosey sympathetically. "But we've got to defend ourselves, Mr. Cheldon, we've got to prepare for danger ahead. I'm not afraid on my own account—the busies will never hand me the bracelets—but there's yourself, a county gentleman with a large fortune. You don't want to be mixed up in no scandal."

He might have been reading Bobbie's thoughts.

"But preparing costs money," Nosey continued in a tone a shade lower, "and I want to be sure where I stand. I'm willing to foot the bill until you are handling the stuff."

The stare from his companion was one of blank surprise, but there were no words of protest or of disagreement.

"So far I've done all the paying out." The simian lips were twisting into all sorts of misshapen repulsiveness. "I didn't get that job done for nothing." He appeared to be glancing at the beer-stained engraving over the dusty sideboard depicting the Sayers-Heenan fight, but the red eyes were on the alert to note and record every change of expression. Nosey had rehearsed in a crude way the scene which he was not acting now, but in despair had been compelled to trust to luck and whatever inspiration the encounter with Bobbie Cheldon might bring. If luck and inspiration failed then he would have to be the truculent bully and undisguised blackmailer as well as the coward prepared to sell his allies to ensure his own safety.

"What job?" The question uttered in a dry, hard whisper, took Nosey by surprise and deleted from his tongue the words which he had carefully and cunningly composed with the object of bringing the critical moment appreciably nearer.

"No need to tell *you*," said Nosey cheerfully. "But you can take it from me as you did from Wake that if you'd waited for chance to get you ten thousand a year you'd have had to wait until you were an old man. See?" The soul as well as the body of Bobbie Cheldon sickened.

"Mind you, Mr. Cheldon," said the human gorilla, smiling through the hideousness of his habitual expression, "I was careful to keep you out of it. You're a gentleman and you're delicate and refined. Nosey Ruslin is the other way about and isn't ashamed to say so. Earned my own living when I was ten and had a fortune before I was twenty-one. So when I began to think over the wickedness of your uncle keeping you and your lady mother—"

Bobbie sprang to his feet, and in his rage tried to grapple with the air.

"Don't bring her into it," he shouted, in a paroxysm of helpless rage.

"Sit down," said Nosey, pushing him into his chair. "I apologise. A gentleman can do no more. Well, as I was saying, when I decided that it was time a clever young gentleman such as you are had the money which ought to have been his years ago I did some quiet thinking. I had that letter from your uncle hinting that you'd been trying to make him acquainted with the business end of my revolver and there was the little note signed by yourself giving me permission to polish the old man off." He rubbed his hands in company with a moment or two of happy reflection. "I'll not try and fool you, Mr. Cheldon, by saying that I didn't expect to scrape a few quids out of it for poor little me." He grinned and as the grin faded into a leer he took a position astride of a rickety chair facing Bobbie's. "There's nothing more for me to say. You've inherited ten thousand a year, and I've old Wideawake on me hands." He shrugged his shoulders.

Had Bobbie been older and wiser he might have been able to deal with a situation his imagination could never have prepared him for, but in his youthful ignorance and nervous condition when he did attempt speech his cheeks twitched and his lips moved noiselessly. He knew it was blackmail, and also knew that he must pay although no one could prove that he had murdered his uncle.

"Who—who did it?" he gasped, two lengthy minutes later.

Nosey Ruslin smiled with his teeth.

"Don't ask dangerous questions, Mr. Cheldon," he advised him seriously. "Wake will be hanging round you again and if you knew you'd only give yourself away."

"But you said I was here to prepare our defence against Wake?" he stammered.

"That's the little game. I was afraid you were under the impression that you'd nothing to do with my worries," said Nosey pleasantly, "and I was getting nervous about Wake's visits to you. The old fox has a way of persuading those who don't know him as I do to talk about dangerous things." He smiled again. "Wake wants to bring you on to his side."

"That's impossible," exclaimed Bobbie.

"It is, now that you know the exact position. Mr. Cheldon, I'll not keep any secrets from you. I know the man who murdered your uncle." Bobbie started with the whole momentum of his body. "Because I wanted to do you a good turn I did all I could to make it impossible for Wake or any of his pals to charge you with complicity. My pal and me have shared all the risks, and so you have ten thousand a year." The repetition of the income of the Cheldon estate which Bobbie himself had so often mentioned in the hearing of Nosey and Nancy had a special fascination for the ex-pugilist and he gave it the honour of a special intonation.

"You have ten thousand a year because your uncle was outed." Nosey tapped him on the knee. "I look to you to help us to leave Wake guessing for the rest of his life and also—"

"Yes?" Bobbie croaked.

"Well, what about it? Do you suppose my pal risked his neck—is risking it now—for nothing? Haven't I had to pay him a bit on account?"

"How much?" The words cost the speaker a real effort.

"A hundred quid," lied Nosey valiantly.

"I shall make it my business to pay you, Mr. Ruslin, the moment I am in possession of the estate," said Bobbie importantly. "You'll not find the interest small either."

There was something of his uncle in his tone and manner, but Bobbie and his companion were not to be bothered by comparisons.

"Thank you." The heavy sarcasm was a threat. "I'm not annoyed, Mr. Cheldon, only amused." The absence of amusement from the foxy eyes stamped the words with a meaning that even Bobbie in his most obtusive mood could not fail to appreciate at its full value.

"How much?" The curtness was unintentional, for Bobbie could not think or speak clearly in his chaotic condition.

"Ten thousand quid—one year's income—and cheap at the price." Nosey, determined to prove how confident and self-controlled he was, went to the sideboard in search of a liquid, but the sideboard was bare inside and out.

"And if I refuse?"

"You won't, Mr. Cheldon," said the pleasant voice from the other side of the tremendous head. "The master of Broadbridge Manor would rather pay fifty thousand quid than stand in the dock of the Old Bailey alongside of his friend, Nosey Ruslin, and—and the other chap."

"So it's come to blackmail, has it?" Bobbie was slowly working himself up into a rage, although fully aware how useless rage would be.

"That's not a friendly remark, Mr. Cheldon. A few days ago you were an underpaid city clerk and Nancy was thinking of throwing you over. Now you're rich and you've a great future. There's no detective looking on you as the villain of the piece. You're Wake's blue-eyed boy even if he does bother you a bit, but he doesn't suspect you and never will unless—"

"Yes—unless?"

Nosey made a face.

"I was thinking of the revolver and the letter from your uncle. I've a copy of it here which you can have for keeps." He took out his pocket-book and extracted a sheet of notepaper. "Never was much good at writing," he explained as he handed it to Bobbie.

> "*I am returning the revolver you lent my nephew and in doing so may I be permitted to point out that to entrust a deadly weapon to a young man on a visit to an uncle whose corpse is worth ten thousand a year to him is to subject him to severe temptation. He yielded to that temptation last night, but the Cheldon motto is 'Courage and Loyalty', and I proved that I lived up to the first part at any rate.*
> "*May I suggest that you look after your armoury yourself?*"

Bobbie read it aloud slowly, Nosey listening with an unctuous smile after the manner of an author conscious of the merits of his masterpiece.

"That's good enough, isn't it?" he asked gently.

"The fool!" he muttered, oblivious of time and place.

He started as a hand touched his back.

"We could talk a lot, couldn't we, but what would be the use? You can't afford to call me names, and it wouldn't be playing the game if you did. I always fought fairly when in the ring, and if I've got you ten thousand a year you ought to be grateful. Look on it as a bit of business and you'll feel happier. I'll keep you out of Wake's clutches. He was a bit sniffy about you, Mr. Cheldon, at the beginning, but I proved your alibi. But then they always suspect the chap who makes money out of a murder, and they're often right. Now be sensible and act sensibly. You're rich. Why? Well, because of a little arrangement by me. Supposing I hadn't done nothing about it? Your uncle would have lived another ten years at least. If it will suit your book better, say, five. Five tens come to fifty thousand quid, and all I want is ten thousand. Your pal Nosey has put fifty thousand, perhaps a hundred thousand in your pocket, and his fee is one tenth. I don't call that unreasonable."

"But how could I pay such a sum? The Cheldon estate will probably bring in less after the death duties have been paid. It would have to be done in instalments." Bobbie marvelled at his detachment from the tragic horror of the situation, but he was incapable of understanding that he was actually defending himself from it.

"Give me an IOU," said Nosey, carelessly. "You can redeem it when it suits your convenience."

"And uncle's letter and mine?" There was a quaver in his voice.

"They'll be handed over with the IOU when the cash is paid and old Wideawake is growing roses in his retirement." Nosey's utter absence of nerves was convincing, and Bobbie became infected by his air of quiet, businesslike confidence.

"All right. Show me what to do. And when I have signed it what then?"

"You can go home and forget all about the London end of the Cheldon affair," said Nosey, not answering the question until he was in the act of placing with reverent ceremony the precious document in his pocket-book. "You can do the squire act at the family mansion and forget Nosey Ruslin and anyone else you want to forget." He looked at him sideways.

Bobbie, half consciously under the influence of the idea that he had settled his debt, took up the remnants of his superiority.

"I will leave London for Broadbridge immediately," he said, lolling in his chair. "I'll not allow myself to be bothered further by anyone."

"The right spirit," said Nosey cordially. "Show Wake the door if he calls. It's the only way to deal with him. Refer him to your solicitor."

The name had an unhappy effect on Bobbie.

"He must never know anything of our arrangement," he said, nervous again. "Either now or in the future. If there is no arrest they will keep the case open for months."

"I had thought of that, and you needn't worry. I'll not pay you a visit at your grand palace, Mr. Cheldon. There's a post-box in every town and village and we can settle our business without anyone being the wiser—unless you want them to be wise."

Bobbie turned away from him with a shiver of disgust. The revolting callousness of his confederate infuriated him, but he was in chains and could do nothing. There was his mother to consider. And his own reputation. He was sure he would be popular at Broadbridge. There were many reforms he would institute at once by way of penance and reparation.

"I wish the papers would stop writing about the case," he said suddenly.

"Oh, they don't rob me of my beauty sleep," Nosey answered readily. "It's Wake who's been on my nerves. He very nearly drove me into a corner where he could have given me one under the chin. I was for leaving London and avoiding my favourite little spots, but I guessed in time the crafty old devil's dodge."

Bobbie walked to the door, expecting Nosey to accompany him, and when the ex-pugilist kept his feet implanted by the sideboard he paused and turned round. Something of the cheerfulness and satisfaction that beamed from the little eyes and the huge cheeks encouraged him to make another attempt to banish his torturing curiosity, for Nosey was obviously in the best of humours.

"Mr. Ruslin, now that I've proved my willingness to treat you generously, won't you tell me who murdered my uncle?" It was symptomatic of his complete surrender that he should see or feel nothing of his cold-blooded detachment from emotion of any kind.

Nosey smiled from ear to ear and from forehead to chin.

"That's a fair question, and before I answer it, will you have a shot at a guess? Who did it, do you think?"

The younger man did not hesitate.

"The fellow you call Italian Charlie," he hazarded.

Nosey's grin became etched into his countenance.

"Italian Charlie was a blind. I always have a blind in a job of work of this kind. For the actual job I try and get the one man the police are least likely to suspect. Of course, I am careful to provide myself with an alibi. That's why I had you to a late, very late dinner on Monday night. No, it wasn't Italian Charlie and never could have been. My business with him was over short weight in cash, a 'fence' in North London gave him. Nothing more. Guess again."

"I can't. There were fellows I've seen in the 'Frozen Fang' who looked equal to cutting any number of throats." Suddenly surprised at the note of flippancy in the only voice he could hear, Bobbie flushed with shame. "I mean I never knew their names," he added, lamely.

"That proves how cleverly I've managed it, and with this little scrap of paper and your letters." How he grinned! "Well, I don't mind putting you wise, Mr. Cheldon. Fact is, you've got to be told." He approached and lowered his voice to the faintest of whispers. "The man who did the knife act on Monday night and put you into a mansion with ten thousand of the best a year was—" the voice was almost inarticulate—"Billy the Dancer—Billy Bright." He slapped him on the back. "Now you know, my boy."

Bobbie's surprise was almost paralysing in its effect. His first effort was to express his disbelief in one blinding phrase of vitriolic contempt, but his faculties refused to function; his next, to give his informant a knowing look as of appreciation of his fantastic humour, and his third, an angry gesture of repudiation of the other's obvious attempt to classify him amongst the most credulous of idiots. But all he could do was to stare vacantly as he wrestled with his conflicting thoughts, while a panorama of the immediate past brought into a jumbled review the persons and places which had become known to him since that night of nights when he had been introduced to Nancy Curzon at the 'Frozen Fang'.

"Never guessed that, eh?" said the husky voice of Nosey Ruslin, "and neither won't old Wideawake. Them Scotland Yard know-alls make a habit of suspecting everybody from the start so that if by chance they get the right man they can boast they spotted him at once. Wake suspects me and you and Italian Charlie and lots of others he's seen me with. He may even be pretending to see the blood on Billy's shirt front, but he isn't thinking of him. That's the way to do a job, Mr. Cheldon, and it's the reason why Nosey Ruslin has the cleanest record in London considering all things."

It was all of a piece with the Cheldon character that Bobbie should in that moment experience a spasm of pleasure at the reminder that in all his moods, good and bad, Nosey never forgot to address him formally. The illiterate ex-pugilist might be familiar now and then, but it was always "Mr. Cheldon". There was comfort in that.

"Billy Bright," he murmured, speaking with an effort. "A nervous wreck without the courage of a mouse."

"Exactly." It was a favourite word of Nosey's. "Exactly." He looked sly and unfathomable. "And the beauty of it is that Billy himself didn't know until the day that he was to do it. I led him up the garden path beautifully and do you know what the carrot was I held in front of his nose, Mr. Cheldon." He rubbed his hands, a sure sign of enjoyment.

Bobbie did not attempt to guess.

"A half share in ten thousand quids," was the startling answer.

"I thought he didn't know—?" Bobbie gasped.

"He knows nothing except what I've told him. He knows less than Wake does about the revolver, in fact he's never heard about it at all. And there's something more." He paused impressively, or with the intention of being impressive. "From first to last he's understood that my little business was being done without your knowledge. I assured him that it would be a waste of time to try and bring a gentleman like you into it."

"But he's keen on Nancy," Bobbie objected, his voice utterly without feeling because of the relief which Nosey's assurance had bred.

"Of course, he is, and would marry her tomorrow if he had the chance." Nosey Ruslin never lied unless a lie promised a dividend, and now he was sharp and cunning enough to realise that the truth would be profitable. "Yes, he's crazy about Nancy, and you and I shouldn't be surprised, Mr. Cheldon. She's one in a million. I'd be crazy about her too if I were twenty years younger. But that doesn't matter. The important point is that Billy prefers hard cash to matrimony, that is, if there is plenty of the cash. He's heavily in debt and there's a bit of trouble with an Italian cousin of his over a cheque—"

"Is Billy Bright an Italian then?" Bobbie exclaimed, a great light beginning to dawn.

"Father from Naples and mother from Athens," Nosey imparted with the succinctness of a one-volume encyclopæ-dia. "The old man was deported years ago by old Wideawake's efforts."

"That accounts for a lot," said Bobbie to himself.

"I should think so. But, as I was saying, Mr. Cheldon, Billy isn't as big a fool as we think he is. He wants money and Nancy, but seeing as how he can't get neither in one hand he prefers the money. That little cheque is threatening to land him in quod."

"Forgery, I suppose?"

"Forged endorsement is what they call it. Billy came to me shaking like a jelly, and it was me who got the Italian cousin to stay his hand for a month, but I had to promise him fifty per cent on the money owing, thirty-three pound ten."

"Doesn't sound much."

"It's a million when you haven't got it," said Nosey feelingly. "But it's not all that Billy owes. He's up against it, or was until he saw daylight and agreed to imitate his Italian ancestors. Nervous bloke, Billy, but when properly worked up can be a regular little demon." Nosey's laughter shattered Bobbie's daydream. When reality became overwhelming he usually had recourse to unreality.

"Anyhow, there's the posish," said Nosey with an air of finality. "I've told you everything so that you can be on your guard. If you see Wake again do none of the talking. Leave that to him. And be prepared for anything, Mr. Cheldon. But if you'll take my advice you'll forget as much as you can, though that won't be easy."

Bobbie laughed sarcastically.

"I can think of nothing else," he said, peevishly.

"But what about your estate and Nancy and your marriage and—and living like a lord?" Nosey's catalogue of earthly joys ended abruptly, for his own was confined to money and eating. "Be prepared for anything," he repeated earnestly, "anything. Now supposing for example I'm arrested?"

Bobbie started with fear for himself.

"You'll get the jumps, but you must keep your hair on. I'll not split, Mr. Cheldon, not even with the hangman telling me it's a fine morning and the warders asking me to choose the menu for breakfast." He laughed the laugh of confidence. "You've kept your part of the bargain and I'll keep mine. And mine is to keep your name out of it."

"Thank you, Mr. Ruslin," said Bobbie, after a pause.

"That's right." The heavy hand was extended.

"And now you'll be wanting to see Nancy, Mr. Cheldon, and she'll be wanting to see you. But don't forget that you've nothing to do now with our little business. You're rich and out of danger. Forget your uncle and forget me until I call for a little cheque. Good-bye."

Chapter Twelve

Chief Inspector Wake sat at his desk listlessly glancing at the latest batch of reports from his subordinates. When he had gleaned a little more than nothing from them he picked up the first of the letters, anonymous and otherwise, which had accumulated during the preceding twenty-four hours. They were all of a familiar type. Eleven contained signed confessions of the murder of Massy Cheldon; twenty-nine named the murderer; eight were devoted to explaining the case against capital punishment; fourteen offered "shrewd guesses"—that was the invariable phrase— as to the identity of the criminal, and sixteen, the majority dated from Service clubs in Pall Mall and neighbourhood, crisply emphasised the more obvious defects of Scotland Yard and its "incompetent underlings," as one of the most virulent of the critics expressed it.

"I suppose these have been looked into?" he said to Detective-Sergeant Clarke, who was standing over him.

"Yes, sir." The question could have reference only to the confessions. "With the exception of one they are all border-line cases."

"And the one?"

"An out of work actor in Brixton who admitted to me that he hoped that after he had been acquitted the film companies would clamour for his services." The sergeant smiled. "He was really surprised when I told him that I didn't intend to arrest him."

The inspector flung the letter which happened to be in his hand across the desk and pushed back his chair.

"Waste of time, Clarke, waste of time, and our time is very precious. Four days since the murder and nothing but suspicion."

"But promising suspicion, sir. You've narrowed the field down considerably. I'm nearly confident."

"That's comforting—coming from you," said Wake gravely. "But, of course, I'm not depressed. Who could be with such a clue as Nosey Ruslin? A big fat, juicy clue." He stood up. "I'll have him, Clarke, but in my own good time and way. The chief rather hinted that he ought to be taken in at once if I really believed what I told him, but that wouldn't do. I wish, though, I could have been present at that con-conference between him and young Cheldon last night."

Detective-Sergeant Clarke became grimmer of expression.

"I'd prefer to know exactly what young Cheldon has to do with his uncle's murder," he said.

"Nothing and yet a lot, Clarke. That's my opinion. Young Cheldon isn't a murderer or a crook of any sort. Of course, he's weak. What could you expect? Brought up by a doting mother and encouraged to be a loafer until the Piccadilly Underground murder gave him a fortune."

"Took him from an office in the city to a mansion in the country, sir. Is there a link between the two? Isn't it probable that it is a case of cause and effect—temptation and—"

The inspector ended the excursion into hypothesis with an impatient gesture. The art of detection was in his opinion chiefly one of acting and thinking. Talking played a small part in it.

"Nosey may be using him, Clarke, as he's used half his friends and acquaintances. You remember the pearl robbery at Norwood and the theft of banknotes at Cricklewood? We know Nosey was in both, but we never got him. Nosey is all secrets so he lives openly and appears to have no secrets at all. He does all his business in restaurants and he parades Piccadilly with jewel thieves and confidence tricksters as though he had nothing to fear. That's the genius of the man—he makes no pretence to genius, but he's got something of it. I wish he would do a bit of bad acting now and then, particularly now."

He turned to the desk and from a pigeon-hole took a half sheet of paper.

"Billy Bright, Nancy Curzon, Italian Charlie, Fred Frescoli, Larry O'Brien, Cora Beamish." He recited the remainder of eleven names to himself before replacing the record. "All pals of Nosey's and all seen with him within a week of the murder."

"I wish we could get a line between Nosey and Massy Cheldon," said Clarke, reviving an old subject. "The registered parcel hasn't led us very far, sir, though I don't agree with you that it's worthless."

"Not worthless, Clarke, but unsatisfactory. It contained a weapon, as Nosey has admitted—if he wasn't lying—but it wasn't a dagger. The dagger is our principal clue."

"The only one, I'm thinking, sir."

"The only one with the exception of Nosey. I prefer human clues to any others. Nosey is on his guard and is pretending he isn't."

"Playing your own game, sir," said the sergeant with a smile.

"That's clever of him, but the trump cards are mine. Still, I was surprised Nosey thought I was capable of being tricked by his blurting out the news that Italian Charlie had got out of the country. He ought to have guessed that I'd be bound to know all about the Italian's movements. Charlie didn't do it, but if ever we want him we can bring him back. I don't believe in being fussy, Clarke."

"Don't I know it, sir."

"There are chaps here who would have arrested Italian Charlie or tried to prevent him leaving the country. That's not my method. I prefer to let the criminal classes agree with the opinion of the newspapers that we're an incompetent lot, and I want Nosey Ruslin to believe it, too. Pretend to let things slide. Be the plodding official regretting his entanglement in red tape. Ask questions and listen to long-winded lies with patience. Don't use the notebook and pencil too often. I've listened to regular speeches by Nosey and the others, and I don't think I've wasted all my time."

"But are we nearer an arrest, sir?"

"We are." The sharpness of the reply startled the phlegmatic sergeant into a prolonged stare. "I've completed my plans, Clarke. You and I will leave Nosey alone for the present and concentrate on Billy the Dancer."

The sergeant wisely refrained from expressing thoughts which might have been treated as mutinous and disrespectful criticism of his superior officer, but his chief went down somewhat in his estimation.

"I think I can guess what's worrying you, Clarke," said the inspector with a patient tolerance which presaged victory. "Billy as young Cheldon's rival in love wouldn't have risked his neck to make it certain that the girl would be carried off by the young heir."

"We have proof that Billy and Nancy Curzon were planning an elopement the day before the murder," Clarke reminded him. "Billy's so mad about her that he's spoilt his career on her account."

"He's heavily in debt, too."

"That wouldn't worry him. It was Nancy he wanted. They've been dancing partners for nearly eighteen months, but he's had to carry her. She's only ordinary—he's the goods. Old Adler, who runs Greville's, told me that he'd heard Nancy Curzon boasting of the well paid continental and American tour Billy had secured a contract for."

"Curious," Wake commented. "I haven't noticed any elation in Billy of late, and I saw him a dozen times before the murder."

"You forget, sir, he's naturally a gloomy sort of chap. It's only his eyes that can smile, and they don't try very often."

"A nervous, cowardly, spineless imitation of a man," said Wake, contemptuously. "I've met several of his kind, but they've all been engaged in the White Slave traffic. Two whiskies and he's drunk."

"One of the reports mentions that he isn't drinking anything now—not since the murder," said the sergeant carelessly.

"I have that report in my pocket-book. Ah, I thought you'd be surprised, Clarke, but it interested me. The difficulty is to find the links that connect Nosey Ruslin with Billy the Dancer, young Cheldon and a few others who are on the suspicion list. So far Billy has kept clear even if he has gone for a holiday."

"He'll be back in Soho soon," Clarke prophesied. "He can't breathe the air properly anywhere else."

"While I'm here I'll go through the statements from persons who were present at the murder and didn't know it," said Wake acidly. He was never patient or tolerant of the unobservant, and that about a thousand persons should have been the unseeing chorus of a tragedy exasperated him.

"We have ninety-five, sir. I've read them so often that I know most of them by heart. But they're all worthless except that elderly woman in Harrow who says she heard a woman scream."

"Yes, that struck me as peculiar. Why didn't any of the others mention it? Yes, yes, I know some did but not until after we had asked them about it. Could the woman have imagined it?"

"Eleven statements contain references to the scream, sir," Clarke reminded him. "Second statement in each case, I know, but I can't imagine why they should lie. They had no reason or cause not to speak the truth. Then more than one of them explained that the shock caused by the discovery of the murder banished everything from their minds."

"The woman who screamed," said Wake, thoughtfully. "If only we could find her, Clarke."

"I'm not so interested in her, sir. If you remember it's been established that she was near the moving stairway and in such a position that she could not have seen Massy Cheldon or the man who attacked him. We have tested and proved that twice."

"Quite so. That's why I'm anxious to meet the woman who screamed—or I ought to say, the woman who screamed first. There were plenty of other screams a minute or so later."

"Unless she comes forward, sir, and—"

"She won't come forward. I'm sure of that. We will have to find her and drag her forward."

"Do you think she was a confederate?"

"I don't know, and when I don't know, Clarke, I suspect. It's a bad habit of mine, but we're dealing with a clever gang, and Nosey Ruslin's the cleverest of them all. You must be prepared for any trickery in anything in which he has a hand."

"But what use would a screaming woman be, sir?" There was a bland patience in the sergeant's tone which amused his senior.

"You fancy it would have interfered with the plot instead of helping it along, eh? I thought so, but, Clarke, have you forgotten the case of Jimmy Waters? You and I arrested him in Lambeth near Westminster Bridge just after he had picked the pocket of a member of Parliament of three hundred pounds in notes. Have you also forgotten Jimmy's neat little trick? There's nothing new under the sun, you know."

Detective-Sergeant Clarke's chagrin and humiliation brought about an upheaval of movement which nearly lifted him into the air.

"What a fool I am, sir! What an ass! Of course, you're right. Jimmy had a girl to scream and focus the attention of the crowd on herself. Why, that's the very dodge that a chap like Nosey would be almost certain to adopt."

"Nosey is like most great crooks, not an inventor. He remembers and copies. Jimmy Waters was a pal of his. If you look into the papers about the case you will find more than one reference to Nosey. Of course, it's only an idea and a guess, but it's worth assuming it's true until it's proved not to be. That's my attitude towards it."

Detective-Sergeant Clarke, however, would accept nothing short of implicit belief in the accuracy of the surmise.

"The woman who screamed could solve the mystery, sir," he said with an emphasis foreign to his slow, cautious nature. "It was a trick, and didn't it come off! Who could she be? I'll have a look through the list again. She must be a pal of Nosey's. Oh, if only we could land Nosey in the Underground at the moment Massy Cheldon was murdered!"

"He has a perfect alibi, Clarke. He was with young Cheldon at least a quarter of a mile away. Both of them have lied—it may be that young Cheldon didn't mean to lie—about the exact time, but I've checked it up and it would be too strong for an Old Bailey jury. Not that I ever hoped for anything from Nosey's timetable on last Monday night. He wouldn't be in the danger zone, Clarke. We know he never is."

For a few minutes the two men preferred to think in silence. Both of them knew that the murder of Massy Cheldon was not of the order of mysteries which are never solved. They also knew that in Nosey Ruslin there lay the solution, and Nosey, even if they suspected with good reason that it was by no means the first murder in which he had been responsible for the preliminaries, must be induced to weaken his defences and somehow tricked into betraying himself, for Chief Inspector Wake and Detective-Sergeant Clarke, however admiringly they might speak at times of the cleverness of the rogues with whom they had to deal professionally, knew that the crook is a fool, in a hurry to betray if his own skin is in danger.

"The papers are not forgetting us, Clarke," said Wake suddenly, "and Piccadilly seems to have trebled its population."

"The manager tells me that yesterday they issued more tickets than ever before," said Clarke grimly.

"Mostly penny tickets, I'll bet."

"You're right, sir." He had guessed that himself before the manager of the Underground had entered into particulars, but it would not have been tactful to refuse a tribute to the perspicacity of one's official superior. "The increase consists almost entirely of people who want to see the exact spot where Massy Cheldon was murdered."

"And the newspapers and the public are clamouring for an early arrest," said Chief Inspector Wake, bitterly. "But if we arrested on suspicion only, Clarke, our prisons would have to be quadrupled. And yet I'm not downhearted. Somehow I can't help feeling that this is going to be one of our really satisfactory cases."

"I hope so, sir." The sergeant's tone did not connote confidence. "All depends if we haven't let anyone we're likely to want escape the net."

"You mean Nosey Ruslin may have a confederate we haven't thought of?"

"We have no proof of any kind against Nosey," Clarke reminded him.

"Except Nosey himself. He's always proof." Wake smiled. "Of course, you may be right, Clarke, and yet in my opinion it's Nosey or nothing. The whole business bears the stamp of his management. Thank goodness, we can bring him in whenever we wish."

"He knows that, sir, and isn't trying to get away."

"As for young Cheldon, well, he won't run away from a fortune."

"It might be a risk, sir, but what if we brought in Nosey, young Cheldon and Billy the Dancer?"

"That would shut their mouths for good. You can't frighten Nosey, and Billy the Dancer never was much use as a talker. As for young Cheldon, he didn't do it, Clarke. I'm certain he didn't even know what was in the wind. That's how I read him. Weak and effeminate. Thinks himself an intellectual Hercules, but is only a pigmy."

"Easily influenced, sir."

"But not a crook. Maybe he is a fool, but you can't jail a man for that. No, as I've already said, it's Nosey or nothing, and when we land the whale the lesser fish will follow. If only I could make more use of the dagger. So typical of Nosey to—" He made a gesture of impatience. "I'm thinking too far ahead again. But the chap who used the dagger didn't himself think of wearing gloves. That strikes me as genuine Nosey just as the time and place for the murder were chosen by him."

"Are we up against a blank wall, sir?" asked Clarke, lured into pessimism by his superior's subdued irritation.

"No, not a blank wall, Clarke. It's a wall though, and the trouble is that we can't pull it down and see what's behind it. But I'll have the murderer of Massy Cheldon, Clarke, I'll have him."

It was at least the twentieth time Detective-Sergeant Clarke had heard the same confident prophecy and he was officially and unofficially tired of it. Yet it had its effect, for his own confidence was oozing now that the days of the investigation were accumulating. It restored his hopefulness to be told by one of the cleverest men in Scotland Yard's service that the Piccadilly murder was not to be added to the list, reprinted at disturbing intervals by the morning and evening papers, of London's unsolved murder mysteries since the termination of the great war.

"You might fetch the dagger," said Wake abruptly. "Trench has it. He was visiting the curio shops on the off-chance of finding someone who could identify it. I have an idea."

The idea took shape when Chief Inspector Wake dined late at Greville's that night and was waited on by the obsequious proprietor himself.

"Your claret is excellent," said the detective, who was no judge of wine or song, but who prided himself on his knowledge of men and women. "How's business in the hot weather?"

The signor answered with a gesture.

"Then it's a pity you can't earn that reward?"

With intense interest and some excitement the signor protested that he had never heard of a reward, and Wake did not admit that neither had he until he had mentioned it. It was simply an idea, one of those harmless and cheap experiments he indulged in occasionally to help his plans and movements.

"You've read that the murderer of Massy Cheldon left the weapon behind? It was a dagger of the sort your countrymen carry."

The signor smiled protestingly.

"There's fifty pounds for anyone who can identify it. I mean give me an idea as to the owner of it. Fifty pounds, signor, and not a word to the public. No publicity—everything private."

The dark eyes gleamed.

"I have seen many daggers," he murmured, "but not in London."

"Where's your private room?" He glanced again at the occupied tables and failed to recognise an acquaintance. "No one here knows me. It will be quite safe." Wake knew the fear of the foreign element of the epithet of police spy.

"My apartment—here," exclaimed the proprietor, who was thinking of fifty pounds and trying to work out the number of dinners which would have to be served to produce such an entrancing profit.

Behind the half closed door he took the dagger from Wake's hands and held it close to his eyes. The detective watched him anxiously, trying to read his thoughts and to anticipate his verdict.

"I have seen poignards that I would mistake for it," the veteran Italian murmured. "Twenty years ago I had one myself though not as long. It is expensive, this one, and sharp." He fingered it almost lovingly. Then the light of a triumphant smile broke across his sallow, withered features. "I remember now, Mr. Inspector. Yes, I remember here in this very room." Wake wished he could shout at him to hurry up. "Carlo Demonico—they call him Italian Charlie—offered me this dagger for a dinner and one shilling. I refused. I am not a pawnbroker, I told him." He drew himself up to the topmost inch of his height.

"Is that all that happened?"

He bowed.

Wake replaced the weapon in its special case and dropped

it into his inside pocket. Disappointment was his predominant emotion.

"'I am no pawnbroker, Carlo,' I said to him." Again the smile of a strength that for a few moments concealed the dirt and the hairs of his face. "'I am a *restaurateur*, my friend.' That's my answer to him, Mr. Inspector, and he went away cursing."

The detective, having hinted at the probability of the fifty pounds coming the way of his genial informant, strolled out in a state of pessimism which blinded him until he was nearly at the corner of Piccadilly facing the Criterion restaurant. Here he recovered his official self and although he had gone off duty it was his official eye that surveyed the crowds that streamed in every direction. A dozen times he overheard references to the Piccadilly murder, and twice loud-voiced females pronounced the words "Scotland Yard" in a tone which left no room for doubt as to their opinion of that famous institution. Wake did not wince nor did he cry aloud. He was inured to criticism of imperfect worldlings who expected perfection in at least one very human institution.

And then something happened which caused an inward revolution as startling in its changes, if not reforms, as any revolution ever could be. He had grown impatient of inaction, and too restless to plan a return homewards, he swung round on his heel. Simultaneously his eyes came into line with the painted word "pawnbroker," and once more Chief Inspector Wake of Scotland Yard had reason to kick himself metaphorically for having taken quite thirty-five minutes to appreciate the importance of the restaurant proprietor's parting advice to Italian Charlie.

"It's a chance, but a winning chance," he muttered, and after the longest night he had ever spent with his eyes open he was at Scotland Yard at half-past eight and holding an impromptu conference of his most efficient and therefore most trusted assistants.

"Clarke, you'll come with me," he said at its close. "Trench and Agate will begin at the end of the list. Graham, you and O'Leary, try your luck in Holborn. I'll 'phone here every half-hour in case there is anything for me to hear. Now be off."

He examined his own extract from the list of London's pawnbrokers within a mile of Piccadilly Circus.

"That would be Italian Charlie's unless he was extra cautious," he said to his companion as they stepped into a taxi.

There had been a murder case sixteen years previously which had involved a visit being paid to each of three hundred and eleven laundries before a vital laundry mark on a collar had been identified. Chief Inspector Wake, then a detective-sergeant, had participated in that weary visitation which remained one of his most seared memories.

"Hope it won't be the Renfrew Street laundry mark again, Clarke," he said as the car was nearing Trafalgar Square.

The sergeant nearly laughed.

"I've heard all about it from Trench, sir."

"Because he happened to have the laundry on his list where the murdered man used to send his shirts and collars? That was a wonderful feat of detection, Clarke," he added, sarcastically. "I wonder how many pawnshops there are in London? A few thousand, I should think." He yawned. "Pity I couldn't sleep last night, but excitement kept me awake." He noticed his companion's surprise. "Oh, I'm young enough to be foolish enough to get excited," he explained cheerfully.

"Something tells me we'll be lucky, sir," said Clarke, whose thoughts had not been diverted by the incursion into past history.

"When a pessimist turns optimist the expected simply has to happen," said Wake with all the weight of his fifteen stone.

Detective-Sergeant Clarke's psychic informant was justified by results. Three pawnbrokers within a quarter-mile radius of Italian Charlie's recently vacated bedroom on the heights of Soho convincingly repudiated previous acquaintance with the sinister weapon Chief Inspector Wake affably tendered to them for examination and, if possible, recognition. The fourth twenty-five per cent philanthropist, whose angular Rialto was situated near the trackless region of Euston Road, identified it with a grin which was reminiscent and not merely a sign of pleasure at the reunion.

"Little dark-faced chap brought it in with a silver watch and a gold-plated brooch. Gave him seven bob on the lot. Want his name and address?"

He went to a safe at the back and sorted out his ledgers.

"Wonder what name he gave?" Wake whispered.

"Here it is," said the pawnbroker, placing the open book on the counter. "May the eleventh. Carlo Demonico, 29, Frederick Alley, W."

"And when were the articles redeemed?" asked Wake, recovering from his surprise.

"May the twenty-seventh."

"Did you know this Carlo Demonico?"

The pawnbroker shook his head.

"Never saw him but once," he said.

"You mean twice," Detective-Sergeant Clarke corrected. "You forget he redeemed the articles."

"I didn't say he redeemed them," was the quiet reply.

The pawnbroker knew he was in the presence of policemen and was wary.

"Who did?" The question was Wake's.

"Ah, now you're asking me one," exclaimed the man on the other side of the counter with inconsequential cheerfulness. "When it's a matter of redeeming seven bobsworth of odds and ends I'm only too glad to be rid of the stuff and take my small profit. I don't ask questions."

"But wasn't the dagger rather unusual in your experience?" Wake's anxiety to preserve his hopefulness was almost pathetic.

"No. I've had plenty. You get everything nearly some time in our business. But now that I come to think of it I remember sizing up the chap who came in with the ticket and the money and trying to guess if he were Carlo Demonico's brother or cousin."

Wake took a photograph out of his pocket.

"Does that remind you of him?" he asked, and in unison with his subordinate waited anxiously for the answer.

"That's the chap," was the almost immediate rejoinder. "He tried to keep his face from me but I saw him clear enough as he turned to leave the shop. Yes. That's him."

"Thank you," said Wake, and would have sat down heavily had there been a chair handy.

"Nothing serious, I hope, gents?" asked the pawnbroker, awed by the set faces that were signalling to each other.

"The Piccadilly murder," said Wake, a trifle sharply.

The pawnbroker threw his hands in the air.

"What! That? Good Lord! I've been reading about it half the night, but it never occurred to me to—"

"There was a photograph of the dagger in every paper a few days ago," said Wake severely. "Didn't you connect it with the one you took in pawn?"

"I saw the photograph, but it didn't look the same—quite different, in fact, gents. The Piccadilly murder!" The twenty-five per cent look came into his eyes. "Is there a reward?" The question was accompanied by a smirk that began with a smacking of the lips.

"No, we don't offer rewards," was the only answer he was vouchsafed. "But keep this to yourself until I call again and you'll have a friend in me and my colleague. Not that it matters very much to us if you do talk, but it may matter something to you. Good morning."

They had only a yard and a half to cover before reaching the pavement, and the taximan was waiting for them with the door open, but to the detectives it seemed that the age of the old coach and horses must have returned as the vehicle trotted to its appointed destination. Half a dozen times Wake thrust his head out of the window to signal to a traffic impeder in uniform information as to his identity, and they did reach Scotland Yard before that June morning was fifteen minutes older, but as Wake waddled vigorously towards the superintendent's room he was lamenting the years he had lost since the interview with the pawnbroker.

"We have traced the dagger, sir," he announced. "It was pawned on May the eleventh by Carlo Demonico, known as Italian Charlie, and redeemed on May the twenty-seventh by Billy Bright."

"Less than a fortnight before the murder," the superintendent of the C.I.D. exclaimed. "And Billy Bright is an intimate friend of Nosey Ruslin's." He spoke as another old acquaintance of Nosey's.

"And Nosey has been very pally of late with young Cheldon who's inherited a fortune through his uncle's death," said Wake, unwilling to break the chain.

"There's only one obvious thing to do and that is to arrest Billy the Dancer. And yet I doubt its wisdom. I've got a constitutional suspicion and distrust of the obvious."

"I would also prefer to wait a little longer, sir," said Wake, in his stolid, matter of fact manner. "Give him more rope so that—"

"We may be in a better position to give him the whole of it," interjected the superior with the smile that invites laughter.

There was an interval of recovery for Chief Inspector Wake, who was not an expert laugher, and when he was himself again he walked over to the window and looked out.

"It's an easy case, sir, and yet somehow difficult. All the time I feel that the murderer is under my nose and I can't see him. I'd bet a million to one that Nosey Ruslin knows all about it."

"That would be a safe bet, Wake," said the superintendent drily. "What we want is someone, yourself for preference, who can boast that he knows all about it, too. But it's something to have narrowed the circle of suspicion down to Nosey Ruslin and Billy the Dancer. You are sure Italian Charlie had nothing to do with it?"

"I wouldn't have let him go, sir, if I hadn't known that at forty minutes past eleven last Monday night he was playing cards in a club in the City Road. I have a dozen witnesses to that."

"So it's Nosey and Billy. What about Cheldon?"

"Can't quite fix him, but he may know something. I am having an eye kept on him in case."

"But the identification of the ownership of the dagger is vital, Wake. That's a real score for you. And yet you don't wish Billy to be brought in at once?"

"No, sir. I'd rather he was provided with opportunities to see his pal, Nosey Ruslin, again. I want to let them talk—talking sometimes leads to quarrels. You remember the Battersea case? If Granger hadn't got unfounded suspicions of his confederate we'd never have secured a conviction. And in my opinion the dagger isn't sufficient even if we can prove it was in Billy's possession twelve days before the murder. A lot can happen in twelve days. Picture Norman Birkett or Patrick Hastings defending Billy at the Old Bailey. Don't you see how much they'd make of those twelve blank days?"

"Too true." The superintendent had had many lively and disadvantageous encounters with famous counsel in the course of his professional career.

"If Billy goes into the witness box with half an alibi the other half will be supplied by his counsel."

"Yes, yes," was the testy interruption. Wake was seldom loquacious, and his colleagues preferred him to be his usual self. "You must have had a dozen reports on Billy."

"About forty, I should say, sir."

"But nothing definite as to his movements on the night of the murder?"

"Up to the present our information would suggest that he vanished off the face of the earth after saying good afternoon to the attendant at the 'Frozen Fang' who was washing the tables. That was at four o'clock."

"But what puzzles me is the entire absence of motive, Wake."

"One can make a guess, sir."

"Have a shot at one then."

"Money. Hard cash. Billy's been on his uppers for months. Can't get engagements, and is crazy about his partner, Nancy Curzon."

"Always a woman in the case, Wake," said the superintendent sententiously.

"Only on the borders of this one, sir. She's completely ignorant of the events leading up to the murder. Nosey would never take her into his confidence. He never does because he feels he can't trust them."

"That doesn't get us any nearer the solution of the problem of the motive," said the superintendent. "If Billy did it for money where did the money come from or if it hasn't been paid who will pay it and when? Nosey hasn't any, and you've ruled out young Cheldon, who will be, actually is at the moment, the owner of the Cheldon estate. There's the weakness of your case, Wake." He leaned back in his chair and stared importantly at the wall beyond. Chief Inspector Wake, who could remember him as a uniformed colleague in the days before he had won the race for promotion, tried to assemble all the humility of which he was capable.

"Very true, sir, very true. But it's less than a week since the murder took place and we've done something."

"You've accomplished a great deal," said his superior generously. "You must forgive my impatience, Wake." He laughed. "You won't be beaten—you never are. The Piccadilly murder will be one of your triumphs."

"Thank you, sir." Wake spoke awkwardly, for compliments unsettled him. "But you are right about the motive. Unless we can secure Old Bailey proof of Nosey Ruslin's participation it wouldn't be safe to arrest Billy the Dancer yet. He's young Cheldon's rival for the hand and feet"—he permitted himself a smile—"of Nancy Curzon."

"A good-looker?"

"Really beautiful, sir," was the enthusiastic reply. "Quite different from the usual Soho dancer. Even when she's made up for her show she's fresh and natural. Got any amount of horse sense too."

"Ambitious?"

"Very. Wants to clear out of the game with the aid of a rich husband."

The superintendent sat bolt upright.

"How's this for a possible solution, Wake? Nancy Curzon has young Cheldon madly in love with her, but he is poor. There is, however, a rich uncle who has only to die to make her lover rich. Well, she has another would-be lover, Billy the Dancer. She goes to him and promises him a small fortune if he will remove the inconvenient uncle."

Chief Inspector Wake smiled the tired smile of the man who has the knowledge and wisdom of which he is about to administer a small dose to a foolish and reckless ignoramus.

"You can take it from me, sir, that Nancy Curzon is as ignorant and innocent of the murder of Massy Cheldon as you and I are. I know that. She was one of the first I suspected but I was soon convinced that I was wasting my time."

The superintendent frowned. The curt dismissal of his colossal brainwave by a subordinate was not flattering.

"I have read all the reports, Wake," he said, with a touch of steel in his voice, "and boiled down they amount to very little. But there is no such thing as an original murder—I learnt that saying from you—and as between us we've been concerned in over a hundred we ought to be able to find a parallel to the Piccadilly one."

"I've searched my memory and failed."

"So have I. That's why I'm theorising. Still, you're so confident about the girl that I suppose I must leave her out. But you can't deny there's strong evidence that the Cheldon estate had something to do with the murder of its possessor?"

"That's the line I've adopted from the beginning, sir."

"Because you suspect Nosey Ruslin, and Nosey's been very friendly with young Cheldon? Of course, if we could get Billy the Dancer to talk a little, to quarrel with Nosey and—"

"He's in mortal terror of Nosey."

"And of you. Didn't he faint when he heard that you'd paid his account at Greville's?"

Before Wake could answer, the door opened and Detective-Sergeant Clarke appeared with a sheaf of papers.

"Report from Margate, sir. Billy Bright left there by the nine-thirty for Victoria. Before he caught the train he entered a telephone booth near the station and remained in it for a quarter of an hour. The call he made was checked and proved to be a post office telephone in the Strand."

"Evidently an arrangement with a friend in London," said the superintendent. "Anything known of the talk?"

"No, sir. Billy Bright didn't say much and appeared to be speaking to someone he addressed as Nancy."

The superintendent glanced triumphantly at his colleague.

"But the name must have been a blind," the sergeant replied. "I've had a special report in since which says that Nancy Curzon hasn't yet left her rooms near Wardour Street. There's no doubt of that."

Chief Inspector Wake could have smiled, but preferred to remain passive.

"Thank you, Clarke," said the superintendent. "There's nothing more. A watch will be kept on Bright."

They were soon alone again.

"Someone's summoned Billy back to London, sir," said Wake, slowly, "and, in my opinion that someone could be only Nosey Ruslin."

"If so your luck's in." The big man rose and concealed the fireplace from human inspection. "The confederates are either frightened at the division of their forces or else anxious to confer in the face of fresh dangers. Either way it's better for us, Wake."

"As I see it, the friend warned Billy that absence from London might be interpreted to mean that he was running away. I've noticed that Nosey has suddenly become confident, even insolent."

"Insolence is either innocence or bluff."

"Bluff, I should say, sir. But the inquest comes on again next Thursday and I am anxious to have a clear cut statement for the coroner."

"We're handicapped by the tenderness of the authorities for the guilty," said the superintendent sarcastically. "If we were in Paris, Wake, we could arrest Billy, Nancy, Nosey Ruslin and young Cheldon, and a dozen more if it suited our book."

"You make my mouth water, sir." Wake actually sighed. "That would solve the problem in a few hours. I'd like to arrest Billy and trust to his fright to open his mouth, but if he kept it shut and we had no case against him there'd be trouble."

He walked to the corner where he had installed his umbrella and gripped it as though it had the form and features of Billy Bright.

"I think I'll try my luck again, sir, and visit Billy's usual haunts. There's always a chance of picking up something."

"Be sure that Billy isn't left a loophole, Wake."

"We can't prevent him committing suicide, but apart from that we can bring him in at five minutes' notice, sir."

"Oh, all right. The less we talk about the case the better." The superintendent moved restlessly to his desk. "It only leads us nowhere. One can so easily invent theories, and the more of them the more difficult it is to think clearly."

"You're quite right, sir. I've been talking too much, and talking is not my speciality. I'll wander down into Soho. Now that Nosey and Billy are coming together again anything may happen. Pity Nosey has his friend so completely under his heavy thumb."

In Whitehall he was reminded that he was hungry, and in a teashop he dawdled for half an hour over tea and poached eggs on toast. The freedom from the office theories of a superior was a distinct relief, and he was refreshed and rejuvenated when he climbed aboard the bus that landed him in Piccadilly Circus.

In Shaftesbury Avenue there was the customary liveliness which created a desire to escape into one of the numerous side streets, but Chief Inspector Wake held his own until he found a convenient backwater in an alley leading out of Wardour Street.

Twice he passed the incurable building which had six months previously nicknamed its cellar a night club with the label of "Frozen Fang." The only sign of life was a constellation of flies which almost concealed the nudity of a cooked ham in the window over the club. Wake, as he sauntered along, identified three newspaper reporters and nodded genially, but he was disturbed by their proximity to the nightly rendezvous of Billy the Dancer, Nancy Curzon and Nosey Ruslin. Did they know anything which was unknown to him?

He walked on with the aplomb of a Frenchman who has just lunched well and economically, asking himself occasionally why he was wasting his time. Did he expect the vital clue he desired to walk up and introduce itself? He was smiling at the simile when he was startled—why startled he was never able to explain—by the totally unexpected vision of Nancy Curzon, dainty in pale blue, talking to Billy the Dancer outside the offices of an American film company. His first decision in a moment when more than one decision had to be made, was to dive into the nearest doorway, but mingled with the same thought was a glimmering of the danger of imitating the police sleuth of fiction.

"Hello, Nancy!" he exclaimed, raising his bowler. "So it's you, Billy?"

The girl met his gaze with a smile that was more than lip-deep.

"Hello, inspector!" she said, shaking hands. Yes, he had been correct in his description of her that morning. She was very beautiful.

"What's the latest news?" he asked, all his face in action as he beamed paternally on her.

Nancy's smile became ecstatic.

"I'm going to be married in September," she said, and there was neither fear nor embarrassment nor guilt in her voice, while her eyes gleamed with a rare sunshine of their very own.

"Not to—" Wake wheeled round to indicate the dancer, but the sentence was perforce left incomplete owing to Nancy's shrill laughter.

"You are a one!" she cried, falling back on the early days of Paradise Alley and its argot. "I'm marrying Mr. Robert Cheldon. We fixed it up late last night." Her candour disturbed Wake.

Suddenly a new light illuminated his darkness.

"That's why Billy the Dancer left Margate," he said, but only to his inner self.

"Billy's expression isn't enthusiastic," he said aloud. Wake's capacity for humour was not large, but he occasionally drew economically on his small stock.

"Oh, that's his way of being funny," said Nancy carelessly. "He's a bit upset because it'll mean an end of our partnership."

"So that's it, is it?" The question was addressed to the swarthy-faced young man who was looking beyond them in an endeavour to appear uninterested.

"She wants money and a gentleman husband," he said, speaking for the first time. "But I've been telling her that she'll not stand for it more than a few months. The clubs and the lights and the dancing—"

Chief Inspector Wake interrupted the rhapsody.

"Well, I congratulate you, Nancy." He paused. "But I must be moving on. Good-bye, Nancy, good-bye, Billy."

He strolled on, apparently conscious only of the presence of the umbrella he was carrying as a challenge to the clouds to do their worst. But when out of sight he increased his pace in the direction of Whitehall.

"I have been lucky today," he said to himself as he entered Scotland Yard, "but to what extent I don't quite know—yet."

Chapter Thirteen

"I don't think we'll ever get anywhere, mother, talking about it," Bobbie exclaimed as he rose impatiently from the table and paced up and down the room.

"But one can't help talking about it," she answered wearily. "It's impossible to think of anything else. The inquest comes on again tomorrow."

He aimed a kick at an imaginary obstacle, his hands deep in his trousers' pockets, his chin nearly touching his chest.

"We'll not be called on to give evidence," he reminded her. "Besides, it's none of our business, mother. It's the police who have to find the man who murdered Uncle Massy."

"Poor Massy!" she murmured, tears in her eyes. "Do you know, Bobbie, I think he was very fond of both of us."

"He was fond of you, mother." He laughed feebly. "There were moments when I thought he was going to propose."

She lifted her pale face towards his and there was no sign of mental discomfort or annoyance.

"I know that—I knew it," she said quietly. "Twice he told me he was a fool not to have asked me years ago. But I didn't encourage him, Bobbie, for there was always you."

He did not reply. Sentiment of any sort outside that which bound him to Nancy embarrassed him.

"I'll be glad when it's all over. I want to take possession of the Manor." He uttered a yawn. "Won't it be great when we leave Galahad Mansions behind us for ever, mother?"

"I'll be glad to leave Galahad Mansions," she said uneasily, "but I don't fancy I'd be happy in the Manor. Somehow I should always be thinking of poor Massy."

How often had she said that and how often had their ensuing discussions brought them no further. From the moment they had heard of the murder of Massy Cheldon they seemed to have talked of nothing else. His mother had infected him with fresh fears every day, and now there was a barrier between them, but neither had the courage to admit its existence. And to Bobbie there was ever in the background the sinister figure of Nosey Ruslin with his threatening amiability, his terrifying good temper, his horrible suavity.

Suddenly he faced her with a defensive scowl of warning.

"Mother," he said, sharply, "when it's all over I'm going to marry Nancy Curzon."

He expected her to start, to flush with anger, and to protest. She merely continued to watch him dully.

"We arranged everything yesterday." How difficult it was to speak clearly! "Nancy's position is not an easy one." He tried to think of an explanation of this statement, but failed. "But she's willing to stand by me."

"Why stand by? Are you in any danger?"

"Of course not." He was weakly irritable again. "But I mean, that is, well, you know what the papers have been saying? We're under a cloud—perhaps, not exactly a cloud." He stopped and wrestled with his nerves. "It's not nice for a girl to marry into a family where there's been a murder, and Nancy has lots of admirers."

"I suppose some of them are rich?" The coldness in the voice swept the room like the blast of a tempest.

"I don't know, mother, and I don't care. You think she's marrying me for my money and nothing else?"

"Do you suspect any other motive?" Ruby stood and shook off her weariness. "Bobbie," she said, once again his mother and Massy Cheldon forgotten, "you know as well as I do that this girl is marrying you for your money and your position."

"She swears she isn't," he protested.

"No doubt she is good at swearing. But never mind. I want you to be happy, and if she is a real help to you, I—"

"Oh, mother, you can't imagine what Nancy means to me!" he cried, with all that boyishness which never failed to touch her heart. "You'll be proud of her when she's the mistress of Broadbridge Manor, and there's many a man and woman down there who'll live to bless the day I married Nancy Curzon." He flung out his arms. "Let's forget the past and look only to the future. The death of Uncle Massy was unfortunate, but it's not our fault. If I didn't benefit by his death someone else would. Had he married you—"

"I should never have married him, Bobbie," she said, with a smile. "It was only my vanity that recalled his efforts to propose. Apart from yourself there is my loyalty to your father. Ah, if only you had known him! He was the finest man in the world."

"I will have a memorial erected to him at Broadbridge," Bobbie said, in his most important manner. "I think I owe that to him. Of course, mother, there will always be a special suite for you at the Manor."

"Nancy mightn't care for that," she remarked. "But never mind. I wonder if the police have finished with it."

"Parker believes they have. At any rate they've returned all the papers they took away with his permission."

"As if old family papers could reveal anything bearing on his murder," she said contemptuously. "Your uncle wasn't a man to collect secrets. His life was an open book. Yet he was murdered." There was a catch in her voice. "Murdered," she repeated, staring into vacancy. "Could he have had a dangerous secret after all?"

She averted her face as the suspicion returned to her that her brother-in-law's heritage was the motive for his death. And if that were true was her son standing in peril of his life?

She brushed the stray hairs back from her forehead and looked at him again.

"How curious everything and everybody, including myself, has changed," she said, speaking at random. "You've just told me you are going to be married and I've hardly referred to it. Have you fixed the date?"

"Early in September." It was wonderful how he brightened up at the change in her manner. "I wanted it earlier, but Nancy thinks it wouldn't do too soon after the inquest. She knows more about these things than I do. It hadn't occurred to me that tomorrow might not see the end of the proceedings. I thought that since uncle has been buried there was little more for the coroner to do. But all that matters to me is that I'm going to marry Nancy."

"You love her very much, don't you, Bobbie?"

"I can't answer that question, mother, because I don't know a language I could express myself in. Nancy is everything to me, much more than the Cheldon estate. That's how I feel about it."

"I have brought you up—watched over you—sacrificed myself for you, and now this girl comes along." There were tears in her voice.

"Didn't your mother bring you up? Didn't—" He paused as he noticed the ghostlike pallor of her cheeks.

"You're right, Bobbie! We all do it. I have no cause, no right to criticise you. But I do hope that Nancy Curzon will not disappoint you—that if ever she is tested she will not let you down."

He smiled complacently.

"I'd trust Nancy with my life," he said earnestly. "She's staunch and loyal. There isn't an atom of treachery in her composition. Of course, mother, you look down on her because she's not exactly in the Cheldon class, but class distinctions were invented by lodging-house keepers in search of a pretence to gentility. When I marry Nancy she'll take the position in the county my wife is entitled to, and—"

"Class distinctions again, Bobbie," said his mother, teasingly.

He was looking at the clock as she was speaking.

"It's nearly nine, mother," he said anxiously, "and I promised to be at Nancy's before a quarter past. She's giving a little party to celebrate our engagement."

"Celebrate? And the Cheldons the talk of the country!" She made a gesture which was intended to express disapproval, but to Bobbie there was only the pathos of jealousy in it.

"It's only a quiet party," he said apologetically. "I shouldn't have used the word 'celebrate'. There'll be no jollification or any ragging. You know what I mean."

"Nancy Curzon will be in the mood for celebrating," she answered with a touch of temper. "It's not often a girl catches a young man with ten thousand a year. You may be sure she'll celebrate right enough."

"You're too morbid, mother, that's the matter with you. And yet I'm not surprised." The tone was lofty, even patronising. "The murder of Uncle Massy has got on your nerves. It got on mine, too, but I've learnt that life belongs to the living and that life must go on."

"But the dead sometimes get their grip on you, Bobbie," she said, with a faraway look. "You can't get away from them when they die as your uncle did. Then there are the newspapers. It's all very well calling them names, but they sometimes hit on the truth."

He walked to the door and opened it.

"I'll not be too late, mother," he said, assuming a cheerfulness that covered his annoyance. "But don't wait up for me. And if you'll take my advice you'll forget the past and think only of the future. I'll make it a happy and a golden future for you if you'll let me."

It was a theatrical but a soothing speech on which he made his exit and the memory of it suffused him with a glow of pride until he turned into Wardour Street and remembered he was within a couple of hundred yards of the loveliest and dearest girl in the world.

Her open-armed welcome took him right out of every temptation to pessimism or moody retrospection, and he was once again the youthful, enthusiastic and unthinking lover of the days—how long ago it seemed now!—when he had shyly shaken hands with a night club dancer and the cellar under the ham and beef shop had instantly assumed the radiant glamour of fairyland.

"You're the first, darling," she exclaimed, as they stepped backwards two paces and found themselves in the tawdry living-room, "and I wouldn't mind if you were the last, but there won't be many, thank goodness. Just push that chair into the corner. It's a bit wheezy about the legs."

A knock on the door and to Bobbie's petrification the voice of Nosey Ruslin penetrated the room like a foghorn through a November fog.

"Had to come along to congratulate you, Nancy. But if you ask me it's Mr. Cheldon who should have all the congratulations. I—" He stepped into the room. "Why, there you are, Mr. Cheldon! I want to wish you a thousand times more than you can wish yourself."

To Bobbie's surprise the over-flavoured personality banished his nervousness and killed his resentment. The renewal of the scrupulously deferential manner of address, the obvious willingness to admit and maintain social inferiority, the familiar and yet not too familiar attitude towards Nancy. All these things separated Nosey Ruslin from the class to which he belonged and entitled him to special consideration by a Cheldon.

"I hope I'm not in the way?" Nosey exclaimed, looking about the room. "I expected to find a crowd."

"You couldn't be in the way, Nosey," said Nancy quickly.

"Of course not." Bobbie shook his hand warmly.

"Won't be a minute," Nancy called as she darted into the next room.

"No worry. Everything all right." Nosey's speech was cryptic but eloquent. "You'll never be brought into it, Mr. Cheldon. Make up your mind on that."

Bobbie awkwardly murmured his thanks, for any reference to the murder of his uncle disturbed him. These were the moments when he was compelled to subdue his conscience, and although he gained the victory each time he was not altogether satisfied with its extent.

"Do you know, Mr. Cheldon," Nosey resumed with a great display of interest and delight, "that when I think you're going to rescue Nancy from all this I can't thank you sufficiently. Again and again I've rubbed that into her, and believe me, sir, she's grateful. Yes, sir." He grinned. "It'll be a wonderful change to Broadbridge Manor, but she'll do the family mansion as well as the family justice."

"I'm sure she will," said Bobbie, touched. "I only hope I'll be able to do justice to Nancy."

"Is it true that you'll have fifteen thousand a year?" Nosey asked from the chair into which he had fitted his ample frame. "It says so in one of the papers."

"Ten thousand at the outside," said Bobbie, pleasantly. Money was the most seductive of subjects when it brought you a girl in a million. "I don't know what effect the death duties will have on the income. My solicitors haven't been able to settle anything yet."

To his surprise and also to his disquiet Nosey unexpectedly disentangled himself from the chair and came across to where he was standing under an engraving of "Queen Victoria receiving her Indian orderlies."

"Mr. Cheldon," he said, with a change of key that intimated he had something fearsome to disclose, "I want you to be yourself tonight and not to worry about the other fellows. I mean to say, if anyone turns up that you don't like, don't show it. Just treat him as if you'd never seen him before." He tapped him on the arm. "Supposing, for instance, Billy Bright shoved his nose in."

Bobbie started as if he had been kicked.

"But he won't come?" he gasped.

"You forget you're with people who live in a world you don't know nothing about," said Nosey Ruslin flatteringly. "We're not my lords and my ladies." This was meant to be humorous. "We have our quarrels and our fights, but we don't bear no malice."

"But Billy Bright, the chap who—"

Nosey's expression became threatening.

"You know nothin' about that—nothin', remember," he whispered, bringing his heavy jowl closer to Bobbie's face. "You've got to treat Billy the Dancer as if you'd never seen or heard of him before. Not that I think he'll turn up. He's too much in love with Nancy."

Bobbie shivered.

"If she had married him," he muttered, horrified.

"That's what I say and have said, Mr. Cheldon." The tone was back to amiability. "And that's why I'm grateful to you.

But you know nothin'? Remember? Billy's a tough guy, but he knows he hasn't a chance and that if he interfered with Nancy's happiness there'd be a certain person to reckon with in a way that would leave him stiff."

Bobbie gazed at the certain person and was discovering fresh reasons for shuddering when Nancy returned, accompanied by a tallish girl with reddish hair and a face which appeared to have been whitewashed.

"Meet Tessie Hodey," she said to Bobbie.

"Congrats, and all that sort of thing," said Tessie with an immense giggle that shook some of the powder off her face. "What about a corpse-livener, Nancy?"

Nosey Ruslin became busy.

"Arthur Yule—not fool." The second introduction was another ordeal, for the dapper little man with the bald head and the mouth of a comedian seemed to have come straight from the ham and beef shop over the "Frozen Fang," as indeed he had when another arrival, Jennie Watts, twenty and already faded, began in a loud voice to talk to Arthur of the time she had spent in his shop as an assistant.

"A good chap," Nosey whispered to Bobbie when he had the chance. "Used to give Nancy all the credit she wanted when she would have starved."

Instantly Bobbie's heart warmed to the little man who was all nerves, loquacity and vulgarity.

"Another cocktail, Mr. Yule?" he said, intercepting his passage to where Nancy was chaffing a heavy, six-foot male in evening dress who might have been a genuine waiter or an imitation actor.

"Thanks," was the reply which accompanied the outstretched hand. "Never refused a drink in my life."

"I'm surprised I never saw you in the 'Frozen Fang'," said Bobbie, glad of an excuse for a conversation which might soothe nerves threatening to spoil the evening because he was certain that the next arrival must be Billy Bright.

Mr. Yule's grimace was eloquent.

"Not in my line. I'm the landlord and that's all. Besides, it takes me all my time to look after the shop. So you're the chap Nancy intends to marry? Well, I congratulate you. She's had many admirers. A clever girl, Mr. Cheldon, and a real good sort."

"You were kind to her, Mr. Yule, and I'm very grateful."

"Oh, that was nothing. Nancy's the sort you can always trust. I knew she'd repay me. Her word's good enough for anyone. Since the—" he emptied the tiny glass and nearly spluttered, for in common with the other guests he had been warned by Nancy not to refer to the Underground murder.

"Hello, Billy!"

Nancy's voice rose above the din of conversation, and Bobbie, listening to Mr. Yule's dramatic account of a certain assistant who carved a ham so badly that he lost heavily on its sales in slices, seized a glass for himself and filled it without noticing what he was doing.

"Very aggravating," Bobbie murmured, his brain clotted with a sickening sense of helplessness not free from terror.

"You know, Mr. Cheldon," said the little man confidentially, "a free and easy life is the life for me, and it suits Nancy, but it's a bit rough having to know a chap like Billy the Dancer." He lowered his voice and appeared to be gazing into his glass. "A blighter who'd lick your boots one moment and cut your throat the next." He lifted his eyes and turned them in the direction of the corner where the sallow-faced dancer, Tessie Hodey and the gentleman in evening dress comprised Nancy's audience. "Mr. Cheldon, when the police hear of a murder within a square mile of where we're standing, they first ask where Billy the Dancer was at the time. That's the sort of chap he is, and he's all the more dangerous because he's not a bully. Never loses his temper. Quiet and polite, and dangerous, damnably dangerous, and yet a coward."

Nosey came up before Bobbie could frame a suitable reply or comment, and a minute later Nancy was at his right with a story of a "hit" she had scored at a now defunct night club which had earned fame by the trouble it had given the police to extinguish it.

"Oh, there you are!" she exclaimed, as a fat woman covered with black silk and a dirty apron came in with the first consignment of sandwiches. "Arthur must have thought we'd eaten the supper before his arrival."

Mr. Yule smiled at the reference which reminded everybody except Bobbie, who had not been aware of it, that the edibles were from the Yule establishment.

"Now, Nosey, get busy. Bobbie, you look after the whisky and keep Bertie from it if you can."

A general laugh passed over Bobbie's head. He did not know who Bertie was and he did not wish to learn.

"There's tea and coffee."

Someone perched himself on the table in the corner, the girls found seats in chairs or on their arms, the men stood or leaned against the wall, and teeth and tongues moved at a rapid pace.

"Tessie, what about that song-hit of yours? If Nosey will get off the piano lid Bertie Desmond can accompany you."

"Oh, no, dear. You dance first," Tessie protested weakly. "I don't feel like singing tonight."

The usual preliminary to the song, and Bobbie, two chairs and a rug removed from Billy Bright, was able to join in the chorus of "The Ocean's Wide and so am I," which Tessie raced through breathlessly.

The pianist next took the floor.

"The Death of Eugene Aram," he announced in a sepulchral voice.

Bobbie had three drinks during the lengthy recitation, and twice to his extreme horror caught the roving eyes of Billy Bright.

"Thank you," said Nancy to the reciter, and Bobbie thought her voice was tart. "Will anyone else oblige with another selection from the mortuary?"

Tessie's peal of laughter saved the situation.

"If you ask me nicely, Nancy," said Nosey Ruslin, "I'll have a cup of tea. Yes, I mean it." He stared at the grins of appreciation of this manifestation of humour.

"It was time we had a joke, Nosey," said Nancy. "The whisky's behind you. Bobbie, fill his glass."

Someone started to sing a popular ballad of the hour, and the momentary confusion sorted itself into less noisy groups. It may have been merely an accident, but now Nosey and Billy found themselves together for the first time.

"A drink, Billy?" The voice was natural and distinct. "Why did you come back?" The voice was a whisper. "You know you haven't a chance." Billy's lips moved. "It's in my pocket now. Ten thousand quid. Keep your head and your nerve and all's well," was Nosey's rejoinder. "But you shouldn't have turned up here, Billy."

"Didn't you tell me to be natural?" Billy had the knack of talking without moving his lips, and to all intents and purposes his only interest at the moment was in his glass. "You swore at me for what you called running away."

"You did it too soon, but never mind now. Keep your head. I've got young Cheldon in my pocket."

"And he's got Nancy," was the growling response.

"We can't have everything," said Nosey warningly. "It had to be money or Nancy, and you'll want your share of the ten thousand."

"Will it stop at that?" The dark eyes were cold and suspicious.

"You bet not," said the big man with the slightest of grins.

"It was the money I came back for—not Nancy." There was a whine in the voice, but his expression retained its slyness.

"Then why did you come here tonight?"

"Because I wanted to see you, Nosey. There's no one else. I'm afraid of my own shadow sometimes, and if you let me down—"

"How could I? If you keep your mouth shut you'll be safe." Nosey affected to be unconscious of the threat in the other's voice. "You've only to deny I had nothing to do with you and they can't touch you."

"Yes, that's right. So you've screwed ten thousand out of him?"

Before he could reply Nancy had pounced on Nosey.

"Call for silence," she commanded him. "I must do my dance at once or else I'll be too drunk."

Her voice was a trifle thick and her movements jerky. Bobbie, who always felt half ashamed of Nancy when she was with her own kind if not kin, shivered and reproached himself for disloyalty. But Nancy in her primitive self was not of the Cheldon standard, not nearly, and he was ashamed of her. She had been talking loudly, slangily and even coarsely ever since the party had found its feet, and he hated loudness. She had a screaming reply for every remark addressed to her, and her determination to force the pace of the gaiety gave to the party an artificiality which even strong drink could not banish. He had never seen Nancy drink so much nor had he heard her talk so loudly. And to make matters worse with the passing of each minute he felt more and more out of it.

These were her friends, the scum of Soho, and she was one of them and one with them. It may have been mere mischance, but Bobbie could not but notice that she was more anxious to please the ramshackle collection of human and sub-human eccentrics than she was to give him any of her society. He tried to excuse her with the plea that in a sense he was one of the hosts and that she was bound by the laws of hospitality to let him fend for himself, but the excuse did not ring true.

The centre of the room had been cleared by now, and Nancy was awaiting the signal from the pianist.

"Bravo!" The cry came from Nosey as the pianist struck a chord.

She danced better than she had ever danced before, but Bobbie, sensitive and detached, failed to detect any beauty whatever in her performance. To him it was a vulgar exhibition, and all the snob in him rose until he could hardly stifle his desire to protest. There was the bounder Bertie handling her with noisome pleasure; here was Mr. Yule of the ham and beef shop bestowing a frantic kiss of enthusiasm on her burning cheek, and above all rose the shrieks of Tessie, the self-elected sycophant to the dancer who would soon be the wife of the owner of Broadbridge Manor.

"Marvellous!—Marvellous!" The shrill voice came from near the door and all eyes turned in its direction.

"Do you really think so, Billy?" Nancy exclaimed, with that gratitude with which the pupil receives the encomiums of a master.

"I do. You've never done better, Nancy. If only you could repeat it the world would be at your feet."

She was so overcome by his praise that to Bobbie's horror she ran to him with outstretched arms.

"Oh, Billy," she cried, with the remnants of a sob in her throat, "you are a darling!" She kissed him on the mouth!

Bobbie felt sick again.

"Come along, Nancy, and give us an encore," cried Nosey Ruslin, who was watching Bobbie as he spoke.

The device to separate the dancer and the man who had murdered the uncle of her lover succeeded only because it was an appeal to vanity.

"You fool!" Nosey later hissed into Billy's ear. "Keep away from her or we'll lose the money and you'll lose something more."

Billy the Dancer looked up at him with a smile that was born of a smirk.

"I couldn't help it, Nosey, and I can't forget," he muttered.

"And I can't forget either." It was a threat.

"We sink or swim together, Nosey, that's what you're always saying," was the covert threat with which the dancer countered it.

"Must I tell you again to keep away?" The words were barely audible, but the speaker's expression spoke volumes. "You'll lose ten thousand quid and more to follow." He pretended to be watching the dancing. "Aye, and Nancy into the bargain. Do you think she'd ever marry you—now?"

"She doesn't know."

"She could be told."

To end the argument he walked over to the piano and entered into conversation with the gentleman in evening dress.

"What about a dance?" Tessie cried when Nancy's individual effort had ended amid the expected applause, Billy Bright defiantly leading it.

"How many of us are there?" As Nancy spoke she began to count. "Twelve. With Bertie to play the piano someone will have to sit out. Come on, Bertie, strike up. Bobbie, you shall have the first dance, but be a good boy and fetch me a whisky. Not too much soda. It's unlucky."

The laughter had died away when, as the pianist was stretching his fingers lightly over the keys, the sound of a loud knock startled the more nervy members of the party.

"Who can that be?" asked Nosey Ruslin uneasily.

Someone uttered a choked cry, but only Nosey and Bobbie detected that it came from Billy Bright.

"Keep him out," Tessie called. "Whoever it is it'll make us thirteen."

A curious and inexplainable nervousness seemed to have infected the whole party as Nancy, slightly unsteady and too obviously hilarious, went into the narrow passage and turned the small knob which opened the door. Bobbie, still feeling oddly out of everything and the only intruder there, listened because there was nothing else to do. He was supposed to be the hero of the gathering of which Nancy was the heroine, but somehow he had escaped observation, and even Nancy's invitation to a dance had not dragged him out of his obscurity.

Suddenly a scream rent the air and their nerves, a scream that Bobbie, unaccustomed to the overworked hysteria of minor Bohemia, interpreted as a signal of danger and rushed forward. Before, however, he came in sight of Nancy another scream revealed that it was her method of expressing delighted surprise at the unexpected arrival of an old friend.

"Why, if it isn't Annie!" The voice with its broad textures of cockney manufacture rose to a scream which thinned out in a sort of minor gasp. "Come in, Annie. You'll find some of your old pals in there."

Bobbie was only in time to avoid a collision in the doorway, and he was back again by the engraving when Nancy appeared with a girl who, under a black coat of unseasonable and suspicious fur, wore a light pink dress that belonged to the gaslight.

"Annie!" exclaimed Nosey Ruslin, and rushed to embrace her. When this ceremony had been performed he held her at arms' length for what purported to be a critical inspection.

"Not a day older, sweetheart," he said, with all the

cordiality and affection of which he was capable. "But where you been all this time?"

Before she could think of a suitable reply she identified Billy Bright and threw a hand in his direction.

"Billy," she cried, reproachfully. "Haven't you a word for your first dancing partner?" Evidently Billy was only of minor importance and her flattery was the current coin of their language, for the next moment she was exchanging abbreviated reminiscences with three of the guests whose lives had crossed hers in the days when she had been the principal dancer in the troupe known as the "Seven Fairies."

"You've kept your figure, Annie," said someone, and, indeed, she had.

Tall, firmly made, well-proportioned, and pretty, there could be no denying that Annie Smithers was still the equal of the beauty once known as Hortense Delisle, a name which was amongst the proudest inventions of Nosey Ruslin. Her eyes were absurdly blue and her skin actually too pretty to require cosmetics. Nearly everyone who watched her now, and Bobbie was fascinated by her, realised that Nancy herself, the beauty of the party hitherto, was eclipsed. Annie bore herself too with something that was not as cheap as her speech and manners. There was a trace of dignity, a suggestion of position, even of power in her carriage. It was only imagination, as Bobbie unnecessarily assured himself, but to Nosey Ruslin, a quick observer of his fellows, it brought a surprise that puzzled him.

"A drink for Annie." Of course, it was Nancy who spoke. It would be Nancy. Bobbie turned to hide his expression of annoyance. Why was she at her worst on this night of nights? Could it be possible that the girl he adored and idealised could be so common and vulgar? She was not drunk but she was on the verge of intoxication, and her alcoholic humour was revolting to the head of the great Cheldon family.

Billy Bright acted as waiter, and Annie with a cheery "Here's everybody," banished the whisky.

"You're tired, Annie," said Nosey, who had become master of the ceremonies by his own choice. "Here's a chair."

The newcomer flung herself into it with an expression of thanks.

"Been travelling all day," she murmured, "and the kid was a drag."

"What kid?" asked Nosey, but before Annie could speak Nancy had seized her left hand and was holding it up for general inspection.

"Look!" she screamed. She was an expert screamer. "A wedding ring! Oh, my Lord, fancy Annie as a wife—"

"And mother," said Annie, with a laugh. "You should see young Jumbo. Not quite three yet and a heavyweight champion."

"You should have brought him along," said Billy Bright, who was enjoying the diversion.

"Yes, you ought to," exclaimed Tessie. "He'd have made us fourteen. We're thirteen now and that means bad luck for someone."

"It may mean bad luck for all of us," said Bertie, whose other name appeared to be evening dress. He had lurched across from the piano with a glass in one hand and a sandwich in the other.

Nancy screamed again, but it was only one of her minor efforts.

"Don't, Bertie, don't. Annie, a sandwich? Never mind about the bad luck. So you're married. Why didn't you let us know. We'd have given you a benefit night at the 'Frozen Fang'."

Annie laughed into her glass.

"Who's the chap?" asked Nosey Ruslin chaffingly. He did not believe that Annie was married at all, being certain that had there been an actual ceremony he would have heard of it.

She looked up at him with a teasing smile.

"The solicitor told me not to talk," she said pertly.

"So there's a secret, eh?" Nosey having taken command was allowed to do the cross-examining. His audience was too interested to care for vocal interruptions.

"Yes. It was a secret marriage to begin with. And then I haven't seen my husband for over two years."

"Where is he now?" Nosey took her empty glass from her and handed it to Bobbie, who happened to be behind him.

"Dead." Her expression was grave as she uttered the word but her hearers with one accord detected the absence of regret or sorrow.

"Oh, bother!" exclaimed Nancy irritably. "We're getting too slow. Bertie, what about that dance?"

"Won't Annie have another drink?" asked the pianist, who evidently preferred Annie's conversation to his own music.

"I'm too tired to dance," said Tessie petulantly.

"What about yourself, Nancy?" asked the latest guest. "You haven't told me anything. Are you married?"

"No, but I'm going to be. That's what the party's for." With a quick and inescapable movement so far as Bobbie was concerned she caught him by the arm and dragged him into reluctant prominence. "My gentleman friend," she exclaimed in a voice that had more alcohol than pride in it.

"Pleased to meet you," said Annie cordially. "What's the name?"

"Bobbie," Nancy replied before the head of the Cheldons could reply with appropriate dignity and distance.

"Any other?" asked the inquirer. "Sounds like a pet dog so far."

A new brand of scream from Nancy inaugurated the applause.

"The same old Annie," she cried, wiping her eyes. "That was a good one, that was." Then she pulled herself together with an effort that was far from easy. "The boy friend has two names, perhaps three."

Someone laughed and most of the guests sought refreshment. The party had developed into an informal gathering with Annie Smithers, once the Hortense Delisle of "Seven Fairies" fame, as the centre of attraction, but had they not all been suffering from physical fatigue she would in all probability have been left to Nancy or to Nosey Ruslin. As it was the other guests languidly looked on and listened, seldom troubling to comment, interested more in the edibles and the liquids than the return of the exile from respectability.

"You're a good looker, you are," said Annie, appreciatively, as Bobbie, feeling the complete ass, approached the horsehair throne.

"You flatter me," he answered, unconsciously a little stiffly.

"That's just how my old man used to talk," she exclaimed and giggled. "But what's the name? Don't answer if there's anything to pay. It'll probably leak out at the assizes."

The joke received its reward of a scream from Nancy and a variety of growls from Nosey Ruslin's throat.

"Bobby, you're a dunce!" exclaimed Nancy, lurching against him and seizing his arm for support. "Kiss Annie and be friends with her."

Involuntarily he drew back, and instantly regretted it, but Nancy provided a diversion.

"When I'm Mrs. Bobbie Cheldon, Annie, and—"

"What's that?" Annie's voice was wholly serious now."

"You're deaf, old dear, deaf. I said Mrs. Bobbie Cheldon."

"But that's my name—I mean the Cheldon. I'm Mrs. Massy Cheldon. You remember the old chap we used to chaff at the 'Broken Tincan' club in Dean Street? Well, I married him four years ago and—why, what's the matter? Nosey, you're as white as the boy friend himself?" She gazed around her until she came to Nancy's stupid grin. "It isn't a joke, is it?"

Bobbie had fallen back out of her line of vision and was leaning heavily against the wall. Nosey Ruslin with face averted was muttering to himself. Billy Bright with a vacant look was trying to seek enlightenment from his partner. And Nancy Curzon, unable to comprehend the meaning and significance of what she had heard as if from the other end of a telephone that buzzed, stood with the assistance of a convenient chair and grinned and smiled and smiled and grinned in turn.

"It can't be true," someone muttered, and no one identified the speaker.

"Ask the family solicitor that and he'll tell you different," said Annie, bridling at the aspersion on her "marriage lines." "He's got them now, and when I showed them to him he had the surprise of his old life when I called on him this afternoon."

"Are you the widow of Massy Cheldon who was murdered a week ago last Monday?" asked Nosey Ruslin, in a voice that croaked and creaked.

"Yes, and if you expect me to do the water-cart act you're jolly well mistaken!" she shouted, mistaking his meaning. "I'm not in mourning and I ain't going to be. Why should I turn myself into a hearse for a man who deserted me when I wanted him and who threatened to take away the kid if I didn't keep our marriage a secret? Five quid a week and him with thousands a year as I've seen from the papers. My God, what do you think I am, Nosey? Dirt?"

She was the raging, tearing harridan now, unable to realise the tragic purport of the news she had disclosed, unable because of lack of the necessary knowledge to appreciate what the secret of her marriage meant to at least four persons in that room.

"I wasn't good enough for his friends!" The whisky had got into her head and inflamed her notions of her pride and importance. "I was to be shut up in lodgings in a God-forsaken village in Cornwall with an allowance of five quid a week on condition I didn't open my mouth. He had me in his power because of the kid. Talked, he did, of my carrying on with another chap when he knew it was only because I had to talk to someone. Nothing more, but he hinted at a divorce and getting the kid to himself."

"I can't believe it," Bobbie gasped, white and trembling, in the grip of a horror that produced sheer physical agony.

"Can't believe what?" Annie screamed. "Well, if it interests you, Mr. Bobbie Cheldon, you shall see my marriage lines and Milton's birth certificate. I've got them safe."

Reared in conditions which conferred a sacrosanct exclusiveness on all documents dealing with marriage and legitimacy, Annie Smithers, claiming to be Mrs. Massy Cheldon, laboured under the delusion that marriage lines and birth certificates once lost could not be replaced.

"Leave her alone, Bobbie, can't you?" exclaimed Nancy irritably. "What business of yours is it? Why shouldn't Annie marry anyone she pleases?"

The intervention restored the outraged guest's good humour.

"Of course, it is, Nancy. You're a dear. My head's splitting."

The usual remedy was applied, and Bertie of the evening dress announced that with it the supply of the most popular liquid had given out. Someone laughed and suggested raiding the bar of the 'Frozen Fang', but Nosey Ruslin, Bobbie, and Billy Bright were unconscious of the interlude. A heaviness of heart had descended on all three, and at least two were balancing the probabilities of escape and the hangman. Billy the Dancer's face was a faint yellow and his forehead was wet.

"I'll go mad if I stay here much longer," Nosey whispered to Bobbie. "Never mind about Nancy. She's too drunk to understand. But in the morning, Cheldon, in the morning!"

Even in that moment of the tragic death of all his hopes Bobbie could wince at the unexpected familiarity of the ex-pugilist. But the wince was replaced by a spasm of fear that recurred again and again before he and Nosey crept downstairs, not because they had any compassion for the slumbers of the queer tenants of the queer building but because they had to keep time and tune with their gloomy and disturbing thoughts.

In the street Nosey stopped first.

"What's the game now?" he asked roughly.

"The game's up," said Bobbie, sullenly.

"And my ten thousand quid?"

Bobbie laughed ironically. It struck him as the worst of taste to talk of money in that moment of moments.

"Where's my ten thousand a year?" he demanded, forcing himself to present an affectation of fearlessness.

Nosey glanced up and down the windless, deserted and ghostly street.

"He's done us in, Cheldon, he's dished us completely. That uncle of yours has got even with the whole blooming lot of us. The old sinner!" He added a few more epithets not to be found recorded except in the more daring dictionaries of slang. "Fancy Annie Smithers scooping the pool, with that brat of hers! I wonder where the kid is."

Bobbie, taking the suggestion seriously, recoiled from him.

"Spent scores of quids and here I am without a shilling." The monologue was Nosey's. "Just when I thought I'd earned something for my old age this knock-out blow comes along. Was ever such cursed luck!" He turned on Bobbie with all the vileness of his type, but the avalanche of filth and reproach was stayed by the heavy footfalls of a policeman.

"I'm off home," said Nosey, crossing the road.

The policeman turned his lantern on Bobbie and bade him "Good night," and the rejoinder was duly memorised by the official protector of the night before he resumed his beat.

For nearly five minutes the dispossessed heir to the Cheldon estate stood, immovable in his uncertainty. Not a sound now came to disturb thoughts which forced themselves into prominence and added to his agony of mind. It was useless voicing a suspicion that it had all been a nightmare, that there was no Annie Smithers....

"I remember now. Nancy did say that uncle had been keen on Hortense Delisle." He could not smile as the name rolled off his lips. "But how could I—what could I—"

A door behind him opened, and he walked away from it to a friendly doorway on the other side which enabled him to watch Billy Bright and the tall man in evening dress they had called "Bertie" walk away together. In the dim light from a street lamp he decided that Billy was so drunk that his companion had to drag him along.

Would it be worth while to return to Nancy? The only answer was a reminder that what Nancy needed was sleep, the only medicine that could cure her.

The other guests appeared in batches, and by way of escape from his thoughts he counted them.

"That makes nine including myself and Ruslin," he muttered. "I suppose my aunt by marriage is staying the night with Nancy."

"I won't believe it—I refuse to believe it," he said aloud when the closing of the door opposite symbolised the end of a day which had encroached on the next one to the extent of three hours. "My God, it can't be true. A job in the city again, and Galahad Mansions for the rest of my life."

In a paroxysm of self-pity he wiped his dry eyes.

"Can I do anything for you, sir?" It was the policeman again.

"No—er—no—thanks—I'll walk home."

When he reached Shaftesbury Avenue, almost rendered virginal by depopulation, he stopped to glance in search of a taxi. In the same moment he dug his hands into his pockets and discovered by contact with the few coins they contained that he had not the fare to the remote hinterland of Fulham where Galahad Mansions reared its head above the woes and worries of its impecunious tenantry.

Measured by his despair and disappointment it was the longest journey he had ever made; measured by the fear that seized him half way it was the shortest, for the arrival at the colourless frame of wood that formed the hall door of Galahad Mansions produced a choking sensation as if the prison walls had closed in on him. But he could not bring himself to pass the block of flats and he dived into the gloomy hall and trudged up the three flights of stairs to where he was wont to fumble for a place in the lock with his key. Not a sound anywhere, not a breath of air, not any sort of rival to his tempest of baffled hopes, gloom and dread.

In the sitting-room he switched on all the lights and drank in, as if it were a dose of poison, all the evidences of poverty it contained. Something of the painful ecstasy of the martyr in his agonies seized him and again a flood of self-pity rose to the surface as he dwelt fondly on the spectacle of himself as a particularly unfortunate victim of Fate.

With a dramatic gesture he seized a siphon and would have found its companion, the whisky decanter in the same manner, had he thought of it, but he was acting mechanically to an audience of himself, and it was of himself that he thought and nothing else.

"Ten thousand a year a few hours ago—and now!" It was very theatrical and stagey, but genuine to him, and he enjoyed the sensation of pain and sacrifice and suffering because he was convinced all three were undeserved.

"What's that?" He started as a noise like the patting of a carpet disturbed the silence which he had claimed as his own.

"Only me, Bobbie."

Through the open doorway his mother appeared, clad in a dressing-gown and looking beautiful and young in spite of her pale face and tear-filled eyes. To Bobbie she was a ghost of all that might have been until he saw the tears and was frightened by them.

Was it possible that she had heard? Perhaps the family solicitor had sent a special messenger with the terrible news!

"Oh, Bobbie," she said in a voice of anguish, "I've had a letter from the solicitor this evening and since reading it I haven't stopped crying."

Then she did know!

"It can't be helped, mother," he said, valiantly.

She looked at him quickly.

"You can't know," she said confidently. "It was about your uncle's will. Bobbie, he did love me, after all, and, perhaps, if he had proposed I might have married him. Who knows! Especially if you married and I was lonely. But he didn't forget me, Bobbie, and although it's only little more than a thousand pounds it's all left to me. I am the only person he names in his will. Do you wonder at my tears now?"

She covered her face with her hands and sobbed, and Bobbie knew that had he been a woman he would have sobbed too, though not for the money she had gained but for the fortune he had lost.

Chapter Fourteen

Mr. Nosey Ruslin sat on the edge of his ramshackle bed, striving to master his rage so that he might be able to evolve a scheme to counter the dangers of his immediate future. He had not undressed on his return home at a quarter to four, but to his surprise he had discovered that since throwing himself on the bed he must have slept for several hours, for it was nearly noon and the world was alive.

The first admission had to be the loss of the fortune for which he had so cunningly marshalled his forces. It was useless drugging himself with doubts of the genuineness of Annie Smithers' claim to be the widow of Massy Cheldon and the mother of the new owner of the Cheldon estate. That thought had occurred to him the very moment she had startled the company with the disclosure of her marriage. He had even tried to persuade himself that it was a trick of Chief Inspector Wake's, but a little reflection had convinced him that such a ruse would be altogether foreign to the stolid, clever and shrewd Scotland Yard detective. Wake was crafty and full of ideas, but not of this brand. He moodily admitted as much as he stared at the yellowish wallpaper confronting him, and deducted from it the necessity to take steps towards self-preservation.

He must be prepared for the worst now, and the worst would begin with the arrest of Billy Bright. They had discussed the possibility and had agreed on the course to be pursued if the dancer found himself in gaol. But that did nothing to lessen the strain of waiting for the sequel to the tragic destruction of his castle of gold.

A smile illumined the gloom of his countenance for a moment and vanished. Poor Nancy! What would she do now? Would she marry young Cheldon for his gentility alone? What would she do if all the details of the conspiracy were revealed? What———?

The shout of a newsboy under the window electrified him, and to the accompaniment of curses which were an antidote for terror he ran to the door. The newsboy had gone, but at the end of the street there was an old man crouching beside a collection of newspapers.

"Quick, give me one. Here you are." He flung a sixpence at the perturbed veteran and with the "early sporting" gripped in his right hand ran homewards.

PICCADILLY MURDER.
SENSATIONAL ARREST.

"It's Billy!" he gasped, and choked.

He had been fully prepared for the news, and yet, now that it was there in print before him it had the startling effect of a totally unexpected catastrophe. For quite five minutes he was helpless in the tentacles of a monstrous terror, but with the gradual return to power of his thinking faculties the imminence of danger compelled him to assert himself.

It was the bulwark of his hopes now that he and Billy had anticipated this disaster and had prepared for it.

"They can hang us together, Billy," he had whispered to the dancer in a corner of Nancy's room the night before. "But they can't hang us separately. If they take you don't forget to deny that you and I were partners. Swear until you're black in the face that you know nothing of the murder and nothing of me so far as the murder is concerned. If they take me I'll do the same. But remember, Billy, that if you turn yellow and give me away you'll only make certain of tying the rope around your own neck. Think it over and see if there's a flaw in that reasoning. It's only suspicion they can arrest you on—nothing more—but the suspicion will be proof if you blab about me. Old Wideawake regards me as the leader and if he can prove that I was behind you—well, God help you, Billy."

He had insisted on discussing that point again and again, afraid lest Billy Bright should not fully understand it. He had never been such a fool as to expect loyalty from the dancer, and from the beginning of the conspiracy against the life of Massy Cheldon he had fashioned his plans in such a manner that Billy at least could not betray him without sacrificing himself.

Yet he was not really satisfied or quiet of mind now. You never could tell what stupidities Billy the Dancer might perpetrate in the initial terrors of arrest. He must be prepared for the worst, although the worst could be brought about only by Billy Bright committing suicide. That was how Nosey put it to himself.

"They may be after me soon," he said aloud, and in that moment swept aside all irrelevant thoughts.

He was fully conscious of the necessity for action based on a frank realisation of the facts of the case. And the first unpleasant fact was that the Cheldon fortune had been lost.

Having assured himself that the door of the flat was locked and barred he excavated from under the boards near the firegrate a small box containing three pieces of paper which a dozen hours previously he had regarded as of almost priceless value. Slowly and with a faintly expressed reluctance he examined them. First, the letter from Massy Cheldon which had accompanied the revolver, then a note from Bobbie, and finally the dispossessed heir's promise to pay ten thousand pounds after he had become the owner of the Cheldon estate. Nosey fingered them with a slowness of movement which revealed his state of mind and he was still in the act of prolonging the farewell when the voice of a newsboy proclaiming that day's "runners and betting" reminded him of the earlier message and he jerked himself into action.

A few minutes later all the once-precious papers were reduced to a tiny collection of ashes, and as if to make assurance doubly sure these ashes were dispatched into the air from the window.

"Now if Billy carries out our plan all will be well," he muttered, and returned to his bedroom to repair and decorate himself for a day which was certain to be a memorable one in the autobiography of Nosey Ruslin.

Carefully and with remarkable steadiness he shaved his two undulating cheeks, and with equal care and precision arrayed himself in such garments as he considered consistent with the weather and the colour of Shaftesbury Avenue. All the time he kept up a noiseless running commentary, interspersed with questions and answers, on the problems created by Billy Bright's arrest. There were many rocks ahead, but he was not afraid of those he could see. It was the unknown and the uncertain that he feared. Thank goodness, he had terrified Billy into a condition of commonsense which, if it lasted, must have the effect of saving his, Nosey's life, even if it did not open the prison gates to the dancer.

In the Piccadilly teashop where he breakfasted with a magnificent disregard of privacy he listened with a smile to the excited chatter of the waitresses about the arrest of the "Soho dancer".

"I've met him," one girl boasted with a fearful joy.

A fresh breeze strengthened the golden wine in the air, and Nosey, replete and confident, sauntered towards Shaftesbury Avenue, the man of means and of leisure to the life. It was one of Piccadilly's glamorous days when the cares of life are forgotten because it is difficult to think of them. All around him was the noise and the traffic and the excitement. At the entrance to the Underground railway where Lower Regent Street touched the Haymarket, he paused to watch the descent into the scene of the crime of a regiment of men and women whose dormant curiosity had been revived by the news of Billy Bright's arrest.

When he had had his fill of watching he resumed his journey to his native land, the stretch of roads and pavements bounded on one side by the Circus and on the other by Tottenham Court Road. He had become anxious for friendly human speech, and he knew it was certain to be found in Greville's restaurant now that the hour of one had struck.

"Why, that means I owe Wake a fiver! Good Lord! I hope he may get it. I wonder if there's anything running today I might have a flutter on." He spoke from the text of a passing newspaper contents bill.

"Hello, Nosey!"

The greeting came from a burly little man with a square face and a triple chin. Nosey identified him as the former proprietor of a night club which had been struck off and its owner fined a hundred pounds. But the feat of memory was due entirely to the ease with which one can recollect the obligations of a debtor, and Nosey fell into line with him hopefully.

"So it was Billy the Dancer, was it?" asked the stout man with the conscious virtue of a crook whose misdeeds had not as yet brought him within measurable distance of the scaffold. "Between you and me, Nosey, I'd never have thought he had the guts."

"You forget he's mostly Italian and has a nasty temper," said Nosey, who was trying to estimate the degree of solvency the new lounge suit indicated. "How are things, Solly? They're a bit blue round the chin with me."

"More than the same here," was the depressing reply. "Was hoping you'd be able to stand me lunch. But fancy Billy!"

Nosey sauntered on alone through the crowd converging on Piccadilly during the lunch hour so as to make the pilgrimage to the scene of the Underground murder. The ex-pugilist identified several plainclothes men with whom he was not on speaking terms, but their proximity did not disturb him. He had less than five shillings and unless the newspapers took his appetite away he would have to lunch at Greville's. No other restaurant would do, for to strengthen and buttress his confidence he must show himself where he was best known.

At twenty-five minutes past one he was on the very doorstep of the Italian restaurant with the Elizabethan name when a newsboy brought into view a contents bill bearing the words "Piccadilly Murder—Victim's Secret Romance." In that moment Nosey, who had successfully withstood the painful sensation created by the news of Billy Bright's arrest nearly collapsed.

"A paper," he gasped, and fumbled with a penny.

The boy snatched at it and resumed his flight, while Nosey, leaning against the wall, ought to have blessed the modern habit of telling the whole of a story in a few headlines.

There it was in all the naked impressiveness of print. Some enterprising journalist had found Annie Smithers and had listened to her.

"The beautiful Hortense Delisle, whom many will remember for her brilliant performances as the leader of the far-famed dancing troupe appropriately named 'The Seven Fairies', has come back into the limelight again with a story no novelist could have invented, a story of a secret marriage to a wealthy Sussex squire, the head of a great county family. Interviewed by our representative, Miss Delisle, or, as she now is, Mrs. Massy Cheldon, told how…' "

Nosey read and read until he became so interested that he quite forgot all that it had meant and still meant to himself. Once he smiled when he reminded himself that not once in the two columns was "Annie Smithers" mentioned. It was Hortense Delisle who had met Massy Cheldon in "a fashionable night club"—the description was good enough for another laugh—and had fascinated the wealthy clubman. They had been married in a Manchester register office and had never disclosed the marriage even to their most intimate friends. Circumstances—that was the word either Annie or the interviewer used, and Nosey thought it very diplomatic— had compelled them to keep it quiet until Mrs. Massy Cheldon, living with her son and heir in an obscure Cornish village, heard of the murder of her husband and came at once to claim her rights.

Not once, Nosey observed to himself, did Annie express regret for the loss of her husband. It was of "her rights" and "my son's rights" that she talked.

"Gorblime!" exclaimed Nosey, nearly tearing the paper in his newer and greater excitement, "what's this?"

The inability to resist a betrayal of his semi-illiteracy was always a sure sign of Nosey's utter abandonment to emotion.

"Good lad!" he cried, unable to restrain himself, and not in the least embarrassed by curious stares.

With the most aggressive of smiles he entered the restaurant and took a table which was a favourite of his.

"Something costing five bob including a bottle of red wine," he said to his friend the waiter, and buried himself in the newspaper again.

"When our representative called on Mr. Robert Cheldon, the nephew and hitherto the generally accepted heir to the late Mr. Massy Cheldon, he was assured that the disclosure of his uncle's secret marriage was no surprise to him. 'I have known it for some time,' said Mr. Cheldon, pleasantly, 'and I am sure my young cousin will be a worthy head of the family when he is old enough to shoulder his responsibilities. I understand that my uncle's widow is the daughter of a solicitor's clerk. If so it is appropriate that she should be the mother of the heir, for the founder of the family fortunes in the late eighteenth century was a clerk in a lawyer's office in the City of London who went to India.'"

There was more, but Nosey's delight was confined to Bobbie's statement that he was not surprised and not at all disappointed to find himself no longer the heir to the Cheldon estate.

"A good lad," he murmured with moist lips. "More brains than I ever suspected he had. Must see more of him when this little bit of trouble is over." A shadow fell across the table. "Hello, Inspector!" He laughed. "If you've called for that fiver you'll have to give me time to collect the fiver first."

Chief Inspector Wake's gravity did not relax.

"The bet was only a joke, Nosey," he said quietly. "I looked in to tell you that the superintendent would be grateful if you'd drop in at the Yard for a few minutes' chat."

"Must have lunch first, inspector," said Nosey complacently. "Never any good at talking until I've stoked and oiled the old tum."

The detective took the chair opposite him.

"I'll lunch too," he said quietly, "and if you're short I don't mind paying the bill."

The arrival of the waiter created an armistice which was not broken until the double bill was presented forty minutes later.

"I'll pay," said Wake shortly. "Ready, Nosey?"

It was a critical moment, a moment which could influence every moment of Nosey's life that was to follow it. Should he show resentment? Dare he display anger?

The answer was characteristic of Nosey Ruslin's easy-going nature when there was nothing to be gained by a display of truculence.

"Righto," he said, cheerfully. "If I can help I'm your man. I must say, inspector, you surprised me by putting the derbies on Billy the Dancer. I should never have suspected him."

He talked all the way and so cheerfully and naturally that he did not notice his companion's taciturnity.

"Not taking it down so that it may be used in evidence, inspector?" was his last attempt at humour as they entered the portals of the building overlooking the Embankment.

He left it two hours and three-quarters later and in the freer air of Whitehall lit a cigar as an oblation to Victory. And it had been a memorable victory, too.

At the beginning of the contest of wits between the combined forces of the superintendent, Wake, and a silent and observant Detective-Sergeant Clarke and the ex-pugilist, the last-named had been in a state of fright which had actually proved helpful, for it had prevented him talking before he had had time to think. But once he had been clever enough to ignore his surroundings he had never feared for the result.

"Of course, I know Billy the Dancer. Of course, I know Bobbie Cheldon." There were numerous other "of courses" to preface the statement that he had had no hand in the murder of Massy Cheldon.

"Ask Billy himself," he had hurled at Wake.

The inspector had merely smiled slightly, but in the smile Nosey had read a confession that Billy was keeping the silence that outwits all curiosity.

"Yes, I know you've traced the dagger to Billy, but what of that? Didn't he sell it for a bob to an out of work Italian waiter? No, I don't know the name of the buyer. That was days before the murder. Oh, you say, Billy was seen in the Underground on the Monday night." He laughed. "That's new to me, inspector, and probably is to Billy also."

These were mere snatches of a conference which at times had developed into meaning silences and meaningless duologues. But out of everything emerged the one glorious fact, Nosey Ruslin was free and unfettered, and Billy the Dancer had more than a good chance of hearing an Old Bailey foreman of the jury pronounce the life-saving words, Not Guilty.

The police court proceedings were not, however, encouraging to Nosey. Wake obviously left a great deal unsaid, and there were many hints of "developments." On the credit side was Billy's calm demeanour, in itself a delicious surprise to the ex-pugilist, who had expected to see a half-fainting prisoner carried into court. To Nosey, who had had a large, if chiefly vicarious experience of docks, the police court investigation was only a formality which meant little. He knew that no matter what happened Billy Bright must be committed for trial.

"And then the real fight will begin," he said to himself as he passed the dock and smiled reassuringly to his dupe while the magistrate was sending the accused for trial.

The enormous crowd outside the police court frightened Nosey out of his assumption of bodily and mental ease, and he lurked within the precincts of the grim building until weariness overcame curiosity and the street emptied.

On his way home he reviewed immediate events with the object of deriving information if not inspiration from them.

That Bobbie Cheldon had not been called as a witness was an indication that the prosecution did not intend to trouble a judge and jury with a motive for the crime.

"Have they sufficient evidence to convict Billy without showing that he had a motive?" he asked himself. "I wonder young Cheldon didn't turn up. 'Fraid to, I suppose."

He walked on, seeking diversion now and then by reminding himself that he was being shadowed by two plainclothes men, and was ever confident and almost urbane.

At nine o'clock he left his flat for a meal at Greville's; and on the doorstep of the restaurant was handed a document which acquainted him with the decision of the prosecution to call him as a witness.

"That means they can't cross-examine you unless you give yourself away," said his solicitor, a bibulous failure whose main source of supply came from fees earned on behalf of swindling bookmakers who tricked foolish backers into entrusting their commissions to them.

"Thanks," said Nosey, and pocketed the piece of official paper again. "I'll be all smiles and help and nothin'."

But for all his affectation of confidence and peace the days of Nosey Ruslin were days of fear, with nights rendered sleepless by thoughts which he could not take captive. He was almost afraid to read the newspapers with their terrifying references to "unexpected developments" into which the ex-pugilist read sufficient to bring the perspiration to his forehead.

To add to his fears there was a curious sense of loneliness which fifty acquaintances could not banish because they did not include in their ranks either Nancy or Bobbie Cheldon. He felt and not for the first time that his natural allies had deserted him. In a state of indecision he sat down and wrote another letter to Billy offering to help him all he could.

"Wake will read it and see I'm not afraid of him," he said with a smirk which was not prolonged. "I want them all to know that I don't desert a pal in trouble. But I'd like to see Nancy. She can't be thinking of marrying that young fool, Cheldon, now."

But Nosey Ruslin was only one of many persons to whom the impending murder trial at the Old Bailey was a source of perpetual worry. In Bobbie it bred a torture which nearly drove him frantic as he waited fearfully with his mother in the cottage twenty miles from London they had exchanged for the dismal Mansions of Galahad. When Mr. Parker, the official solicitor of the Cheldon family, wrote to announce that Annie Cheldon, *née* Smithers, and formerly Hortense Delisle, was with her massive infant installed in Broadbridge Manor, Bobbie hardly felt surprise or annoyance. The story had become old and stale, and there was the overwhelming competition of the constant preparation for his appearance in the witness-box when Billy Bright was on trial for the murder of Massy Cheldon.

But he still could think of Nancy with a wistfulness that hopelessness intensified. If only…

He had come to London for the day to settle accounts with the agent for Galahad Mansions when he met Nancy outside the Trocadero. Their encounter was no coincidence, for he had been pacing her regular haunts for nearly four hours on the chance of running into her.

"Oh, it's you, is it?" was her ungracious recognition of him.

Nancy had been and still was utterly bewildered by the inexplicable blow Chance had dealt her, but she had a suspicion that she had been tricked by someone, and that someone, Bobbie Cheldon.

"I am a pauper now, Nancy," he said with the passion of the weak and the feckless for sentiment and self-pity. "I am thinking of going abroad and—"

She left him standing and phrase-making, but within ten minutes she was smiling and happy. A penny exchanged for an evening paper had effected the transformation.

"The beautiful young dancer," she read from the latest information about the forthcoming sensational Old Bailey murder trial. "Well known and popular in London's exclusive Bohemian circles."

She could not resist the lure of lavish praise.

"Poor Bobbie," she said to herself as she examined the coins in her handbag and went in search of a tobacconist who stocked her favourite brand of cigarettes.

The days sped by to the date of the trial as London waited impatiently for the fulfilment of the promises of sensations. Nosey Ruslin grew haggard and apprehensive to such an extent that when he was at last ushered into the witness-box and was confronted by what seemed to be several acres of faces he could hardly hear his own voice, and on his return to the corridor outside was none the wiser for his experience. But a few hours later as he and Nancy were having tea together an evening newspaper explained to him why the jury had found Billy Bright guilty in less than twenty minutes. Five witnesses whose names Nosey had never heard of before had identified Billy as the man they had seen near Massy Cheldon at the time of the murder, and three more witnesses had proved that instead of selling the weapon to an out of work waiter the prisoner had had it in his possession on the evening of June the eighth, the last day of Massy Cheldon's life.

"Bit of luck for me that that all came after Billy had sworn in the witness-box he'd never mentioned Massy Cheldon to me or to anyone else. He couldn't go back on that without pleading guilty, and he couldn't guess what the jury would say." He mopped his forehead, and watched sympathetically the tears in Nancy's eyes.

"Have another cup of tea," he said gently. "It's all right. There's no one looking our way."

They had a table in the corner of a gigantic teashop in the Strand at a time when most tea-drinkers had departed satiated, and already the conviction of Billy Bright was nearly as stale as the result of the three-thirty race.

"I can't help feeling sorry for Billy," she whispered, all the colour gone from her cheeks and all the life from her eyes.

"You must forget, Nancy. Go away and forget. You are too lovely and dainty for this sort of thing." He patted her cheek and she smiled her gratitude.

"I'm going to stay and remember," she said with an attempt at pertness. "Loneliness would kill me."

"You're not—not marrying—"

She made a gesture of impatience.

"Marry a chap I'd have to keep? Not bloomin' likely, Nosey."

He smiled placidly.

"If I were only twenty years younger, Nancy."

She laughed now.

"You dear old thing! If you were twenty years younger you'd have been married long ago. But still, Nosey, you can be a darling." Her mood and her tone changed suddenly. "Coming along to the 'Frozen Fang' tonight?"

"Is it re-opening?"

"Yes, and it'll be an extra-special night, too. I'm to be the star. Old Battray is shouting about it already. He's expecting a crowded house and a triumph for me. I'll not disappoint him, Nosey. I won't let him down. I'll dance as I never danced before." The light vanished and the eyes became dull. "Poor Billy," she sobbed, collapsing.

"Don't," he implored her, embarrassed by her too spectacular emotion.

She rose to her feet and they walked out together, Nancy with averted face and Nosey erect and scowling.

"You mustn't cry, Nancy," he whispered in the street, and drew her into the shelter of a convenient doorway. "It's all in the game, you know. I might have been in Billy's place and he in mine. The next time I may not be lucky, for you never know. Look at yourself. It was only the other day I was thinking of you as a great lady with a rich husband and a mansion. And now what's the position?"

Nancy pressed the arm she was holding and met his gaze with a smile.

"It's the 'Frozen Fang' and the struggle again, Nosey, but I shan't mind. It's what I love most. I want to be with my pals and not with people who look down on me. See, I'm not crying now. I'm brave and happy. Let's have dinner and talk before we go to the 'Frozen Fang'. If you're broke I have a quid which Battray advanced me. He's paying me five to dance tonight, Nosey. More than I've ever had before."

"Will the boy friend be there?" he asked, attempting to introduce a less serious note.

Nancy made a grimace.

"The boy friend won't be able to afford it. His darling mother whispered to me as we were leaving the court that as he's got to earn his own living she hopes to get him a job in the colonies. But no colonies for me, Nosey, as long as London's where it is."

"Good old London," he murmured sentimentally.

"And good old 'Frozen Fang'," she said, almost reverently. "But see you later, Nosey. Must run home and change."

At a quarter past eight they had their favourite table at Greville's.

"Tell me honestly, Nosey," said Nancy, "which of my dances do you think is the best? I simply love the Dancing Apache, but that requires a partner." She looked at him earnestly as he carefully considered the question before replying.

And at that moment Billy Bright, lying under sentence of death, was almost dead with terror; Ruby Cheldon was explaining to Bobbie that he was well out of it; Bobbie himself was declaiming that he had lost his faith in women, and at Broadbridge Manor Mrs. Massy Cheldon, *née* Smithers, was beginning to learn how irksome and how difficult it was to be a lady at short notice. All four were miserable, but Annie was nearly the most miserable of them all.

"How I wish I could get back to Nancy and Tessie and all the old crowd," she muttered to herself when West, the stately butler, entered in a procession of one bearing a silver salver on which reposed the telegram from the family solicitor announcing the result of the trial of Billy Bright for the murder of her husband.

And as Annie was opening the envelope Nancy in the Soho restaurant was anxiously awaiting her companion's reply to her question.

"Why not revise the Silken Dagger dance?" he said solemnly. "It used to go with a bang."

"Nosey, you're a genius," she exclaimed rapturously. "It's the very thing. I wonder I didn't think of it myself." Then her face clouded. "It was Billy who taught me how to do it," she mumbled tearfully.

"Never mind about Billy now," he said impatiently. "You must think of your art, Nancy."

She smiled with pleasure.

"Yet I can't help thinking of poor Billy." She sighed and played with some crumbs on the table. "Nosey?"

"Yes?"

"There's one thing about the—the case that puzzles me." She hesitated again.

"Well, what is it?" he said good-humouredly.

"Who was the woman who screamed just before old Cheldon was knifed?"

Nosey waggled a playful finger in her direction.

"You mustn't be jealous, darling," he said, capturing her waist. "Waiter, another bottle of wine. Nancy, we must drink to your success tonight. May it be the beginning of good fortune."

"You're swell," she whispered, stretching out a hand to press his.

To receive a free catalog of Poisoned Pen Press titles, please provide your name and address through one of the following ways:

Phone: 1-800-421-3976
Facsimile: 1-480-949-1707
Email: info@poisonedpenpress.com
Website: www.poisonedpenpress.com

Poisoned Pen Press
6962 E. First Ave. Ste 103
Scottsdale, AZ 85251

CPSIA information can be obtained at www.ICGtesting.com
Printed in the USA
BVOW08s2356060415

394730BV00001B/1/P